Y0-BZM-221

SOUL FIRE

Mr & Mrs Charles E Bissell
11815 E Mapleton Rd
Mapleton, OR 97453-9631

SOUL FIRE

JOHN McRAE

Packer Press
Ithaca, New York

© 1999 John McRae

All rights reserved. No part of this book may be reproduced in any form or by any electronic or mechanical means without the written consent of the publisher. Contact the publisher at Packer Press, P.O. Box 6728, Ithaca, New York 14851-6728.

Packer Press
Ithaca, New York 14851-6728

Printed in the United States of America

ISBN 0-9656875-4-6

Cover illustration by Thomas Saffle.

CHAPTER ONE

SALT LAKE CITY
LATE JULY, 1858

An open carriage pulled by a pair of black mares turned onto East Temple, the main street through Salt Lake City. The driver, a muscular black man named Henry Washington, and his two passengers were engulfed in noise and dust.

Henry brought the carriage to a stop in front of the Galloway & Tregale emporium, located less than a block south of the walled Temple Square. He glanced back at the two men behind him.

General David Galloway was in his early sixties, wearing a black suit, white shirt with stiff, starched collar, and a billowy black and gray striped cravat tucked stylishly inside the vest. Slightly sunken cheeks made Galloway's face appear long and thin, clean-shaven except for a small, neatly clipped mustache. He was hatless and his full white locks were blown into disarray by the trip to town. Though Galloway had retired from the British army years ago, everyone still respected the title he had earned commanding a Scottish regiment.

Beside him sat Carn Tregale. Half the age of the General, Tregale looked trim and fit in a plain white shirt and dark trousers. The clothes fit loosely on him over a lean, firm stomach and narrow waist. Tregale's face was deeply tanned, with no beard but long sideburns. Most women thought he was handsome, in a rugged sort of way, and constantly whispered to his wife, Heather, how much they envied her.

"How long will you be staying downtown, General?" Henry asked. "I can wait, or come back later—"

Before General Galloway could answer, two hands seized the door frame on the street side. A face shoved forward, glaring angrily

1

at the two men in the carriage. The face was flushed, eyes red and watery, thick lips twisted in a challenging snarl. Even before he spoke, the strong smell of whiskey and the dust and dirt soiling the rumpled suit attested that the man in the street was falling-down drunk.

"I want a word with you, General," the man in the street said belligerently. The eyes blinked rapidly, as if the man was trying to focus his vision. "And I want it now, sir."

Both General Galloway and Carn Tregale recognized the man and were instantly alert. Confronting them was the Right Honorable Delano R. Eckles, newly arrived Chief Justice of the Utah Territorial Supreme Court.

Eckles was in his fifties, stodgily built, with a large, protruding paunch. The white of his long sideburns emphasized the red flush of his face. He made a feeble attempt to sound imperious but was too drunk and the words slurred badly.

"I am addressing General David Galloway, am I not—?"

Eckles momentarily lost his balance and held tightly to the door to avoid falling. He continued to peer at the man in the carriage.

"You are," Galloway replied sternly. "However, I suggest you address no one, sir, until you are sober. Your condition does not invite conversation, nor does it invite respect for your position as Chief Justice."

"You insult me, sir—" Eckles spluttered.

"You insult yourself by appearing this way in public," Galloway retorted.

The General's stern gaze took in the two army lieutenants standing in the street a few paces behind the judge. They didn't appear quite as drunk as Eckles but were not far from it.

"If you consider this man your friend, gentlemen," Galloway called to them, "you'll get him off the street."

Eckles shook the door angrily, causing the carriage to rock. "You will address me, sir, not my companions. And you cannot order me or anyone else off the streets. You Mormons need to be taught respect for authority—"

Tregale leaned over and unlatched the carriage door, slowly but firmly pushing it open. Eckles was forced to stagger back, still holding on to the now open carriage door for support.

"And you, Judge, need to respect other people's property," Tregale said quietly, stepping out into the street. "You're making the horses nervous, sir. I must ask you to stand away from the carriage."

Eckles leaned forward, peering at Tregale. His glance dropped to Tregale's left arm. There was no hand, just a curved steel hook protruding from a metal casing at the end of the arm. The hook was a constant reminder for Tregale of far away Crimea, of a futile charge up a hill on a cold, snowy November morning, and a cannonball that left a shattered, bloodied stub of an arm. That had happened over four years ago, but the sounds of battle, the screams of wounded companions, the sightless stares of the dead, never left Tregale's memory.

"I've seen that hook," Eckles mumbled, staring harder. "You're that Englishman who brought all those messages to Ecklesville last winter—"

Ecklesville was the camp of civilians located a half mile from the soldiers and teamsters trapped in the mountains last winter during General Albert Johnston's disastrous attempt to invade Utah Territory. An angry division between Johnston and the civilians appointed to Territorial offices by President James Buchanan resulted in the two groups separating from each other. Because Johnston would have nothing to do with any Mormon, Carn Tregale had served as liaison, traveling between the two opposing sides through a savage winter.

Tregale nodded. "That's right, sir," he told the judge. "Now, if you have something to say, please do so and we'll all go about our business."

Eckles swung his attention back to Galloway. "My business is with you, sir. No one else."

"What business would that be, Judge?" Galloway asked.

"You robbed and swindled two upstanding citizens of this territory," Eckles said, letting go of the door and swaying unsteadily. "I will see you in my court, sir—and I promise you will rue the day you joined these Mormons."

"Who are these men I'm supposed to have robbed—?"

"You know as well as I do, sir. Mr. Livingston and Mr. Kinkaid. Their business establishment is only a few doors from your own—"

"If you are referring to the inventory of their former mercantile," Galloway interrupted, his voice now edged with anger, "I bought that merchandise at the price they set themselves."

"You stole it from them. They made that claim to me not an hour ago."

"Over quite a few whiskies, no doubt," Galloway said caustically.

The merchandise that the judge was referring to was sold by the two Gentile merchants last year when word of the approaching army reached the valley. Apparently the two were afraid the Mormons would confiscate the merchandise and they asked only pennies on the dollar just to get rid of it. Galloway had bought a large part of the inventory, and was now selling it in his own recently opened emporium. Livingston and Kinkaid had found it a bitter pill to swallow, now that business was booming.

"I strongly resent being accosted with such false charges," Galloway continued, "especially by an officer of the court who can hardly stand up."

"Be careful with your insults, sir," Eckles shouted, anger reddening his face even more than the whiskey had already flushed it.

The General stepped down from the carriage. "You're a disgrace, Eckles, to yourself and this community. Even more disgraceful is what you do for these officers, and others like them."

"What do you mean by that?" Eckles demanded, struggling to keep his balance. "What are you accusing me of doing, sir—?"

"You know very well what he means, Judge," Tregale said. His words were slow and deliberate. "Everybody knows you use your office to threaten and intimidate people so you can supply these—" he paused, his voice heavily tinged with sarcasm "—these gentlemen with innocent young girls, and wives and widows for that matter, to satisfy their lusts. You're a pimp, Judge, plain and simple."

Eckles appeared on the verge of apoplexy. "That is slander, sir—most foul and vicious slander. I will have you in irons—Tregale, isn't it? I'll have all you treasonous Mormons in irons—"

"You'll find no treason in this territory, Eckles," Galloway snapped. "You'll have to go back to Washington for that. I don't need to tell you it's becoming clear how deeply treason nests within the ranks of your Democratic party."

Eckles could hardly speak for the anger gripping him. "This whole territory reeks with treason, sir. I intend to make every one of you Mormons answer for it, too."

"You have no authority to bring charges of treason against any-one," Galloway said disgustedly.

That infuriated Eckles all the more. "I am the Chief Justice of the highest federal court in this territory, sir. You say there are no trai-tors in Utah—let me tell you, Galloway, I am in possession of signed affidavits that prove otherwise. Dozens of them, in fact, all swearing to rebellious and treasonous acts committed by Mormons against the federal government."

"Even if that were true," Galloway said, "which it isn't, you seem to be forgetting that President Buchanan signed a pardon for every citizen in this territory."

"I have not forgotten it, sir," Eckles snapped back. "That pardon only proves my point."

"What point would that be, Judge?" Tregale asked.

"If you Mormons hadn't committed treason, you wouldn't need a pardon. I'm going to see that action by Buchanan gets reversed in a court of law."

"Let these officers take you back to Camp Floyd and sleep this one off, Judge," Tregale suggested quietly.

"You're giving orders again," Eckles shouted. He took an un-steady step forward and swung a roundhouse blow at Tregale, who caught the judge's fist in midair. Tregale held it for a moment while he brought his temper under control, then disgustedly shoved Eckles back into the two army officers. All three went sprawling into the dirt.

Just as Tregale turned away, three teamsters stepped off the side-walk, fanning out as they fastened truculent stares on Tregale and Galloway. The flush of whiskey was showing plainly on their faces.

"You Mormons think you can get away with anything," the teamster in the middle grated. "Well, you cain't. That there's a federal judge—"

"That there's a drunken fool," Tregale corrected contemptuously.

Tregale saw the teamster's eyes set into a narrow squint. This man wanted trouble, he decided. Tregale motioned for Galloway to step back.

"These men seem bent on doing something foolish, General," he said softly. He spoke directly to the three teamsters. "Don't get yourselves in a spot you can't get off," he warned.

Up on the driver's seat, Henry Washington poised himself to jump down and back up Tregale. All three of the teamsters slowly moved hands closer to the guns in their belts, keeping their attention riveted on the man with the hook. Tregale raised his left arm and waved the hook in a threatening circle. His right hand drifted toward the gun in the holster at his side.

"You don't want any part of this," Tregale warned again. "Just back off and no one will get hurt."

From the ground, Eckles raised up on an elbow and shouted at the teamsters. "You men know who I am," he yelled. "This man attacked me—everybody saw it. He has a gun—shoot him. Shoot all of them—I am the law, and I order you to shoot—"

All three teamsters suddenly drew their guns and fired. General Galloway gave a sharp cry of pain, grabbing at his chest. Tregale felt a sharp sting in the upper part of his left arm. Henry came flying down from the carriage seat, getting to his feet and raising the whip high as he lunged toward the teamsters. One of them fired point blank at the black man, but missed. Tregale drew his own revolver but before he could fire, three shots rang out in quick succession from somewhere close behind him.

The teamsters looked surprised, each staring down at a stain of red suddenly spreading across his chest. Then the knees of all three folded and they fell face down into the street. The crowd had seen enough death to know the teamsters wouldn't be giving any more trouble.

Tregale wanted to find the source of the shots but his first concern was for General Galloway. He and Henry reached the general's side about the same time. Galloway was wincing in pain, clutching a hand tightly to his upper chest.

Henry knelt beside the general, anxiously looking at the wound. "Miss Agatha ain't never going to forgive me for this," he muttered.

"Wasn't you who shot me, Henry," the general wheezed. "I'll make sure my wife understands that."

Tregale ripped open Galloway's shirt, not liking what he saw but relieved the wound was no worse. A lot of blood was pumping out of the hole, but the general was a lucky man. Any lower, and Galloway might not be alive.

"It'll take a while, General," he said, "but you'll heal."

Galloway looked at the red stain on Tregale's arm. "What about you—?"

Tregale looked down, almost surprised to see the blood. He tugged up his shirt sleeve and looked at the wound. "Just a scratch," he shrugged. "Glad those men were drunk—"

"It's them being dead that pleases me," Galloway said, pressing his hand against the hole in his chest. "Who shot them, anyway? Didn't see you firing—"

"That was me, General Galloway."

A man stepped toward them. He was dark complexioned, short, wearing a thick black beard. A mustache had the ends twisted and waxed, and curled upward. His eyes were deeply set under a wide brow, bushy eyebrows doing little to hide the hot fires blazing in them. The pants of his suit were tucked into worn boots and despite his lack of size, the man looked powerful and dangerous. Perhaps that impression came from the two Colt pistols still held in his hands. He took a step forward, shoving the pistols cross-armed into twin holsters belted outside his coat.

"William Hickman at your service." The voice was gravelly, without a trace of warmth or friendliness. "Friends call me Billy."

Tregale stood up and shook the man's hand. "Appreciate you jumping in, Mr. Hickman. I was a little slow—didn't think they'd really start shooting."

Tregale suddenly remembered Eckles and the two drunk army lieutenants. He looked around, saw the three of them melting into the crowded sidewalk on the other side of the street. Apparently the judge wanted no part of the justice Billy Hickman was dealing out.

"If you'll forgive me, Mr. Hickman, I'll thank you properly later. Right now, we need to get this man tended to."

Hickman nodded. "I know their kind," he said, glancing at the dead teamsters. "Best to settle in a hurry. Me and my partner just opened a law office on Second South, a couple blocks down from you. Hickman and Williams. Happy to visit with you when you get a chance."

With that, he turned and pushed back into the crowd.

CHAPTER TWO

SALT LAKE CITY

H enry Washington kept the horses at a gallop all the way back along South Temple. The carriage skidded as it turned into the circular driveway of the Galloway mansion, stopping in a cloud of dust before the columned entranceway as Henry pulled in the mares. The front door opened before Henry could jump to the ground.

Agatha, the general's wife, crossed swiftly to where her husband was slumped in the carriage seat. She looked anxiously at Carn, who read the question in her eyes.

"He'll be all right, Agatha," Carn assured her. "He's been shot but it's nothing that won't heal."

Agatha looked quickly up at Henry. "Don't just sit there, Henry—get a doctor."

Henry glanced uncertainly at Carn. "Best I help carry the General, with that arm of yours—"

For the first time, Agatha noticed Carn's bloodied shirt sleeve. "You've been shot too—"

Carn gave a quick shake of his head. "Barely a scratch." He turned to Henry. "We can manage. You get a doctor here quick as you can."

Heather Tregale appeared in the doorway and gasped as she saw the bloodstains on her husband's shirtsleeve. "Carn, you're hurt—what happened?"

"Nothing to worry about," Carn told her. "You and Agatha grab the General's feet and we'll get him inside."

The doctor arrived and treated General Galloway's chest wound, confirming that the bullet had passed cleanly through, missing all vital organs. Barring infection, which was always a risk, it would just be a matter of rest and Agatha's care before the General was up and about again.

Heather was relieved when she saw that the wound on Carn's arm, with all the blood cleaned away, was merely a shallow groove. Bandaged, and with a clean shirt, Carn showed no effects of the encounter with the teamsters.

Still, as they stood alone for a moment in their bedroom, Heather couldn't help clinging tightly to her husband. She pressed her head against his chest, her whole body trembling with fear and relief. Carn was again aware of how lucky he was. A few inches to the left and that bullet would have smashed into his heart. No matter if there was a life after death, as the Mormons believed—he couldn't imagine an existence without this woman who had come into his life.

He could still see her that first time as she stepped from the carriage onto the dock at Liverpool, minutes before the sailing ship Horizon was to leave for America. She still had that wonderful eagerness for life he had seen that morning. It had survived the grueling journey to the valley, blossomed even brighter when she held their newborn son. Heather still possessed the serene gentility of her upbringing amid the wealth and graces of London's high society, but strength and character underlay those outward impressions. Carn's breath still caught when he saw how beautiful she looked with those long, dark curls framing the oval face, and how fine a figure had matured with the birth of their child. Carn Tregale knew how fortunate he was to have such a wife, and now a bright healthy child. His life of emptiness and despair was replaced with happiness and contentment.

The sound of horses and a carriage arriving below came through the bedroom window. Heather crossed and glanced outside. "It's Governor Cummings and his wife. Bob Burton and Colonel Cooke are with them."

"They probably heard about the General being shot," Carn said.

"I'd better get downstairs," Heather said quickly. "Agatha won't want to be leaving the General—"

Henry Washington had already admitted the visitors by the time Heather and Carn came down the wide, curved stairway. Governor

Cummings looked anxious as he took Tregale's outstretched hand.

"How bad is it?" Cummings asked. "We came as soon as we heard about the shooting—"

"The General took a bullet in the chest," Tregale told them, "but he was lucky. Went through clean. The doctor says he'll recover."

"I'm relieved to hear that," Governor Cummings wheezed. He had hurried from the carriage into the foyer and was out of breath. There was no concealing the governor's heavy Southern accent, the unmistakable stamp of a gentleman from Georgia.

The new governor of Utah Territory was of average height but well over two hundred and forty pounds. A short, bull-like neck and a rotund midriff made the governor appear heavier than he was. Gray hair, wavy and well combed, was turning to white. His concern for General Galloway heightened the intensity of wide-set eyes, tightening a thin mouth that curved downward on each side, giving an impression of a scowl. Appointed by President James Buchanan to replace the popular Mormon governor Brigham Young, Cummings surprisingly became friends with Brigham Young. The Mormons accepted Cummings with respect and a warmth shown to few other federal appointees.

Bob Burton, a colonel in the Utah militia, gave Carn a quizzical inspection. The two had become close friends during the long months of the clash with the U.S. forces.

"Heard you got shot too, Carn—"

Tregale motioned to his left arm. "Just a scratch. Those teamsters didn't get a second chance."

Burton grinned. "Yeah. Heard you met Billy Hickman."

Colonel Philip St. George Cooke, of General Johnston's command, flashed a smile. "From what I hear about the man, Hickman could just as well have shot the two of you, instead of the teamsters."

"Don't know anything about him," Carn said, "but I owe him a debt of gratitude."

Cooke, looking thin and dashing in his uniform, shrugged. "Never met him myself, but by reputation he's somewhat of an outlaw. I understand he has a close relationship with Brigham Young though—goes back to when Hickman acted as bodyguard back in Nauvoo."

Heather reached out to clasp the hand of the governor's wife. "It's so thoughtful of you to come. Agatha will be pleased."

Mrs. Cummings looked like the wife of a gentleman from Georgia, although she actually was raised in Boston, the daughter of a prominent physician in that city. The years had rounded her but she carried herself with dignity. Her graying hair, not as white as her husband's, was always neatly arranged. She had endured extreme hardships this past year and a half with her husband on the hellish journey from the frontier and the winter-long nightmare at Bridger. Still, she seldom complained about being so abruptly relocated from the comforts and social circles of Boston and Atlanta to the comparatively primitive life of a Mormon colony, isolated from the mainstream of civilization. She was pleasant by nature, and always had a ready smile for those around her.

"How is Agatha doing?" Mrs. Cummings asked, with genuine concern. "Can we do anything to help? I'm sure Alfred could get a doctor from the Army post to look at General Galloway—"

"That isn't necessary, Mrs. Cummings, but thank you for the offer," Carn said quietly. "General Galloway is in no danger and getting very good care."

Agatha Galloway heard the visitors arrive and now came down the stairs to greet the people in the foyer.

"This is so nice of you," she said, looking around. "The General is resting comfortably—well, as comfortably as he can be with a hole in his chest. He's a little groggy from the laudanum the doctor gave him, but I'm sure he'll be glad to see you all."

There was the sound of another carriage outside in the driveway. Agatha went to the door and opened it, a pleased expression coming to her face as she saw the woman alighting from the carriage.

"Sister Eliza," Agatha said, stepping out to give her visitor a warm embrace.

"You are so kind to come—"

The petite, fashionably dressed woman who entered was well known to all of them. Eliza Snow Young looked fragile, but her energy and talents were boundless. She was wearing an immaculately pressed dress, full-skirted and lavishly trimmed with lace. Eliza loved

11

lace, and it was always somewhere on her attire. She was wearing a gold chain around her neck. Eliza was famous for that chain and wore it constantly, though without any hint of flaunting wealth.

This tiny woman was considered the most influential woman in the entire Territory. A widow of Joseph Smith, prophet and founder of the Mormon Church, she became a polygamous wife of Brigham Young back in Nauvoo, after the assassination of her husband. It was a marriage of respect and caring, and everyone knew Eliza was a wife to Brigham Young in name only. She was constantly at his side whenever important visitors were hosted, and had gained a national reputation for writing and poetry.

"I just heard about the General being shot," Eliza said, looking at Agatha.

"Is he going to be all right—?"

Agatha nodded. "It will take time, but the doctor says he's in no real danger."

"Thank goodness for that," Eliza said. Her glance swiveled to Carn. "We heard that Judge Eckles was involved. Is that true?"

"He was there," Carn said, "but some drunken teamsters did the shooting. Billy Hickman dropped them before they could do any more damage."

Eliza shook her head. "That Billy—a saint and a sinner if there ever was one."

"Well," Agatha said, "why don't we all go up and let the General know you're here. He probably won't carry on much of a conversation, but he'll certainly appreciate seeing his friends."

The visitors spent only a few minutes at the bedside of David Galloway, for it was obvious the wounded man was indeed feeling the effects of the painkilling drug. General Galloway's eyes closed in sleep almost as soon as the door closed behind his visitors.

When everyone was again down in the foyer, Governor Cummings cleared his throat and spoke up. "Ladies, I wonder if you would excuse us gentlemen for a few minutes. We need a moment or two in private with Carn."

The ladies followed Agatha back into the kitchen area, Eliza assuring them she would be delighted to spend some time visiting.

Carn motioned toward the parlor off from the foyer. The parlor and dining room were now restored to their former elegance. For the long months of the campaign against the U.S. troops, both rooms functioned as headquarters for the Utah militia leaders, where they planned and strategized away from the crowded confines of the Council House downtown, where just a few weeks ago Buchanan's peace treaty was formally accepted. The rooms were no longer cluttered with maps and papers, although no one dismissed the possibility of the peace treaty being violated. General Johnston openly resented not being allowed to treat the Mormons as a conquered enemy, and draw at least some blood to avenge the losses and humiliation suffered by his troops.

The men settled into the comfortable overstuffed sofas and chairs in the parlor, as Carn could barely conceal his curiosity.

Cummings got straight to the point. "We all know there is no trust between the Mormons and General Johnston. Carn, you're as aware of that as any man in this room, having spent most of last winter as liaison between the two camps."

It was true. General Johnston refused to have direct dealings with the Mormons. Carn, not a baptized member of the Mormon faith nor having declared intentions of becoming one, was accepted by both sides to intermediate between them. As a result, Carn spent the long, bitterly cold and stormy months of last winter traveling between the Echo canyon headquarters of the Utah militia and the U.S. forces snowbound at Camp Scott, a forlorn encampment hastily improvised near the burned-out ruins of Fort Bridger.

"We have a difficult situation confronting us," Cummings continued. "Half the population still hasn't returned from the south and there is absolutely no contact with General Johnston."

Governor Cummings was referring to the evacuation of tens of thousands of citizens from Salt Lake and all other settlements north of Utah County in preparation for carrying out Brigham Young's order to burn and destroy the entire territory, rather than let it fall into the hands of the invading military. The peace treaty seemingly ended that threat but people were reluctant to return to their homes, waiting to see if the Army and the new federal officials considered themselves bound by Buchanan's pardon.

Frustration flashed across the new governor's face. "I respect Governor Young and he has been very gracious in turning over the powers of his office, but it's almost as difficult setting a meeting with him as it is with General Johnston. He's locked himself inside his estate with his own private army of guards."

Burton gave an apologetic shrug. "He doesn't meet with anyone these days, not even his own people."

"Why has he gone into such seclusion?" Cooke asked. "With all due respect to Governor Cummings, the people in this territory do whatever Brigham Young says. Seems like his voice, his leadership, his direction are needed now more than ever."

"What would you do, Colonel," Burton replied, "if you had as many men as he does sworn to kill him—?"

"The army has issued no such orders," Cooke said quickly. "General Johnston's orders are to protect the safety of all civilians in Utah Territory. No matter what his personal feelings might be, the General will follow those orders."

"And what about all those teamsters and the other riffraff who came in with the Army?" Carn asked. "They don't take orders from anyone. Every one of them brags about wanting to put a bullet into Brigham Young."

Governor Cummings was nodding in agreement. "I certainly understand his reluctance to leave the safety of his estate—I would exercise the same cautions. He's given full cooperation, even if it has been through third parties."

"I understand all public meetings—even weekly church services—have been canceled until further notice," Cooke said.

"That's correct," Burton said. "We need to be sure all sides want order and stability restored. When we're confident of that, things will quickly return to normal."

"Mrs. Cummings and I just returned from spending a very pleasant few days with him and some of the other church leaders—you people call them apostles, don't you—in Big Cottonwood canyon," the Governor said. "It was cool and delightful and we all had a good opportunity to exchange views."

Cummings's heavy jowls shook in the earnestness of his feeling. "I want the Mormons to feel it's safe to return to their homes. I want peace and tranquillity restored throughout the whole territory. That's why it's so frustrating not to be able to communicate with Johnston."

Colonel Cooke frowned as he stroked the blackspade beard on his chin.

Cooke undoubtedly was the most popular among the Mormons of all the officers in Johnston's command. As a young major, Cooke had commanded the Mormon Battalion of youthful volunteers on its long march south during the Mexican War. He won the respect of his command, and that was reinforced during the army's recent march into the valley. Riding beside General Johnston, Cooke had bared his head in honor of the many in the Utah militia who previously served with him. It was an act of respect appreciated by every member of the Nauvoo Legion who witnessed it. Cooke now commanded the six companies of the Second Dragoons, sent to reinforce the troops of the Utah Expedition.

"You know how General Johnston feels about Mormons, Carn," Cooke said quietly. "He made that plain enough on many occasions. Being forced to accept this peace treaty is particularly galling to him. He sees the Mormons accepting Governor Cummings—and I'm afraid he considers the governor almost as much an enemy as they are. So it's extremely difficult to communicate between parties at a time when communication is absolutely essential."

"The man is rude. He ignores all my requests for meetings between us," Cummings said, his mouth pulling down at the corners. "I have complained to his superiors in Washington, but I doubt if anything will convince him to work in harmony with civil authorities—certainly not with me. He seems less prejudiced against Messrs. Eckles and Sinclair, probably because both of our esteemed new federal judges are openly opinionated against all Mormons. Of course, Eckles is hardly sober long enough to have an opinion about anything. From what I've seen, the man is an absolute disgrace. Don't know much about Sinclair, since he arrived only a few days ago, but I do know he's also hard set against the Mormons. Can't understand what they're doing back in Washington, sending out men with such strong prejudices. We certainly can't count on either Eckles or Sinclair to help accomplish a peaceful turn of events."

"Which brings us to the purpose of this meeting," Cooke said, looking directly at Carn. The Virginian's slow, accented drawl served to emphasize his words. He cut an almost dashing figure, tall, slender, a stiff military bearing, his uniform brushed clean of most of the trail dust gathered since leaving Leavenworth. Signs of the years were beginning to show in the slight edging of gray around deep side-burns. Still, he gave an impression of almost youthful agility. Cooke was a soldier's soldier, firm, determined to obey any order of his superior, a patriot who so far betrayed none of the uncertainties and personal conflicts going on inside him over the mounting crisis of loyalties between North and South.

"Carn, we're asking you to continue as liaison, not only between the army and the Mormons, but between General Johnston and Governor Cummings. I'd do it myself, but the General will not allow me to compromise my position as an officer of the Expedition."

"Does this pose any difficulties for you, Mr. Tregale?" Cummings asked, studying him anxiously. "It will mean a lot of trips between here and Camp Floyd, as Johnston is calling the new encampment, but nothing like the journeys of last winter."

Carn was silent, considering the governor's question. It certainly posed one difficulty, for which he didn't have a direct answer. Bob Burton saw his hesitancy, and understood.

"There is one major consideration, Governor," Burton said, "and I'm sure Carn is reluctant to bring it up. With your permission, Carn—?"

Carn nodded. The friendship between them was solid, and he knew Bob understood the problem.

"Last winter, Carn was not a Mormon," Burton continued. "However, with the recent birth of his son, and the feelings that have grown within him, Carn has requested to be baptized into our faith—a decision, I might add, that has made his wife extremely happy. I'm sure Carn is thinking that if he accepts your offer, Governor, he can't go through with that baptism. That undoubtedly would make him unacceptable to General Johnston. Have I stated the dilemma correctly, Carn?"

Tregale nodded. "Tight in a nutshell, Bob. I'd be happy to serve, but I feel I must tell my wife about the need to postpone my baptism. Under the circumstances, I'd like to consult with her before giving a final answer. Is that acceptable, gentlemen—?"

"More than fair, Mr. Tregale," Cummings said, leaning back in his chair, "but I should tell you, I already have a sizable stack of communications for that old goat sitting on my desk—"

When the men emerged from the meeting, Eliza Snow Young left to return home, and shortly after, Governor and Mrs. Cummings left. Carn walked outside with Colonel Cooke and Bob Burton. Both officers swung up into the saddle.

"If you accept the offer, Carn," Cooke told him, "I'll have horses set aside for your use, and a place to billet. I'm a soldier, and I respect the authority of my commanding officer, but the General can be stubborn and more than a little exasperating at times. You'll be doing all of us a great service, Carn. He's already indicated he'll accept you as a liaison."

"That's an improvement," Tregale grinned. "There were times last winter when he wanted to put a bullet in me. I don't expect we'll become close friends."

Cooke shrugged. "All that's needed is a voice acceptable to one and all."

"Just so you know," Burton said, "our people also give this their full approval."

"I'm not sure 'full approval' applies to General Johnston," Cooke smiled.

"More like pragmatic sanction. By the way, did you hear that the four companies of mounted riflemen brought up from New Mexico are on the way back?"

"When did that happen?" Carn asked.

"Left yesterday. One of the companies of teamsters left the same day, headed back east—under military guard."

"More guarded than you know," Burton grinned at him. "We posted extra guards around the homes of church leaders, and hid men all the way up the canyon in case any teamster tried to double back to Salt Lake."

"I see the Legion's on top of things as usual," Cooke said wryly. "You boys should go back to Washington and give lessons on intelligence gathering."

The two visitors gathered up their reins and prepared to leave.

"Remember what the Colonel said about Billy Hickman," Burton cautioned Carn. "Don't count him as a friend, even if he did save your life. Hickman's a schemer and his reputation as a killer goes a long way back. If he tries to befriend you, he's probably up to no good."

"I think you're being harsh," Carn replied, shaking hands with the two officers, "but thanks for the warning."

"I have a few more matters to take up with Governor Cummings," Cooke said, "then I'll be heading back to Camp Floyd. If it all works out, I'd like to visit with you before you meet with General Johnston."

"I'll be talking to Heather in the next few minutes. She'll understand, I'm sure. You can count on me being there."

"Good. I need to brief you on the Indian situation, too."

"Trouble—?"

"This whole territory is in serious trouble."

Carn watched the men leave, then returned into the house. He found Heather and Agatha in the rear kitchen, and to his surprise, Maude Tate and her fifteen-year-old daughter Beryl. The two had come up from Provo, and as usual, brought their small wagon up through the back road of the estate. Maude appeared upset, and kept looking at Beryl. Defiance was written all over the young woman's face.

"I'm sorry to bring trouble, Carn, especially after hearing what happened today," Maude said, her frustrations showing through, "but Beryl insisted we come. Seems that running off with that boy from Arkansas didn't teach her much—"

"That's not fair, mother," Beryl blurted angrily. "One has nothing to do with the other."

Heather looked across at her husband. "Beryl wants to get into acting. She met Mercy Tuckett last week during a theater performance in Provo. Even got a part in the play."

"Just a small part," Beryl said quickly. "Miss Tuckett always gives parts to local girls—saves her money, she told me, and helps draw bigger audiences."

"Beryl says Miss Tuckett invited her to come to Salt Lake and join her theater company," Heather added.

"She did, Brother Tregale. She thinks I have a natural talent for the theater—and I do. It's what I want to do with my life. I'm certainly more suited to acting than I am to feeding pigs in Provo."

"We've never asked you to feed the pigs, Beryl—"

"That's not the point, mother," Beryl said, exasperated. "I was wrong about running away with Amos—I've admitted that a hundred times—but this is about my future, not my past."

Last summer, Beryl had fallen in love with a young cowboy, Amos Gray, passing through Utah with a wagon train bound for California. The Tate family lived in Parowan, in southern Utah, at the time, but were in Salt Lake City visiting other members of "Tregale's Twenty" during the Pioneer Day holiday. Against her parents' wishes, Beryl ran away with Amos and married him—a wedding forced on Amos by members of the wagon train who would not condone an illicit relationship with the Mormon girl. A short time later, Amos told Beryl he didn't consider himself legally married, didn't want to be married, and ordered her back to her parents. The wagon train was attacked by Indians a few hours after Beryl left. Amos was killed, along with all the other emigrants of the wagon train.

Beryl went back to her family. The pain inside her was slow to heal but she finally accepted the bitter truth that Amos had only used her for his pleasure. Moving back home was difficult, for her childhood was over, no matter how hard it was for her parents to accept it.

Carn saw the tension between mother and daughter. "Are you set against this, Maude?" he asked.

"Not so much the acting, as the fact she has no place to live."

Beryl gave her mother an impatient look. "I told you Miss Tuckett said I could probably share a room with one of the other girls in the company."

"Probably—" Maude snorted. "And what if you can't? I suppose Miss Tuckett thinks you could also move in with one of the boys in the company—"

"Is that what you think of me, mother?"

Agatha had not been paying full attention to what was being said, her thoughts more on her husband upstairs. Now she put an arm around Maude's shoulders.

"Don't worry about it, Maude. Beryl is more than welcome to stay here. We've plenty of room."

A smile jumped across Beryl's face. "I'll pay, Agatha. Whatever you think is fair."

"You have no money, child," Maude snapped, "and neither does your father or me."

"There'll be no talk of paying," Agatha said, dismissing the subject with a wave of her hand. "Beryl can help with the housework. Both Heather and I will be spending more time helping out at the emporium, so some help with the household chores will be greatly appreciated. That meet with your approval, Beryl?"

Beryl rushed over and gave Agatha a tight hug. "You are so wonderful, Agatha—all of you are," she added, looking around at Heather and Carn. "I know this is the right thing for me."

Maude gave a resigned sigh. "I hope so, child. I hope it brings you happiness. Goodness knows you've had more than a child's share of sorrow."

A short while later, Carn closed the door of the bedroom and met the curious stare of his wife.

"What's this all about, Carn. Is something wrong—?"

"We have a decision to make."

He related the events of the meeting downstairs. Heather felt a rush of disappointment. She was eagerly looking forward to having her husband a baptized member of the Church. That was now going to be pushed aside, it seemed. Something in the back of her mind resented, even if just for a moment, that the priorities of other people were being placed before her own. To cover the guilt of that fleeting thought, she gave her husband a long embrace.

"This won't change your mind will it, about being baptized?"

"Of course not. You're not too disappointed—?"

"Disappointed, yes, but proud that people think so much of my husband."

"Maybe they won't for long. General Johnston is—well, an exasperating man to deal with."

She reached up and cupped his face in her hands, looked into his eyes, then gave him a warm, lingering kiss. She pressed against him, whispering into his ear.

"I know you've been shot, but—"

CHAPTER THREE

SAN PETE RESERVATION— CENTRAL UTAH

White smoke rose almost vertically into the hot summer air from the Ute camp sprawled across a grassy clearing in the mountains overlooking the San Pete reservation, some one hundred miles south of Great Salt Lake City. The plume of smoke could not be seen by settlers in the township of Manti, located in the San Pete Valley below the encampment, although everyone knew the Indians moved up to the same mountain campsite every summer, long before the reservation was established two years ago.

Had the white settlers seen the unusual number of tepees dotting the camp, it would have alarmed them. Several tribes, including the Piedes, Paiutes, Pahvants, and the Sanpitch Utes, were answering a call to attend a council. Even some of the Cumumbahs, part of the Shoshone nation, were in attendance.

The gathering included the powerful Arrowpeen, and Peteetneet, Sanpitch, Tintic and Yampants, four of the most powerful chiefs of central Utah, Kanosh from the southern Pahvants, and Little Soldier from the northern Cumumbahs.

The smoke came from a large fire burning in the center of the camp, the dry wood crackling noisily. However, what surrounded the fire held the unsmiling attention of every man, woman and child gathered in the high vale.

Six poles were imbedded into the ground in a circle about the fire. An Indian woman was roped tightly to each of the poles, and piles of wood were stacked at the feet of each of them. The women had spent themselves hours ago in screaming and wailing against the fate decreed against them. Now they slumped silently in the ropes holding them, no longer able to hold up their heads, resigned to the judgment of their chiefs. They looked asleep, except for an occasional moan and the deep shudders that shook their bodies. Each of the women knew how little importance was attached to their life. They were a possession, given from father to husband, their only purpose to provide comfort and children. Perhaps the presence of Chief Arrowpeen, brother of the great Chief Walkara, brought a fleeting reminder that when Walkara died three years ago, among the possessions buried with him were two women, two children, and fifteen prized horses, all killed to accompany the chief on his journey to the Great Spirit.

The chiefs made their appearance from inside the teepee of Peteetneet , where they had been in council. They stood in a half circle, Chief Arrowpeen in the center. Arrowpeen remained aloof, arms folded across his chest, staring stonily into the sky and not looking at anyone. Enough time had passed, the chiefs decided, for all assembled to absorb both the crime and the punishment of the six women. The chiefs wanted an unforgettable lesson seared into every heart.

The low buzz of voices stopped as Chief Peteetneet raised both arms and let his gaze circle the people standing before him. Suddenly he let out a fierce, pained screech, his hands began beating against his breast. Then he stretched out his arms again toward the gathered throng.

"Our people have angered the Great Spirit. Our people share in the great sorrow fallen upon us because we have let the soldiers and the 'Mericats steal our pride and stamp it into the dust."

The Indians drew little distinction between white men invading their lands. Mor-mons were friendly and helpful, even as they stole tribal lands. Other whites, usually called 'Mericats, referring to the hordes of immigrants in the wagon trains passing through Indian lands, were all considered enemies. The blue coats, and the hated wagon drivers and gamblers and others who traveled with them, were all lumped together as 'soldiers,' or sometimes they too became simply 'Mericats. All blue coats were hated. White people were not to be trusted, for they trampled sacred lands and killed animals given to the Nations by the Great Spirit. Even the Mor-mon settlers were barely tolerated. To accept the Mor-mons among them would be accepting a finality that Indian lands and freedoms and the gifts of the Great Spirit would be lost forever.

Peteetneet's stare fastened on the six women at the stakes. They had all raised their heads at the chief's pained outcry. They looked at Peteetneet but their eyes showed no real emotion, no grasp of what was happening. The eyes of all six were dark and glazed, showing the merciful effects of the leafy weed they were given to chew when first tied to the stake. The leaf lessened pain and dulled their ability to grasp the reality of the punishment about to be inflicted upon them.

Peteetneet began to speak again. "All of our nations must fight the 'Mericats who bring a stench to our lands. No Indian woman can allow herself to be taken by them. It is better to die by your own hand than bring such shame upon yourself and our people."

His glance hardened as he looked at the men in the company. Most tried to avoid meeting those angry eyes, knowing the accusation before it was spoken. "No man must ever again sell his woman to a 'Mericat, as many of you have done. No man must lose his honor and the greatness within him for whiskey or a few coins. All our nations are weakened by this. Any man who gives his woman to be used by a 'Mericat will be banished from our lands." He glared once again at the people around him. "Now hear the words of Chief Yampants."

Yampants stepped forward, his face as hard and set in anger as Peteetneet. He pointed to the women tied to the stake. "These must die. They have been with soldiers and 'Mericats many times, bringing shame to our nations. Their bodies have a sickness given them by the soldiers—a sickness that has swept through our brother nations to the south and destroyed them. These women must die so that our people will always be strong.

"And we must be strong, for the Great Spirit is calling to us. Soon, all of our nations will band together and drive the 'Mericats from our lands forever," Yampants continued. "Only by doing this can we make our forefathers proud. Only this will make us worthy to have the Great Spirit smile upon us."

Now Chief Little Soldier stepped forward. "The women—and the men—of the Cumumbahs are among those who offended the Great Spirit when the soldiers first came to our lands. Our women were defiled by many soldiers during the long winter moons in the mountains. Some were taken by force, but many were given to the soldiers by their own man for whiskey, as Chief Peteetneet has told you. I took our people away from the soldiers' camp, but it was too late. The sickness already was planted inside some of our women. I will not allow such shame to fall upon my people again. Any warrior of the Cumumbahs who does not protect his woman from the men of the 'Mericat nation will die with her. That is the oath I make to the Great Spirit."

There was silence for several moments. The chiefs glanced at each other, then Peteetneet raised his arms again. His voice this time was lower.

"Let the fires be lit."

The piles of wood and faggots about each stake licked into flames. The women tied to them began to struggle as pain bit into flesh, overcoming the numbness of the drugs. Screams once again filled the clearing. The smoke darkened and the circle about the women widened, as if those who watched feared they too might be devoured.

The assembly of chiefs, faces showing no trace of emotion, watched the pyres for a few minutes then turned and went back into the teepee of Peteetneet.

There were matters to be discussed of more importance than disease-ridden squaws. The Great Spirit was speaking strong language to all sixteen nations. The time of reckoning with the hated 'Mericats was fast approaching.

Outside, the screams fell silent one by one.

CHAPTER FOUR

CAMP FLOYD
EARLY AUGUST

General Johnston had chosen an unfriendly site to build Camp Floyd, the new army headquarters. Cedar Valley was unknown even to most settlers, lying beyond the uninviting Lake Mountains, the small, little-known range bordering the western side of Utah Lake. The valley stretched flat and forlorn at the southern end of the Oquirrh Mountains, isolated and dusty, swept by fierce wind much of the year, by howling blizzards in the long months of winter, and searing sun in the summer.

The Oquirrhs ran south along the western edge of the Salt Lake Valley with neither the forests, the wide canyon streams, nor the grandeur of the Wasatch peaks that rose majestically along the eastern edge. Here in Cedar Valley, some forty miles south of Salt Lake City, the Wasatch could be seen only as a distant line of peaks towering above the barren slopes of the nearby Lake Mountains. The short stretch of the Lakes, looking more like hills than mountains when compared to the two main ranges, cut off Cedar Valley from any view of Utah Lake and the many settlements clustered along the eastern foothills of Utah County.

A line of low hills ran out from the southern end of the Oquirrhs, serving as a dividing barrier between Cedar Valley and the equally desolate Rush Valley to the west. The only use of these valleys was by a handful of Mormon ranchers as grazing land for their cattle.

Johnston was pleased to find only two small settlements in Cedar Valley. Cedar Fort was located in the northern end, and Fairfield was in the middle, on the north bank of Cedar Creek, the valley's lone, shallow stream that meandered down from the western hills. As the Union forces approached, most of the families living in Fairfield fled to Cedar Fort. General Johnston decided to erect the new army post along the southern bank of Cedar creek, almost directly across from the now virtually abandoned settlement of Fairfield.

As unfriendly as it was, Cedar Valley impressed Johnston as being ideally suited for the army's purposes. It provided easy access to the most populated Mormon settlements, from Brigham City in the north to Cedar City in the south. If a crisis developed in any of the larger cities, such as Great Salt Lake, Provo, or the capitol city of Fillmore, troops could respond quickly. In addition, Cedar Valley was in a central location to provide protection for the wagon trains heading for California along the main immigrant trails running south and west through Utah.

In the past month or so since arriving in Cedar Valley, the army had turned it into a site of frenzied construction. Buildings were rising everywhere, and the sounds of hammers and saws and shouting men could be heard even over the winds that swept the valley day and night. There was good reason for the urgency in building the camp; not one soldier or teamster wanted to spend another winter like the one just past, trapped out in bitter stormy weather with only tents for shelter and little food.

Thousands of wagons already had beaten a wide, dusty roadway between Cedar Valley and Great Salt Lake City. Veering northeast across the valley, the road passed through a gap between the Traverse and Lake ranges and continued north to Salt Lake City. The army's supply wagons followed a rutted trail worn by the Cedar Valley settlers, grinding and broadening it into a double-wagon roadway. Now it was almost constantly marked by a pall of dust overhead as wagons loaded with milled lumber, building supplies, and foodstuffs bought from Mormon businessmen and farmers, traveled to the army outpost. It was galling to General Johnston to deal with people he still considered his enemies, but there was no other recourse if Camp Floyd was to be completed before winter. Army supply trains were en route from the east but they were a thousand miles away and could not be depended upon to arrive on time.

Carn Tregale entered Cedar Valley the day after meeting with Governor Cummings. He was briefed again before leaving, and listened carefully to the requests Cummings wanted put before Johnston. The saddlebags slung behind him were stuffed full of official papers. It would be interesting to see, Carn thought, if the military commander even bothered to look at them.

With all the construction and confusion, Carn crossed the bridge over Cedar Creek and entered the camp without challenge. That would change, Carn knew, for Johnston was a stickler for military procedures. It would not be long before guards were posted day and night.

A sergeant led him to the far western edge of the encampment where the stone walls of a long line of buildings, running north and south, were already up to the rooflines. It looked like there were at least nine or ten of them, although in the confusion of construction it was difficult to tell exactly. The sergeant pointed at the unfinished buildings and a line of Sibley tents a short distance east of them.

"Those will be the administration buildings," he said, "and the officers are temporarily quartered in those tents, sir," the sergeant told him. "General Johnston's tent is the one in the middle, with the pennant outside. I believe Colonel Cooke's tent is the second or third south of that, sir. There's less noise and not so much dust in that end of camp."

Tregale thanked him, then walked his horse slowly down between the buildings and officer's tents. Over a hundred men, he guessed, were working to complete the administration buildings, some of them soldiers but mostly civilians. Timbers for roof supports were ready to be hoisted into place on some of the walls. It was the same throughout the huge encampment, buildings going up in every direction. Tregale was astonished at the enormous size of the place. It was far larger than anything he had imagined, and it was indeed taking shape in a hurry.

Colonel Cooke came out from one of the buildings under construction and hailed Tregale as he passed. Carn stopped, leaning down from his horse to shake the colonel's hand.

"Trust your wife understood the situation," Cooke said, looking up at Tregale. "Don't wish you any undue burdens."

"Heather was very understanding," Carn replied, swinging out of the saddle. He looked around again at all the construction. "I heard the camp was going up fast, but this is amazing—"

"Isn't a man here eager to spend another winter like the last one," Cooke grimaced. "Everybody wants a roof and a fireplace this time."

Cooke led Tregale toward the row of tents. "There's someone who'll be pleased you rode out today." He stuck his head into one of the tents, spoke to someone, then motioned for Tregale to follow him inside.

Tregale ducked through the tent flap and a smile broke over his face as he confronted the tall, white-haired officer stuffing belongings into a travel bag. A grin was as broad on the face of Colonel Edmund Alexander as they gripped hands warmly.

"Carn—"

"Edmund—Colonel, sir," Carn corrected with a smile. "You leaving—?"

"Been ordered back to Leavenworth," Alexander said. "I was hopeful I'd see you before I left."

Colonel Alexander, who gave substance to the phrase "an officer and a gentleman," had been in charge of the advance force of the Utah Expedition, leaving the frontier a couple of months before Johnston. He and Tregale shared the hope that new orders would be received recalling the army to Leavenworth, but that hadn't happened. Tregale stayed with the advance force through the savage weeks of early storms and the two men had grown to like and respect each other.

Carn glanced at Alexander's hair. It was neatly combed as usual, but considerably more white than Carn remembered. "You've more snow than there's left in the passes, Edmund," he joked good-naturedly. "Don't remember it being that white."

"It wasn't," Alexander sighed. "Distinguished silver, was the way I overheard a lady describe it back at Fort Leavenworth. That was before the Utah Expedition and last winter."

"What's your new assignment?"

"Won't know until I get to Leavenworth. I'm hoping they'll send me some place where the winters are warm." Alexander motioned for his two guests to sit, the only places for that being his cot and a rickety folding chair. "Has Philip had an opportunity to brief you about the situation here—?"

"Just going to do that," Cooke answered, "before he meets with the General." He glanced at Carn. "Saw your saddlebags. I suppose they're full of papers for the General—"

"Cummings had more," Carn grinned, "but I convinced him this was enough to get the General's attention."

"Don't be surprised if it doesn't," Alexander said, echoing Carn's own thoughts earlier. "The General has a full plate of problems of his own."

"Anything I should be telling Cummings about?" Carn asked.

Cooke gave a frustrated shake of his head. "The General is concerned with military matters, and the Governor views every-thing from a civilian perspective. Neither of them is likely to put much priority on the other's agenda. That may well create serious problems for all of us."

"I take it all is not going smoothly here," Carn murmured.

"Problems on top of problems," Cooke answered. "Teamsters are a big headache. They're off the government payroll and don't like it one bit. We give them as much work as we can, but that takes away jobs from the regulars who rely on them for extra pay. So the two groups are constantly fighting. General Johnston finally ordered all the teamsters out of camp, and most of them moved across the creek into Fairfield."

"Thought all problems like that were in Salt Lake," Carn smiled.

"One night across the creek will convince you that isn't true," Alexander grunted. "Fairfield is the devil's playground, for sure. It's been put off limits, but that doesn't stop anybody."

"Then there's all the civilians working here," Cooke muttered. "Close to two thousand—probably more—and nearly all Mormons. That rubs the soldiers the wrong way—they'd rather shoot Mor-mons than work with them. Makes for a lot of tension, and a lot of bloody noses."

"Noticed the civilians on the way in," Carn said. "Surprised to see so many, though I heard the army is paying top wages."

"That's what's drawing them, right enough," Alexander said. "You can tell they feel the same anger toward us, but for three dollars a day—more for those with building skills—a man can swallow a lot of pride."

"They'll earn more money in the next few months than most would see in a whole year—or two or three years, for that matter." Cooke was again shaking his head. "But teamsters and the Mormons aren't the real problem."

"Who's left?" Carn asked dryly.

"Indians," Cooke said soberly. "The Indians pose a more serious threat than all the other problems put together. The whole Territory could be affected."

Carn's interest sharpened. "So you said in Salt Lake. How bad is it?"

"Raiding westward all along the California trail, up into the Sierras," Cooke said. "Shoshones mostly, but also Utes. Been a lot of trains attacked and burned, and a lot of people killed. We've already sent out several patrols and more will be dispatched as soon as the camp gets better organized."

"Tell you what," Alexander said, tying up his travel bag. "I've already said my farewells to the General. No regrets there for either of us, I can tell you. The General always thought I was too soft for command, and I think he's too harsh. How about you two escorting me out of camp—give you a chance to look around, Carn. Then I'm on my way into Salt Lake."

"You planning on staying awhile in the city—?"

"Heading east tomorrow," Alexander said. "I'm hoping to meet with Brigham Young. You think he might agree to it?"

"He's staying pretty much behind locked doors these days," Carn told him, "but I'd be very surprised if he didn't see you, Edmund. He has a lot of respect for you."

"I suppose I owe much of that to you—"

"Brigham Young respects honor and decency. I'd consider it a favor, Edmund, if you'd spend the night at our place. General Galloway would like to meet you, as would my wife."

"I'll be pleased to accept that offer," Alexander replied. "Heard a lot about General Galloway, and it will be the first time I've met an angel. The way you talked about your wife last winter, Carn, has me convinced she wears wings."

Mounts were brought for the two officers and the three men started a tour of the new army encampment. Once again, Carn found himself overwhelmed by the size of the camp and the rapid progress being made in its construction.

Camp Floyd was laid out in a giant rectangle. On the shorter western side was the complex of administration buildings. Along the northern boundary, facing Cedar Creek but not close to it, stretched rows of barracks for the Tenth, Seventh and Fifth Infantry. Located next to them were the two battalions of the Third and Fourth Artillery, their light and heavy caissons already lined up in place nearby. Then came barracks for the six companies of the Second Dragoons, Colonel Cooke's command, stretching to the eastern edge of the camp. The walls of the barracks were being built out of orange-colored sandstone quarried from a canyon about five miles out of camp. It made the buildings stand out brightly from those constructed of lumber, adobe and stone.

South of the barracks, filling the rest of the massive rectangle, were scores of buildings and workshops all in various stages of construction, too confusing even for Cooke and Alexander to sort out. The number of workers swarming throughout all the building sites defied an estimate. That would take close scrutiny of the Paymaster's records. There were at least three or four thousand engaged in this frenzied construction of Camp Floyd, counting the soldiers.

Tregale and Cooke accompanied Alexander to the wooden bridge fording Cedar Creek, and made their farewells. It was clear that Alexander was sorry to be leaving friends but felt only relief that he was no longer under General Johnston's command. The Utah Expedition would not be a pleasant memory for anyone, particularly someone like Colonel Edmund Alexander who knew only too well how military integrity had been twisted by political deceit.

Riding back to the administration area, Colonel Cooke gave a few last words of caution to Tregale.

"I'm sure General Johnston will prove aggravating," he said. "Just try to remember he's under a lot of pressure. Lawlessness is out of control here at Camp Floyd, as well as in Salt Lake. I know Governor Cummings isn't sympathetic to military problems, but an army without discipline cannot be tolerated, especially by a man like General Johnston. I thought he was going to use a firing squad more than once at Camp Scott. Nothing will be more important to the General than restoring that discipline. So expect him to be curt to the point of rudeness when it comes to discussing Governor Cummings's requests."

"I'm wearing my thick skin, Colonel," Carn smiled. "Not expecting anything but the worst in my conversations with him. Like you said in Salt Lake, I'm not here to make friends, or to prove points. Just passing papers between the parties."

"You can be glad you postponed that baptism, too," Cooke added. "For a man who hates Mormons, he's now surrounded by thousands of them every day. It's bitterly galling to him, though he knows he has no choice but to employ them."

"I'll be sure to remind him of my Gentile status," Carn grinned.

"Have you ever met Lieutenant Colonel Smith, the General's second in command?"

"A couple of times, just briefly. Don't think we've ever exchanged direct words."

"Well, he'll probably be there when you meet with the general. Smith's in charge of getting Camp Floyd up and running, so the two of them spend a lot time together these days. Smith's a fine officer. He not only graduated from West Point, he served in it as instructor, adjutant, and commandant. Distinguished himself in just about all the major battles in the Mexican war. He's as much a stickler for the rules as Johnston, if not more so, but the thing to keep in mind is, Colonel Smith hates Mormons every bit as much as the General."

Not too long after, Tregale was admitted into the command tent of General Johnston. Colonel Smith was indeed sitting beside the General, both men studying maps spread out on a small table.

Lieutenant Colonel Charles F. Smith was about Johnston's age, looked similar to him in many ways. Smith had a bushier mustache, one that drooped down on each side of a tight-lipped mouth, isolating a strong chin from the rest of his face. His eyes were spaced wide apart under bushy, overhanging eyebrows, just as piercing as those of his commanding officer. His hair, turning gray like Johnston's, was much more combed and well kept. Johnston's hair usually looked as if he had just been out in a windstorm, like it did now. Both officers wore the same unhappy scowl. The differences, and the similarities, were very clear as they sat close at the table.

Smith noticed Tregale was not really standing at attention, but was standing stiffly enough to show respect. That was proper, and a mark of the man, Smith thought. In his book of rules, even a civilian should show courtesy to a commanding military authority. Another good thing about the man, Smith remembered, was this Tregale was not a Mormon.

General Johnston was looking at the saddlebags Tregale was carrying. A dour look crossed his face. "I assume those are papers from Governor Cummings?"

Tregale nodded respectfully. "He said he is most anxious to receive a prompt response to several of the items—"

"Well, he won't get it," Johnston interrupted. "Tell him I have a military command that takes priority over any civilian matter. You might remind him that my command also includes all of Utah Territory—and beyond."

"I'll do that, sir."

Johnston reached out to take the saddlebags, dropping them on the ground beside him. He frowned up at Tregale. "You're a military man, aren't you, Mr. Tregale?"

"British army, sir. Served in the Crimea."

"Well, I'm going to tell you some things I normally wouldn't say to a civilian. I'm going to do that because I hope you can communicate them to Governor Cummings—I know that's beyond any power of mine. Mr. Tregale, I don't believe Cummings is capable of seeing the full scope of the problems in this Territory. We are facing an explosion of trouble, sir, and I resent being pressured by Governor Cummings to assign men and resources I can't spare to solve his problems." The General's glance went down to the saddlebags. "I know he's going to make accusations that I am opposing him by refusing to answer his beck and call." He stared with hard eyes at Tregale. "May I trust you to place the facts before Governor Cummings, sir?"

"That's why I'm here, General," Tregale said without hesitation. "Thoughts and reasoning are often more important than words on a piece of paper. Can't vouch for what Governor Cummings may or may not do, but I'll certainly put it in front of him."

"Good enough," Johnston grunted. He glanced at the man sitting beside him. "You have any problem with briefing Mr. Tregale on military matters, Colonel?"

"If it gets that man off our backs," Smith muttered, "I'd agree to making Mr. Tregale an honorary colonel."

Tregale held back a smile. He'd already been given that honor by Utah militia officers.

Johnston motioned to an empty chair in front of the table. "Sit down, Mr. Tregale. I want your full attention for the next few minutes."

There was silence for a couple of minutes as the General gathered his thoughts. Then he kicked a foot at the saddlebags. "No doubt Cummings has some genuine problems in there, but I'll wager not one of them is as serious as those the army is facing.

"Don't know if you are aware of this, Mr. Tregale, but I have already sent several patrols out to deal with Indian problems. It's going to get a lot worse and we're going to need a lot more patrols."

His hand went up to stroke his mustache. "While we're talking about Indians, let me put to rest the report that I placed a bounty last winter on Mormon scalps. Not true, sir. I am sworn to protect the lives of every American citizen, and that includes Mormons. I placed no bounty, sir."

"I have already expressed such thoughts to Mormon authorities, sir," Carn said quietly. "Some believe you did it, like you said, but most do not lay it at your door, General."

"If there is a bounty," Johnston frowned, "I recommend someone interrogate that scoundrel of an Indian agent who came to Camp Scott last winter with a band of Utes he had led off the reservation—Herd, or Hurt, or something like that. He wanted me to approve the Utes attacking Mormon settlements. I was also approached at Camp Scott by Chief Washakie, of the Shoshones, and another Shoshone chief, Little Soldier, wanting the same thing. Turned them all down, of course. Told them not to connect themselves with the trouble between the army and the Mormons, to go home and stay out of it. I don't trust any Indian when it comes to choosing between killing Mormons, immigrants, or soldiers."

Colonel Smith was wearing a somber expression as he nodded in support of what the general just said. "A lot of innocent people lost their lives to Indians these past weeks. Every train on the trails to California is at risk."

"That's disturbing news," Carn said.

"I'm sure the Mormons are aware by now that General Harney has arrived at Fort Bridger with the Sixth Infantry Regiment. That puts six thousand troops at Camp Scott. Those will be held there in reserve until Washington decides what new orders will be issued."

"There is now over a third of the entire United States army stationed outside Great Salt Lake City, sir," Colonel Smith emphasized. He cast a quick, under-the-eyebrows glance at the General. "That fact amazes me, if not the Mormons. It isn't as if the country has no other problems. In my opinion, we are facing an imminent national crisis—but that is another matter."

"Civilian shortsightedness again," Johnston grunted. "Cummings isn't the only politician who can't see beyond his nose. However, those things have no bearing on the present situation, other than pointing out that even if we could use all those troops, we still wouldn't have enough to control the number of Indians now on the warpath."

"I suppose we should tell Mr. Tregale, so he can pass the information along to the Governor," Smith added, "that we expect serious reductions in force in the very near future. The companies of riflemen from New Mexico are already en route back, and there undoubtedly will be more reassignments of Expeditionary forces back East."

"What the Colonel is telling you, Mr. Tregale," Johnston said heavily, "is that while I don't have sufficient troops to do Cummings's bidding at present, he can expect even less support in the future if matters continue to deteriorate."

"The Governor probably won't appreciate that, General," Carn said, "but I'll be sure he understands the situation."

"I hope so," Johnston said, his scowl deepening. "He'll have his own troubles if the Nations unite and attack settlements in the heart of the Mormon corridor, instead of these random raids along the California trails. And I greatly fear that will happen."

"Do the Mormons think such a thing could happen—the Indian nations uniting against them?" Smith asked.

Tregale shrugged. "Nobody knows the answer to that, Colonel. The Mormons have worked hard to make friends with the Indians, ever since coming into the Territory ten, eleven years ago, but there's been bad blood of late. As you stated, General, nobody can trust them. They're open about their hatred for the army and the immigrant trains. The general feeling is they have the same hatred for the Mormons, though they don't come out and show it so plain."

Both officers looked at each other, then Johnston again fastened a heavy look on Tregale. "You heard about the burning of the squaws up in the San Pete reservation?"

Tregale shook his head. "No, sir. When did that happen?"

"Just awhile ago. Some trappers brought word—they were up in the hills and saw it happen. A whole bunch of different nations were up there in the San Pete camp, they said."

"Why did the Indians burn their women, General—?"

"Trappers think it was because they caught the Mexican dierhed disease—no doubt from teamsters at Camp Scott, and probably from some of my men, too. It's highly contagious and it appears the chiefs made an example of them. Point is, it shows the local nations are already uniting, and they're pretty riled up. If they're mad enough to burn their women, isn't much of a leap to be burning settler's homes."

"I'll pass that along, General."

"I take it you've never fought Indians, Mr. Tregale," the General said, studying him.

"No, sir."

"I have, sir, and learned respect for them."

"General Johnston fought in the Blackhawk war, as Adjutant General of the Illinois militia," Smith said, glancing respectfully at his commanding officer.

"That was a long time ago, Colonel," the General said gruffly. "I only brought it up to make sure Mr. Tregale understands—and hopefully can make Governor Cummings understand—that Indians are wily fighters and it's no easy task to best them. This could turn into a hard campaign, put a real drain on the command. It's important for Governor Cummings to realize that."

"I believe I can make the governor fully aware of the situation," Tregale assured him.

"Good." General Johnston looked down at the maps on the table. "I've said all that needs to be said, Mr. Tregale. You can tell the governor I'll get to his papers as soon as the opportunity presents itself."

Carn turned to leave but just then Colonel Cooke and a captain abruptly entered the tent. The colonel's face was grim as he addressed General Johnston.

"Rider just in, sir," Cooke said, without waiting to be asked. "Trouble in Oregon Territory. Report is that Colonel Steptoe was killed just a few days back. A large force of Shoshones, near a town called Colville, up near the Canadian border. His whole command of over one hundred and fifty men died with him, sir."

Johnston was on his feet, his face stern. "His whole command—?"

"Hundred and fifty-six officers and men was the report, General," Cooke said grimly. "Seems to be reliable."

The commanding officer in Johnston instantly took over in the face of crisis. He addressed the junior officer.

"Captain, I want you to ride to Camp Scott. Tell General Harney what happened. My suggestion is that Harney express back for orders to march the Sixth up into Oregon—probably headquarter at Fort Walla Walla. With a massacre of that magnitude, the army needs to reassert its presence before the whole territory goes up in flames. Tell General Harney I can't spare a large enough force, and besides, it would leave Utah and the California trails stripped of protection. The relief has to come from the Sixth. Get riding, Captain."

The officer left and the general turned his attention to Cooke.

"Colonel, I want a meeting with the head chiefs in this part of the country, here in Camp Floyd. I need to talk to them, try to stop the same thing from happening in this part of the country."

Cooke was thinking.

"That would be Arrowpeen, Peteetneet, Tintic, Sanpitch and

Yampants. Kanosh, of the southern Pahvants—they massacred a big train last summer. Then there's Washakie and Little Soldier of the Shoshones up north—though they don't mix too often with the Ute tribes. Won't be easy, General. They don't trust the military—"

"Just get them here, Colonel, as soon as possible," Johnston said irritably. "Put them under arrest if that's the only way. We need to—"

He was interrupted by a young lieutenant bursting into the tent. He gave Johnston a hurried salute. "Sorry sir, but there's a rider outside who needs to see you immediately. That's what he said, sir—"

"Show the man in, Lieutenant."

The rider was a sergeant, covered in dust, almost overpowering with the smell of sweat. Fatigue was etched on his face. "Report from Captain Jewkes, sir." Jewkes was in charge of one of the patrols recently sent west toward the Humboldt. "Indians raiding up in Thousand Springs. Three trains that we know of, sir. Maybe forty, fifty immigrants dead. Captain Jewkes requests reinforcements. Must be four or five hundred redskins raiding up there along the Thousand Springs trail."

Johnston digested the news, then nodded at the sergeant. "Get some food inside you, sergeant. Not much time for rest, but get what you can. You'll be needing to ride back with the reinforcements."

"One thing more Captain Jewkes wanted passed on, sir," the sergeant added. "Some survivors said they saw white men in the raiding parties. They was painted to look like Indians, but they was white."

"White renegades," Colonel Smith grated. "Worst sort of killers. Tell Captain Jewkes to show no mercy if you run into them. Don't leave one alive."

The sergeant saluted and left the tent. Johnston and Colonel Smith quickly studied one of the maps on the table, the general tracing a finger to the area of Thousand Springs.

He looked up at Cooke. "Colonel, get a hundred and fifty of your dragoons ready to start for Thousand Springs. I want them on the trail soon as you can. Put a reliable officer in charge—they'll undoubtedly be seeing action."

"I'll assign Captain Hawes," Cooke said. "Jim's no stranger to Indian campaigns. This will be an extended sortie, I assume."

"However long it takes to bring these savages under control," Johnston said grimly. "Have Captain Hawes establish a camp in Thousand Springs Valley. Jewkes' command can use it, too, while they're patrolling the Humboldt trail."

He swung again to Colonel Smith. "Colonel, put more men to work completing Camp Floyd. Double the number of civilian workers if you have to. We need this fort fully operational."

The General looked at Tregale. Carn answered his question before it was asked.

"I'll head back to Salt Lake right away," he told the general. "I'll make sure the news reaches all the proper authorities."

"Thank you, Mr. Tregale," Johnston clipped. "Tell those people none of those renegade whites better be Mormons. Now we all have things to attend to."

Outside, Colonel Cooke shook Carn's hand. "Got to get those dragoons into the field," he said. "Let me know how Governor Cummings reacts to these new events."

"I'll do that, Colonel."

As Tregale cantered up the roadway, heading for the Cedar Creek bridge, he was surprised to see a familiar face. It was Calvin Gray, standing beside his horse as he talked to a sergeant, seeming to be pleading with the man. The sergeant was stockily built, bare-chested in the heat, wearing only boots and work pants held up by a pair of sweat-stained suspenders. Sergeant stripes were pinned to the suspenders, Carn noted. The soldier had a lean face and long dark hair, or it would have been dark if the greasy locks hadn't been heavily coated in reddish dust. Evidently the sergeant was working near the sandstone barracks.

Calvin looked rugged and lean, burned brown by the long months of working a farm near Provo, owned by General Galloway. Calvin's hair was sandy and fell to his shoulders. His features were pleasant but ordinary, giving no strong impression about him. A person could see just about anything they wanted to in Calvin, for nothing was yet clearly stamped as a mark of the man inside.

In his early twenties, Calvin was working his way to California with his younger brother, Amos, riding herd for the large train from

Arkansas. Curiosity brought them to a Mormon celebration last summer commemorating the passing of a decade since the first Mormon pioneers entered the Great Salt Lake Valley. Calvin met Harriet Hilliger, a young woman who had traveled to Utah with her sister the previous winter. Calvin and Harriet fell in love and were married a few days later. That was when the ill-fated relationship between his brother Amos and young Beryl Tate began. Warned about an imminent attack by Indians, which Amos and the rest of the wagon train dismissed, Harriet convinced Calvin to leave and return to Parowan. The massacre occurred shortly after that, and Calvin never really forgave himself for leaving his brother and friends to die at Mountain Meadows. He knew there was nothing he could have done, but it still left a feeling of guilt.

Shortly after the massacre, the Tate family, along with Calvin and Harriet and another young couple, Jim and Beth Wilson, left troublesome southern Utah and moved onto a ranch and adjacent farm just outside Provo, both owned by General Galloway. Tregale had thought everyone was content there, until now.

Tregale rode closer to Calvin and the sergeant.

"Calvin," he said, "what brings you to Camp Floyd?"

"Trying to enlist, Mr. Tregale. This here sergeant—"

"Sergeant Pike, sir," the sergeant told Tregale. He'd seen this civilian, easily recognized by the curved hook where a left hand should be, in the company of officers both here and back at Camp Scott. It was always best to be polite to people who moved within circles of authority, Pike knew. "Trying to tell this man we're not taking new enlistments. Nothing personal. It's orders from the Department of the Army in Washington."

At that moment, Colonel Cooke rode up, on his way to where the dragoons were camped on the east side. He saw Tregale and reined in his horse.

"Trouble here, Carn?" he asked.

"Not really, Colonel," Carn answered. "Sergeant Pike was just explaining to a friend of mine, Calvin Gray, that the army is not accepting enlistments." He looked over at Gray. "Calvin, meet Colonel Cooke. He commands the Second Dragoons."

Calvin nodded respectfully. "That's what I dearly want to be, Colonel Cooke. A dragoon."

Cooke studied him, looked at the saddle, Calvin's clothing. "You look comfortable in the saddle, Mr. Gray."

"Born in one, sir. Was riding before I could walk."

"Can you shoot?"

"Rifle or handgun, sir. I'll peg a rabbit between the eyes at fifty paces."

"Think you could peg an Indian at a hundred paces?"

"I've beaded on a few, Colonel. Just never squeezed the trigger."

"How soon you ready to ride, Mr. Gray?'

"Right this minute, sir."

Cooke looked at Sergeant Pike. "Get this man sworn in and outfitted, Sergeant. There's a hundred and fifty dragoons leaving for Thousand Springs in the morning and I want Mr. Gray with them." He saw the wide grin break across Calvin's face. "You'll do a lot of hard riding and probably a lot of killing, Mr. Gray. Let's hope you're still wearing that grin when you get back."

"Thank you, sir," Calvin said, giving Cooke his version of a military salute.

"I deeply appreciate this, Colonel."

Cooke directed a brief nod at Carn, then continued eastward across the camp. Calvin reached out and shook Carn's hand so hard it shook the Cornishman's whole body.

"Tell Harriet about this, will you, Mr. Tregale? Didn't expect things to happen this fast." He paused, flashing an uncomfortable smile. "Harriet don't know about me wanting to enlist, Mr. Tregale. I've been real uncomfortable about being a farmer—just ain't my nature, I guess. I was going to tell Harriet after I made inquiries, but won't get the chance to do that now. Don't know where this Thousand Springs is, or how long I'll be gone, but tell her I'm happy about being in the army, and I'll miss her and the baby."

CHAPTER FIVE

SPANISH FORK
MID-SEPTEMBER

The smell of fresh-cut hay wafted from the fields behind the Markham farm just outside Spanish Fork. It was the last cutting, better than expected, and was still scattered waiting to be gathered and baled. The evening was warm and pleasant, cooled by a breeze drifting from the nearby canyon. Through the open window of the kitchen, Anna Maria Markham heard her husband hammering on the metal anvil in the barn, telling her the task of shoeing the horses wouldn't be completed much before dusk. On an impulse, Anna Maria took the hand of her nine-year-old daughter and headed for the door.

"Let's pick some pretty flowers for the table," Anna Maria smiled.

The two of them strolled through the fields, sometimes chasing each other, sometimes running to be first to reach a bunch of wild flowers, laughing and twirling together, enjoying the freedom and freshness of the evening. Finally, Anna Maria glanced back over her shoulder and realized they'd traveled farther from the farmhouse than she normally went. It was a family rule that everyone always kept the farmhouse clearly in sight. These were uncertain times, what with drunken soldiers and teamsters just a few miles away in Cedar Valley, and several hundred malcontent Uintahs on the Spanish Fork reservation just a short ride from the settlement. Both parents agreed it would be safer to stay close to the farmhouse. Anna Maria could barely see the roof of the house from where they were now, and she was suddenly nervous.

She called to her daughter, who just moments ago ran behind a clump of trees a few yards away. There was no answer and she called again, starting for the trees. Two Indians stepped their horses out from behind the trees, one of them holding her wildly struggling daughter, his hand clamped tightly over the child's mouth.

Anna Maria screamed and started running toward the Indians as both men slid to the ground. She reached the one holding her daughter, fighting to free her from his grasp. She hit the man with her fists, screaming and clawing at his face. Her fingernails dug in deeply, drawing lines of blood on his cheeks. Then the other Indian had his arms around her, pulling her away, throwing her roughly to the ground. The smell of whiskey reeked strongly from both of them. The second Indian now had his knees on her arms, pinning them, and he started slapping her face with savage force. Her screams died into painful sobs.

The other Indian took his hand away from the daughter's mouth as he watched the mother being beaten. The child began screaming loudly, fighting to free herself. The Indian hit her twice on the head with his clenched fist and the child slumped in his arms, unconscious. The Indian dropped her onto the ground and crossed to join his companion.

What happened next was so brutal the mother would have nightmares about it for the rest of her life. She was stripped naked, tortured, and repeatedly raped. The worst part came when the savages finally finished with her and turned to her daughter. Anna Maria tried to scream but she was too brutalized to move or even force sound from her throat. She tried to hold on to consciousness, wanting desperately to save her child from the horror engulfing her, all the while knowing there was nothing she could do. Mercifully, blackness overcame her and Anna Maria no longer could hear her daughter's tortured cries.

Markham found his wife and daughter late that evening, after becoming alarmed when he didn't find them in the farmhouse. He searched the darkening fields for almost an hour before discovering them behind the clump of trees. Anna Maria was huddled on the ground, shuddering and moaning even in her unconsciousness. Markham's heart shredded as he picked up his daughter, naked and cruelly cut, still bleeding. She tried to put her arms around her father's neck, but her little body had suffered too much. She fell back limply in his arms, lapsing into a coma that mercifully shielded the pain. Weeks later, when she finally regained full consciousness, memories of her ordeal were pushed back into a hazy world that everyone hoped would never clear.

Word of the rape and torture of the mother and daughter spread like a wildfire through Spanish Fork and along the line of settlements. A family who lived close by the reservation remembered seeing two Indians riding back into the compound, yelling drunkenly and waving what looked to be part of a woman's dress. They recognized the two riders—Pangunts and Namowah.

They were known troublemakers, part of a rebellious band of young Indians angry at the whites who had shepherded them onto the confines of a reservation and tried to force warriors into becoming women. Farming was a way of life that violated every nomadic tradition of their people. What little tilling and planting was done was women's work, on a level with weaving blankets. A warrior provided for his family by hunting and could only be degraded by working in the fields. All the young men held a particular hatred for the Mor-mons, for they had stolen ancestral lands and bought Indian children to raise them in a white man's world, deliberately trying to destroy the very lifeblood of the nations.

By the time Pangunts and Namowah were identified as suspects, it was too late and too dark to follow them onto the reservation. Besides, the most urgent concern was caring for Anna Maria and her daughter. Neighbors took them in, doing what they could for the cuts and bruises, unable to do anything for the agony still stark in Anna Maria's eyes. Throughout the night, Markham never left the side of wife or daughter.

With daylight, a force of some two hundred men descended on the two-storied stone headquarters of the Spanish Fork reservation. Not only were there the men of Spanish Fork, but they were joined by militiamen from Springville and Payson and other small nearby settlements. The attack upon the Markhams demanded immediate justice, for what had happened to them was the secret nightmare haunting every family in the valley.

There was not an Indian in sight as the Mormon horsemen surrounded the building. A bearded, grim-faced man in his gray militia uniform dismounted and pounded a fist loudly against the front door. The door shook but there was no answer from inside.

"This is Colonel John Fullmer, commander of the Spanish Fork militia," the man shouted, looking up at the small window openings on the second floor. "Doc, if you're in there, better open this door before we smash it in."

The militia commander was calling to Garland Hurt, the Indian agent appointed in Washington three years ago to assist Brigham Young in his duties as Territorial Superintendent of Indian Affairs. Young had recently been relieved of those duties by a new superintendent, Jacob Forney, who had arrived in company with the new governor, Alfred Cummings.

Hurt, a lean and darkly surly man in his early thirties—young by the standards of most federal appointees—professed to the title of doctor, although it wasn't clear what kind or how official it was. From the outset, he had opposed the Mormon approach to dealing with the Indians. He had become so at odds with the Mormons that they now considered him more troublesome than the Indians themselves.

Hurt strongly favored imposing reservation farming on the Indians, believing that would eventually make them self-sustaining, preserve their native cultures, and protect their rights to the land. He believed the Mormon approach of providing gifts and annual subsidies only made the Indians unproductive and dependent on begging and stealing. Hurt also objected to Mormon missionary activities among the "Lamanites", as they called them, claiming it was solely for the purpose of absorbing the Indians into a way of life that was not their own.

In the last year, Doc Hurt had become an implacable enemy of the Mormons. Many suspected he encouraged his Indian charges to harass and steal from the settlers—and possibly commit far more serious crimes.

So the anger and belligerence on the faces of the mounted men surrounding Hurt's headquarters could almost be felt. Fullmer pounded on the door again, stepping back to get a view into the upper windows. This time, there was a fleeting glimpse of a man looking down. Many recognized him as Ute Pete, the Indian servant of Garland Hurt. A few moments later, the front door opened a few inches and Ute Pete peered out nervously at Fullmer.

"Doc Hurt," the colonel repeated. "We must talk to Doc Hurt."

Ute Pete shook his head. "Not here."

Fullmer stepped forward and pushed the door all the way open. The servant cowered back, his face fearful.

"Bring Doc Hurt—" Fullmer ordered harshly.

Again the shaking head. "Not here. Not here all day gone."

"When is he coming back—?"

Ute Pete pointed up at the morning sky, then down at the floor. "Be here. Soon."

He couldn't have been more prophetic. Everyone turned as they heard, then saw, a horseman galloping toward them. He was coming out of the north, and riding hard. Moments later, Garland Hurt reined up in front of them. His eyes took in the large number of horsemen and a hard expression came to his face. He raised a hand to cut off Fullmer as the militia commander started to speak.

"I know about it, Colonel. Heard it in Provo this morning. That's why I'm here." He glared frostily at Fullmer. "There's no mistake about this—?"

"No mistake, Hurt," Fullmer answered, equally cold. "No mistake about who did it, neither."

Hurt was surprised. "You know who did it—?"

"Pangunts and Namowah. They're the two we want. And we want them now."

"You planning a lynching, Colonel?" Hurt asked.

"A woman and her daughter were raped and brutalized by two of your bucks, Hurt. The little girl may never come to her senses. Those bucks are going to pay for that."

"You can't be sure—"

"Dead sure," Fullmer said, cutting the agent off. "You bringing them out, or are we going in after them?"

Garland Hurt turned to his Indian servant standing in the doorway. He asked him something in Ute. Ute Pete started shaking his head, pointing off into the west. His reply was grunted in hurried Ute, difficult to pick up. Hurt turned back to the commander.

"Ute Pete says they're gone, Colonel. Both of them. They left last night."

Fullmer frowned at the servant. "Ute Pete say where they went?"

Hurt asked his servant the question. The answer came quickly and Hurt again turned back to Fullmer.

"Ute Pete says they went to Camp Floyd."

Fullmer stared at him, distrust on his face. "Why would they do that?"

"If you was them, Fullmer, would you wait around for two hundred angry Mormons to come and get you—?"

"You guarantee those two aren't on the reservation—?"

"Ute Pete don't lie to me," Hurt said angrily.

One of the horsemen spoke up. "My Ute's passable, Colonel. Ute Pete did say they was both gone to the soldiers' camp."

"Then I guess that's where we're headed," Fullmer said grimly.

"Don't advise that, Colonel," Hurt said quickly. "Those soldiers see two hundred of you militia boys coming, there won't be any talk. People just went to a lot of trouble to avoid that kind of a fight."

"You got something else in mind, Hurt?" Fullmer asked. "We can't help wondering whose side you're on in this. None of us have forgot how you tried to turn the Indians against us last year. If you'd had your way, wouldn't be a Mormon alive in this whole territory today—"

"That isn't true," Hurt protested. "Those were just rumors. There's no evidence that proves I did that—"

"If there was," Fullmer said grimly, "you'd be dead, Hurt. But you understand why we don't consider your word good for much."

Hurt's face reddened with a flush of anger. "If Pangunts and Namowah are guilty—"

"They're guilty, Hurt. No room for doubt on that."

"—then I want justice done as much as the rest of you. I'll ride out to Camp Floyd and bring them back myself, with an escort of soldiers."

"You'll deliver them over to us?" Fullmer asked suspiciously. "Last year, about this same time as I remember, you and about three hundred of those redskins skeedaddled up Spanish Fork canyon—"

"You were after my hide," Hurt reminded him.

"No fault of ours," Fullmer said. "Brigham Young offered you a carriage and safe escort to Camp Scott."

"After he dismissed me for no cause—"

"After you stole government property," Fullmer corrected. "It was your choice to run up into the mountains with all those Indians from the reservation. You're lucky we decided not to go after you, Doc. You wouldn't be here now if we had."

"This is different," Hurt said curtly. "I'm not doing the running. I'll deliver Pangunts and Namowah to the sheriff in Provo, where they got a proper jail. You boys can meet me this side of the Lakes if you don't trust me to do that. But you got to promise there'll be no lynching. No matter what they did, those two got a right to have their say in court."

Fullmer looked around at the other faces, saw general agreement. He nodded at Garland Hurt. "No funny business. If there is, we'll take you in their place and let you rot." He noticed the agent glance furtively westward, toward the hills of the reservation. "No need to go up there, Doc. We'll all feel a might easier if you just head out from here, right now. We see more than two Indians in one place and we're cutting loose. And count on it—we will be waiting for you this side of the Lakes."

◆

After Pangunts and Namowah made their triumphant return to the reservation, the excitement of their attack upon the white woman and her child, coupled with the euphoria of the whiskey, gradually gave way to an awareness of the enormity of what they had done. They began to realize that the Mormons would hunt them down relentlessly and make them pay for every savage moment of pleasure. Fear and panic finally drained all other emotions.

The two braves slipped away from the reservation as soon as full darkness blanketed the valley. They considered fleeing south and hiding out with the Piedes or one of the smaller tribes, but then they decided there was a better way. They set out at full gallop for Camp Floyd to find a man they were sure would help them—for a price, of course. Even with whiskey pain now hammering inside their heads, they knew anything was better than falling into the hands of the settlers.

Sergeant Pike was roused out of sleep by one of the guards who had challenged Pangunts and Namowah. The guard made no mention of the gold piece he'd been given to bring Pike to the two Indians, now crouching as part of the shadows beside the bridge.

Pike recognized Pangunts and Namowah. These two had brought him many squaws last winter at Camp Scott. All it cost the sergeant was a few bottles of whiskey and some stolen rations. Pike ordered one of the guards to rouse an Indian interpreter and soon they were all crouched inside one of the unfinished adobe buildings. With the aid of the interpreter, Pike heard a greatly understated version of what happened earlier that evening in Spanish Fork.

"So you want me to hide you out until things cool down," Pike muttered. "That ain't gonna be easy. Doing what you did is gonna bring down the Mormons, the Territorial peace officers, and probably the army on your tails."

"You do this for us," Pangunts said through the interpreter, "and we get all women you want, as long as you are here."

The grin that spread across the sergeant's face could be seen even in the shadows. "Sounds mighty enticing," Pike said, "specially the way prices are going up in Frogtown."

Frogtown was the current name for Fairfield, just across the creek from the army camp. With its flamboyantly festooned streets of saloons and brothels, Frogtown already had more residents than the three thousand soldiers at Camp Floyd. As Pike said, greater demand for Frogtown's pleasures kept pushing prices higher.

Pangunts was looking anxiously at the sergeant. "You hide us from Mor-mons?"

"I'll hide you," Pike grunted, "but it's gonna cost you more than squaws." His glance fell to the leather pouches each carried at his waist.

"Let's start with those coins I hear clinkin' in those pouches. I'm thinkin' you wouldn't steal nothin' but gold."

Pangunts and Namowah looked at each other, both knowing they were not in a position to argue with the sergeant. They untied the pouches and each emptied a pile of gold coins into Pike's outstretched hand.

"That's good," Pike said. "Now you got to do one more thing then I'll make sure you ain't touched by no hand of the law. You get me some young things I can use to go into business." He could see they didn't understand and another grin flashed across his face. "Frogtown is about to get another whorehouse, boys. You get me some prime stock and I'll even cut you in on the profits. You'll both be so rich you can buy yourselves all the white women you want."

The interpreter had to explain it twice. Then both Indians started shaking their head.

"Must wait. Can't go back now."

Pike's face hardened. "You bust back to that reservation. You can hide out for one day with your people. Bring the girls tomorrow night. I'll meet you at the south end of the Lakes about midnight. You boys better show, or I'll be coming after you myself."

CHAPTER SIX

CAMP FLOYD

This better be a matter of urgent importance, Colonel Cooke," General Johnston snapped. "I left specific orders that Colonel Smith and myself were not to be disturbed while we were meeting with the chiefs."

He scowled at the three men waiting for him in the small ante-room in the administration building. The building, completed three days before, still smelled strongly of the white paint covering the interior sandstone walls. Colonel Cooke stood nearest the door; Carn Tregale beside him. Johnston did not even bother to nod. If he'd been pulled out of an important meeting to deal with a request from Cummings—well, Cooke would find out how displeased he was. His glance fastened on the third man in the room. It took a moment, then he recognized him. The Indian agent—the one he had dismissed so curtly at Camp Scott last winter. What was he doing here—?

"I'm waiting, Colonel," Johnston said. "I assume there is an emergency of some sort—"

Quickly Cooke told him what had happened in Spanish Fork the previous afternoon. "Mr. Tregale is here on behalf of Governor Cummings," he added, "and I'm not sure why Doctor Hurt is here."

Hurt spoke up quickly. "The two Indians accused of this crime were reported to have fled here to Camp Floyd," he said. "As agent in charge of the Spanish Fork reservation, I need to question them to determine if they are indeed implicated."

Johnston's scowl deepened. "Why do you think they're in Camp Floyd?"

"I was told they came here for safety from the Mormons," Hurt answered. "I myself was accosted this morning by more than two hundred of them—I felt my own life was in danger. There's no proof of guilt, as far as I know, but the Mormons intend to vent their anger on these two, guilty or not."

"Just what do you want the army to do?" Johnston asked irritably.

"If there is cause to take them back to Provo for trial, I need a military escort to make sure they, as well as myself, get there safely."

Johnston switched his attention to Tregale. "I assume Governor Cummings has heard about this and wants me to send my entire command after these two Indians—"

"Something like that, sir." Tregale resisted smiling, the look on General Johnston's face not inviting levity. There was a letter in Carn's pocket drafted by Governor Cummings during the night which was pretty close in demanding just that. Producing it would not help the general's temper, Tregale decided. "The Governor is naturally anxious that the persons responsible for the attack on the Markhams are apprehended, but he is even more concerned that the civilian population see the army put on an immediate show of force to let them, and the Indians, know such lawless acts will not be tolerated."

"You may inform the Governor I do not need to be reminded of my duties, sir," Johnston said. "I am far more aware of the dangers of an Indian insurrection than he is. You may assure him I will act swiftly and firmly once the facts are clear and a course of action is determined. I will not, however, order my men to ride around in circles firing their guns in the air just to frighten people—as I'm sure the Governor would prefer."

Tregale simply nodded. No reply was needed or wanted.

There was a knock on the closed door behind Johnston. Cooke crossed swiftly and opened it. A private stood there, at attention and looking very nervous.

"Private Williams, sir. I was told to report to the Colonel, sir."

"You were on guard duty at the bridge last night, Williams—?"

The private nodded, looking even more nervous. "That's right, sir."

"Did you see any Indians approaching the camp—?"

"Yes, sir," Williams said, making a quick and wise decision. Part truth would be harder to unmask than whole lies. The gold coin still in the pocket of his pants was beginning to burn. "Two of them, sir. Both bucks. Shortly after I went on duty at midnight, sir."

"Did they enter the camp?"

"No, sir."

"Tell us what happened, Private—"

"They wanted to see an officer, sir."

"Why—?"

"I believe they wanted sanctuary, sir. Couldn't understand what they were saying exactly—don't know any Indian talk."

"So the two Indians are here in camp—?"

"No, sir," Williams said quickly. "Sent them packin'."

"They left—?"

"That's right, sir."

"You're sure they're not in camp—?"

"Not unless they slipped in somewhere on the perimeter," Williams replied. "Don't know why they would do that though. They knew from my rifle in their noses they weren't welcome at Camp Floyd."

"Thank you, Williams," Cooke said. "You're dismissed."

The colonel closed the door and turned to Johnston. "That's the last of the night watch, General. Only Williams even saw any Indians. I ordered a search of the camp this morning after hearing what happened. I doubt if those Indians are here, sir."

"You seem to have matters under control, Colonel," Johnston frowned. "Why interrupt my meeting—?"

"Thought you should be aware of this, General. If we're going to send troops to the reservation—which seems called for—those Indian chiefs probably should be told. Didn't want them thinking you spoke with a forked tongue, so to speak, or have them react the wrong way. If they jump to the wrong conclusion, we could have an all-out Indian war on our hands."

"Thank you, Colonel Cooke," Johnston muttered. "That was good thinking. I just hope we don't already have that war."

Cooke's efforts to get the Indian chiefs to Camp Floyd had met with only partial success. Only Chiefs Peteetneet, Tintic, and Sanpitch had shown up this morning for the meeting with the "Big Soldier," General Johnston. The officers knew the other chiefs stayed away because they didn't trust the army and had no intention of allowing a trap to be sprung around them all at the same time.

Johnston had already spent three frustrating hours in negotiations with the three chiefs next door in the meeting room, during which he and Colonel Smith accomplished absolutely nothing. There were no promises, no commitments, no real communication despite the presence of two interpreters. For the most part, the chiefs had sat silent, listening to the interpreters repeat the officers' words. Johnston thought of asking Hurt to join the meeting, but immediately rejected it, not trusting the agent to be truthful even with army interpreters present.

"Colonel," he said, "I need to get back to that meeting. Take what action you feel is necessary, including sending a company of dragoons to the reservation. I'll tell the Chiefs what's happening and try to head off any overreaction on their part. If one of our officers sees the Markhams, give them my personal and deepest sympathies. You may assure the family we will find the persons responsible and bring them to the bar of justice."

The general left and returned to his meeting. It didn't last much longer.

"We must find your people who did this evil thing," Johnston said, after telling the three chiefs what happened in Spanish Fork. "Soldiers will be sent to Spanish Fork, but only to arrest those two. After that, they will be tried in a court of law to determine their guilt or innocence."

The chiefs listened to the interpreter, frowned at each other, then grunted an answer. The interpreter nodded.

"The Chiefs do not understand when you say 'trying'," the interpreter said, "but they say it would be better for warriors to be dead than kept in a white man's prison. The Chiefs also say they are angered and insulted by your words, and this meeting is at an end."

The chiefs rode out of camp a few minutes later. Out in front of the headquarters building, Cooke, Tregale and Hurt watched them go.

"This could be bad trouble," Hurt muttered. "General Johnston should not have insulted three such powerful chiefs—"

"The General did not insult them, I am sure," Cooke told the man stiffly. "They had no intention of being cooperative and this was just an excuse to end the meeting."

"I'd better get back to the reservation," Hurt said. "I'll need that escort now more than ever, Colonel. The Mormons are waiting for me. They see me coming without those two bucks, I'm a dead man."

Cooke glanced at Tregale. "Would you go with Hurt, Carn? The Mormons will listen to you, and I'd like you to be on the reservation when the troops get there. I'll send a report to the Governor."

Dawn broke over the reservation farm at Spanish Fork several days later to reveal a circle of soldiers around the outer perimeter. The force of one hundred and sixty dragoons and infantrymen was under the command of Major Gabriel Paul. They took positions silently during the night and as the order to advance was quietly passed, the troops began to close in. It was confirmed just the day before that the two Indians sought in the Markham attack were indeed still hiding out on the farm and Major Paul intended to tighten the noose until the suspects were chased out and taken into custody.

It didn't take long for the Indians to become aware of the encircling troops.

Chief Tintic was awakened, and he in turn awakened Pintuts, son of Chief Arrowpeen, who was at the reservation to obtain a full account of the recent meeting with Big Soldier at the camp of the blue coats.

"We must leave," the older Tintic told Pintuts. "Soldiers are coming to take Pangunts and Namowah, but perhaps they will take me and the son of Arrowpeen prisoners if they find us."

"Why are the Mor-mons so angry about what happened to this woman and her daughter?" Pintuts asked, frowning. "They were not killed—"

"That is true," Tintic said.

"It was not a good thing, what Pangunts and Namowah did," Pintuts said, "but if all they did was take pleasure with this woman—"

Tintic shrugged. "They beat and cut both mother and child, but the Mor-mons are angry mostly because Panguts and Namowah have skin not the same as theirs."

A few minutes later, the two chiefs sat on their horses in an arroyo near the eastern edge of the farm. Tintic silently pointed both to the right and the left, making sure Pintuts saw the four soldiers coming toward them. The soldiers, intent on keeping as quiet as possible, had not spotted the two Indians in the arroyo. A nod passed between Tintic and Pintuts and suddenly they charged out of hiding, heading straight through the widely scattered line of advancing soldiers.

It almost worked.

The soldiers were caught by surprise, unnerved by the sudden appearance of the two Indians. At first the four soldiers thought they were being attacked but quickly realized the Indians were simply trying to break through their line. A volley of shots rang out.

Pintuts cried out in pain as two bullets smashed into his back. He flung out his arms and fell from the galloping horse. Tintic looked back, saw the son of Arrowpeen fall, and despite the continued shooting of the soldiers, turned his mount around and raced back, jumping to the ground and taking Pintuts in his arms. Pintuts was already dead.

Tintic looked up as the soldiers closed in, rifles pointed at him. The soldiers didn't need words to tell them the flight and the fight, if one was ever intended, was gone. A sergeant, a veteran of other Indian campaigns, understood enough Shoshone and Ute to put together what Tintic was saying.

"The son of Chief Arrowpeen was only going back to his father," Tintic muttered, looking down at the dead man he still held in his arms. "This must end. I will take you to Pangunts and Namowah—they are the ones who attacked the white woman and her daughter."

When word of the killing of Pintuts reached Garland Hurt at the farm headquarters, he was visibly upset. The agent looked at Carn Tregale and Major Paul, directing the attempt to capture the two suspects in the Markham assault. Hurt looked angrily at the major.

"Arrowpeen will avenge the death of his son," Hurt warned grimly. "There will be much blood spilled over this. Your soldiers should not—"

"My soldiers saw two Indians trying to break through our lines," Paul interrupted. "They thought it was the two we were after. Chief

Tintic had no reason to do what he did."

"Tintic had no reason to trust your soldiers," Hurt snapped. "They are killing Indians throughout the whole Territory."

"Indians who have killed innocent settlers and overland immigrants—"

"The Indians kill only because they are being killed, and mistreated, and robbed of their lands—"

"There's no time for this, Hurt," the major interrupted. "My men have Pangunts and Namowah in custody. We'll be returning to Camp Floyd immediately." Paul glanced respectfully at Carn Tregale. "I trust a proper account of what happened here today will reach the Governor, sir—"

"Be assured of it, Major."

Tregale decided to accompany Major Paul and the troops, along with the two prisoners, back to Camp Floyd. He was impatient to return to Salt Lake but felt it would be more satisfying to Governor Cummings if he could report he had actually witnessed the two Indians locked up in the guardhouse. While he was in Camp Floyd, he could also find out if there were any new problems that would concern the civilian authorities.

Pangunts and Namowah were put in a cell together in the new sandstone guardhouse. Tregale reported the facts about the shooting of Arrowpeen's son to Colonel Cooke, supporting Major Paul's account and heading off any false rumors that might be started by the Indian agent Hurt. There were no reports from the patrols up in the Thousand Springs area or along the headwaters of the Humboldt. Several fur trappers visited Frogtown with hair-raising stories about Indians raiding and killing all along the California trails, but no official credence was given to them. General Johnston was waiting for his officers to report. There was a growing conviction, however, that when the reports came, they would simply authenticate the stories of the trappers.

Tregale was heading out of camp when he ran into Aaron Cunningham. Aaron insisted Carn come with him to the carpentry shop where his father was working. Both Cunninghams were among the first to go to Camp Floyd and since both were skilled carpenters, they'd quickly been given high-paying, supervisory responsibilities in the building of the camp. They had done extremely well, even managing to keep their carpentry shop in Sugar House operating while working at the army camp.

Alfred, his wife Esther, and Aaron were among the close-knit group of handcart families who had been under Tregale's supervision during the grueling trip to Utah in the winter of '56. Alfred and Aaron were of special help, for they built extra strength into the group's handcarts, and provided much needed maintenance along the way. Alfred saw his son approaching in company with Carn and came out of the carpentry shop smiling, with hand extended.

"Heard you were a regular visitor out here," Alfred said, shaking Carn's hand, "but we've never been able to catch up with you."

"Good to see you, Alfred," Carn smiled. "Been hearing good things about the work you and Aaron are doing. Even General Johnston had some words of praise when your names came up a couple weeks ago."

"That's good to hear," Alfred said. "The general's always wearing a frown whenever I see him."

"That's his happy face," Carn grinned. "He was born frowning."

"What's all this we hear about Indian trouble?" Aaron asked anxiously. "Are mother and Lydia in any danger—?"

Tregale shook his head. "Nothing to worry about, Aaron—not in Sugar House, anyway. There's serious trouble other places, though."

"Lydia said something about Calvin enlisting," Aaron said. "That true—?"

Aaron's wife Lydia was Harriet's sister, and she had worried, like everyone else, when Harriet married the Arkansas trailhand so quickly after they met. Carn had told Harriet about Calvin enlisting and riding off to patrol the Thousand Springs trail, and she had taken it hard. The news was such a shock she was unable to hide her feelings from anyone.

"He's a dragoon right enough," Carn said. "Went with a large patrol up into Thousand Springs. That's up in the northern part of the Territory, a little west of the Great Salt Lake. A lot of wagon trains take the Thousand Springs trail to California."

"Sort of sudden, wasn't it?" Alfred said. "Last I heard, he and Harriet and the baby were doing just fine on that farm near Provo."

"Calvin wasn't cut out for farming, I guess," Carn said. "That's what he said, anyway."

"Well, Lydia is sure worried about her sister," Aaron said. "She never did take a strong liking to Calvin."

"And he never took a liking to Mormons," his father added. "That's part of his problem, I'll wager."

"Looks like the post's nearly finished," Tregale said, changing the subject.

He felt uneasy talking about Harriet. He knew how much she was still suffering. Since Calvin left, she had gone to Sugar House several times to visit her sister, and usually came on into Salt Lake to spend some time with Heather and Agatha. She always asked if he'd heard anything about Calvin's patrol, but of course, there was nothing to tell her. Carn changed the subject by looking around at the surrounding construction, then back to Alfred and his son. "This place is going up fast. Still can't believe how huge it is."

"Biggest army camp in the whole United States, they tell me," Alfred said. There was a note of pride in his voice. "Over three hundred buildings. Well built, too. Had to tear down a few and start over, but mostly there's been good work. It's almost finished now— should be dedicating the place in a month or so."

"Sure has changed life for a lot of people," Carn mused.

"Our family among them," Alfred agreed. "When we get back to Sugar House, we can build mother any kind of home she wants— even something as big as General Galloway's place."

"Is that what Esther wants?" Carn asked, surprised. "Didn't think she'd be up to a place that big."

"Esther's changed," Alfred said, giving a little shake of his head. "She sure surprises me these days."

"Get ready for another surprise," Aaron grinned. "Me and Lydia may be going up to Brigham City."

Alfred stared at his son, startled. "Brigham City—? That's Indian country. Why would you want to move there? Soon as we're finished here at Camp Floyd, I thought the plan was to open up another carpentry shop in Salt Lake City—"

"We can do it in Brigham City instead," Aaron said. "Lydia and me been talking serious about this." He glanced at Carn. "Our bishop asked us to go. He said the call came right from Brigham Young."

"You're thinking about going to Brigham City?" Alfred repeated, still not believing what he was hearing. "We got the world by the tail, Aaron. Someone hit you on the head, boy?"

"There's a lot of opportunity up there, father," his son insisted. "That whole Brigham City area will grow fast."

"If the Indians don't burn it down first," his father snorted. "You'll break your mother's heart, Aaron. You know she's counting on having you and the grandchildren near her—"

"You can both move to Brigham City—"

Alfred shook his head firmly. "Your mother won't do that. She likes her life among the social circles now. We need to talk about this, Aaron." He shrugged apologetically at Carn. "My son's having a crazy spell. He'll come out of it."

Carn slapped Alfred on the shoulder. "Whatever happens, let's all stay in touch. Now that I know where you spend your time, I'll drop by and visit." He glanced at Aaron. "Know you'd do well up there, Aaron, but think it through carefully. You don't want to be giving your mother a heart attack—"

CHAPTER SEVEN

SALT LAKE CITY
LATE SEPTEMBER

T here's a card game every night at Jackson's stage office—low stakes and friendly-like," Billy Hickman told the man sitting across the desk from him. "Carpenter never misses it. You show up and sit in the game."

"Carpenter won't pay no attention to me—"

"Yes he will. He thinks you stole his money."

Ferguson, sitting in a straight-back chair in the shabby, one-room upstairs law office of Billy Hickman and his partner Thomas Williams, blinked his eyes and sat up straighter.

"Why does he think it was me—?"

Hickman brushed aside the question. "It don't matter. Carpenter downs a couple of drinks and he'll start accusing you. All you got to do is let him pick a fight, in front of witnesses. You kill him, and everybody will testify it wasn't your fault."

Ferguson thought about that. A pale, sickly looking man in his late twenties, Ferguson stared down at muddy boots that looked several sizes too large for him. Thinking didn't come easy to Ferguson, and he had the uneasy feeling he was being out-thought by the two men with him. Ferguson was dressed in a dirty, rumpled suit that fitted badly. It looked like it belonged on someone a lot bigger. It did, actually—a man Ferguson found dead in an alley a month or so ago. Since the dead man didn't need a suit and Ferguson did, there was a quick exchange. Suit and boots. A few people asked about the two holes in the back of the coat, but Ferguson didn't care about that any more than the dead stranger buried in his longjohns because the clothes found beside the body didn't fit.

61

"What if Carpenter kills me—?" he asked finally, not knowing what else to think about.

"He ain't no hand with a gun. Shoot him first."

"You'll get me off?" Ferguson frowned. He'd already asked the question twice before but it kept bothering him. "I'd be in a fix if you didn't, Billy—"

"Won't even be no trial," Hickman assured him. "Just do like I said. Everyone will swear it was self defense, and you're scot-free with a hundred dollars in your pocket."

"I ain't got a gun—"

"Tom will get you one."

Hickman and Williams watched Ferguson leave the office a few minutes later, no doubt headed for the nearest saloon. The ten-dollar gold piece Hickman had given him as advance payment would buy a lot of courage. Williams, a scraggly, longhaired young man who came West a few weeks ago after being tossed out of law school in his first year for cheating, looked doubtfully at his new partner.

"Ferguson isn't too smart, Billy," Williams muttered. "Can we trust him?"

Hickman shrugged. "What's he going to say?"

"He might figure out why you hired him to kill Carpenter—"

"I ain't so sure. He knows six hundred dollars was stolen from Carpenter's store on Temple Street, and now he knows people are blaming him for it. After a few drinks, Ferguson will probably be convinced he really did steal the money."

"You don't think he'll figure out that you—"

"I didn't do nothing, Tom. I'm a respectable lawyer, remember." A smile flickered somewhere in the midst of the thick, dark beard circling mouth and chin. He tugged at the belt around his waist carrying the two holstered pistols, slung outside the dusty black suit. "Hickman and Williams, Lawyers. We got us a shingle, boy, and we're about to get our first case. Feels right strange, though, sitting on this side of the law."

◆

In another part of town, Mayor Abraham Smoot was shaking his head and staring out the window from his office in the Council

House. The man sitting across from him, federal marshal Pete Dotson, felt uncomfortable.

"I know that ain't what you wanted to hear, Mayor, but it's the truth. Even if there was money to hire people, which there ain't, it ain't in my jurisdiction. I already asked Judge Sinclair about it. The federal marshals cain't do nothing about law and order within city limits."

Judge Charles E. Sinclair, appointed Associate Justice of Utah Territory, under Chief Justice Delano Eckles, had arrived in Utah about six weeks earlier. Eckles assigned him to the Third Judicial District, headquartered in Salt Lake City. Only twenty-eight years old, Sinclair was considered a "baby judge" by his contemporaries, but was also known for being very astute when it came to legal matters. Openly displaying his resentment toward the Mormons, Sinclair was harsh and antagonistic in his dealings and judgments. He practically threw Pete Dotson out of his chambers when the inquiry was made about providing federal help in combating the staggering increase in violence and crime in Salt Lake City.

"It's a federal problem," Smoot insisted. "We didn't have none of this trouble before the army and all those camp followers got here."

"I told Sinclair those same words. He told me if I was going to step in anywhere—which I cain't, of course—it would be Frogtown. You ain't got no problems, Mayor, compared to them."

"Frogtown ain't a city—"

"It is now," Dotson told him. "Third biggest in the Territory, they tell me. No place bigger, though, when it comes to raisin' hell. There just ain't no law a-tall in that town."

"My concern is here, in Salt Lake City," Smoot grunted, bringing the conversation back to where it started. "This lawlessness that's taken hold must be stopped. Do you realize, Marshal, we've had more shootings and murders in the past few months than we had in the whole six years since Salt Lake County was organized. It's cost more than double in law enforcement in those months than what we spent in the past eleven years put together."

"I know the situation is bad," Dotson muttered. "You need more police officers, Mayor. How many you got now—about forty, isn't it?"

"City Council is meeting tonight to add another two hundred officers," Smoot said. "They'll be on the street tomorrow."

"Well, that will help. Any roughneck steps into federal jurisdiction, you let me know, Mayor. Until then, Judge Sinclair ain't giving me no slack. I get the feeling it wouldn't upset him if this whole town went to hell."

"Hell is coming to us, Marshal," Smoot said grimly, "and ridin' fast."

◆

General Galloway was almost fully recovered now. A little stiffness in the chest muscles still, but the wound had healed without any infection or disabling complications. Galloway didn't feel up to bouncing around in the carriage much, so he worked a lot in the comfort of his study. Agatha and Heather were spending considerable time clerking at the store downtown, and surprisingly, both seemed to like it. Henry was with them at the store most of the time, ready to keep any unruly teamsters in line. Business had actually increased as more women responded to service from two such prominent and well-liked ladies. It was difficult for either Agatha or Heather to consider herself any different from when they were walking across the plains, but fate and their husbands had changed that. There wasn't hardly a person in the valley now, Mormon or Gentile, who didn't know and respect the names of Galloway and Tregale.

Galloway was in his study, enjoying a rare visit with Carn. Tregale had returned from Camp Floyd, made his report to Governor Cummings, and now was looking forward to a few days at home. The duties of liaison were far more demanding than expected, requiring almost constant travel.

The general leaned back in his chair. "You're looking fit. Must be all that riding."

Tregale gave a wry smile. "Already wore out a couple of good horses. Colonel Cooke has a stable of prime stock put aside just for me."

"Don't understand why General Johnston is acting so stubborn. The man hasn't come off that military reservation once since he got here. Won't come to Salt Lake City, won't talk directly to either Cummings or Brigham Young. He's causing a lot of frustration."

"Not sure he's just being stubborn," Carn said. "He's dealing with a lot of Indian trouble. There's talk of closing the California trails and making a no-man's-land out of all the overland routes."

Galloway frowned. "Will that affect our plans to open a store in Ogden this fall?"

"I'm even uneasy about going into Provo until things are more settled," Tregale answered. "The whole Shoshone nation is at the flash point. Shoshone bands are raiding all through Weber and Cache counties, and you know what just happened down in Utah county—"

"Tragic affair," Galloway nodded. "I agree with Johnston—his first priority has to be getting the Indians under control."

"Then there's Frogtown," Tregale grimaced. "That place causes almost as many problems as the Indians. It's a cesspool. Soldiers come back to camp drunk, robbed, stabbed or shot. In fairness to Johnston, he has his hands full without any of the civilian problems Cummings dumps on him."

"Talking about civilian problems," Galloway said, "did you hear Jim Wilson left the farm in Provo?"

Tregale was surprised. "Thought he was happy there—"

"It was too much after Calvin went into the army. He talked to me about it—I told him to do what he thought was best for his family."

"So no one is running the farm—?"

"Willie found a family to move in. Couple with four sons old enough to help. Told Willie we'd pay him extra to manage both places. That meet with your approval?"

Tregale nodded. "I'm comfortable with it. Sorry I wasn't around to help—"

"What you're doing is more important," Galloway said quickly. "Not your fault it's taking up so much time."

"What's Jim going to do?"

"Joining the police force here in Salt Lake City."

"I heard about that. The city is adding a lot of new officers—"

"Jim says the pay's good. He's thinking maybe staying in police work—although Beth isn't exactly in favor of it."

"And Harriet—?"

"She's living right here, taking care of your son while Heather's filling in at the store. Which reminds me, any word about Calvin?"

Tregale gave a shake of his head. "His patrol is still out chasing Shoshones. There's been some fighting, but I haven't heard anything about casualties." Without any reason, Galloway suddenly thought how nice it would be to have Agatha bring in a plate of her fresh-baked biscuits about now, like she usually did when there was a meeting going on. But she and Heather were working at the store. He realized he was really missing Agatha, not her biscuits.

"Our wives are turning into real charmers at the store," he told Carn. "Word's out that we're getting more than our share of the Mormon trade. The ladies like them, and both Agatha and Heather seem to be enjoying themselves."

"I worry about them, though," Carn said. "Too many rough characters wandering around town—"

"Henry keeps a close eye on them," Galloway said, "and I'll soon be putting in a lot more time at the store."

"Heather told me she and Agatha want to keep on working there even after you go back."

"Told me the same thing. Don't see any harm in it, do you?"

"If it helps keep Heather's mind off me being away so much," Carn said, "I'm all for it."

"Agatha mentioned buying a gun to keep handy in the store. Probably a good idea. I know I'll feel better if they have some protection whenever Henry's not there."

"Derek Pitts works in a gun shop—"

Galloway nodded. "Beezley's—bought a few guns there myself. Charlie lost his wife about the same time I did. Got a young daughter—Sarah, I believe her name is. He keeps a good stock."

"I'll take the ladies down to Beezley's tomorrow," Carn said. "Give us a chance to catch up on how Derek and Gwen are doing."

◆

Two hundred new Salt Lake City police officers were sworn in that evening in the courtyard near the livery stables of the Beehive House, the residence of Brigham Young. The Mormon leader, concerned about the lawlessness now gripping the city, personally ordered the larger force of police deputies. He told the assembled men this marked the start of a major assault upon the violence and crime taking over city streets. He expressed particular concern for the large numbers of young people who had forsaken their values and beliefs and joined a way of life that threatened to destroy the entire Mormon society.

Jim Wilson, standing attentively in the crowd of recruits, listened to Brigham Young and all the other speeches and warnings, and felt even more convinced he had made the right decision. This was going to be as much a fight for survival as it was for the soldiers who engaged the Union army forces last winter. In some ways it was even more important, for the destruction of values and principles among the Mormon population was not only threatened, it had already begun.

Jim was an intense young man, with strong feelings about being a Mormon and keeping Zion, as most converts called the Salt Lake Valley, the refuge it had been in his mind since first joining the church in England. Now that he and his family were here, he wanted it to stay a place uncontaminated by worldly influences—and that certainly wasn't what was happening.

Jim Wilson had dark hair and a fair complexion, though not the peaches and cream look of his wife Beth. He was about average height for an Englishman, which made him a little short by American frontier standards. In his mid-twenties, Wilson was broad-shouldered, his body kept trim by the hard regimes of mining down in Cedar City, then working the farm in Provo. He had none of the stockiness often found on Englishmen raised on a diet of potatoes, gravy, heavy homemade bread, and suet and bread puddings. Jim was clean-shaven, mostly because Beth believed he looked younger and more handsome without any trace of beard. Looking at Jim, you felt there was a depth to him, a quickness of mind. When he raised his arm to take the oath, a determination was on his face that did not bode well for those attempting to destroy the peace.

The next day, the enlarged force was organized and given assignments. Seven special guard groups were organized, comprising twenty deputies in each one. These select groups were to be available for assisting the regular officers on a twenty-four hour basis, one group for every day of the week. These special forces would be spearheading the effort to bring law and order back to the streets. They were all issued blue woolen shirts and given a metal badge with "Marshal" stamped on it.

Jim Wilson was selected to be in the First Company of twenty, and at six in the evening of the next day, he began his first twenty-four hour tour of duty. He was paired with Bill Hennefer, a burly, surly, bearded man who was a blacksmith by trade. Bill worked with his brother James in their shop at the south end of the city until deciding to help out the family finances by responding to the call for more police officers. A veteran officer, John Sharp, was placed in charge of Jim's twenty-man company of special marshals. It was decided the marshals would patrol on foot through town. They wouldn't be able to give chase to anyone on horseback but it would give them an opportunity to do some face-to-face stare downs.

The First Company went directly to East Temple, the center of crime and rowdiness. They split up, ten starting down each side of the street, in pairs but spaced close together. It was intended the new marshals make a show of force among the denizens who took over the town after regular businesses closed for the day. The windows of most mercantile shops were shuttered and doors padlocked. The scores of saloons and brothels, the few hotels and restaurants in the area, and a scattering of other small stores would remain open most of the night catering to the crowds that became bigger and drunker and noisier with every passing hour.

They stayed on East Temple Street, avoiding the side streets that ran east to west. Orders were to take control of the main north-south thoroughfare first, however many days or weeks it took. The marshals patrolled down to Fourth South, then turned around and began working their way north again toward the temple block. The crowds were brazenly antagonistic to the blue-shirted officers, and there was a lot of cursing as the marshals stiff-shouldered their way through those who tried to force them into the street to pass. The officers wanted to make a point, and they didn't back off from anyone.

Wilson and Hennefer were the first to go into action. Two huge black men, teamsters judging by the look and smell of them, burst out of a saloon beside Jim, almost knocking him down. The two men were bare-chested and sweating, pants held up by suspenders, one wearing a red stocking cap. Jim noticed neither was wearing shoes. They were shouting angrily at each other, each holding a knife in his hand. They ignored the two officers after one quick glance, then crouched threateningly and started to slowly circle one another in the street.

"Better put down those knives," Hennefer told the two men, taking a step toward them.

"Why would we do 'dat," the one in the stocking cap growled, keeping his eyes riveted on his opponent. "You ain't got no part of this, fellah—"

"I ain't putting my knife down," the other hissed, "I's stickin' it in him—"

The two men lunged at each other, arms swinging, the blades slashing. They collided, grappling, each man locking up the arms of the other. They stumbled, kicking up dust in the street, cursing and sweating. Hennefer and Wilson started toward them. Hennefer pulled his pistol and fired two shots into the air. At the sound of the shots, the man in the cap swerved his eyes toward Hennefer. In that second of distraction, the other man broke free and stabbed him in the side. With a bellow of rage, the wounded man lunged at the other man, his blade cutting deeply into an upper forearm. The man cried hoarsely in pain, his knife dropping to the ground as he grabbed at his forearm in an effort to slow the blood streaming down his arm. He stumbled backwards and fell to the ground.

The teamster in the red cap stepped forward, knife held ready for a second, killing blow. Jim Wilson fired a shot directly between the man's feet. It did what it was supposed to. The man in the cap looked from the man on the ground to the dust still rising between his legs, then to the guns in the hands of the two marshals. Cold reality sank through the man's rage. He dropped the knife and raised both hands.

"Don't shoot," he said, looking from Wilson to Hennefer. "I ain't doing nuthin'—"

"You're going to jail," Hennefer grated, "both of you. Jim, get a doctor to look at their cuts while I escort these two gentlemen to their new lodgings." He waved the gun in his hand menacingly as the teamster on the ground stood up. "You'd be doing me and the city a big favor if you decided to resist arrest—"

An hour later, Wilson and Hennefer were back on East Temple. It was almost dark now and the whole atmosphere of the street had changed. Piano music jangled discordantly from bars on both sides of the street, and the air was filled with the sounds of men and women laughing and quarreling and shouting with the happy abandon that comes with too many drinks. It was all so loud that the two marshals had a difficult time making themselves heard across just the few feet separating them.

"Don't see any of the other marshals," Hennefer shouted. "Stay together. I'd say the fun is just gettin' started."

They reached the corner of Second South when a man came running down the street onto East Temple, He was wheezing for breath, occasionally glancing with terror over his shoulder. He saw the two marshals, turned so fast he almost fell down, and came running toward them. Behind the frightened man, a stream of people came into sight, obviously chasing him. The man fell down as he reached Wilson and Hennefer. The two officers took a position between the terrified man huddled on the ground and the angry crowd streaming onto East Temple.

Hennefer held up both hands, seeming not to realize he held a pistol in one of them.

"Far enough," Hennefer told the crowd. "Someone tell us who this man is and what he did to get you folks all riled up—"

"That's Ferguson—he don't go by a first name. He shot Carpenter," one of the pursuers nearest the officers blurted, pointing an accusing finger at the man on the ground. "Shot him in cold blood."

"And who might Carpenter be?" Hennefer asked.

"He owns a store in town. Got robbed a few days ago—by that there murderer."

"Shot him in cold blood—?" Jim Wilson queried, looking down at the man on the ground. He was sallow, wild-eyed, chest heaving wildly as he struggled for breath. He was wearing a suit too large for him, Jim noticed.

"They was in a card game at the stage office. Carpenter accused Ferguson of robbin' his store. Ferguson pulled a gun and shot him. Everybody saw it—wasn't no cause for Ferguson to go for his gun."

"Did Carpenter threaten him?" Wilson asked, again looking at the man at his feet. The man's eyes were still swerving wildly about.

"Never did," the self-appointed spokesman said quickly. Others in the crowd shouted agreement. "Wasn't no argument or no threats. Ferguson just pulled his gun and shot him dead. Bullet went right through the heart—it's still in the wall."

Hennefer holstered his gun and looked at Wilson. "I'll take him in and send one of the regular officers to check out the stage office. You want to come, or stay here—?"

"I'll stay," Jim muttered. "Get back quick as you can though. I got a hunch the night is just beginning."

Hennefer left, practically dragging the now sobbing Ferguson off to jail. Wilson walked only a half-block when it suddenly sounded like the hordes of hell were riding down East Temple behind him. Jim whirled, eyes narrowing as he saw some dozen riders coming at full gallop, people scattering hurriedly to get out of their way. He knew with a sinking certainty this was one of the wild gangs they had been warned about.

Lately, bands of young rowdies had taken to riding recklessly down the main street of Salt Lake City, racing their horses, yelling at the top of their lungs and more often than not, shooting at anything that amused them. The shutters on all the store windows were now mostly double-planked, hopefully thick enough to stop the bullets of the gangs. Occasionally, one of the gangs would ride through town after the drunks and gamblers were mostly off the streets, and a store would be broken into. But many of the looters were shot or jailed and such forays were becoming less tempting. Now the rowdies mostly wanted to vent their high spirits and gain whatever reputation they could.

Jim quickly determined the bunch of riders coming down the street were not hard-case rustlers who didn't care if someone got trampled or shot. Those men lived outside the law and rode through town to show their contempt for anyone who got in their way— Mormons, Gentiles, peace officers, or hopefully, angels from heaven. They looked and rode like the outcasts they were, and the police rarely challenged them.

The riders now approaching Jim, however, were a group of the new breed of rebellious youths who reveled in flaunting their disregard for a society that no longer could control them. The rigid structure of authority existing before the advent of the army and the flood of Gentiles into the Territory, was broken down. Now there were freedoms to taste and things to do never even imagined before. Hardly a family in the valley had not seen their youth swayed and mesmerized by the myriad pleasures now available for the taking.

Wilson had no doubt these yelling riders were mostly young rebels. It showed in the flashy attire, bought with money earned in greater quantities than many of their parents had seen in their whole lives. They wore embroidered buckskin jackets, with fringes flapping along the arms, wide buckskin chaps, and the brightly colored flannel shirts that all Gentile emporiums now stocked. Many wore silver spurs, and most sported the tall, steeple-crowned felt hats that merchants assured them were what every hard case on the frontier was wearing these days. There were sheathed knives and holstered pistols with ornate, expensive handles. It was all new, all pretentious, all fashioned to fit an image in young minds. They all looked the same, a fantasy world come to life, a sight that made real cowboys spit in disgust.

The first of the horses thundered past Wilson as he stepped off the wooden sidewalk. This gang might not be particularly dangerous, but they had to be taught that law had come to Temple Street. The next rider veered toward Jim, trying to throw a scare into him and make him jump back onto the sidewalk. Instead, Jim reached out as he rode past, grabbed the foot in the stirrup and gave the youth a heave upward. Caught by surprise, the rider went flying up into the air, falling to the ground and narrowly missing being trampled by the riders behind him. He shook off the pain of landing mostly on his backside, then glared angrily up at Jim Wilson. Just as Jim thought, the youth on the ground was probably no more than sixteen, still looked fresh, no hard lines of rebellion etched yet on his face. Those probably would come, Wilson thought, but this young man was no hard case yet. The youth started to reach for the gun at his side, but Jim already had his pistol out and pointed.

"I wouldn't do that," Jim warned him. "All you done so far is disturb the peace. Draw that gun and you're looking at jail time."

The other riders in the gang stopped, They rode back, staring at Jim Wilson with angry hostility.

"You must be crazy, mister," one of the rowdies growled at Wilson. "You stepped right into his way—"

"Maybe you got a hankering to die," another said. His hand drifted to the handle of the pistol in his belt.

"Don't touch that gun, kid," a voice came from the middle of the street. "You draw on a city marshal, and we'll cut you down."

All heads jerked around. About ten blue-shirted marshals were standing just a few feet away, all with guns drawn and pointed at the gang of rowdies. Shock and surprise wiped away everything but fear from the faces of the youths. Jim saw the man speaking was Marshal John Sharp. He recognized the other men of the First Company nearby.

"What we ought to do is toss you tough guys into jail for a few days," Marshal Sharp continued, "but I think you get the drift. This ain't your private playground no more. None of you ever rides down this street again at more than a canter—you boys hear what I'm tellin' you?"

Every one of the riders nodded, including the one on the ground. Marshal Sharp waved the pistol in his hand. "I'd be leaving now, if I was you, before I change my mind. Next time you ride hard down Temple Street, you won't be throwed off your horse—you'll be shot off."

The young rider got back on his horse and the gang trotted south at a slow canter, none of them looking back.

Marshal Sharp continued across the street and clapped a hand on Jim's shoulder. "That was a crazy thing to do, Wilson. Might've got yourself killed—"

"Didn't want to shoot," Jim shrugged. "They didn't look like hard cases."

"Never can tell if there's a bad apple in the barrel. Like what you did, Wilson, but next time don't take chances. There's only a couple hundred of us, and there's thousands of them."

About that time, Assistant Army Surgeon Edward Covey was finishing a late dinner at the nearby Globe restaurant. He was in company with Captain Turnley, and both men looked up as the inn keeper, David Candland, approached their table.

"Everything satisfactory?" Candland asked. "There's more apple pie out in the kitchen—"

"No more pie," Covey said. He cast a quick glance at his companion, then stared up at the inn keeper. "However, if you've any sweet young pastries out there for sale, we'll pay a good price—"

Candland stifled the anger that surged through him. Instead, he smiled at the army doctor. "Nothing that would satisfy the tastes of you gentlemen. Any pastries in my kitchen are too plain, judging from what I've seen you sampling before."

"Don't have to be beautiful," Covey leered. "Just warm and willing."

"Sorry—"

"Well, Charlie Kinkaid's throwing a party tonight at one of the taverns for some of us officers from Camp Floyd," Captain Turnley smiled. "There'll be enough pastries there for all of us. Charlie knows what it takes to make an officer and a gentleman happy."

The door of the inn opened and an army lieutenant entered. He saw Covey and Turnley and crossed to their table.

"You two about ready? A bunch of us just rode into town, and we're ready to party." He gave the two officers a wide grin. "Saw a lot of pretty ladies going into that tavern—wouldn't take too long if I was you, unless you don't mind leftovers."

"Appreciate the warning, Sanders," Covey said. "We'll be joining you soon as we settle up here."

The lieutenant left and Covey looked up at the innkeeper. "How much we owe you, Candland?"

"Just for the dinners, gentlemen. The pie's on me."

"You Mormons should be so generous with your pastries, Candland. Never had you come up with anything but pie—"

"Most of our young girls are afraid of you Army people. They've been warned about—"

A scowl darkened the face of the army doctor. "I know what's being said." Covey growled, "and I know who's doing the telling. Some of your so-called bishops been taking it upon themselves to make sure every girl in the Territory thinks I'm a demon."

"Don't think it's a personal thing—" Candland began, but the doctor cut him off.

"I'll make it personal if I ever run into one of them," Covey said angrily. "They're getting their jollies with a dozen wives each, and who knows how many concubines, so they have no call to object to me taking on a few pleasures—"

Captain Turnley slapped a hand hard on the table.

"Things would be a whole lot different if they'd turn us loose to make law-abiding citizens out of you Mormons."

"Some think you've already been turned loose on us, Captain," Candland said quietly.

"When I get back to Washington," Covey said, now thoroughly angry, "I won't leave a stone unturned to keep Utah from becoming a state. I'd rather let the Shoshones into statehood than you people."

"Sorry you feel that way, Doctor Covey." Candland gave both officers a curt nod. "Looks like you both might be getting some indigestion. Won't charge you for the dinners."

Candland turned away and went back in the direction of the kitchen. After a few moments, the two officers stood up and Covey contemptuously tossed a five dollar gold piece onto the table before leaving. It was more than double what Candland would have charged, but Covey wanted to make it plain there was no debt between him and any Mormon.

◆

It was almost 2 a.m. when the call came for the First Company of marshals to respond to a party getting out of control at a tavern on East Temple. Apparently Livingston and Kinkaid were drumming up favor with the army in a way they knew no Mormons would compete.

All twenty marshals arrived on the scene a few minutes later. Lamps inside the tavern showed it was packed with uniformed army officers and women with tight dresses and bare shoulders. Judging from the noise blasting into the street, most of the people inside were drunk. The front doors were open and men would occasionally stumble outside, needing either to urinate or throw up. A group of a dozen or so women approached the building and there was little doubt why they were joining the party. Marshal John Sharp stepped forward, holding up a hand to stop the women.

"Sorry, ladies," he told them, "but this party is about over. No one in there will be needin' your services. They'll either be ridin' or spendin' the night in jail."

There was an angry shout from the open doorway. It was the lieutenant who had showed up at the Globe a few hours earlier.

"Mr. Kinkaid—Doctor Covey—we got a situation here," Lieutenant Sanders shouted back inside the shop. Moments later, Covey and Kinkaid came to the door. They frowned as they saw the marshals grouped in the street.

"You officers want to join the party?" Kinkaid called.

"Don't think so, Mr. Kinkaid," Marshal Sharp replied. "We come to close it down."

"What's the matter," Covey shouted, for it was hard to hear any conversation over the noise from inside, "you Mormons can't stand people enjoying themselves?"

"More like us marshals can't stand a bunch of drunks disturbing the peace," Sharp replied evenly. His glance settled again on the merchant. "Party's over, Kinkaid. You tell your guests, or we will."

Covey took a couple of steps toward the officers in the street. "Fun's just getting started, marshal. I'm Doctor Covey, of the United States Army. Most of the people in there are also army officers, and in case you don't know it, we don't take orders from civilians."

By now, people inside were aware of the confrontation. They spilled out into the street and soon there were about forty of them facing the company of marshals. Everyone was belligerent, and, of course, drunk.

"Mr. Kinkaid here is a civilian and I'm ordering him to shut this party down." Marshal Sharp was staring hard at the merchant. "Five minutes, Mr. Kinkaid. After that, everyone goes to jail—army or not," he added, swiveling his stare pointedly to Covey.

"We got something to say about that," Lieutenant Sanders growled, moving to stand beside Covey. "Don't start something you can't finish, marshal."

"Better listen to him," Covey warned.

More army officers began to line up across from the marshals. Kinkaid could see things were about to turn ugly. He wanted the officers' business but not at the cost of going to jail. Kinkaid turned to Covey.

"Maybe we better call it a night, Doc," he muttered. "We've all had our fun. No sense in anyone getting hurt—"

Without warning, Covey and Sanders pulled their weapons, both pointing them at Marshal Sharp.

"Call your marshals off, mister," Sanders hissed, "or I'll put a dent in that badge."

Jim Wilson and Bill Hennefer were standing off to the side, out of the direct line of sight of the two officers confronting Sharp. They both drew their pistols, looked at each other, then stepped forward.

"You just gave us legal grounds to blow off your heads," Hennefer grated, causing the two army officers to twist toward them in surprise. "One twitch, and we'll do it—"

It was more of an unconscious reflex than a deliberate action, but the guns in the hands of the army officers started to turn toward Wilson and Hennefer. Both marshals fired at the same time, Wilson smashing a bullet into Sanders' right arm, and Hennefer shooting Covey high in the shoulder. Both army officers remained on their feet, shocked at the sight of their own blood. The officers around them, however, howled in anger. The street erupted into a swirling brawl as the two groups crashed together.

Both sides had seen blood flow and were leery of more gunplay, so it became a melee of fists and billyclubs and gun butts. The fight engulfed the whole street in front of the tavern. It was a bedlam of noise, shouts and cries of pain from struggling men mingling with shrill, piercing screams of frightened women. Most of the army officers were drunk and no match for the determined onslaught of the marshals. Soon the street was littered with men, groaning in pain or silent, unconscious. At least two thirds of the army officers were no longer on their feet when the brawl finally ended. A dozen or so marshals had cuts and bruises, but every one felt grimly satisfied as they looked around. The battle was won, and for the first time in weeks, there wasn't a whore in sight on East Temple. So far, it was a good night for the keepers of the peace.

CHAPTER EIGHT

FAIRFIELD
EARLY OCTOBER

Carn Tregale arrived at Fairfield late in the afternoon, tired from the long ride from Salt Lake City. He had met with Governor Cummings until almost noon, then pushed his horse hard to make the ride south in just a little over five hours.

He went directly to the Carson Inn, the newly-built two-story hotel on the main roadway, near the bridge across Cedar Creek that marked the entrance into Camp Floyd. There was business to be done with General Johnston but it was better left until morning, Carn decided. He knew the general would be tired and testy after a day of dealing with army problems and in no mood to discuss anything the governor wanted brought to his attention.

John Carson, the innkeeper, greeted Tregale warmly and assured him that "General Johnston's room" was available. During these months of construction, Johnston frequently availed himself of the comforts of the inn. Carson always gave the general the upper room on the southwest corner of the hotel. It was private, and the farthest removed from the noise and distractions of Front Street. The room had windows on the south and the west, providing a pleasant cross-breeze. From the southern window, or from the verandah just outside, the general could watch the swarming activity of the new army post taking shape. Colonel Cooke arranged for Tregale to have the same room at army expense whenever he stayed overnight in Cedar Valley.

Carn went upstairs, flopped back onto the thick, quilted coverlet on the bed and closed his eyes for a few moments, letting the motion of the ride slow in his head. The Carsons always kept a tight rope supporting the straw mattress and it was so comfortable, Carn had to fight falling off to sleep.

A little later, he got up and stepped to the dresser. This was one of the many things Carn appreciated about staying at the Carson Inn. The Carsons always provided clean sheets, a clean towel, and a full pitcher of water beside the wash basin, along with a bar of yellow soap. He washed the heavy coating of dust from his face, wishing there was time to relax in the metal tub he knew was downstairs in the men's washroom. The sifting alkali dust covered his entire body. By the time he finished washing up, the smell of food was coming up through the rag carpet covering the floorboards. Elvira Carson would soon be serving supper and that was something no guest wanted to miss.

There were two empty seats at the dining table and Tregale took one of them. The table was always set with a white cloth and tableware. The coal oil lamps fastened on each wall were lit, for dusk was already gathering. A flickering glow was cast against the white-washed walls, giving the room a friendly warmth, accented by the multicolored rag carpet underfoot, feeling soft and cushiony from the layers of straw between it and the floorboards.

Tregale exchanged greetings with the other men, most of whom he'd met before. There was Andrew Miller, one of the founders of the company now known as Russell, Majors and Waddell, the largest freighting and mercantile operation in the Territory.

Sitting beside Captain Miller, as he liked to be called, was Richard Ackley, who ran the company store Miller recently opened in Frogtown. Ackley, a bullish man in his late twenties, was a teamster before deciding he'd probably live longer if he quit the freighting business. Miller liked the fact that Ackley was burly and intimidating, and so he had offered the teamster a job.

Sheriff Bill Coates was also at the table, Tregale saw. Coates was a regular at mealtimes, though he didn't stay at the inn. The county picked up the twenty-five cents it cost for a full breakfast, and the thirty-five cents it cost for supper. No one objected to Coates eating at county expense, for no one expected a sheriff in Frogtown to live very long.

Tregale didn't recognize the man sitting next to Coates. The man leaned over and shook hands with him. "Jim Rodeback," he said. "I'm staying the night. It's my unfortunate duty to collect taxes here in Fairfield. People don't like me much."

"Wouldn't worry about it," Tregale smiled. "People probably like you more than they do Sheriff Coates."

"That's a true fact," Coates grunted.

A teenaged youth, Ebenezer Crouch, waved a hand in greeting to Tregale.

"See you're back again, Mister Tregale—"

"Where's your father, Ebenezer?" Tregale asked, returning the greeting.

"At the store. Those soldiers and teamsters are still stealin' us blind."

Tregale first saw Ebenezer, who was about sixteen, standing on the counter of his father's store on Front Street, spotting who was buying and who was stealing. The Crouch store was one of the more popular in Frogtown because it had a whole row of forty-gallon barrels lining the back of the store, all containing a different kind of liquor. Crouch was a Mormon but he found it convenient—and very profitable—to put religion on the shelf during such prosperous times. A lot of Mormons were doing the same throughout the Territory.

Miller smiled at Ebenezer. "I envy you Crouches," the merchant told the youth. "Always a crowd in your place—"

"That's mostly because of all the Valley Tan we got," the youth replied honestly. "Call it Tiger Sweat, Tarantula Juice, whatever you want, there ain't a man in Frogtown who don't down it. Our stuff's double rectified, we give people a choice, and we sell it cheaper than they pay for it in the saloons."

Ebenezer was referring to a cheap whiskey brewed mostly by mountain men and Mormons in nearby communities, although some was freighted in from the Missouri frontier. Young Ebenezer took a swallow a few months ago and spent the next hour throwing up. Valley Tan was foamy and foul, smelled terrible, and tasted worse. Some compared it to drinking kerosene. It was powerful stuff, a pint enough to put almost any man flat on his back. Someone once said about it, "Ain't nothing bad about this whiskey; only fault is, it ain't good."

In saloons with the best-looking dancing girls, the home brew cost fifty cents a shot, or more. The Crouches bought it for eight dollars a gallon, sometimes less, and sold it for three dollars a pint. Enough profit to make a little theft bearable, the elder Crouch had decided months ago. No sense worrying over the fact that many of the men who bought it worked all day to earn that three dollars. Everyone had to make their own choices.

John Carson was sitting at the head of the table, smiling and affable as usual, his thin face clean-shaven except for a bushy mustache. There was quite a story behind Carson building this inn. He and his four brothers were part of the original group of settlers who came to Cedar Valley a little over four years ago. They built a small rock-walled fort, about twenty-two feet square, for protection from the Paiutes who roamed Cedar and the nearby Rush valleys. It was hard just keeping the families alive those first years. Two of John's brothers were killed in brushes with the Indians.

But the real trouble started a few months ago when the Union army marched into the valley. It wasn't the soldiers as much as those who followed them—the teamsters, the gamblers, the prostitutes. The army settled south of the creek and the camp followers took over the north side surrounding Fairfield and the Carson Fort. Front Street sprang up almost overnight and Frogtown was booming in less than a week.

John won the protection of General Johnston when a gambler took over the stone fort. After getting rid of both the gambler and the pigsty the man built along the creek, John dismantled the walls, using the stone and adobe bricks to build this inn. The cistern the Carsons had dug in the fort now provided fresh running water for the inn. Water was channeled into the kitchen at the back of the inn, stored in a barrel, then flowed into the men's washroom, and finally out into the garden. There wasn't a house anywhere south of Great Salt Lake City with such a wondrous convenience. The two-storied building, with its imposing wooden front, astonished more than one traveler to this barren Valley. The five bedrooms upstairs were all clean and adequately furnished, and freshly-washed bedding and towels always were hanging from Elvira's clotheslines in back.

The door to the kitchen swung open and Elvira entered with the first of the dinner, a huge platter containing a beef roast already carved into slices. She was followed by two of her young daughters, carrying platters of potatoes and vegetables. Elvira was a plain-looking woman, probably still in her early thirties, but her face was pinched and wrinkled into looking much older. Harsh summer sun, even harsher winter cold, and the cruel harshness of just surviving in this desolate Valley, all had left their mark. With her hair drawn severely back into a bun, Elvira looked like many of the frontier wives; worn out, unhappy, cross with life and everyone in it who wore trousers. She was a wonderful cook, though, and only John had to worry about the rest.

After dinner, topped off with a large slice of delicious apple pie, Tregale excused himself and went back up the narrow stairway separating the dining room from the large recreation room that ran the whole length of the western side of the house. This room was the gathering place of guests who wanted to sit and talk, and was furnished more elegantly than the rest of the house with chairs and sofas and chests hauled in from the East. Sometimes guests would be entertained by visiting artists of music and the theater, even dancers at times. Carson, who was bishop of the flock of Mormons now living in Cedar Fort, banned all liquor from the premises. It was no surprise that most of Carson's guests usually spent the evening hours sitting outside, hoping Elvira would not complain about tobacco smoke or the smell of liquor drifting into the inn.

Stepping out onto the verandah from his room, Tregale saw Captain Miller sitting in front of the inn, watching the lights and noises coming from Front Street. Miller saw him and called up, waving an arm in invitation.

"Join me, Mister Tregale. Some things I'd like to discuss with you, if you have a few minutes—"

Reluctantly, Tregale went downstairs and took a chair beside the merchant. The bed had looked awfully inviting but he knew the meeting with Miller wouldn't last long. Though it was cool now in the evenings, an unpleasant number of skeeters still swarmed about. Unless you were shrouded in tobacco smoke, you didn't offer yourself up to the bloodthirsty pests for too long.

Tregale glanced at Miller, glad the man was puffing hard on a pipe that smelled like it hadn't been cleaned in a long time. The mosquitoes probably wouldn't like it, either. Captain Miller was a native of Pennsylvania, same as John Carson, though both men had spent most of their lives in the West. For a time, Miller was a cook on a Mississippi keelboat but in ten years became captain of one of the steamboats wheeling up and down the river. He left the river and became a successful faro dealer and gambler, often dipping outside the law. He never lost his fondness for the title of Captain and had used it ever since. A series of events drew him into a freighting venture with Bill Russell. They bribed their way into getting a huge share of the enormous army contracts to haul goods to Utah Territory, and Bill Waddell was invited into the partnership since he could find the goods and money needed. For mostly political reasons, the firm became Russell, Majors and Waddell, and the success of the freighting company became legendary. Miller now directed operations of all the company stores.

"Found out something today you should pass on to Governor Cummings, "Miller said, taking the pipe out of his mouth. "There's four hundred and fifty men being discharged from Camp Floyd in a couple of weeks. Soldiers and teamsters. No place for them to go except Salt Lake City. They'll all be broke in a week—and you know what that means."

"More trouble," Tregale muttered. "More robberies, more killings."

"You got that right," Miller agreed, sliding the pipe to the corner of his mouth and giving a few more puffs into the air. "That's not all of it. Another two hundred wagons is headed this way from Leavenworth, as we speak. There's about six hundred teamsters, I'm told, all pushing to get discharged in Salt Lake. Some plan on going to California in the spring, but they'll all be here for the winter."

"That's bad news, Captain," Tregale frowned. "A thousand more roughnecks—don't know if the valley can handle them all."

"I paid off thirty-five teamsters myself yesterday," Miller said, anger edging into his voice. "Just found out they robbed me blind. Headed for Salt Lake with everything they could carry, which was a lot," Miller added, "because they stole two of my wagons. I'll be looking them up when I get back to Salt Lake."

"Must be something we can do about all those teamsters being turned loose—"

"There is," Miller said, "but it'll need the governor, the mayor, and Brigham Young to agree to it. And General Johnston, of course."

"Sounds like you have a plan—"

"Only way we're going to get those teamsters out of the Territory is to organize wagon trains ourselves and escort as many of those devils as we can to California. If it's done fast, we can still beat the winter."

Tregale thought for a moment, then started nodding in agreement. "A right good plan, Captain Miller. Can't see anyone disagreeing with it."

"Cummings should know what's happening as soon as possible. You got the governor's ear and you'll be seeing him before I do—I have to visit more of our stores here in the south before going back. And you're one of the few civilians privy to General Johnston. If you can get Cummings and Johnston to agree on putting those wagon trains together—and bring Brigham Young in on it—we may not have as wild a winter as it threatens to be."

"I'll do what I can," Tregale assured him.

Two youths passed in front of the Stagecoach Inn. They saw Tregale and hailed him excitedly.

"Brother Tregale—remember us?" both called in unison.

Tregale smiled back. It was hard to forget Fred and Ted Tate, the redheaded twin sons of Willie and Maude. He was surprised to see them here, though.

Miller was looking at him with a surprised expression. "Didn't know you was a Mormon—"

"I'm not. They're just used to calling me that," Tregale replied. His stare went back to the twins. He excused himself from Miller and went out into the street to join the two boys.

They had grown, he saw. They couldn't be much over fourteen, but looked at least seventeen or eighteen, even older. Working on the ranch in Provo had certainly broadened them out, put on muscles. And with that thought came a question.

"How come you boys are here in Frogtown?" he asked. "Run out of work helping your pa with the ranching—?"

"We ain't doing that no more," Ted said. "We're working at Camp Floyd. Started five days ago. You can't believe how much money they're payin' us—"

"Doing what—?"

"Just walkin' around," Fred grinned. "All we do is stomp clay floors in the barracks until they get hard and shiny."

"I thought they brought in Mexicans to do that—"

"Mexicans and a bunch of kids like us. Soldiers want things hurried up and finished. Guess they think we cain't do nuthin' that takes brains. For the money they're payin', they can think anything they want."

"Surprised your parents let you come out here."

"They weren't too happy about it—had us quite a row, in fact," Ted said. A smile came to his face. "But pa had to admit that ranchin' don't pay like this—no offense intended to you or General Galloway. They still ain't feelin' easy about it, though. Ma thinks some whore is going to get us, and pa's afraid we'll join the army."

"I hope you're not thinking of letting either of those things happen—"

"We been talking about the whores," Fred grinned. "Might be worth a dollar. Don't sound as bad to us as it does to ma."

"But we sure ain't going to join the army," Ted added, "not after what we seen these past few days. I ain't never goin' to be no soldier."

"So where are you headed now?" Tregale asked. "Surprised they let you off the post—"

"We're civilians," Fred said quickly. "They cain't stop us."

"Thought we'd take a look at Frogtown," Ted added. "We ain't never seen no whores—"

"Mind if I walk with you?" Tregale said. "I can point out a few places you don't want to go into."

"Pleased to have you do that, Brother Tregale," they said in unison.

The three of them started down toward the noise blaring out from the saloons and garishly-signed buildings lining both sides of the street. Across the main roadway from the Stagecoach Inn, on the western end of Front Street and stretching for about fifty yards or so, was the only semblance of a normal town.

The merchants who came to Fairfield, like the Crouches and another Mormon shopkeeper, Charlie Bailey, and the Miller emporium, all congregated in this short stretch, separating themselves from the half-mile of ramshackle buildings that continued up Front Street and housed the "social" enterprises. There were seventeen saloons in that half-mile, packed side by side with dance halls, gambling dens, and gaudy houses of prostitution. The buildings were mostly rough planking, some still half canvas. A few were two-storied, providing quarters for proprietors and cribs for the finer collections of whores. The buildings were connected together in long lines on each side of the street, some with wooden walks in front but most opening directly onto the thick, swirling dust of Front Street. Walking a few steps beyond the Carson Inn and those few mercantile establishments brought a person quickly into the heart of everything that was Frogtown.

Behind Front Street was a rough crisscrossing of dirt lanes, marked by a jumbled maze of tents, wood and canvas shacks, wagon boxes converted to sleeping quarters, and shelters no more than holes dug into the ground. This was where the camp followers and gamblers and drifters lived and slept, in those few hours each day they didn't spend plying their trade, whatever it might be, along Front Street. The population of this shantytown, officially Fairfield, already was swollen to well over three thousand, with more arriving every day.

Tregale and the Tate boys didn't even get beyond the stores before they found themselves surrounded by violence. Tregale took the boys into the store of Captain Miller. He'd seen Miller leave the inn and go into the store and wanted to ask him a question about his plan to move the teamsters to California before winter. There was an army sutler store on the post, but Miller's mercantile had a much better variety of goods and the prices were slightly better. Since they hauled in all of the merchandise for both stores, Miller, Russell and Waddell made a profit on everything sold on or off the post.

It was late enough for most men to be seeking pleasures, not merchandise, and the Miller store was almost deserted. Tregale saw the burly manager, Richard Ackley, with his arms propped on the counter near the wire-protected cashier's cage. Ackley was reading a dog-eared copy of the Deseret News, a newspaper most Gentiles resented because they felt the stories printed were strongly biased in favor of the Mormon point of view. There was talk of another newspaper starting up, this one published by outsiders, but for the present the Deseret News was the only way to find out what was happening in the Territory and back in the States. Occasionally there was a copy of a newspaper from New York City, or Boston, or some other big eastern city, brought west by a traveler, but that news was always several months old.

Two other men were in the store, browsing the merchandise and talking quietly. Tregale recognized one of them as George Harney, a rough and tough teamster who claimed to be a nephew of General "Squawkiller" Harney. No one challenged him on that. It wasn't worth dying over.

A man entered the store behind Tregale and the boys. He was wearing a dusty, dark suit, looked pale and unhealthily thin. He glanced at Ackley.

"Cap'n Miller around?"

Ackley nodded toward the office at the rear of the store. He knew Oliver Rucker, a gambler who drifted from one saloon to another, wherever a game could be drummed up. Ackley had watched him enough at the tables to know he never wanted to get in a game of Monte or anything else with the Kentuckian. Whatever Rucker's business was with Miller, it was no concern of Ackley. Rucker knocked on the door of the office, identified himself, and Miller opened the door for him.

Tregale and the boys wandered through the shop, waiting for the Kentucky gambler to end his visit with Miller. In a few minutes, another man, scowling angrily, pushed into the store.

"I'm Peale," he growled at Ackley. "Saw Rucker come in. Where's he at?"

Ackley didn't even look up. "Back in Cap'n Miller's office. Probably be out soon."

"I'll wait," Peale grunted. He stared around the room, taking in Tregale, the twins, and the other two men. He apparently saw no threat and stood waiting near the front door.

A few minutes later, Rucker came out of the office. He closed the door and frowned as he saw Peale glaring at him from the far side of the store.

"You got a problem, mister?" Rucker asked.

"I ain't got a problem," Peale rasped, "you do, Rucker."

Rucker's stare narrowed. "Do I know you?"

"I know you," Peale replied. "You're the man who cheated me last night at Monte."

"Don't remember," Rucker said thinly, "no more'n I remember anyone ever accusing me of cheating."

"I was drunk then," Peale hissed, "but I ain't now."

"So what do you want with me?"

"I come to kill you, Rucker."

The Kentuckian tensed, his hand clawed over the handle of the gun hanging from his waist. "Then you'd best be about it, Peale."

There was barely time for Tregale to grab an arm of each boy and drag them down onto the floor beside him before the shooting started. The two men were about twelve paces apart and the sound of their guns in the confines of the store was thunderously loud.

Rucker beat the other man to the draw. His first shot struck Peale in the jaw. Peale staggered back, clutching the shattered bone, firing as he started to slide down the wall. His shot hit Rucker in the thigh, and the gambler fell to the floor. Both men kept shooting, though both were now sprawled on the floorboards. Rucker fired again at Peale's head but the shots missed, slamming into the wall beside the fallen man. Peale kept firing. Three shots hit the floor about three feet in front of Rucker. Two of the bullets whined and ricocheted up to sever both the middle and index fingers of the Kentuckian. Peale fired twice more, both bullets striking Rucker near the heart.

The shooting finally stopped and Ackley rushed over to Rucker, sprawled on the floor near the office door. Rucker looked up at him, whispered something, then fell back dead. Peale was lying in a pool of blood beside the front door. He gave a final gasp, then he too was dead.

Tregale stood up, and the boys followed, eyes wide as they stared at the two dead men. They looked at each other, mirroring their disbelief they had just been in the middle of a gunfight. Ted couldn't help asking a question of Richard Ackley.

"What'd he say, mister, when you bent over him?"

"Said he was a dead man," Ackley muttered. "Guess we all knew that."

It wasn't long before Sheriff Coates arrived at Miller's store. He talked to everyone present at the shoot-out and finally shrugged his shoulders.

"I'd say this was settled." He glanced at Miller. "I'll have Ben come by and pick up the bodies. Don't look like these gents shot up anything but themselves but let me know if you're looking for damages. Usually this kind don't leave enough even to pay Ben for planting them."

When Tregale and the Tate boys left the store, they found a small crowd outside. Killings usually went unnoticed in Frogtown, but word was quickly spreading that this was one those shoot-outs people would be talking about for a long time. Two men, dead game, facing each other and shooting until guns were empty and both of them down. Most shootings in Frogtown involved a bullet in the back from ambush.

Tregale saw Colonel Philip Cooke riding down the street toward the store. The officer reined in and reached down to shake Tregale's hand.

"Carson said I'd find you down here. Been a shooting, I hear—"

"Couple of gamblers settling a debt." Tregale looked at the Tate twins standing beside him. "Hope you boys won't get an urge to sit in on any card games—"

"Not after that, we won't," Fred said quickly.

"Besides," Ted added, "we don't know no card games."

Three youths in the small crowd pushed forward to stand beside the twins. Tregale frowned, for he'd heard stories about the
young hard cases who had drifted out to Camp Floyd. These three
definitely were hard cases. It showed on their faces and in the arrogant way they held themselves.

"Did you see it?" one of them asked the twins.

"We wuz on the floor and they wuz firing right over our heads,"
Fred replied. "Just kept pumping bullets into each other—"

"Blood all over the place," Ted added.

Fred looked over at Tregale, pointing to the three youths. "These
are our friends, Brother Tregale." He pointed at the one who had
asked the question. The youth looked older than the others, by
several years, Tregale guessed. "This is Rod Swazey," Fred continued, "and these are Ike Hatch and Jim Warthers. They been here
since work started."

Colonel Cooke interrupted. "Carn, there's some things General
Johnston would like to discuss with you—"

"Tonight?" Carn asked, surprised.

Cooked nodded. "He's waiting in administration."

"Must be important."

"It is," Cooke said.

Tregale looked at the twins. "Just remember, we only made it to
the good part of town. It gets a whole lot worse down the street—"

"We know Frogtown," Swazey spoke up. "We'll see they don't
get into no trouble."

Seeing the grins that passed between the youths, Tregale didn't
put much stock in Swazey's assurance. He'd have to talk to the
twins about who they mixed with, but that would have to wait.
General Johnston wouldn't have sent Colonel Cooke to find him
this late if he didn't have something important on his mind.

The youths watched the two men leave, then Swazey clapped a
hand on the shoulder of each twin.

"Got some good news for you two," Swazey grinned. "You remember meetin' Charlie Drown a couple days ago?"

"The man you work for—"

"Well, he's agreed you two can join us—if you don't mind doin' a little night ridin'."

"Doin' what?" Ted frowned.

"Making four, five times more money than you get stompin' floors," Ike Hatch told them. "A lot easier, too."

"You interested?" Swazey said.

The twins didn't need to look at each other. They already knew what the other was thinking.

"We're in," they said at the same time.

Swazey squeezed their shoulders again. "You made a smart choice. In a few weeks, you'll have more money than you know what to do with."

"You said we'd be riding at night—"

Swazey nodded. "That's the best time to rustle cattle." He saw the startled looks that crossed the face of each twin. "Don't worry. We only steal army cattle. That ain't really stealin'—just helpin' the Mormon cause. But tonight, let's just rustle up some ladies worth spending a dollar on—"

In General Johnston's office, Tregale accepted the invitation for him and Colonel Cooke to sit across the table from Johnston and Colonel Smith. The table was covered with papers and maps as usual, but the expressions of the two commanding officers were grim.

"Appreciate you coming, Tregale," the general said gruffly. "There's some new developments. Governor Cummings needs to be apprized as soon as possible."

"We don't expect you to ride back tonight, of course," Colonel Smith added, "but every hour may be important."

"What's happened, General?" Tregale asked.

"This whole Territory is about to blow up in our faces," Johnston replied. He tapped one of the maps. "The Indians are out of control in the north. I've ordered George Chorpenning to close all his mail stations between Salt Lake and Placerville—too dangerous. I've also ordered all the overland trails closed, so there'll be nothing coming or going to California. It's now a no-man's-land. Washakie and Little Soldier have the Shoshones running wild, and the Snakes and

Bannocks have joined them. Cummings needs to know Salt Lake is cut off from the west."

"Do you expect the overlands to be closed all winter?" Tregale asked.

"Maybe longer," Johnston grunted. "Depends on what Washington does with the rest of Harney's command at Camp Scott."

"We don't have enough troops to patrol that whole stretch," Smith explained. "General Harney's gone to Oregon with the Sixth Infantry, but there's still the First Cavalry, Seventh Infantry, two companies of the Second Artillery and two additional companies of the Second Dragoons, along with some eight hundred raw recruits, left at Camp Scott. Colonel Canby's in charge now, and he's standing by to reinforce us if needed. Perhaps we can get some of those troops assigned to Camp Floyd—"

"It won't happen," General Johnston growled, "not with all the trouble up in Oregon Territory, and Harney assigned to command the Oregon Department. Those troops are headed for Oregon, no matter how much we need them here."

Tregale glanced at Cooke. "Does this mean your dragoons are being recalled—?"

Cooke nodded. "Already headed back. Should arrive in a day or two."

"We expect the Shoshones and Bannocks to stay up north," Johnston continued, "but Cummings should know there is now the threat of a general uprising. Every settlement north and south of Great Salt Lake is in danger of attack."

Tregale realized the situation was indeed serious. Johnston wasn't given to exaggerating and his concern was plainly evident.

"Any special cause for the uprising, General?" Tregale asked.

"Arrowpeen's at the bottom of it," Johnston grunted. "He wants revenge for the killing of his son—Pintuts, wasn't it?"

"The Indian agent—Garland Hurt—can't he help?"

"He's in the thick of it," Colonel Smith snapped. "He's encouraging the Indians and stirring up trouble. Why does he hate the Mormons so much?"

"It's mostly between him and Brigham Young," Tregale answered. "There's been bad blood between them from the start. Hurt's set on blocking everything Young wants done."

"How does he expect to do that?" Smith frowned.

"Any way he can. Write letters to congressmen back East to keep Utah from becoming a state. Try to get all the Indians out of Mormon settlements—they took in a lot, especially children. Mormons say it's to help civilize them, but Hurt claims they're deliberately destroying Indian traditions. He's also fighting Young on establishing a land office. If Young gets that, people can claim legal title to all the land they settled. Hurt says those lands still belong to the Indians. Fact is, he just hates Mormons—Brigham Young in particular."

"Well, he has more than Mormons to worry about," Johnston said. "Chief Tintic and a bunch of Indians on the Spanish Fork reservation sacked and burned Hurt's headquarters a couple days ago. Drove off all the horses and cattle, then left the reservation and headed down to join Sanpitch and Arrowpeen in San Pete."

"What happened to Hurt?" Tregale asked.

"Major Paul reports he's in hiding," Cooke answered. "Hurt has his enemies, but he has friends, too."

"Met some of them at the reservation," Tregale agreed. "Ute Pete, of course—he's been with Hurt since he came out to Utah three years ago. There's Joseph Waters, Sam, and Shower-socket—don't ask me where that name came from. If Hurt's in hiding, he's probably with one of them."

Johnston was frowning at inner thoughts. "Apparently Arrowpeen has gone south, trying to pull the Navajos into the uprising, I suspect. The Indians are quiet for now, waiting for Arrowpeen to get back. Peteetneet and Kanosh are reported ready to join Arrowpeen whenever he's ready to go to war." He looked grimly at the three men seated around the table. "Gentlemen, if the nations band together, all hell is going to break loose in this Territory. Cummings and Brigham Young need to be made aware of the danger."

Tregale gave a worried frown. "You really think they'll attack the settlers?"

"Guess you haven't heard," Johnston told him. "A patrol found two dead ranchers this afternoon. They went missing four days ago running a herd from Juab Valley down to Fillmore. They'd been shot, scalped, and had their throats cut."

"Doesn't leave much doubt, does it?" Tregale muttered.

Cooke gave Tregale a questioning look. "Do you know any way to make peace with Arrowpeen before this becomes an all-out uprising?"

"Don't know much about him," Tregale said. He gave General Johnston a sidelong glance. "He's near fifty years old, and a baptized Mormon, I heard—"

"He's what—?" Johnston exploded.

"Baptized about eight years ago, with his brother Walkara. Heard he was even ordained an Elder in the Mormon priesthood."

Johnston was staring at him in disbelief. "The man's a murderer of women and children—"

"So was his brother," Tregale said. "Mormons were just trying to keep the peace, maybe change his nature."

"A Mormon—" Johnston repeated, shaking his head. "Well, it won't stop him from spilling blood."

Tregale ventured one more comment about Arrowpeen. "Obviously, the Mormon settlers aren't safe, but if Arrowpeen goes on the warpath, General, he'll come at the army. He's hated soldiers long before they killed his son."

Johnston nodded soberly. "That's true, Mr. Tregale. I've ordered Major Paul back to Spanish Fork with two hundred reinforcements. Colonel Smith has doubled the watch around the camp—that's in place, isn't it, Colonel?"

Smith nodded quickly. "Two hour night duty, four hours during daylight. At least a hundred men assigned, General. No Indian, or anyone else, is going to sneak up on us."

The general nodded in satisfaction. He looked again at Tregale. "You might pass on to Governor Cummings that I've ordered the construction of four outposts, strategically placed to detect a major assault. What are those locations again, Colonel—?"

"Rush Valley, Tintic Valley, San Pete Valley, and Chicken Creek—that's about twenty miles south of Nephi, in case the governor isn't familiar with it. The forts are being built out of stone, so our men should be able to hold off an attack and give us plenty of warning."

"We've sent troops to protect cattle herds in Rush Valley, Steptoe Valley, and Skull Valley—although they'll see more rustlers than

Indians, I suspect," Johnston growled. "We've been losing a lot of stock but haven't had the manpower to ride herd. Got to do that now, for the safety of the camp."

"Sounds like the army is prepared, General," Tregale said. "Let's hope it doesn't come to fighting, but I'll let Governor Cummings and Brigham Young know the seriousness of the situation. As hard as the prospect seems, I'll ride out tonight."

"You just got here a couple hours ago," Cooke reminded.

"Wouldn't feel comfortable sleeping on this news," Tregale replied.

The seriousness of the situation came home with a knock on the door of Johnston's office as a junior officer entered without waiting to be invited. It only took one look at the young lieutenant's face for the men in the room to know his news was not going to be good.

"We got us a problem in Provo, General—" He suddenly realized he not only had burst into the general's office uninvited, but he hadn't saluted. He did so, and Johnston nodded.

"You going to tell us what the problem is, Lieutenant—?" Colonel Smith asked curtly.

"Two little girls were kidnapped this afternoon by some Indians," the lieutenant blurted. "A ranch just outside Provo. Indians rode right up to the house and grabbed them. Weren't any menfolk around and the Indians were gone before the mother could grab a gun."

Alarm was tingling in Tregale. "Do you have the girls' names, Lieutenant? I have friends in those parts—"

"Girls were named—what was it—Maggie and Dolly. Tate is the parent's name—"

CHAPTER NINE

UTAH COUNTY

Tregale got a fresh horse from the dragoon stables and an hour later was galloping through the darkness down Cedar Valley. The trail curved around the southern end of the Lake Mountains, skirted the edge of Utah Lake, then turned east toward Provo. He promised General Johnston he would make it back to Salt Lake City as early as possible, but needed to visit the Tates before doing that. Major Paul had a troop of soldiers trying to locate the missing girls, but Carn knew Willie and Maude would be out of their minds with worry. He thought of looking up Fred and Ted before leaving, but there was no telling where they might be and there wasn't time to go searching for them in Frogtown. Colonel Cooke assured Carn he would locate the Tate boys and tell them about their sisters.

Moonlight rimmed the edges of scudding clumps of clouds and deepened shadows around hillocks and stands of trees. Carn was still several miles from the ranch house when two riders emerged from the dark outline of some cottonwoods just ahead of him.

Startled, he pulled in the reins and his hand went to the revolver at his side. The riders were only a few yards in front of him, blocking the trail. Now washed in moonlight, he could see they were Indians. The gun cleared its holster but both Indians raised a hand in a gesture of friendship. Tregale stepped his horse closer, the gun pointed and ready.

"Tree-With-Crooked-Hand," one of the Indians said. He raised both hands into the air, showing he held no weapon. "No fight. Talk."

Tregale was surprised by the greeting. He'd heard the Indians had a name for him, but this was the first time he'd heard it. Tree-With-Crooked-Hand. He had to admit it fit. Tree-gale. A man with a hook on his hand. He put the gun back in the holster, but the tension inside did not lessen.

"Talk about what?" he asked.

The Indian pointed back into the hills to the east. "Chief Arrowpeen. You come."

Tregale was again surprised. "Arrowpeen? I thought he was in the land of the Navajos—"

"Arrowpeen here. Wants talk to Tree-With-Crooked-Hand."

Tregale frowned. "You been waiting for me—?"

Both Indians nodded.

"That doesn't make sense," Tregale said, studying them closely. "You didn't know I'd be riding—"

"Know Tree-With-Crooked-Hand at soldier camp," the Indian said. "You know family of little girls. You come—we know."

That caused Tregale to straighten. "The little girls—where are they? Take me to them—"

"Take you Chief Arrowpeen. No more talk."

They rode in silence for another hour, skirting ranches and farms, heading up into the hills. Tregale tried to figure why Arrowpeen would want to talk to him but gave up. He would know soon enough. They climbed high into a canyon—Tregale was pretty sure it was Spanish Fork canyon but wasn't familiar enough with the country to tell in the darkness. Suddenly the trail rolled over into a grassy clearing and he found himself in the midst of what must have been a hundred Indians. His two guides led him toward a man sitting a horse stiffly in the middle of the band. Tregale knew this must be Arrowpeen. The guide who had done the talking in the valley turned to look at him.

"Chief Arrowpeen. You talk."

Arrowpeen dismounted, followed by four other Indians beside him. Tregale followed their lead and also swung to the ground. The five Indians—Tregale guessed the men beside Arrowpeen were subchiefs—all sat in a semi-circle. Arrowpeen motioned for Tregale to sit with them.

The moonlight was bright enough for Tregale to get a good look at the most powerful chief of all the Ute nations. Arrowpeen looked taller than he probably was, thin and muscular, moving smoothly like a man many years younger. His features were stern and unsmiling, without a trace of emotion. He wore the coat and pants of a white man's dark suit, but was bare-chested. Tregale saw several strands of ornate, beaded jewelry hanging around the man's neck.

Arrowpeen stared silently at Tregale for several moments. Finally he raised a hand in the sign of friendship. "Arrowpeen welcomes Tree-With-Crooked-Hand. You speak with straight tongue. You speak with Big Chief of Mor-mons. You speak with Big Chief of Mericats. You speak with Big Soldier at fort."

Tregale was surprised the chief spoke English so well. It was barely halting. Then he reminded himself this man had been exposed to the white man's language for ten years—longer than that, counting the years trappers roamed this country. He nodded deferentially toward the chief.

"It is an honor to speak with Chief Arrowpeen."

"Soldiers killed my son, Pintuts."

Tregale nodded again. "I was at Spanish Fork when it happened. It was a sad day."

"Soldiers must pay for my son." Arrowpeen's voice was harsh, his face seeming to harden even more. "Much blood will avenge his death."

"Much blood of your people will also be spilled," Tregale said quietly. "If Arrowpeen makes war on soldiers, they will make war on you. Many of your people will die—there are too many soldiers, too many guns. It will not be a good war."

"They must pay for life of my son. Must pay for suffering brought to all my people. Because of soldiers, my people get hungry, sick, lose honor."

"More killing will only bring more sorrow."

"My people ready to make war on white soldiers. Many nations. Many thousands of warriors. When word of Arrowpeen is given, our enemies will drown in blood."

"I understand your sorrow and your anger," Tregale said, "but my heart is also heavy because of two little girls your people have taken. I would like to see them, take them back to the mother and father who grieve for them."

Arrowpeen seemed not to have heard the request. He glanced at the four men seated beside him, then turned again to Tregale. "You take message to Big Chief Young. Tell him sixteen nations ready to kill all soldiers. Tell him Mor-mons must join with Indians—then we are seventeen nations."

"Big Chief Young will not order Mormons to attack soldiers," Tregale said swiftly. "He will not approve Arrowpeen and his people going to war. He will not join with you."

"If Mor-mons not join with us, they are our enemies. We kill soldiers and we kill Mor-mons."

"Has Arrowpeen already given this order?" Tregale asked. "Your people killed two Mormons at Chicken Creek—"

"Not my people," Arrowpeen interrupted. "Pahvants. Chief Kanosh. Young braves angry at all whites. They kill men at Chicken Creek."

"There will be no more killing of Mormons—?"

"Not if Mor-mons join with us to fight blue coats. Arrowpeen gives word."

"I will tell Big Chief Young," Tregale promised, looking Arrowpeen squarely in the eyes, "but he will not do it. It will be a terrible war, Chief Arrowpeen. Even if you kill many soldiers and many Mormons, you cannot win this war. The soldiers and the white people are like sand blown by the winds of the desert. They will come against you until your people are no more."

"It is for the gods to decide," Arrowpeen muttered.

"Is there some other way for the soldiers to pay for the life of your son?" Tregale asked. "Something that will bring honor without shedding blood?"

The five chiefs looked at each other. Evidently they did not all understand English for Arrowpeen began talking rapidly in his own language. Nothing could be read in their expressions as they talked among themselves for almost ten minutes, then finally fell silent again. Arrowpeen fastened his stare on Tregale.

"Two things. Big Soldier at fort may choose."

"Arrowpeen is a wise chief," Tregale said quickly. "What are the choices?"

"Give us soldier who kill my son."

Tregale shook his head. "Big Soldier will not do that. It is not the white man's way—"

"Then one more thing," Arrowpeen said. "Soldiers pay for Pintuts' life with one thousand cattle, one thousand blankets, one thousand pounds of grain. Then there will be honor."

Tregale felt a surge of excitement. He couldn't be sure how General Johnston would react, but in Carn's opinion, it was a small price to pay for avoiding a bloody conflict.

"If Big Soldier does this," Tregale asked, "will Arrowpeen send the nations back to their homes?"

"Arrowpeen will not make war on soldiers, or Mor-mons, if Big Soldier does this. That is my word."

"I will go back to Big Soldier and tell him," Tregale said. "Then I will bring his answer to Arrowpeen."

"Must be word of Tree-With-Crooked-Hand," Arrowpeen grunted. "Do not trust word of Big Soldier."

"Now I must ask again, Chief Arrowpeen," Tregale said, "about the two little girls taken by your people. These children and their parents are my friends—"

"They are safe," Arrowpeen said.

"I ask the word of Arrowpeen that no harm will come to them—"

"No harm will come. When you bring back word of Big Soldier, I will give them to you."

They all stood up. Tregale nodded at each one, then turned and swung up into the saddle. As he rode out of the clearing with the same two guides, Tregale thought for a moment of riding to the ranch and telling Willie and Maude what Arrowpeen had said about Maggie and Dolly, but decided against it. It was more important to ride back to Camp Floyd and stop a war.

It was full daylight before Tregale gratefully took a seat in General Johnston's office. Colonel Smith was present, as was Colonel Cooke. Fatigue beat in the back of Tregale's head; it was a long time since he last slept. Johnston leaned both arms on the table, scrutinizing Tregale.

"Hear you had a busy night, Mr. Tregale," he began. "Is it true you met with Arrowpeen?"

"Yes, sir," Tregale answered. "Up in Spanish Fork Canyon, I believe."

"So Arrowpeen's not in the south. Did he mention the Navajos?"

"No, sir. But I think he's willing to end this war before it begins."

"An interesting comment, Mr. Tregale," the general said. "Why do you think that?"

Tregale quickly outlined his conversation with the Ute chieftain. When he finished telling the three officers about the two choices Arrowpeen had offered to avoid a shooting war, Colonel Smith slapped a hand angrily on the table.

"The arrogance of the man," he snapped. He frowned at Johnston. "I say we send out a regiment and teach these Indians a lesson—"

"Like the lesson we taught them up on the Humboldt, and Thousand Springs, or like Steptoe taught them up in Oregon country," Cooke said caustically. "That's the worst thing we could do. We'd be knee deep in blood through the whole Territory—more of it from settlers and soldiers than Indians, I'd wager. Take on sixteen nations in their own land—we'd be wiped out."

Colonel Smith started to protest but Johnston raised a hand to silence him. "He's right, Charlie. The army would win the war eventually, but I doubt if any of us would live to see it."

Tregale was staring at the officers angrily. "Why are you talking about fighting? Arrowpeen has offered to end hostilities without a shot being fired." He stared frostily at General Johnston. "I realize, sir, that I'm a civilian and don't have a military point of view, but if you're thinking of not accepting Arrowpeen's offer—"

"At the moment, we're reviewing the options, Mr. Tregale."

"Well, you may consider that losing the lives of a thousand or more of your soldiers is worth proving you're better fighters than the Indians, but no one in this Territory—or back in Washington, for that matter—is going to think it's worth the lives of hundreds, perhaps thousands, of innocent settlers. That's what will happen, gentlemen, if you turn down Arrowpeen."

Johnston stood up abruptly. "I resent your comments, sir—"

Tregale was also on his feet. "And I resent you even thinking about putting my wife and child, and the lives of every other person in this Territory, in needless jeopardy. Are you putting a higher price on the head of a thousand cattle than on the lives of all those people—? You lose more cattle than that to rustlers every month. You don't have options, General—sir."

Colonel Cooke stood up, putting a hand on Tregale's shoulder. "You've misunderstood the General, Carn. No one here would deliberately put civilian lives at risk."

"That's not what I'm hearing," Tregale said angrily.

Johnston glared at him a moment longer, then sat down and motioned for Tregale to do the same. "We owe you a great debt, Mr. Tregale. You're right—we have to accept Arrowpeen's offer, no matter how galling it may be. Cows and blankets aren't worth a single life—not one of my men, not one civilian. It just rubs the wrong way to have an Indian dictating terms to the United States army."

"When those terms will save untold lives, however," Cooke added, giving a reassuring glance at Carn, "there can be no thought of not accepting them."

"He's right, of course," Colonel Smith muttered. "My apologies to you, sir," he added, glancing at Tregale.

"There will be conditions, however," Johnston said sternly. "You said Arrowpeen has promised to order the Indians to return to their reservations. That must be done, and let him know soldiers will be posted to guard the reservations until I feel it's safe to recall them. No Indian will be allowed to leave the reservation without written permission from an Indian agent or officer in charge."

"Don't see him objecting to those conditions, sir," Tregale said.

"One more thing," Johnston said. "Arrowpeen must agree to a council of all the chiefs—all those within, say, a fifty mile radius of here—meeting with me here at Camp Floyd, within a month. Those are my conditions."

It was mostly a matter of pride, Tregale knew, but he nodded. "I'm sure Arrowpeen will agree."

"And tell him," Johnston added, "the army will see to it his people don't go hungry this winter. They can draw from the quartermaster's warehouses whenever there's a need."

"That's a generous offer, sir. All the chiefs will be grateful, and it will go a long way toward keeping a lasting peace. We all want to stop this uprising before it happens, and I want those two little girls back with their parents. The Tates don't know about any of these developments, so I'm sure they're thinking the worst and going through hell."

Johnston scrubbed at his bush of mustache. "Philip, get those cattle cut out. Should be a big enough herd in Rush Valley for that." His glance swiveled to Colonel Smith. "Charlie, you round up the blankets, and the grain—how many wagons will be needed to haul all that stuff, anyway? No matter, get it loaded." This time he had a question for Tregale. "Arrowpeen say where he wants this delivered?"

"Probably the San Pete reservation. That's central, and he stays there most of the time. He can easily move it north or south to other farms."

"You ride back to Arrowpeen and tell him the beef and the wagons will be heading south in the morning." Johnston paused, then added in a lowered voice, "Tell him I'm truly sorry about his son. I have a son of my own, and know how he feels. Wish it hadn't happened."

Johnston stood up. "Gentlemen, if Arrowpeen keeps his word, the uprising is over." He reached out a hand toward Tregale. "My thanks again, Mr. Tregale. If it means anything to you, I trust you as much as the Indians do."

Tregale took his hand. "It means a lot, sir. I am to tell Arrowpeen his offer is accepted, then—"

"He has my word, Tregale."

Tregale thought it best not to tell General Johnston that Arrowpeen wouldn't accept the word of the Big Soldier. Tregale would simply pass it along as his own. Tregale didn't have a great fondness for Johnston, but he, unlike Arrowpeen, believed the general was a man of his word.

Late that afternoon, Tregale rode slowly toward the Galloway ranch outside Provo. He was leading an Indian pony with Maggie clinging tightly to its mane. She was frightened, but she kept smiling and talking to the pony, her little hand patting its neck. Dolly rode in front of Carn, almost asleep as she leaned back against him. Tear tracks showed down the cheeks of both girls, a grim reminder of their frightening experience.

Willie and Maude came running out of the house when they were still a quarter mile away. Shading their eyes to see who was coming, Maude was the first to recognize her two little daughters. Tregale could hear her scream even as far away as they still were. Despite the distance, Maude broke into a run toward them, skirts flying. Willie was behind her, moving slower but no less eagerly. Dolly came fully awake and saw her mother running toward her. The tears started to flow again as the little girl began to call out to her mother, holding out her arms. Maggie straightened on the pony's back, and despite her fear, kicked her legs into the pony's flanks. Luckily, the pony did nothing more than break into a trot. Tregale let go of the lead rope, letting Maggie ride toward her parents.

There were long moments before anyone could say a word. It was all tears, and kisses, and hugs, and more tears. Finally Willie, holding Maggie in his arms, came toward Tregale. He tried to say something but couldn't, the sobs in his chest too deep. Tregale dismounted, and Maude fell against him, sobbing and holding on to little Dolly.

CHAPTER TEN

SALT LAKE CITY
MID-OCTOBER

Esther Cunningham was sitting with Agatha and General Galloway in their formal living room. Agatha would normally visit
with her friend back in the large kitchen, where people gathered most of the time, but Esther had arrived decked out in finery: a
deep purple brocaded dress with a high collar, puffing out from a
tightly-fitting bodice into a multilayered bustle with a large matching bow; new black leather shoes, high-topped and ladylike, much
too fragile to be practical; a fancy knitted shawl with daringly bright
stripes of colors, and a sewn label identifying it as coming from
Paris. She was also wearing black lace gloves, and a stylish pearl
choker—Agatha supposed they weren't real pearls—around her neck.
Her hair looked as if a long time had been spent on it, and for the
first time in Agatha's memory, Esther's face had a pink blush applied. Overall, Esther looked so startlingly different from the drab
woman she had been that it had taken Agatha two looks to recognize her standing in the doorway. Prim and proper, Esther obviously wanted to show off her new clothing and Agatha decided the
front room provided a grander setting for the occasion.

What that occasion was exactly, neither Agatha nor her husband knew. Esther talked incessantly, almost giddily, for ten minutes without saying much of anything. She was effusive about the
wonderful shops now in Salt Lake City in which one could find high
fashion dresses and millinery for ladies. The prices were high of
course, she pointed out, but ladies now could dress as finely in

Utah as they did in London or Paris. That was an exaggeration, but Agatha wasn't going to challenge Esther's exuberance. She exchanged glances with her husband, amazed at this new Esther who seemed to have suddenly burst from a cocoon. Esther finally got around to the reason—the other reason—for her visit.

"Well, what I really came to tell you," Esther said, putting her gloved hands together excitedly, "is that Alfred and I will soon be your neighbors."

Agatha's eyes widened in surprise. "You're leaving Sugar House—?"

"Yes," Esther beamed excitedly. "I'm so excited!"

"Where are you moving?"

"Right here on South Temple—not a half-mile east of you!"

"That is good news, Esther," General Galloway said. "Is Alfred building a new house?"

"Oh no. We bought the Mellencamp mansion."

"Doctor Mellencamp's place?" Galloway was really surprised at that. Mellencamp was a well-known physician who came West to Utah two years after the first pioneers. A lot of people walking around the valley today owed their lives to old Doc Mellencamp. Galloway attended the funeral of Mellencamp's wife two years ago. The large house the Mellencamps had built, about the same size as the Galloways, seemed large and lonely for the doctor after that. Galloway understood that feeling only too well.

"So where is the doctor going?" Galloway asked.

Esther seemed a little hesitant to answer, then flashed another smile. "He's going to stay with us. Keeping his office, although he doesn't see patients any more, and Alfred is making one of the rooms on the main floor into a bedroom for him. Poor man has no relatives and the mansion is just too large for him. And at his age, he's having trouble with stairs."

"I'm so happy for you and Alfred," Agatha said warmly. "You'll be the envy of our friends."

"Alfred and Aaron did such a good job working at Camp Floyd." Esther's voice dropped, and she leaned forward, as if to make sure her next words did not go outside the room. "Did you know the army is paying Alfred three thousand dollars as a bonus for doing his job so well—and giving Aaron fifteen hundred dollars extra. I know Alfred doesn't want me telling anyone about it, but it makes me feel right proud. They're both so good at carpentry. Colonel Smith told Alfred that if it wasn't for them, the camp couldn't have been finished before winter."

"I suppose Aaron and Lydia are moving in with you. There'll certainly be plenty of room—"

For the first time since Esther arrived, the smile dropped off her face. It was a moment before she answered. "That's what we were expecting, but Aaron has been called to go to Brigham City. He's decided to do it."

Agatha frowned. "Called—? He's not going on a mission, is he?"

"Same thing," Esther said, the anger plain in her voice. "The Church thinks because he's young and so skilled, he can help build up the settlement. I'm told Brigham Young does this all the time—uproots people and sends them wherever he thinks they're needed, with no mind to their own feelings. It's absolute foolishness for Aaron to go. He and his father can make a fortune right here in the valley, with all the building going on."

"Well, I'm sure Aaron will do well in Brigham City, too," Galloway said, trying to comfort Esther.

But the tiger was loose and fire flashed in Esther's eyes. "Everything is so primitive in Brigham City—Indians camp there all the time. Aaron needs to think about Lydia and bringing children into this life. They don't have any good doctors there—don't have hardly any doctors at all. Why, we'll have one of the finest doctors in the whole Territory living right in our own home. There's so much more here in the valley—better schools, a theater, a library, all the activities the Church offers—"

"Not much of that going on at the moment," Galloway cautioned. "Don't know when the Church authorities will allow all those things to start up again but we're on our own for awhile, I suspect. We'll have to wait and see what happens with the soldiers and all those teamsters. It's certainly not safe for anyone to be about in the valley these days."

"I told Alfred we should go to Brigham Young. I'll tell him what I think about sending Aaron up to Brigham City and putting his family in danger. Alfred won't hear of it, of course—he can't believe I'd really speak my mind, for that matter."

Agatha couldn't hold back a laugh. "I confess, I can't either, Esther. You wouldn't talk to a church mouse a few months ago, and now you're going to scold the prophet—"

Esther smoothed her dress, tapped her feet, then a little smile tugged at her mouth. "I suppose I have changed. Alfred says he hardly knows me any more. Just because I have opinions now, and speak them. You've always done that, Agatha—"

Agatha nodded. "You're right, Esther, but people expect it of me. It's a surprise, to say the least, coming from you. Seems like you didn't have a tongue before you came to the valley." She was smiling, so there was no sting in the words. "Now you seem to be—"

"—making up for lost time," Esther finished. She smiled back. "I'm growing to like the sound of my voice, Agatha—I admit it. I'm learning that the more you speak up, the more people listen to you."

"Good for you," Galloway said. He stood up. "If you ladies will excuse me, I have a few items of business to attend to in my study. Good visiting with you, Esther. We'll be looking forward to having you and Alfred drop in frequently once you've moved into the Mellencamp place."

"That's nice of you, General Galloway," Esther smiled back. "We'll have all of you over once we're settled. Alfred says it will be a few weeks more before he's completely finished at Camp Floyd. We won't be moving until after that."

Galloway was almost out of the door when Esther called to him. "I forgot to ask you, General—have you heard anything about Calvin? Lydia made me promise to ask. She's worried about Harriet and the baby."

Galloway gave a shake of his head. "Haven't heard a thing, Esther. I suppose Calvin's company will be heading back to Camp Floyd before too long, though. They've been out in the field quite awhile, and I hear all the troops are being recalled for the winter."

He looked curiously at Esther. "Is Lydia worried about her sister? Harriet and the baby are in good health, and she seems happy enough living here with us—"

"I know she enjoys taking care of little Carn while Heather's at the store," Agatha added.

"It's Calvin coming back that has Lydia worried," Esther explained. "She's afraid Harriet will move out to Camp Floyd when he does, and we've heard such terrible things about the place. Some of the goings on Alfred tells me—well, I can hardly believe such things actually happen."

"An army camp is a rough place to raise a family," Galloway agreed, "even in the heart of civilization—which Camp Floyd certainly isn't. But Harriet will be all right—"

Esther gave a little shudder. "That Fairfield, or Frogtown, as everyone calls it, is such a horrid place. I worry about Aaron being there. Goodness knows what might happen if Alfred wasn't with him—"

"If Harriet doesn't like it," Agatha added, "or feels she and baby Calvin aren't safe, she can always come back here to live. It won't be all that far for Calvin to travel for the weekend, if it comes to that."

"Come to think of it, she can come live with us," Esther said, "now that we're moving into a big house. I'd like that. She might convince Lydia to put her foot down and bring Aaron to his senses. I just get sick at the thoughts of them going to Brigham City—"

While Esther and Agatha chatted, Heather was busily dealing with a half dozen customers still in the store downtown. It was near closing time for most stores on East Temple, for respectable people wanted to be safely home before nightfall and the violence and crime that came with it. It was less dangerous on city streets now that the special marshals patrolled them, but still, no one was really safe.

It had been a busy day. Agatha worked at the store in the morning, then Heather relieved her for the afternoon hours. It worked out well, because Heather was able to spend precious time with little Carn for the first part of the day, then Harriet cared for the baby until Heather returned in the evening. She knew it was selfish, but Heather was dreading the time that Calvin returned and Harriet and her baby moved out to Camp Floyd to be with him. Harriet was so good with little Carn. Still, Harriet's son needed his father too, and when the day came for the reunion, Heather would be happy for them.

This was a particularly draining day for Heather, waiting on customers and trying to unpack some of the new goods that arrived a few days ago from the frontier. Henry did most of the heavy lifting, but it still was a lot of hard work, stocking shelves and finding places for the new items. She looked at the clock, relieved to see it was only an hour to closing.

Carn hadn't returned for several days and she didn't know when to expect him. He was gone most of the time now, sometimes coming home only for a few hours sleep, then riding out again. Heather was worried, for she felt they were losing the closeness that had always been between them. He was tired after a day of riding, she was tired after dealing with customers and caring for the baby, and lately there was little conversation between them even when they did spend time together. The strained silences were becoming more and more frequent.

To be truthful, Heather told herself, she was feeling really resentful over the fact that her husband seemed to be putting everyone and everything ahead of her and the baby. His being gone so much was bothering her much more than she had expected it would. In those times alone—which was most of the time lately—she felt neglected and unloved. That was foolishness, she tried to convince herself. Carn still loved her—at least, she wanted to believe that. If he would just show a little more interest in what was happening in her life, hers and the baby's. The only things that seemed important to him now were troubles with Indians, and soldiers, and all the political squabbling.

She knew Carn felt badly about being gone so much, but she had begun to resent hearing her husband tell her over and over again that these were times of trouble and turmoil, that one day things would be normal again. Heather felt she no longer knew what normal was.

Nothing had been normal since the day she left her parents in Liverpool over two years ago and boarded ship for the Americas. Certainly not during the grueling journey of pulling a handcart over thirteen hundred miles of wilderness, not in the past winter campaign against invading federal soldiers, nor these last few months of Carn so involved in keeping the lines of communication open between the U.S. army, the Territorial administration, and Church officials. Hardly a day in all that time that Heather would call normal.

The little bell attached to the front door jangled and Heather looked up. An army officer entered, smiling and nodding his head politely as he met her glance.

For some reason, she felt a warm flush go through her, followed instantly by a feeling of guilt.

The officer worked through the other customers and came back to where she was standing beside the counter. He was tall, fair complexioned, with a small, neatly clipped mustache. He looked like a man of breeding, Heather thought. His uniform was dusted, his boots shined. He took off his hat and again nodded politely.

"Captain Geoffrey Edwards, ma'am."

"What can I do for you, Captain?" Heather asked. Again she felt that strange flush of warmth. This was ridiculous. She was a married woman, not a schoolgirl. "Is there something I can get for you?"

The officer smiled. She couldn't help noticing the white, even teeth, showing against the deep sunburn of a face she could only describe as handsome. You're not a schoolgirl, Heather, she told herself again. Just a lonely married woman.

"To be honest, ma'am," Captain Edwards said, "I came in to speak to you."

There it was again, only this time she noticed a quickening beat to her heart. Only natural, she reasoned. A natural womanly response to a compliment tendered by a handsome man. But then, she was assuming it was a compliment.

"Why would you want to speak to me, Captain?" she asked. "Have we met before?"

"No, ma'am," he answered, "but you remind me of people back home."

"Not your mother, I hope," Heather smiled.

"No, ma'am," the officer said quickly. "Although I do see images of my sister. Takes me back home, for sure."

"Where is home, Captain?"

"Boston, ma'am."

"I'm from London. I spent a few hours in Boston when we first arrived in America—"

"It's not the city, ma'am," he smiled, "it's the grace I see stamped on you. No doubt you were a delightful member of London society, and a great loss when you left for the Americas."

Heather didn't know what to say. "I take it your family is prominent in Boston—" It was awkward, but she couldn't think of anything else for the moment.

"My father is in banking, ma'am," the captain said quietly, "and yes, I was fortunate to be raised in good circumstances."

Heather glanced down at her dress, a plain brown garment wrinkled from the day's work. She put her hands on her hips. "I'm hardly dressed for a gala, in London or Boston. You flatter me, Captain Edwards—and surprise me, I might add. What on earth would draw such an opinion about social graces?"

"You have the bearing, ma'am. It's easily recognized. Both my mother and my sister have it. They would see it in you, too."

"I see myself as having lost any such distinction in the last two years—"

"Not in twenty years," he interrupted.

"And when did you see all this in me, Captain? I don't remember us meeting—and I'm sure I would have." She wished she could have taken back those last words. It would be possible to mistake them.

"I have to confess to a very ungentlemanly action, ma'am—"

"Please call me Heather—Mrs. Heather Tregale," she added hurriedly. What was the matter with her. This man was a total stranger, and there was no reason to do anything but distrust a stranger in uniform. "What ungentlemanly act are you guilty of, Captain Edwards? Will I be embarrassed?"

"The embarrassment is mine, Mrs. Tregale," he smiled. "I walk past this store a dozen times whenever I'm in town, hoping to catch a glimpse of you. I learned you are here mostly in the afternoons, seldom in the mornings."

She felt her cheeks redden. "You are observant, Captain," she smiled. She hesitated, then decided it was time to distance herself from this man she felt uncomfortably comfortable with. That undoubtedly had something to do with the memories of London and all the pleasant luxuries she enjoyed while growing up. Captain Edwards was uncannily accurate in placing her among the socially elite. Her family was prominent in London and surrounding areas for the dozen or so haberdasheries bearing the Lee name. Yes, it was time for the married woman to come to the fore. "I usually spend the mornings with my baby."

Again to her surprise, the captain nodded. "A son, named after his father," the officer said. "I've heard your husband speak of little Carn."

That was a shock to Heather. "You know my husband—?"

"I've seen him quite a few times," Edwards replied. "Last winter at Camp Scott and recently at Camp Floyd. He's well respected, Mrs. Tregale."

"It's nice of you to say that, Captain Edwards." Despite her inner concerns, she gave him a warm smile. "I appreciate your honesty, Captain, about peering at me through the window. I find no offense in that. It's not often a woman enjoys flattery in these times, and in this part of the world."

"May I drop in now and then just to chat?" the captain asked. "It also is not often one meets a lady that reminds me so strongly of the good life awaiting me after I get out of the army."

"When will that be, Captain?"

"A matter of months," Captain Edwards said, his face plainly showing pleasure. "Then it's back to Boston."

"I'm happy for you, Captain," Heather said. "I easily picture you sitting behind a desk at your father's bank—a better occupation than charging the enemy with upraised sword."

"I'm grateful for any picture you carry of me, Mrs. Tregale," the captain said softly. He put on his hat, nodded, and left the store.

CHAPTER ELEVEN

CAMP FLOYD
LATE OCTOBER

The Second Dragoons under the command of Captain Jim Hawes returned from Thousand Springs late in the afternoon, dusty, bedraggled, and bone tired. They had been on the trail for thirty-eight hours, riding day and night with only brief stops for meals and to rest the horses. Every man felt a sense of relief when they crossed the bridge over Cedar Creek and entered Camp Floyd, the long, frustrating campaign of chasing the Shoshones finally at an end. The Indians had proven wily and difficult to engage, eluding the most carefully set traps. As a result, casualties were light; eight wounded riding in wagons, a score of bandaged troopers, but not one life lost.

The horse soldiers lined up before their barracks, remaining in the saddle as Colonel Cooke delivered a few words of welcome, then dismounting and breaking ranks with wild yells as Captain Hawes gave the order to dismiss. Grooming and feeding the horses was first priority, then a lineup at the paymaster's for the small cash draw allowed each month until the pay-train arrived from California sometime next spring. Soon after that, the noise in Frogtown noticeably increased.

A half dozen troopers from Company D, with Calvin Gray in the middle of them, were among the first to wade across Cedar Creek at the eastern edge of Camp Floyd. The group stood on Front Street, dripping wet and staring in eager anticipation at the line of saloons and whorehouses. A short distance from them, three gaudily-dressed women leaning against a rickety two-storied frame building stepped out into the street, beckoning to them. A red-painted sign on the building proclaimed it as Lila's Love Nest and Bath House.

Calvin stripped the suspenders off his shoulders. "Getting a bath and having a couple of those lovelies sounds like fun to me," he said, grinning at his buddies. "Always time to get drunk."

If Harriet could have heard her husband, and seen the raw lust on his face, it would have broken her heart.

Two days later, the afternoon stage from Salt Lake City pulled up in front of the Carson Inn. Carn Tregale climbed down from where he had been riding beside the driver and opened the stage door. Three women inside waved handkerchiefs to clear away the dust still swirling through the windowless doors. One of these was Harriet Gray; the other two were officer's wives returning to Camp Floyd after spending a few days in Salt Lake shopping and visiting friends. The two men in the stage were traveling salesmen hoping to sell their wares to merchants in Fairfield, such as Crouch and Gilbert & Gerrish, and to the base sutler. Tregale didn't envy them the task of competing with Andy Miller and the stranglehold of the Miller & Russell Company stores.

He stretched out a hand to help Harriet down onto the ground. Two officers waiting beside the fence came forward to assist their wives. Tregale glanced uncertainly at his horse tied behind the stage but the driver called down to him.

"Go ahead and help the young lady. I'll see your horse gets cared for."

Tregale gave him an appreciative nod and led Harriet up the pathway to the inn. She looked back just before entering, studying the few men on horseback passing in front of the inn.

"He doesn't know you're coming, Harriet," he told her. "Soon as you're settled, I'll go look him up. Calvin will be here before you know it."

With Harriet waiting impatiently in the room on the upper southwest corner where Tregale usually stayed—General Johnston's room, as John Carson still called it, although the general hadn't stayed at the inn for several months—Carn rode his horse across the bridge onto the grounds of Camp Floyd.

He was well known by sentries now and directed to the administration building where he was told he would find Colonel Philip

Cooke. The colonel was working at his desk when Carn was admitted, and he quickly rose to greet him with a handshake.

"Good to see you, Carn." His glance fell to his visitor's empty hands. "Not carrying much from the Governor this time."

Carn grinned. "Got a full saddlebag back at the inn. Rode out with the stage—Harriet Gray was on it. Word in Salt Lake is your dragoons are back from Thousand Springs and she's hoping to see her husband. Calvin left sudden, as you recall."

Cooke called out through the open office door. "Corporal Sanders—go find Calvin Gray. He's with the dragoons—Company D, I believe. When you find him, bring him here."

A voice acknowledged the order. Cooke closed the office door, motioned to a chair in front of his desk, and both men sat down. The colonel studied Tregale with a quizzical frown.

"Something troubling you, Carn?"

Tregale hesitated, then shook his head. "Nothing. Just a little tired. Anybody thought about putting in a railroad between here and Salt Lake? Sure would make life easier."

Cooke smiled. "I'll see it gets mentioned in one of the dispatches to Washington."

Tregale looked up at his friend. "Maybe there is something, Philip." He hesitated again, then reached a decision. "You know a Captain Geoffrey Edwards?"

Cooke was surprised. He thought for a moment, then nodded. "Attached to the Tenth Infantry. Comes from a prominent Boston family, I believe. Good officer. Getting out of the army in a few months, I hear." He stared curiously at Tregale. "What makes you ask about Edwards?"

"Heard his name mentioned awhile ago, that's all."

Cooke wasn't going to be satisfied with that. "In connection with what—?"

"Doesn't matter. I was just curious—"

"Don't give me that," Cooke snorted. "You have an interest in this man. What's he done?"

"He hasn't done anything," Tregale said quickly. "I was just curious what you thought about him." Another hesitation. "Is he married?"

"Is some woman interested in Captain Edwards?" Cooke smiled. "Is that what this is all about?"

Tregale expelled a deep sigh. "Can this stay just between the two of us, Philip?"

"Of course."

"You won't feel obligated to make it official, no matter what I tell you—?"

"Not without your permission. What's this all about, Carn?"

"Nothing, really. I guess I just need to talk it out with someone—someone who isn't directly involved, if you know what I mean."

"You have my word as an officer and a friend."

The quiet reassurance satisfied Carn. "Well, you know Henry Washington—" Cooke nodded. "Henry mentioned something the other day—got me thinking, the way he said it."

"Something about Captain Edwards—?"

"It was, but it was more about my wife, I think."

Cooke was instantly frowning. "Hope this isn't going where I think it might—"

"Henry was real careful," Carn continued. "It was plain he didn't quite know how to say what was on his mind, and didn't really want to be saying anything."

"What did he say—?"

"He mentioned that Captain Edwards is a frequent customer of late in our emporium downtown, always when Heather is in the store. Henry said Captain Edwards is a real gentlemen, and made a point to let me know Heather thinks highly of him."

"Thinks highly—?" Cooke asked. "What does that mean?"

"Didn't ask."

"So what was Henry saying that he didn't say?"

"I think Edwards might be courting my wife."

Cooke stared at him. "Find that hard to believe. Not that Edwards might try making up to your wife—she's an attractive woman. I can't believe Heather would ever allow such a thing to happen, though. If I've ever seen a woman in love with her husband, it's Heather."

"It's probably nothing," Tregale muttered. "Just me reading something into what Henry said that isn't really there."

"On the other hand," Cooke frowned, "Henry wouldn't have said anything if he didn't think there was cause."

"If there is some kind of attraction between Heather and this Captain Edwards—and I'm not saying there is," Tregale added quickly, "I put only myself to blame."

"What blame is on you?" Cooke asked.

"I've been on the trail a lot these past months," Tregale muttered. "Haven't spent hardly any time with Heather and the baby."

"Can't blame yourself for that."

"Still, it's been hard on Heather—hard on both of us, for that matter. We don't talk much, or enjoy each other's company like we used to. I know she's unhappy about me being gone so much, not spending more time with little Carn. Truth is, I'm not good company when I am home—tired, usually, and always a lot on my mind. You know better than I do how close we are to things blowing up in the Territory. That's no excuse for not being a good husband, but things are different between us. I can see how she might be grateful for another man's attention. I consider it my fault, Philip, but it's hard to accept it might be happening."

"I could talk to Captain Edwards—"

Tregale quickly shook his head. "He's done nothing except pass some polite conversation with my wife, from what Henry said. I'm sure Henry would have told me if there was anything more. But it's eating at me, Philip, more than I want to admit."

"Maybe you should quit being a liaison for all sides. I don't know who'd fill your shoes, but it's not worth losing your family—"

"Don't think I'm facing that," Carn told him, "leastwise, I hope not. It's my own guilt I'm living with, and I have to deal with it."

"I still think a word with Edwards—"

Another firm shake of the head by Tregale.

"At least let him know people are noticing he's spending an unusual amount of time at the emporium—"

"He'd mention it to Heather. I don't want her to think she's being watched."

"Well, let me know if you change your mind."

"Thanks, Philip. Hope you don't mind me dragging you into my personal affairs."

"I'm your friend, Carn." He gave Tregale a warm smile. "So, if we're changing the subject, I hear Brigham Young has approved sending some of those teamsters off to California."

"Wagons leaving in a few days. We'll be rid of more than six hundred."

"The Territory's gain," Cooke murmured, "and California's loss."

"The army intending to cut any more of those hellions loose before spring?"

"Don't think so," the colonel said. "Not before the post is dedicated, anyway."

"Has a date been set for that?"

"General's mentioned the ninth of November. Wouldn't want to be the person responsible for missing that date."

The two men chatted about various matters for the next few minutes, particularly about General Johnston's continued refusal to have any direct contact with either Governor Cummings or the Mormon leader, Brigham Young.

There was a knock on the door. When Cooke opened it, Calvin Gray was standing at attention outside, a worried look on his face.

"At ease, soldier," Cooke told him.

Calvin saw Tregale and the worry was replaced with a grin of relief.

"Glad you made it back, Calvin," Tregale said, coming forward to shake Gray's hand. "Got a little surprise for you—"

A few minutes later, Harriet burst out of the front door of the inn and ran toward her husband. She wrapped herself in his arms, clinging to him, tears streaming down her cheeks. Calvin seemed a little awkward at first, aware that Tregale was watching them, then his arms tightened around his wife and he lifted her off her feet, swinging her around.

"Well," Tregale said, "guess you have a lot to talk about. Colonel Cooke cleared you for a two-day pass, Calvin. Room's reserved for the whole time. I have a lot of stuff to go over with General Johnston and I'll be staying in the officer's quarters. Good to see you two together again." He flashed a smile at Harriet. "Don't want to rush your time together, but remember Calvin has to answer roll call at eight o'clock on that third morning, and the stage leaves an hour after that."

Harriet quickly became aware that her husband had changed. She saw it in his eyes, in the harder set to his face. At first, she put it down to what he had gone through these past months in the campaign against the Shoshones, but she couldn't ignore for long that the changes went much deeper.

It showed when she tried to explain why she had left baby Calvin back in Salt Lake City.

"I hope you're not too disappointed," she said, when they were alone in the room. "I know how much you must have missed your son, but I wasn't sure I would get to see you, let alone spend time with you—"

"It's all right," Calvin said, his tone almost gruff. "Sure, I want to see the kid, but—" he added, putting his arms around her waist and drawing her hard against him, "I'm glad it's just the two of us. I've been thinking about doin' this every night since I've been gone—"

The change in him was painfully obvious when he made love to her. It was completely different than before. It was natural that he was hungry and impatient, she told herself, but she could feel no warmth in him. She sensed that the act held no love; not the first time, not any of the times after that. It hurt her, left her confused. She could feel none of her love returned. Calvin seemed to want only to satisfy his needs.

They came down for lunch the next day, chatted briefly with Elvira in the kitchen, said little to anyone at the table during the meal, then left right after.

Calvin started walking down Front Street, Harriet holding his arm. He stopped on the corner outside Crouch's store.

"We shouldn't go no farther," he told her.

"Why not?" she asked, looking down the street. It didn't look inviting but she had heard so much about Fairfield that she was curious to see it.

"Ain't no place for you," Calvin muttered. "No place for the kid, either."

She looked up at him, surprised. "You said you wanted us to be here with you—"

"That was just talk," Calvin said, avoiding her eyes. "I do want you with me, of course, but Frogtown ain't no place for a person like you to live."

"I hear there's more people living here than—"

"Not people, Harriet," Calvin interrupted harshly, "only gamblers and thieves and prostitutes and murderin' teamsters—that's who lives in Frogtown. Any decent, God-fearin' person lives up in the north end of the valley, in Cedar Fort. That's where all the Mormons live, 'cepting for John and Elvira Carson and their kids."

"So I'll live in Cedar Fort. How far is it—?"

"It ain't how far it is, Harriet. That don't matter. I'm in the army—I cain't come and go whenever I please. Even if I could, folks in Cedar would shoot any soldier before letting him inside the fort. They hate soldiers—and that's what I am, Harriet."

"Then I'll stay here in Fairfield—Frogtown, as you call it. I could stay at the inn—"

Calvin grunted in disgust. "Even officers cain't afford to stay there regular."

"There must be some place—"

Harriet winced as Calvin gripped her arm. "All right, you want to stay in Frogtown. Let's go find you a place."

Calvin kept a hard grasp on her arm as they walked north about fifty yards from Crouch's store. There, the hard-packed dirt street gave way to a maze of rutted, muddy trails that seemed to go everywhere and nowhere. At first, Harriet thought there was only a jumble of junk stretching in every direction, as far as she could see. As Calvin walked her into the muddy ruts, she suddenly realized she was in the middle of a pitiful collection of improvised shelters.

"This is Frogtown," Calvin grated harshly in her ear. "You tell me when you see a place you'd like to stay with our son."

It was a sight Harriet would never wipe from her memory. Scores of dirty little tents supported on sticks, with only mud to sleep on. Holes dug into the ground, with a canvas over them to keep out snow and rain. Some of the dugouts were boxed in with rough timbers, a few even had slanted timber roofs to protect those who lived there. There was little room inside the dugouts to do anything but crouch down, or stretch out on dirty, wet straw scattered as flooring. A few wagon beds, the wheels gone, were sunk into the earth to provide a little more protection from cold and wind. Some of these converted wagons still had their canvas tops, but many had only bare iron rings that offered no protection for occupants of the boxes. Off in the distance, on the northern edge of the pitiful clutter, Harriet could see several rows of dilapidated shacks. Most looked like they would collapse under the first onslaught of winter wind. Still, the shacks were mansions compared to the squalor of the muddy holes in which most of the citizens of Frogtown were living.

Walking through the muddy clutter of dugouts and canvas shelters was shattering for Harriet, but catching glimpses of the people living in them was even more heart wrenching. Dirty, suspicious and antagonistic faces of men, women and children looked out at Harriet. It was haunting and frightening. Finally she could take no more, and breaking free of her husband's grasp, she turned and ran back to the realities of Front Street.

Calvin caught up with her as she leaned against the wall of the Crouch's store. He felt sorry as he saw the pallor of her cheeks, but knew he had made her understand.

"You and the boy can't live here, Harriet," he muttered. "You know you can't. I had to show you that for your own good."

Silently, Harriet nodded. She started walking back toward the Carson Inn. Something inside her had died in these last few minutes. She didn't know what it was, but there was an empty space in her heart that hadn't been there before. It had something to do with Calvin, with the army, with their marriage, with this horrible town. She really didn't want to know what it was. It was painful enough just to know it was there.

When the morning of the third day arrived, Calvin had little to say, groping for words and thoughts that wouldn't form in his mind. He regretted taking Harriet through shantytown, knew that something had happened inside her. Finally he left with only a brief hug and a cold kiss between them. Harriet went out onto the balcony and watched him ride away. Tears started to fall, but she didn't try to understand what was causing them.

CHAPTER TWELVE

SALT LAKE CITY SOCIAL HALL

I t looked like a Bedouin encampment, with small individual tents filling the entire main floor of the Social Hall. The tents were simple makeshift affairs, a sheet or a blanket hanging over a central support, closely packed together and extending from the back of the hall to the front stage. There must have been a hundred and fifty tents, leaving barely enough room to find pathways between them.

With all those tents, there wasn't a person to be seen in the upper hall. It wasn't difficult to tell where everyone was, however, for the noise coming up the stairs from the lower hall was loud enough to be heard two blocks away: a babble of voices, all of them female, all sounding like they were enjoying themselves immensely.

And they were, women enjoying each other's company, enjoying the refreshments spread out on tables against the walls, and enjoying this rare opportunity to be a guest at a costume party, if you could call it that. Everyone looked pretty much the same, as if they had stepped out of ancient Hebrew times. They wore simple tunic dresses and their heads were covered with shawls. Their attire went with the collection of tents in the hall above them.

This was a latter-day celebration fashioned after the ancient Feast of Tabernacles, which for centuries was commemorated as a festive occasion. This evening's social followed the same happy, yet solemn, tradition.

The event was the idea of Agatha Harbon, who would never forget the horror and pain endured by so many at this time two years ago in the savage winter fury of the high Rockies. Tents were the only protection then for those in Ed Martin's handcart company, so there was a special significance to this celebration for all those who had survived that ordeal.

All the ladies present were invited guests of Agatha and Sister Eliza Snow Young, who had joined with Agatha in hosting this special social. Many prominent families were represented, families who had made their own sacrifices in crossing the plains in wagons a decade earlier. However, survivors of the ill-fated handcart companies were special guests, for their suffering could still be seen in gaunt eyes and extremities crippled by frostbite. Many of the surviving families were now scattered in settlements throughout the Territory but most of the women of families still in the Salt Lake Valley were in attendance.

Eliza was surrounded by a group of admiring women, and she was shaking her head as she answered the question just asked her. It was one that had been asked a dozen times already this evening.

"I don't know when the meetings will start again," she said. "The President is anxious to do it, of course, but there still is no assurance people will be safe. Those horrid teamsters are no longer under army control and hardly a day passes without them brutalizing someone. We can't even be sure the soldiers aren't planning to attack us. General Johnston certainly gives no guarantee of that."

The sister who had asked the question was near tears. "It will be so nice to attend sacrament meeting again. I worry about what the children are missing—"

"Don't let them miss a thing," Eliza told her quickly. "Your husband has the priesthood—make sure you have the sacrament every Sunday. And you can hold Sunday School for your family—the children need to draw spiritual strength from the scriptures these days more than ever before."

"Our bishop leans on us sisters to keep in touch with all the families of the ward," one of the women in the group said. "We meet socially from time to time, and we're always rendering service to each other, but I'm wondering if the Female Relief Society will ever be activated again. Seems like it would be a great help to all of us."

Eliza was familiar with what the sister was referring to. Back in the days of Nauvoo, the women of the church were organized into the Female Relief Society. When church members were driven out of Illinois, the women's society was dissolved. Many settlements had recently formed unofficial groups to help one another, but there was no official recognition or direction like there had been with the former Female Relief Society.

"The President and I have talked about bringing it back," Eliza responded. "I'm sure it will happen. There are just so many things that need attention at the moment. So keep working together, and helping each other. We'll have our Society back one of these days."

"Will you be leading us, Sister Eliza?" another asked.

Sister Eliza raised her hands quickly and shook her head. "I'm sure the President will find the right person to be in charge."

He would. And it would be Eliza. But that was still a few years in the future.

In another part of the hall, Agatha spotted Maude Tate. Moments later they were hugging each other tightly. Maude and her husband Willie, along with their five children, were family to Agatha now. Without expressing it, the extra warmth of the hug was gratitude for the safe return of Maude's two young daughters after their recent kidnapping by Arrowpeen's braves.

"How are the girls doing?" Agatha asked.

Maude gave a wry smile. "They tell anyone who'll listen how they weren't frightened for one minute. I let them tell it that way—better to have a good memory in their mind than a bad one. But they do love Carn for rescuing them and bringing them home safe—as do Willie and me. Don't know what I'd have done if I'd lost those girls."

"Well, I hope you're being cautious these days, living out on the ranch. My heart breaks when I think what happened to Sister Markham and her daughter—"

"Willie stays close, and I always carry a revolver now. I can assure you, the girls don't get far from my apron strings."

"These are such dreadful days," Agatha sighed. "I hope things change for the better before too long."

"Just think of those poor families in Cedar City," Maude muttered. "There's not thirty or forty families left, I hear—almost a ghost town. They've all scattered, in fear of being hounded by these new federal judges."

"Jim Wilson has never said a thing about what happened back in Mountain Meadows—"

"Nor does anyone else," Maude muttered. "Whatever really happened in the Meadows, it must have been horrible for it to affect so many good Mormons. I know we'll never go back to Cedar."

"Well, we have enough problems of our own right here in Salt Lake City," Agatha murmured. "Not a day goes by without a killing or a shooting or a stabbing. The new marshals have helped a lot, but only a fool would be out on the streets after dark."

"Perhaps it will help when Camp Floyd is dedicated," Maude said.

Agatha quickly shook her head. "It's not the soldiers causing the trouble. It's those gamblers, and those drunken Irish teamsters, and all those prostitutes. No one is going to be safe until the lot of them has been cleared out."

The two friends looked over and saw Esther Cunningham moving toward Sister Eliza.

"That could be trouble," Agatha muttered. "Esther's found her tongue and doesn't give much thought to when she wags it."

She was right. Esther pushed close to Sister Eliza and blurted out a question.

"I'm wondering, Sister Eliza, if I might ask you a question about plural marriage—"

Eliza looked at her, the faintest hint of a smile tugging at her lips.

"Of course, Sister—it's Esther Cunningham, isn't it? You're a friend of Agatha, I believe."

"Yes. My husband is Alfred Cunningham, the carpenter. We'll be moving soon to a house on South Temple, not too far from the Lion House."

This time the smile was plainly evident. "Happy to hear that, Sister Cunningham. Our husbands have a common interest in carpentry. The President loves working with wood—he's always engaged in some carpentry project, it seems. What is your question, Sister Cunningham?"

"I can't help wondering how you ladies do it—share your husband with so many other women. It certainly isn't a natural thing, is it—"

A little frost edged into Eliza's tone. "I must disagree, Sister

Cunningham. It is part of a woman's eternal nature to live in a plural relationship with her husband."

"But it's not in her nature now, is it," Esther pressed. "I mean, I can't imagine allowing my Alfred to be with another woman—"

The conversation around the two women hushed. People were staring at Esther as if they couldn't believe what they were hearing. How could anyone confront a plural wife of Brigham Young with such a question—especially a woman so loved and respected as Sister Eliza?

Esther seemed oblivious to the unfriendly stares, her mind wrapped in the questions going through it. This was something that she truly didn't understand about Mormon women. It was completely unnatural to her, just as she'd told Sister Eliza.

"If you are in harmony with eternal principles, Sister Cunningham," Eliza said quietly, "you do not think of your husband as 'being with another woman'. You think of him, and yourself, as participating in a holy and exalted state of marriage that has existed through the eternities."

"Well, I don't know anything about the eternities, do I?" Esther frowned.

"It seems you don't, Sister Cunningham. I believe it would be helpful for you to learn more about these eternal principles. Perhaps you would allow me to deliver some scriptures to you, so you may study the subject at your leisure."

Agatha and Maude reached her side before Esther could reply. Agatha took Esther's arm firmly, smiling at Eliza.

"That's very thoughtful of you, Sister Eliza," Agatha said. "Esther will be most happy to receive them, won't you, Esther—"

Esther nodded, feeling the pressure of Agatha's grip. For the first time, she was aware of the tension in the other women around her.

"I would indeed be appreciative, Sister Eliza," she said quickly. "Please forgive me if my questions seemed rude. It was not my intent—"

A short while later, the women moved up into the hall of tents. They sat on the floor in front of the small booths as Agatha and Eliza threaded their way up onto the stage. Agatha stepped to the podium.

"Welcome again, sisters," she began. "It is such a pleasure to meet with all of you on such a special occasion. This was a very sacred and a very joyful time for the ancient Hebrews. The Feast of Tabernacles, as you are aware, was a time when families gathered together, erected a small tabernacle, or booth as some called it, and offered prayers of gratitude in remembrance of the deliverance of their forefathers after wandering in the desert of Sinai for forty years. This isn't the exact date of the feast but it's close enough."

Agatha smiled, looking around the hall. "Some of you may feel you've been out in the wilderness for forty years, too. It seems almost that long since I set sail from England, I know. But while we have our problems, we also have much to be thankful for, and that is why we're gathered together this evening."

"In this month of Tishri, the seventh month of the Hebrew calendar, the Hebrews not only thanked God for deliverance, they dedicated themselves to a purification of their souls for a whole week of repentance in order to cleanse themselves from individual sin. This day of dedication was known as the Day of Atonement, and it was so holy that it was the only day in the whole year when the High Priest entered the Holy of Holies in the temple."

Agatha gave the gathering another smile and shrugged her shoulders. "That's all I know about the Feast of Tabernacles, and I have my husband, General Galloway, to thank for most of that."

It brought a ripple of laughter throughout the hall.

"But it's not the survival of ancient Israel that should be uppermost in our thoughts this evening," she continued. "It's the suffering every one of us have endured, in one form or another, in making the journey to our Promised Land. And it's a time for all of us to recognize our need for repentance. Though most of us have tasted the bitter, we remember the sweet. This evening, we should give thanks to our Father in Heaven for his love."

Once again she looked around the hall.

"That's all you'll be hearing from me. Sister Eliza has written some of her beautiful poetry especially for this occasion, and I know our souls will be touched and refreshed. So if all of you will bow your heads in two minutes of silent prayer, thanking Him for what is most precious to you, we will turn the rest of the evening over to Sister Eliza—"

CHAPTER THIRTEEN

SALT LAKE CITY

Three U.S. marshals and five Salt Lake City police officers escorted the four prisoners to the city jail. Paperwork was brushed aside as the prisoners were taken back and locked up, two to a cell. Bill Cooke, the city jailer, would have preferred keeping them separated in individual cells but the jail was too overcrowded, as usual. Seven prisoners had been moved and crowded in with other inmates just to get the two empty cells. Cooke wanted to take every precaution. These men were not only hard cases who had spent most of their lives outside the law, but because of their connections, Cooke believed they posed a threat to the life of every lawman in the building.

The four men had been spotted gambling in a downtown saloon about an hour ago. All were known killers, with prices on their heads, and all of them were known to be members of Billy Hickman's gang of rustlers. The existence of such a gang was not officially admitted, and only spoken about in whispers. No one was willing to challenge Hickman's public image of a citizen living within the law, at least not while he was still in favor in high places.

Cooke personally checked both barred doors, making sure they were securely locked. Other prisoners, at least two dozen of them, mostly drunks and petty thieves, watched the proceedings but made no sound. Normally, they would be yelling and clanging on the bars in a thunderous protest against authority, but these new prisoners were known and feared. No one wanted to do anything that could be misunderstood by them, or passed on to the man they worked for.

Cooke returned to the front of the jail. The lawmen who had brought in the prisoners, along with the three regular officers on duty, were bunched near two small windows, all staring out into the street with somber expressions.

"We got company already, Bill," muttered Stan Diggs, one of the regular jail officers.

One glance out the window showed Cooke there was reason for the concern on Digg's face. Over a dozen men were grouped about fifty yards away, armed and staring truculently at the jail.

"Let's arrest the whole bunch," one of the U.S. marshals grunted. "Ain't one who don't look like he belongs in here."

"Recognize any of them?" Cooke asked.

"They're part of Billy Hickman's gang, that's for sure," Diggs answered.

"Ain't nobody proved Hickman is running a gang of rustlers," Cooke reminded. "Until we get hard proof, or until he don't have friends in such high places, Hickman ain't nothing but a lawyer."

"That's reason enough to hang him," another lawman muttered. It brought a round of chuckles from the others.

"Stay alert," Cooke snapped. "I'm asking all of you to stick around awhile, until we see what those hard cases got on their minds."

"This ain't no federal case. We got no jurisdiction—" one of the U.S. marshals protested, but Cooke cut him off.

"They was rustling army cattle, riding stolen army horses, and they shot up two federal marshals. Don't get any more federal than that. Like it or not, you men are part of this. Besides, I got a feeling we'll be needing some extra firepower before this night's out."

"You thinking they'll come after the prisoners?"

"They ain't planning no prayer circle."

The crowd outside the jail grew steadily, until fifty or more could be seen.

Evening shadows deepened and when it was almost dark, the men outside the jail spread out and took cover. Minutes later, a hail of bullets whined toward the jailhouse. Chips flew from the brick walls, the glass in the two windows was shattered, and dozens of bullets thudded into the thick wooden door. The shooting kept up for several minutes, the lawmen inside not returning fire, just crouching down close to the floor to escape the storm of lead whistling through the windows and ricocheting around the room.

The shooting stopped. The sound of gunfire was suddenly replaced with the sounds of angry shouts and running feet. Diggs, crouched below one of the windows, raised up to peer cautiously outside.

"They're coming," he told the others. "Going for the door—got some kind of battering ram."

Cooke stood up. "Four of you go upstairs. Good angle from the windows up there. The rest, pick a window, take your shots as quick as you can, then duck out and make room for the next man. Go for the rammers first—and shoot to kill. They see a few bodies lying out there, this fight is over."

The mob outside didn't have a chance. Exposed to the shooters inside the jailhouse, they started falling with the first volley. The four men running with the battering ram never made it to the door. Three went down dead, the fourth jumped to get out of the way of the falling log, then howled and clutched his thigh as a bullet shattered bone. Men charging behind started falling as the marshals upstairs began firing. Even before all the lawmen got to shoot, the mobbers were gone. They left behind six dead and five wounded.

Cooke and the other officers waited for a few minutes, making sure there was no regrouping for a second charge. The only sounds from outside were the wails of wounded men. Cooke was edging open the door when again there were the sounds of men approaching. This time, however, it was the First Company of special marshals who had been patrolling the downtown district, heard the shooting, and came on the run.

An hour or so later, the bodies and the wounded had been carried away and things returned to normal at the jailhouse. The U.S. marshals left, as did the other Salt Lake City officers. Two of the special marshals, Jim Wilson and Bill Hennefer, were assigned to remain at the jail for the rest of the night, just in case Cooke and his jailers needed assistance again.

A couple more hours passed, the darkness outside quiet with no sign of trouble. Still, it was decided to keep the front part of the jailhouse dark so as to present no targets to anyone outside. Cooke asked the two special marshals to watch the front while he made a check of the prisoners. It wouldn't take long, Cooke said, then the marshals could grab some sleep or do whatever.

Stan Diggs and one of the other jailers left to get something to eat. Jim Wilson took station beside the downstairs windows, while Bill Hennefer went upstairs. Neither of the marshals were aware of what happened after that in the cell block behind them.

Cooke entered the cellblock and locked the door. He went straight to the two cells holding the four new prisoners. They were sitting on the beds and said nothing—just stared belligerently at the jailer.

"You lost some friends awhile ago," Cooke told them. "Six went real sudden, and a bunch more got shot up pretty bad. I expect some of those will cash out before morning."

Hank Simms, one of the four, glared angrily at him. "You ain't never going to hold us, Cooke. And I ain't forgettin' about those friends, neither."

Cooke nodded slowly. "No doubt about you being trouble, Simms. That's why I'm willing to cut a deal."

All four prisoners stared at the jailer. Simms stood up and crossed to the front of the cell. "What kind of a deal?"

"They'll come again—I agree with that," Cooke said. "Your boss don't want you boys talking in no court of law."

"We don't work for nobody but ourselves—"

"Personally, it don't matter to me," Cooke continued, "if they pin something on Billy Hickman or not."

"We ain't got nothing to do with Billy Hickman—"

Cooke raised a hand to cut him off. "I told you, Simms, it don't matter to me. What matters is, I'm not hankering to go through another shoot-out just to keep your hides in jail."

Simms' eyes narrowed. "Don't follow what you're sayin', Cooke."

"If it was up to me," Cooke said, "I'd push the four of you out the back door and be rid of you. None of you is worth me or any of my men getting shot."

"What kind of deal you offering—?"

"Cain't let you all go—I'd be behind those bars myself if I did that. I'm offering to let two of you slip out through that back door.

You decide amongst yourselves who goes and who stays."

The four rustlers were all on their feet now. They looked at each other, then back to the jailer.

"Why do that?" Simms growled suspiciously.

"Don't like being shot at, Simms. I let two of you go, the other two sees through whatever happens, and nobody shoots up the jail again. That's the deal, clean and simple."

Simms was still staring at him. "When does this happen?"

"Right now. Soon as you pick who's going, I unlock that door and they're gone."

The four again looked at each other, but whatever anyone was going to say, never got said. Simms made the decision for all of them.

"Me and Banks," Simms growled, motioning to the man in the cell with him. He looked at the other two rustlers, Ryan and Wills, neither seeming surprised at the choice. "I got a good lawyer in mind, boys. You'll be out legal-like before you know it."

"Countin' on it, Hank," Wills replied.

"And I'm counting on you keeping your end of the deal, Simms," Cooke warned. "Any more shooting, and Wills and Ryan here is almost certain to catch a couple of strays right between the eyes."

Cooke stepped to the end of the cellblock, unlocked the back door and withdrew the two heavy crossbars, leaving the door slightly ajar. He returned and unlocked the cell holding Simms. He met the rustler's stare for a few seconds, then went to the door leading to the front of the jail, closing it behind him.

Jim Wilson was leaning on the sill of one of the front windows when he heard the shooting start. It sounded like it came from the back of the jail, six to eight shots in quick succession. Hennefer came down the stairs, revolver in hand.

Bill Cooke came up the hall, joining the two marshals.

"You hear that?" Hennefer asked the jailer.

Cooke nodded. "Out back, sounded to me."

"We best check it out," Hennefer growled. "That door locked?" he asked, pointing toward the one leading to the cellblock.

Cooke nodded again and reached into his pocket. Just then, there was a pounding on the front door. Jim peered out into the darkness and made out Diggs and the other jailer. He unbarred the door and the first thing everybody saw when it opened was the guns in the hands of each jailer.

"Everybody all right in here?" Diggs asked.

Cooke glanced at the guns. "I take it you boys was doing the shooting back there—"

"Two of those rustlers broke loose," Diggs said. "Got 'em both. How'd they get out—?"

"Just two—?" Jim asked.

"That's all we saw."

Cooke was staring at Diggs. "Both dead. You sure about that—?"

"Ask 'em if you want," the other jailer said.

Jim looked from Cooke to the two jailers. Something wasn't being said. He could see it in the eyes of all three men. Well, couldn't be much wrong with two rustlers shot dead trying to escape. Not worth asking about, he decided.

The two special marshals had begun their daylong stint of duty at six o'clock the previous evening. When morning came, about seven, Cooke told Hennefer and Jim Wilson they could leave if they wanted, because there wasn't much chance of an attack on the jail in daylight. The marshals decided that since they had been officially assigned to help out, at least one of them should stay. Jim Wilson volunteered, asking only that Hennefer bring back some hot food before too long.

After Hennefer left, Jim sat in the front with Bill Cooke. Finally, Wilson asked a question that had been bothering him since the shooting of the two rustlers last night.

"How do you suppose those two got out?"

Cooke, who was smoking a short, black pipe, took a couple of puffs before answering. "Don't rightly know," he said. "Probably picked the lock. Those hard cases learn to do that."

"Sure was fortunate Diggs and that other jailer happened to be passing by just when it happened."

"Sure was."

Jim stared hard at him. "You checked them a couple minutes before, didn't you?'

"I did."

"Could they have taken your keys without you noticing it?"

"No chance."

"Must not have been two minutes after you left that Diggs saw them out back and started shooting."

"Not much more."

Cooke took several slow puffs on the pipe, then met the marshal's stare. "You got something on your mind, Jim?"

"Just curious about the timing. Seems it happened mighty fast."

"That's the way these things happen."

Jim's stare hardened. "Does that mean it's happened before—?"

"Happens all the time. I thought every lawman in the city knew that."

Shock rippled through Jim. "This one didn't."

"Well, it's time you did. Ain't an hour goes by any day of the week without two or three getting arrested and thrown into this jail. You ever figured out how many prisoners this place holds? How long it takes to put them in front of a judge? And how many get slapped with thirty, even ninety days, as my guests? This jail ain't big enough, Jim, and nobody seems able or willing to do the counting."

"You telling me that arranging for prisoners to escape out the back door is a regular thing?"

"They don't escape—not more'n fifty yards, anyway. I ain't got no choice, Jim. There just ain't room to hold 'em. Besides, saves the city and the county a whole lot of money—which they claim they ain't got anyway."

Jim shook his head, trying to deal with what Bill Cooke had just told him. "Who knows about this?"

"Thought everyone did. Politicians don't ask, but they know. You new marshals ain't been exposed yet, I guess."

"How many prisoners get killed thinking they've been let loose?"

"Nobody keeps count of that. Leastwise, I don't."

Jim fell silent. Cooke gave him several minutes before asking a quiet question.

"This a problem for you, Jim?"

Wilson took a long moment before answering. Then he gave a

reluctant shake of his head. "Guess not, Bill. It's something I wish I didn't know, though."

Half an hour later, Hennefer hadn't returned to the jail with food, and although he wasn't hungry, Jim used it as an excuse to get away. It meant Bill Cooke would be alone, but it wouldn't be for long and Jim needed time to settle the churning inside him. The shocking realization of what was happening at the jail brought a real conflict. It wasn't easy to accept murder as a justifiable way to save money and control the jail population.

Wilson was gone only a few minutes when someone knocked hard on the front door of the jail, calling out to Cooke.

"It's Cunningham. Need to talk, Cooke."

Cooke was still sitting in the darkened front area of the jail. "You alone, Cunningham?"

"Got Foster and Ingram with me. No one else. We ain't aiming to shoot you nor anybody, Cooke. Just talk."

Cooke knew Cunningham and the two men with him, knew they were part of the inner circle around Billy Hickman. Hickman probably had already heard about Simms and Banks, and he'd know Ryan and Wills were on a short rope.

Wouldn't hurt to hear what Cunningham had to say. Cooke unbarred the door and let the three men inside.

"Dark in here," Foster grunted. "Ain't there no lamps?"

"Don't need a lamp," Cunningham snapped. "What we got to say can be said in moonlight."

"Who's talking, Cunningham?" asked Cooke. "You or somebody else."

"It ain't about talking, Cooke, so much as it is about not talking."

"I don't talk much to nobody."

"Ain't you I want to talk to, Cooke. Need a few minutes with Ryan and Wills."

"You don't want to talk to Simms or Banks?"

"They ain't in no condition to listen, from what I hear."

"Wouldn't want Ryan or Wills to get all riled up over what you got to tell them—"

"Nothing like that, Cooke. Need a few minutes with them in private. Then we're gone and you ain't got no more trouble with anybody."

"Billy Hickman feel that way?"

"Didn't say nothing about Billy—but you could say nobody wants any more trouble. Now, can we have a few minutes alone with Ryan and Wills?"

Cooke shrugged. "Don't make it long."

He went back, unlocked the door to the cellblock, and led the three men down to the cell containing the two rustlers. He started back but Cunningham had another request.

"Don't want everyone hearing what we got to say, Cooke," he said. "Appreciate you letting us in with them. We'll keep it short."

Cooke shrugged again. "Ain't no harm in that, I guess. Most people want out, not in."

He opened the cell door for the visitors then went back toward the front part of the jail. Behind him, Ryan and Wills looked expectantly at their visitors.

"You getting us out, Cunningham?" Wills asked.

"That's what Billy asked us to do," Cunningham told him, his voice low. "Billy don't want you talking about his business—"

"We wouldn't do that—"

"Billy don't want to take no chances. So you two are leaving."

"When we doing that?" Ryan asked.

Cunningham reached into his pocket and handed Ryan a key. "That'll get you out the front door."

"Cooke won't let us out—"

"Cooke will be coming with us—we'll tell him somebody important wants to meet with him. That's when you two do it."

"Where we supposed to go—?"

"Out to Cedar Valley. Billy will meet you at the ranch."

Wills had been listening closely, now started shaking his head. "We ain't doin' it, Cunningham."

Cunningham looked at him with narrowed eyes. "You ain't got no choice, Wills."

The rustler gave a firm shake of his head. "We ain't going. People get dead trying to walk out of this place. We know what just happened to Simms and Banks."

Cunningham's face twisted in sudden anger. He reached into

his coat pocket and pulled out a revolver, pointing it at Wills. "You can get dead in here, Wills. Forget the key—you two just follow us out. Cooke ain't going to buy into no serious trouble."

Just then, the door opened and Cooke walked into the cell block. He saw the gun in Cunningham's hand and went for his own. Cunningham fired two shots, the noise loud in the narrow confines. The jailer fell back, the half-drawn gun slipping back into the holster as Cooke clutched at the holes in his chest.

"What'd you do that for?" Foster grated. He lunged for the door, Ingram close behind. "You just brought the law down on us hard—"

Cunningham glared at Ryan and Wills, who retreated to the back of the cell. They wanted no part of this murder. Better to stay in jail than run with a price on their heads for something they didn't do. Cunningham knew there was no time to argue with them. He started after his two companions, stepping over Cooke. He glanced down at the lawmen. The amount of blood gushing out of the two holes told him Cooke would soon be a dead man.

Jim Wilson was on his way back to the jail when he heard the shots. He started running, saw three men race out of the building, but decided against trying to chase them. The fact that he hadn't seen Cooke in pursuit told him something was wrong.

Jim found Cooke on the floor, and one look told him, as it had Cunningham, that the jailer had just a few breaths left. Cooke reached up and grabbed Wilson by the blue shirt, pulling him close.

"It was Cunningham what shot me," he whispered, struggling for breath. "Tell Scottie. Tell him I said to even the score—"

Cooke's whispers trailed into silence.

News of the murder of the Salt Lake jailer spread quickly. It was only a few hours later that Jim Wilson, who had been asked to stay on duty at the jail until the shooting was officially put on record, was able to put a face to the name Cooke had muttered as he died.

Edwin Jones, known to everyone as Scottie, pushed his way into the crowded jail and loudly called out Wilson's name. Scottie was a mail carrier between Salt Lake and the Missouri frontier, bearded and burly, a man who delighted in intimidating people who saw only the rough giant, not the almost gentle person inside the exterior.

Wilson came to the front of the jailhouse in response to hearing his name.

Jones glared at him, and Jim wasn't quite sure whether or not to get ready to draw. The man had a ferocious look on his face.

"You with Billy when he checked out?" Jones demanded.

Wilson nodded. "Didn't see the actual shooting, though I got here in time to see three men hightailing out of the jail. Bill Cooke was on the floor when I got to him, two bullets in the chest."

"You know the men who shot him?" Scottie growled.

"I don't, but Bill did." He looked curiously at the man in front of him. "You wouldn't be Scottie, would you—?"

"That's me," the man said. "Scottie Jones."

"Last words Bill spoke were to tell Scottie to even the score for him."

"That I will," Jones grunted. "Billy give you the names of those who shot him?"

"Cunningham. Didn't name the other two, but he said it was Cunningham who shot him."

"Heard about that skunk. One of Billy Hickman's gang. Any idea where he is now?"

"There was a report three men were seen riding hellbent up the canyon awhile ago. Probably Cunningham and the two with him. Cunningham's been seen lately with two men named Foster and Ingram. Police are putting together some wanted posters with a price on all three."

"Headin' east, you say," Scottie muttered. "Goin' that way myself with a wagon of mail later today. I'll take some of those wanted posters and spread 'em along the trail. And you can be sure I'll be on the lookout for Cunningham and his pals myself. That kind usually ain't too hard to find."

Two days later, Scottie Jones pulled the mail wagon into Fort Bridger. He was tired, for the weather was bitterly cold and he kept running into heavy squalls of snow. The way station was crowded with travelers, but he sat down at a table with three other men and wolfed down a meal and several beers. Scottie wasn't in a mood for chatter, and said little to the other men. When he was finished, he downed another beer and left.

He slept that night in the wagon, buffalo robes pulled tight around him. With first light, he was up and soon had the mules hitched and ready. A couple of mugs of coffee later, he cracked his whip and the mail wagon pulled back onto the eastbound trail.

Jones was well on the way to the Green River station when he met the westbound mail wagon. They pulled up, exchanging greetings. Jones told the other driver about Bill Cooke getting murdered. He was reaching under the seat to get a handful of wanted posters, when he suddenly straightened and loosed a wild stream of oaths.

"That was them," he yelled at the other driver. "I had dinner two days ago with the murderin' scum back at Fort Bridger. I was sittin' right at the same table with all three of 'em—"

Jones loosed another outpouring of angry oaths, beating himself on the head, the battered floppy hat almost coming off.

"I'm a damn fool—didn't connect 'em. Too tired to think straight, I guess."

"Give me some of those posters," the other driver said. "If I see 'em at Bridger, I'll sound the alarm."

"Got a better idea," Scottie grimaced. "Do me a favor, Willie. Trade me wagons. You take this one back to Missouri, and I'll take the westbound on into Salt Lake—after I take me another looksee at Bridger."

"Sounds like you're takin' this personal, Scottie."

Jones nodded grimly. "Bill Cooke was a friend. Last words was to ask me to square things for him. I aim to do that."

Minutes later, Scottie Jones was cracking the whip over the mules of the westbound mail wagon, keeping them at a full run toward Fort Bridger. When he finally pulled into the station, he jumped off the seat and went straight for the main building. He pushed open the door, glaring around the room. The bushy beard parted in a pleased smile when he saw Cunningham sitting at a table, a bottle of whiskey beside him. He was alone, with no sign of the other two anywhere in the room. Scottie was in no mood to wait. He marched straight toward Cunningham.

The fugitive must have sensed him coming. Cunningham whirled around in the chair, saw the rage on Scottie's face, and went for his gun. Scottie drew and both men fired. Jones bellowed as Cunningham sent a bullet into his upper arm.

Cunningham stood up, blood spurting from a gaping hole in his neck. He put up a hand, squeezing in a futile attempt to stop his life from pumping out. Then he slumped to the floor, dead.

Scottie yelled in triumph, waving his gun and firing off a couple more rounds into the roof before putting the weapon back into his holster. Then he knelt over Cunningham, took out a large Bowie knife and grabbed the dead man's hair. With two quick slashes, Scottie scalped the man who had murdered his friend. He held up the bloodied scalp for everyone in the room to see.

"This puts to right the wrong this man did to my friend, Bill Cooke, who he shot down in cold blood. May this murderin' scum rot in hell."

You could almost see Bill Cooke smiling.

CHAPTER FOURTEEN

SALT LAKE CITY

The feel of snow was in the air, heavy gray clouds with a dark foreboding that the storm would break soon. It was still only late October but the weather these past couple of weeks had been cold and miserable. It made people wonder if the Territory was in for another long, cold winter like the two previous years.

Crowds were thinner than usual on East Temple Street, probably because people with any distance to travel didn't want to risk being caught in the approaching snowstorm. Business was slow in the Galloway & Tregale emporium so Henry Washington was standing looking out the front windows at the people hurrying past, coat collars turned up, scarves wrapped around faces to protect against the bitter wind now blowing.

His attention was drawn to a young black woman coming down the sidewalk. She was bundled in a long dark coat, and he couldn't see her features because of the bonnet covering her head, tied tightly under the chin. Something about her held Henry's gaze. Perhaps it was just that young black women were not often seen walking down East Temple.

Then two roughly-dressed, bearded men, easily recognized as teamsters, stepped in front of the young woman, blocking her path. She stopped, looking frightened. One of the teamsters reached out to grab her arm, pulling her toward him. She screamed and Henry was out on the sidewalk, lunging toward the two men. He crashed into the back of one, sending him sprawling into the street. The other man let go of the young woman and turned to Henry with a snarl of rage, his hand clawing under his coat. Henry smashed a fist solidly into the bearded face. The teamster staggered, but remained on his feet. Henry rammed three more hard blows into the face and the man fell backwards. He was unconscious even before his head cracked on the boards of the sidewalk. Henry wheeled to face the man sitting in the frozen dirt.

"You want some more?" Henry gritted threateningly. The man shook his head, looking bewildered about how he got where he was. Both men had been drinking; Henry could smell whiskey strong on the man sprawled on the sidewalk. "Then you best be moving on—and take this one with you," he added, pointing at the unconscious teamster. "Next time either of you puts a hand on this lady, I won't be so polite."

Heather had seen the ruckus and was out on the sidewalk. The young woman was still upset, breathing jerkily. Heather invited her into the store and the woman gratefully accepted. Henry pulled up a chair for her, and moments later, brought a mug of steaming chamomile tea.

A customer entered and Heather excused herself. Henry pulled up another chair and stared curiously at the woman he had rescued. With the bonnet off, he could see she was pretty, about twenty years old, he guessed. He glanced down at her hand, saw there was no wedding band. She looked a little embarrassed at his scrutiny. Henry quickly introduced himself.

"I'm Henry," he said. "Henry Washington. Forgive me staring like that, but I don't very often see a pretty young Negra woman in Salt Lake City. You live here, Miss—?" He hesitated, then asked, "It is Miss, isn't it?"

"Woods," she smiled, "and yes it is. I thank you, Mr. Washington, for coming to my aid out there."

Her voice was soft, educated. She obviously had been raised in the North—like himself, he realized. He felt a flutter in his stomach. Hold on, he told himself sternly. You're probably fifteen years older than she is—of course, that don't particularly matter, he found himself adding to his thoughts.

"Is there some place I can escort you, Miss Woods?" he asked. "If you've shopping to do, might be well not to delay. Looks like a hard storm is blowing in."

"I was coming here, as a matter of fact," she replied. "Need to buy a large stew pot. One we got is almost burned through."

"Got some good ones," Henry told her. "Fair prices, too. You live close, Miss Woods? Those stew pots get pretty heavy if you have to carry them far."

"I don't live here, Mr. Washington. I work for a family traveling to California. I help care for the children and do most of the cooking. The trail's closed, so a lot of families are camping across the Jordan. Army won't be letting anyone through until spring. Too late to beat winter now, anyway."

"You walked from the river?" Henry gasped. "That's a long way— too far to carry a heavy stew pot, even for me."

"It was farther than I thought," the young woman admitted. "Didn't expect walking to take so long—and didn't expect it to get so cold."

"Miss Heather has a carriage out back. I'm sure she wouldn't mind me running you back across the river—you and the stew pot."

"I couldn't impose like that—"

"You don't know Miss Heather. It would please her to help out, especially with this storm coming."

She looked up, studying him. He had already proved himself to be a gentleman, and she felt comfortable about accepting his offer. She nodded. "If you're sure Miss Heather won't mind, it would be most appreciated, Mr. Washington."

"Call me Henry, please."

"Then you must call me Rose."

Henry said it aloud. "Rose Woods." He smiled at her. "That's a pretty name—fits you real good." Suddenly afraid he had let his tongue get ahead of his manners, he pointed across the store. "Stew pots are over there—"

Shortly after Henry left to escort Rose Woods back to the River Jordan camp, the bell over the door jangled again and Captain Geoffrey Edwards stepped into the store. Heather saw him, and came forward to greet him.

"Good afternoon, Captain Edwards."

He doffed his hat and gave a little nod of his head. "Thought we'd agreed to Geoffrey. Does this mean I'm back to calling you Mrs. Tregale—?"

Heather smiled. "Of course not. You've become too good a customer. Well, at least a friend—you don't buy much. But you're right, it's Heather and Geoffrey."

"I hope so, Heather," the officer said quietly, "—that you consider me a friend, that is. I'm bold enough to tell you that you're in my thoughts a great deal of late. Does that offend you?"

Heather hesitated, again fighting the two worlds she always found herself in with this man. "No, Geoffrey. I must say it confuses me a little—but it doesn't offend me."

The captain looked around the store. There were only a couple of customers, and they were across the room. He and Heather were almost alone.

"Would you mind if I told you what some of my thoughts were, Heather?"

She was flustered and showed it. This man just had a strange effect on her, especially when he looked at her as he was doing right now. Very intense. His face was serious, and she had to admit, very handsome.

"I'm not sure, Geoffrey," she told him. "Is this something I would want to hear?"

"It's something I want to tell you," he replied. "You know I respect you greatly, and I think it's time I was open with you."

"Then proceed, Captain," she smiled. "I admire openness and honesty."

"First, let me say I am only too aware that you are married, and have a son," Edwards began. "And I greatly admire your husband. But my time in Utah is running out, and I must follow the choice I have made."

"What is that, Geoffrey?" she asked quietly, realizing how serious a matter this was for the man in front of her.

"You may think this foolish, Heather, for we have done no more than talk to each other in this store," Edwards continued, "but you have touched me deeply. It happened the first moment I saw you, and my feelings have grown until I must ask if you have any affection for me— if you could consider having such feelings were you not a married woman."

She stared at him, not knowing what to say. The devil of it was, there was a stirring inside her that said she could indeed have affections for this man. There was even a slight sense of dread that it might already have happened, despite the stern control she had tried to exercise over her feelings. She couldn't imagine such a thing being real, but neither could she pretend it wasn't there. How was this possible? she asked herself. There was no reason for it—but there was.

Anger.

Hurt.

Loneliness.

It was the bad side of love that was causing this confusion, bubbling and festering from frustration. She suddenly wasn't even sure Carn was to blame. Perhaps she was the person really at fault, not being patient, not being understanding. Whatever was happening, or had happened, there were obligations that could not be ignored. Even if Carn turned from her, or she no longer found him the center of her life, there was little Carn. Her child must be nurtured and protected and loved. Woman, wife—each was less than mother, and mother was more important than self. And what had any of this to do with this man, a virtual stranger, standing in front of her? Why was her life, so wonderful and complete such a short time ago, now so unhappy and so complicated? Why was she even thinking such things? Had some madness been unleashed inside her?

Captain Edwards interrupted her flow of thoughts. "I want you to know, Heather, that my intentions are honorable. Nothing would please me more than to have you return to Boston with me." He saw her eyes widen in shock and hastily added, "My family is connected with fine lawyers, who will handle all the details of divorce for you. I assure you all will be proper until we're married. Of course, I would expect to raise your son as my own."

Heather turned and walked to the rear of the store. She reached the counter and leaned both hands on it, closing her eyes. She looked up as the captain joined her, staring searchingly into his face.

"You hardly know me, Geoffrey. How could you think of marriage—"

"I can think of little else, Heather. And you should know that our conversations have touched me in another way. You've told me much about your religion, and I find the Mormons to be completely different from all that I've heard. When I return home, even if it is without you, I want you to know I will seriously investigate your faith. There is much that has a ring of truth and sensibility about it. I've come to see the Mormons are much misunderstood and unfairly maligned."

She reached out and took his hand. "It pleases me very much, Geoffrey, to hear you say that." She gave a despairing shake of her head. "You are indeed a cause for much upheaval within me, and a great deal of confusion. I don't know what to say—"

"Don't say anything," he interrupted, "not yet. I needed to tell you what is in my heart. It's not what I would have planned, and I know many will misjudge my motives. Still, it's happened and I must at least try to win you."

The doorbell jangled again. Heather froze as she saw her husband walk into the store. His glance fell to their clasped hands and she quickly broke the contact. Edwards' eyes locked with Carn, neither man saying anything. The captain put on his hat, nodded politely at Heather, and walked toward the front door. He paused in front of Tregale, their stares again locking.

"Mr. Tregale," Edwards said quietly. "Good to see you."

"Did you find what you were looking for, Captain Edwards?" Tregale inquired, keeping the tone flat.

"I'm not sure, Mr. Tregale," the captain replied, his voice equally flat. He turned his head to look back at Heather. "It's been nice chatting with you, Mrs. Tregale." With that, he continued on out of the store.

Tregale fastened his wife with a stare that held both hurt and anger. Heather returned the look with one of defiance.

"Seems we have things to talk about," he muttered.

"That would be different," Heather said coldly, "you and me talking to each other. Are you getting back, or leaving?"

"Just rode into town. Won't be leaving again until day after tomorrow."

"A whole day. Maybe you can spend a few hours with your son—unless, of course, you'll be in meetings. I realize those come before your family."

"Don't do this, Heather. We need to talk."

"About what, Carn? Probably not the things I want to talk about. I want to know why everything is more important than you spending some time at home with me and the baby. I want to know why you never mention getting baptized, like you did before. Are you still planning on that, Carn, or has that changed along with everything else?"

"Maybe it has," Carn flared. He didn't really feel as set as it sounded, but he was hurt. "From what I've seen of Mormons these past months, a lot don't practice what they preach. Never did like a two-faced person, and I've run across a bunch lately who don't live up to any of the things they're supposed to hold sacred. But that's not what's on my mind, Heather."

"What is on your mind?"

"Our marriage. Our son." He paused, then added, "and Captain Edwards."

"And of course, you consider Captain Edwards the most important of those three."

"How important is he to you?" Carn asked quietly. "You and little Carn are the most important people in my life, though that seems difficult for you to accept. So the question is, where does Captain Edwards place with you?"

Heather looked around. There was only one customer in the store now, and Henry had not yet returned, although he would be back at any moment. "This is not the time or the place for such discussions."

"Can we talk later—?"

Heather sighed. "Not if we're going to fight, Carn."

The doorbell jangled again and this time it was Jim Wilson. He looked agitated as he approached Tregale.

"We got a problem, Carn," he told him.

"Can it wait?" Tregale asked, mindful of the despairing look that had jumped across his wife's face. "I just got into town."

"Personal request from Governor Cummings and Colonel Burton," Wilson said. "The colonel sent me looking for you, said it was important you come."

"Do you know what it's about?"

"Horse thieving."

Tregale stared at him. "Horse thieving—?"

"Somebody stole the matched pair of white mares belonging to the governor. He's madder'n—well, you know what," he finished, casting a quick glance in the direction of Heather. "Colonel Burton said to tell you the governor is about to explode."

"He wants the police—"

"We've already been there," Wilson grimaced. "The governor let us know how incompetent and useless we are—especially when it comes to catching horse thieves. He wants to talk to you, Brother Tregale."

"Probably wants me to ride to Camp Floyd," Carn muttered, "and get Johnston to assign the whole army to getting back his horses."

Tregale glanced at his wife, but her face was expressionless. She merely shrugged her shoulders. "This obviously comes before family. Don't worry about little Carn—I won't tell him you were here."

◆

The storm struck a couple of hours later. It roared out of the north and quickly turned into a howling blizzard, blanketing the city and the whole valley. The ground was cold enough from a week of near-freezing temperatures that the snow began to pile up with the first flake. Soon it was a foot deep and the weather-wise knew it would be double that before long.

Derek Pitts looked out the window of the Beezley gun shop and realized he had a problem. Derek and Gwen lived about three miles south of the city, and a little east, in Sugar House. It was a good walk to and from work most of the year, but an unpleasant, even danger-ous, ordeal in weather like this. Seeing how the blizzard had already cut visibility to a few feet, and darkness was rapidly closing in, Derek knew he wasn't going to make it home tonight.

He was joined by a pretty young woman, Sarah Beezley, daughter of Charlie Beezley, owner of the gun shop. Sarah stared morosely at the driving wall of snowflakes.

"We might as well close up, Derek," she said. "There'll be no more customers now."

"Think you're right, Sarah." He looked at the sixteen-year-old, thinking again how pretty she was. Not only pretty, but smart about guns. She could talk the good points, and the bad, of any weapon in the store, from handgun to rifle to scattergun. "When will your father be back to pick you up?"

Sarah shook her head. "He won't. Not in this storm."

Derek was alarmed. "How will you get home? It's over a mile to your house. You can't walk it in weather like this—"

"Don't intend to. There's a cot in the storage room. I'll just spend the night here." She looked questioningly at him. "How about you, Derek? You're not thinking of walking, are you—?"

Derek was embarrassed. "Actually, I was planning on staying, but

I didn't think about you being stranded, too. If me being here makes you uncomfortable, Sarah, I can still head out before it gets any worse."

"That's foolishness, Derek. They'll find you dead in a drift come morning. Father will be grateful for you staying. This will be fun—you can tell me about England, and pulling those handcarts all the way from the frontier." She smiled warmly and clasped his arm. "I'm glad it's storming—now we can enjoy each other's company the whole night."

Derek felt his arm burning under her touch. That was foolishness, he told himself sternly. He wasn't much older than she was, but he was married. Sarah was an innocent young girl, and he was sure she had none of the thoughts he was trying to keep out of his mind. It would be fun, like she said, just to sit and talk.

They did talk, for several hours, huddled near the stove in the center of the store. And it was fun. Derek felt more lighthearted and carefree than he had in the past two years. There was a connection between them, a pleasant touching of spirits. Then it got cold in the store, even with the warmth of the stove, the heat dissipated by the bitterly cold temperatures outside. They began to run out of things to talk about, at least, that's what Derek told himself was the cause for the longer pauses and quiet. The truth was, being this close to Sarah was having an effect upon Derek. More and more, he felt a physical attraction to her. What was even more disturbing, he could tell she was feeling something, too. He kept pushing that realization into the back of his thoughts, but it was there, and both of them knew it. Finally, Sarah stood up.

"It's been so good spending this time with you, Derek. I hope you've enjoyed this evening as much as I have—"

"One of the finest of my life, Sarah. I mean that. Seems like we've known each other forever."

"Perhaps we did," she smiled. "Perhaps we knew each other before we ever came to this earth. Father says we did."

"I feel that might be true," Derek said earnestly. "I wish I'd known you in England—" He stopped, realizing what he was implying behind the words.

It had not escaped Sarah. She moved closer to him, taking his hands in hers. "Derek, would you kiss me—"

The first kiss was gentle, restrained. But there were more, and passions became more inflamed and demanding with each one. Finally, Derek pulled away, shaking his head.

"This is not fair to you, Sarah—"

"Because you're married?" she whispered.

"Mostly because I can't allow myself to take away from you what is so sweet and innocent."

"You take nothing, Derek," she breathed, pulling him closer. "I ache with wanting to give my love to you."

Derek groaned and pushed away again. "Sarah, I want you more this minute than I've ever wanted anyone, but it isn't right. It's all so sudden—too sudden—though I know I'm not just feeling passion. Sarah, I love you, and I want you to be my wife."

"But you have a wife—"

Derek nodded. "I know—and strange as it must sound to you, I love Gwen. But I love you too, Sarah, so much I can hardly breathe."

"So what can we do?"

"Would you consider becoming my wife, Sarah—even though I have Gwen?"

"Your second wife—a polygamous wife, Derek? Is that what you're asking of me?"

"I see no other way, Sarah. We could be happy—all of us. I know we could."

"But you have to get special permission to take another wife—not everyone can do it. That's what my father says."

"If two people love each other like we do, Sarah, who could deny us?"

"Your wife, maybe—?"

"Gwen will love you like I do."

"I hope not," Sarah said, flashing an impish smile. She put her arms around his neck, drawing his face down to hers. "I'd be happy to be your wife, Derek, first or second won't matter—just as long as we have our nights alone."

CHAPTER FIFTEEN

SALT LAKE CITY

Storm clouds were still dark overhead the next morning, though the wind had dropped to occasional gusts and snow came only in scattered, light flurries.

Some two feet of snow covered the valley floor, with much more on the ground in the higher benchlands. By midday, the skies were again clear, bringing a cold that crisped the snow and made it difficult for Derek to shovel off the sidewalks in front of the store. He had just finished that chore when Charlie Beezley arrived. Derek came in, took off his coat, and stood in front of the stove to warm himself.

"Turned bitter," Charlie said. Beezley was in his sixties, a widower since Sarah's mother died in childbirth. He was gruff, and a little testy in his manner, but people respected his knowledge of guns. "Sarah tells me you two had quite a night."

Derek's glance slid to Sarah, standing nearby at the counter where a dozen or so handguns were displayed. She spoke up quickly.

"I told father how bad the storm was," she said, "and how grateful I was you stayed with me."

"Sounds like you gave Sarah quite a thrill," the elder Beezley said.

Again Derek looked quickly at Sarah. She smiled at him. "I told father what you said it was like being a Mormon in England, and the troubles coming across the plains in the handcarts."

Derek nodded. "Glad all that's behind me, sir."

"Our family's American born," Beezley grunted. "Came West from Iowa."

Derek saw the urging look Sarah was giving him. She was right. What he had to say to her father wouldn't get any easier by putting it off.

"Something I'd like to ask, Brother Beezley," he began.

Beezley nodded. "Don't hurt to ask."

Derek drew in a deep breath, then blurted it out. "I want to marry your daughter, sir."

Beezley frowned at him, then turned to look at his daughter. "Anything happen last night you didn't tell me—?"

Sarah's face flooded red. "Of course not, father. How could you think such a thing—"

"Well, if you're approving this, can't help thinking something had to happen to bring it on so sudden."

"I do approve, father," Sarah said, coming over and taking hold of his arm, "but the only thing that happened last night was we fell in love."

"You're sixteen, daughter. You sure you know what love is?"

"Yes, I do," Sarah told him, "and I know I feel it deeply for Derek."

Beezley's glance settled on Derek. "Seems there's a problem here, Derek. I recall, you already got a wife."

"Yes, sir," Derek said. "I do, sir, but I also love your daughter."

Beezley looked at Sarah. "You know what he's saying, child? He wants you to be a polygamous wife."

"I know that, father. We talked it all through. Nothing wrong with being a second wife, not when you love each other like we do."

"How long you two been planning this?"

"Wasn't planned, sir," Derek said. "It just happened."

"Last night—?"

"Yes, sir." Derek felt color rising in his cheeks. "Don't want you to think anything wrong happened between us, Brother Beezley. Wasn't anything like that. We just discovered we were in love."

"Awful sudden, ain't it."

"I agree, sir. But I can't fight what came into my heart."

"You talked to your wife about this?" Beezley asked. "She has to agree before the authorities will even consider allowing it."

"No chance to do that yet, sir," Derek said. "Wanted to get your approval first."

"Ain't up to me," Beezley muttered, studying his daughter. "You're all growed up, child, but this is mighty sudden. You sure you want to go polygamous? You already had a couple offers of marriage, and you can count on there being more."

"I know what I'm doing, father. I love Derek and I want to be his wife. First or second doesn't matter to me. It's being with him my whole life that counts."

"You feel that way, son? You feel capable of supporting two women and making both of them happy?"

Derek nodded. "I do, sir."

Beezley reached out a hand toward Derek. "Decision's made then. Can't imagine it, myself—hard enough living with just one. But, can't complain about having a son-in-law who knows as much about guns as you do."

Derek left for his home in Sugar House a short while later, anxious to break the news to Gwen. He felt sure she would understand and be supportive, ready to welcome Sarah into their family.

Derek had never been more wrong in his whole life.

Gwen happened to be washing the dishes when he told her. A heavy metal skillet flew out of her hand and if he hadn't ducked in time, it would have flattened him.

"Get out!" she screamed. "Get out. I never want to see you again!"

Derek had never seen such a look of anger—it was hatred, really—on his wife's face. He was shocked.

"What's got into you, Gwen?"

"It's not me who's getting into things," she shouted at him. "You just go back into town and spend all the time you want with your little harlot. Only don't ever come back to me—"

"Nothing happened between me and Sarah," Derek shouted back. "And she's not a harlot. I told you—she's a fine young lady."

"A fine young lady who spends the night with another woman's husband."

"It was the storm, Gwen. We had no choice—the storm trapped us."

"You were trapped all right," Gwen said bitterly.

"I can't believe this," Derek said, staring at her. "I told Sarah you would be happy for us—"

"Well, I'm not. This is about you and me not having any babies, isn't it."

Derek was stunned again. "Of course it's not. That has nothing to do with it—"

"You're cruel, Derek. You know I want babies—"

"This isn't about babies," he said angrily. "I don't understand you, Gwen."

"Well, you're easy enough to understand. Take this girl if you want, Derek, but you can't have her and me. I'm not agreeing to you having a polygamous wife—especially not some sixteen-year-old girl with only one thing on her mind. Get out, Derek—I mean it. And I don't think I ever want you back."

CHAPTER SIXTEEN

CAMP FLOYD
EARLY NOVEMBER

Camp Floyd was dedicated on the morning of the ninth of November, exactly according to the schedule set by General Johnston. Ceremonies were brief, held under a threatening, cloudy sky. The weather was cold but neither rain nor snow marred the ceremony, and even the hard winds that usually whipped Cedar Valley were quiet.

After General Johnston officially named the post in honor of Secretary of War John Buchanan Floyd, the howitzers of the Fourth Artillery thundered a twenty-gun salute. Next came probably the most impressive part of the whole ceremony, the raising of the Stars and Stripes, accompanied by the playing of the Star Spangled Banner by the combined bands of the Fifth, Seventh and Tenth Infantry. No one could not be touched by the sight of nearly three thousand United States soldiers in full dress uniform standing rigidly at attention as they saluted the raising of their country's flag.

And an impressive raising it was. The flagpole rose ninety feet into the air. Its base, a little over four feet in circumference, was imbedded nine feet into the ground, the cross-tree forty-five feet up the pole. The flag was equally impressive, measuring over twenty feet in length. When it first reached the top, the flag curled close to the base. A short while later, however, the wind began blowing hard enough to unfurl it, and the huge flag flapped majestically over what was now the largest military post in the United States.

In the four months since General Johnston first rode into Cedar Valley, the post had been laid out, constructed, and now dedicated.

It was an enormous undertaking, and General Johnston was first to admit it could not have been done without the skills and assistance of thousands of the Mormons he had come to quell.

The post now had nine fifty-foot wide avenues running between a city of over three hundred buildings. The hard-packed clay streets pointed toward the administration building that marked the western edge of the post, actually a series of fourteen buildings all connected into one structure. Over a million-and-a-half bricks of bluish clay were made by Mormon craftsmen to construct all the buildings in the new camp, most of them low and sturdy, with pine-pole, brush and hard-packed dirt roofs. Floors were covered with straw and canvas, providing surprising warmth and comfort. Windows in the barracks were small and shuttered to give extra protection from winter storms. The barracks were divided into rooms about twelve by fifteen feet, each with its own fireplace.

The only break in the symmetry of the neat rows of buildings were the cluster of adobes constructed by the Seventh Infantry in the northwest section of the post, just south of Cedar Creek. The Seventh had won permission to build their quarters out of low circular walls of adobe bricks, topped with the new-issue Sibley tents. No one knew at the time, of course, but it would take only one harsh winter for the Seventh to realize the brick and canvas quarters were a mistake.

Workshops, warehouses, ordnance buildings, and storehouses for the Quartermaster Department marked the southern border of the giant army post. More than a dozen of the warehouses were over six hundred feet in length, holding a staggering amount of goods and supplies—enough to last the post a full two years.

Scattered throughout the post was housing for officers and civilian employees, four hospitals, five guardhouses, and numerous bowling alleys, canteens, and sutler stores. Also on the northern edge of camp, near the entrance bridge over Cedar Creek, was a post theater. The building was not quite completed, although rows of slab benches, some smoothed and shaved for officers and their guests, were in place. It was far enough along for the first performance of the Military Dramatic Association to be scheduled for tonight. Comprised mainly of troopers from the Fifth Infantry, the acting group was under the direction of Sergeant Richard White, and it was rumored a program of ribald skits was to be presented. The theater was expected to become a popular pastime for many on the post.

Camp Floyd's massive central parade ground was edged by acres of wagons stacked side by side, a forest of tongues sticking into the air. There were at least two thousand wagons, essential to moving such a large army from the frontier with all the necessary supplies, but now of little use. Near the sea of empty wagons were mountains of firewood gathered by soldiers and teamsters for the long winter ahead.

Not only was Camp Floyd the largest military post in the nation in terms of size, it also housed the largest concentration of U.S. forces ever put together in one place. Not one officer in the whole command understood why this huge post had been ordered built in the virtually empty western desert, especially when the nation stood on the brink of civil war between the North and the South. It was no secret the federal treasury could ill afford the more than two hundred thousand dollars the post had cost so far, not counting the enormous expense of bringing the army and its supplies to Utah and continuing to feed and maintain them. It was a growing belief that treason had reached into the White House, if not to the President, then to some of his top advisors. The term "Buchanan's Folly' was now used in connection with more than launching a war against the Mormons.

Such thoughts did not bother the troops who, after being dismissed from the parade ground, began enjoying a daylong celebration with a liberal ration of whiskey. Ordinarily, officers could drink alcohol in the privacy of their own quarters at any time, but enlisted men could consume hard liquor on the post only when the commanding officer suspended the rules for a holiday or some special occasion. The men could purchase beer at the sutler exchanges, but anyone who got drunk would find himself fined a month's pay and consigned to a month of hard labor in the quarries in the Oquirrh Mountains. Intoxication was a crime not tolerated on the post.

However, General Johnston ordered this day be observed as a special occasion and the quartermaster doled out whiskey rations for one and all. With barrels unplugged and accessible, it became a challenge to see who could obtain the most extra rations. It wasn't too difficult, not when every man in the quartermaster corp was willing to be bribed with whatever was offered in trade. It was the first time in four months that anyone got drunk on the post—not counting getting drunk in Frogtown, of course. All five regimental guardhouses were soon filled to capacity with happy guests.

The whiskey barrels were finally ordered put under lock and key again. With the supply of free whiskey cut off, groups of soldiers started wading across the creek into Frogtown. They were eagerly welcomed by the gamblers and the whores, beginning a wild celebration that lasted through the night.

The officers celebrated in a more restrained manner, with punch and light refreshments served for them and the invited guests. It was a social event, with many Territorial dignitaries and their wives in attendance. Conspicuous by his absence was Governor Cummings. General Johnston did not take this as an affront, for he had not issued an invitation to the governor nor any Mormon official.

Carn Tregale was among the invited civilians, and after an hour or so of mingling and listening to the chatter, he answered Colonel Cooke's silent invitation and slipped away from the crowd, joining the colonel in a stroll down one of the quiet avenues.

"Quite a day for the general," Tregale murmured. "He and Colonel Smith should be proud of what's been accomplished."

"It's a fine post," Cooke agreed. "However, I can't help feeling it belongs somewhere in Kansas or Iowa, not out here in the Utah desert."

"Does seem strange," Tregale said. He gave his friend a curious glance. "Never realized there were so many nationalities in the force. Seeing the troops all together like that on the parade ground, made me think of the French Foreign Legion."

Cooked nodded. "Army recruitment has been fierce the last couple of years," he said. "The men are mostly Irish and German immigrants, fresh off the boat. We have lots of other nationalities— Mexicans, Italians, Scandinavians, and a fair share of Negras."

"Explains some of the frictions," Tregale mused. "With that many backgrounds, communication must be difficult."

"Not so much communicating," Cooke grunted, "as it is dealing with all the different ways they look at the same thing. Abolitionists denounce the pro-slavers—there's more fights over that than any-thing else. The slavers are just as angry with those who would deny them their right to own slaves. Then there's those with religion who favor temperance—not many, mind you—but they're dead set against the evils of alcohol. No more hard drinkers than the Irish, and they're mostly stubborn Catholics. So it's not just politics. We have the evan-gelists pounding on the Catholics, the Catholics pounding on the Baptists, and the Baptists convinced the Catholics are all members of the great and abominable church of the scriptures. We've even got an active bunch of Masons, who don't get along with anybody. It makes for an ugly mess. About all anyone agrees on are Mormons and Indi-ans—the Territory would be better off without either of them."

"No wonder General Johnston looks grim all the time," Tregale smiled.

"It's not just the enlisted men, either," Cooke added. "Tensions are tight among the officers, especially the southerners who come from landed families. They damn the Republicans for trying to change their traditions—owning slaves is the big one, of course. It's causing some real stresses, because most of us fear it will come to fighting, the North against the South. That probably means we'll be fighting each other, sooner or later, for we come from both sides of the fracture."

"Fighting Indians might relieve some of the stress."

"And what about your stress, Carn?" Cooke asked. "What about Captain Edwards—is that matter put to rest?"

Tregale walked on without answering. Cooke waited, and fi-nally Tregale stopped and turned to face him.

"Saw Edwards in the store a few days ago," he muttered, "hold-ing hands with my wife."

Cooked stared at him, a shocked expression on his face. "Cap-tain Edwards was holding hands with Heather—?"

"Walked in on them," Carn said. "What really hit me, though, was neither of them seemed too upset."

"I'll talk to Edwards," Cooke said firmly. "This must be stopped."

"If it is," Carn said quietly, "it won't be me or you who does it. Heather has to be the one to settle this."

"Did you talk to her about it?"

"Tried, but about that time, Cummings lost his mares. Guess I took the easy way out by staying here at Camp Floyd since then. I know we have to talk it out, but I also want both of us to have time to think it through."

"Won't presume to tell a man his business," Cooke said slowly, "but if you were to ask me for some friendly advice, I'd tell you to get home and clear the air."

Carn nodded agreement. "Be doing that tomorrow, Philip. I want to talk to Captain Edwards though before I leave. I need to hear from him how serious he is about this."

"Want me to arrange that?"

"Better to let things happen natural, if that's possible. If it's not, I'll take you up on your offer."

The occasion presented itself that evening. It began to rain heavily as Tregale accompanied Philip Cooke to the theater, along with some six hundred others who paid from fifty cents to a dollar for admission. Carn sat through the first half and laughed along with everyone else at the crude humor that ripped apart the Mormons and their strange ways. Nothing was sacred—far from it, in fact. Tregale saw many of the ladies in the audience pale as they watched some of the skits.

The air inside the theater became as foul as the language of the performers, resulting from a mixture of coal oil from the lamps, thick tobacco smoke, stale bodies, and damp clothing.

By intermission, lace fans were whirring in ladies' gloved hands and judging by the looks on their faces, few would be back for the second half of the performance. The men in the audience had been rolling off the benches, however, and there were enough soldiers waiting outside, drawn by the gales of laughter from the theater, to ensure a full house even without the ladies and their escorts.

Tregale and Cooke stepped outside to get some fresh air, and it was then that Captain Edwards, in company with two other officers, passed near them. Tregale surprised himself by calling out to the captain.

"Captain Edwards. Might I have a few words with you, please—"

The captain turned, saw who had called to him, hesitating for a moment then excusing himself from his companions. Tregale walked to meet him, leaving Cooke behind.

"Mr. Tregale. Didn't see you inside."

"Not surprising, considering all the smoke. They ought not to allow cigars in such close quarters. It upset quite a few of the ladies."

"You want to talk about your wife—"

"Thought it might be a good idea."

"You want to do it now—here?"

Tregale glanced around. "Seems private enough. I'll be heading back to Salt Lake in the morning, so the time seems right too."

The two men walked a few yards farther away from the crowd milling outside the theater. Finally, Captain Edwards swung around to face Carn, his features serious.

"Are you seeking satisfaction, Mr. Tregale?"

"Do I want to kill you—?" Tregale shook his head. "My satisfaction will be in getting some honest answers, Captain Edwards. That's all."

"I want you to know, Mr. Tregale, there has been nothing between your wife and me."

"Saw you holding hands. I count that as something."

"Heather was merely expressing her pleasure at something I told her. It wasn't what it looked like."

"Maybe if you told me what was said, I might be more inclined to accept that, Captain."

"I had just told her I was going to investigate the Mormon faith when I returned to Boston. It was a result of some of the things she told me about the Mormons, and it pleased her."

"Sounds like Heather, right enough," Carn nodded. "When are you planning on going back to Boston, Captain?"

"My tour of duty will be up in a few months. I'll probably be leaving in April—maybe March."

Carn decided not to sidestep anymore.

"You planning on taking my wife with you, Captain Edwards?" Edwards didn't flinch.

"I've asked her to do that, Mr. Tregale. Your wife has had a profound impact on me, sir. Can't explain it, and she certainly had nothing to do with it. Most certainly she did nothing to encourage such an interest on my part."

"Has she said she's going with you?"

"To the contrary, Mr. Tregale. Unfortunately for me, your wife holds you and your son very dear. I suspect you are much to blame for her allowing me to express my feelings as I have."

"What are those feelings, Captain?"

"I love your wife, sir. I did not seek such emotions—I had no control over them. I have told her how I feel, and that my wish would be for her to divorce you and come back to Boston and marry me. I'm sorry to be so blunt, sir, but I'm sure you agree this is the time for honesty."

"I do, Captain," Carn replied, "and I appreciate how difficult this must be for you. However, I believe the situation is much more difficult for me. Do you intend to keep pursuing my wife, Captain Edwards?"

"Honesty again—?"

"Absolutely."

"Yes. I will not give up hope until rejection is clear in her words and in her heart."

"Do you feel you have a place in her heart—?"

Edwards hesitated briefly. "I don't think so, much as it hurts to face that fact. I'm hopeful that might change, however, before it's time for me to leave."

Tregale gave him a curious stare. "You said a moment ago you felt that I was partly to blame for all this. What did you mean by that?"

"I don't think Heather would have given me more than a friendly smile if there hadn't been such pain and loneliness inside her."

"She told you she felt that way?"

"I've seen it on her face, Mr. Tregale. I'm surprised you haven't."

"And you think I'm responsible—"

"Don't you—?"

The people were beginning to return into the theater. Tregale saw Cooke waiting, trying not to be too obvious about watching the two of them.

"I don't condone your actions, Captain Edwards," Carn told the officer, "but I appreciate the respect you obviously have shown my wife."

"I must be truthful with you, Mr. Tregale," Edwards said firmly. "I have not given up the hope of enticing your wife away from you, sir."

"And I haven't given up hope of holding on to her, Captain."

CHAPTER SEVENTEEN

FROGTOWN

C alvin Gray was half-drunk even before he crossed the Cedar Creek Bridge into Frogtown with a dozen other troopers from D Company. They found the place already swarming with soldiers and teamsters, for the orders of the day also lifted the ban on frequenting what was referred to by God-fearing folks as "a den of vipers and a refuge for all sin." A soldier caught in Frogtown when it was off limits was fined fifty dollars and given twenty days at hard labor in the quarries of the Oquirrh Mountains. That didn't stop soldiers from going to Frogtown, but it made them more cautious about getting caught.

The men from D Company checked out several saloons on their way down Front Street, but inevitably the first stop was the section of whorehouses. Calvin chose one of the girls standing in front of a two-storied frame building with a red and yellow sign that proclaimed it the Love House. Some of his companions followed him inside, while others made their choices in such places as the Soiled Doves Of The Wasatch, Gentle Annie's, LuLu's Lovelies, Love's Dreams, and other houses of ecstasy. If all the girls were busy, there was plenty of gambling and whiskey to keep troopers occupied until one became available.

When Calvin and some of his buddies left the Love House, they headed west up Front Street, intending to see where they might find a game that offered at least a chance of winning. Most of the card sharks inhabiting the saloons won too many hands not to give warning, although once a man got really drunk, he tended to believe he was better than any black-suited gent who invited him to sit in on a game.

Calvin was walking down the middle of the street when two Indians on horseback raced past, both narrowly missing him. Gray bellowed his anger, turning to see the Indians wheel their ponies around and start racing back up Front Street again. Both were whooping shrilly and waving tomahawks wildly in the air. They were so drunk it was surprising either stayed on his horse.

Gray waited, and as one of them thundered by he jumped up and grabbed a handful of long black hair. The rider was jerked off his horse, hitting the ground with a groan and a swirling cloud of dust. He tried to get to his feet, but in his condition, that was going to take a long time. The other Indian looked back over his shoulder, saw the crowd of soldiers gathering about his fallen friend, and kept on riding out of town.

Gray knelt on top of the Indian in the street, pinning both arms as he began smashing his fists into the man's face. His buddies yelled encouragement, but when the Indian was hammered into unconsciousness and Calvin kept on hitting him, some of the dragoons dragged him off.

"No sense killin' him, Gray," one of them muttered. "He ain't nothin' but a crazy drunk buck."

"We're supposed to kill 'em," Gray mouthed, struggling to get free. "Ain't we supposed to kill 'em—?"

"Not in Frogtown," another dragoon grinned. "Let's go find us a game—"

They crowded a reluctant Gray into a nearby saloon, leaving the Indian unconscious in the roadway. Some teamsters were already eyeing the fallen man, trying to figure if he was worth robbing. As soon as the bat-wing doors swung closed behind the soldiers, the teamsters went into the street and rolled him over. He had no money, so they settled for taking his tomahawk. Twenty minutes later, the second Indian trotted warily back into town, leading his friend's pony. He helped the beaten and still dazed man onto the pony then both slipped away into the shadows.

Inside the saloon, the dragoons dragged up chairs and crowded around a table. A worn-out-looking bar girl brought glasses and a bottle of whiskey and one of the soldiers grabbed her arm, pulling her onto his lap. He whispered something in her ear, the girl gave a weary nod, and led the soldier toward the back rooms amid a chorus of yells from his companions.

Calvin calmed down after a few drinks were poured, and looked around the room. One of the dragoons poked him in the ribs, motioning toward a nearby table where five men were playing cards.

"See that dude with the beard and the black suit—?"

"The mean lookin' one with the pistols slung backwards?"

"That's Billy Hickman."

Calvin peered through the smoke. "A lawyer, ain't he? Heard his name—"

"Don't get on his bad side. People lost count of how many men he's killed."

"What's he doin' in Frogtown?"

"Bought a ranch in the south end of Cedar Valley. Needs a place to keep all the cattle his gangs rustle from the army."

The others grinned and went back to drinking. The man who had left with the bargirl came back, a satisfied smirk on his face.

"Better'n I thought she'd be," he told his companions. "Only charged fifty cents, too."

The bottle was emptied, followed by two more. By now, it wasn't just the thick smoke inside the saloon that was making things hazy for Gray and the other dragoons. One of them suddenly closed his eyes, leaned back in the chair and fell to the floor. The others looked down at him, unsure whether to pick him up or let him lie there.

"Maybe it's time to head for the barracks—"

"Not me," Gray growled, getting unsteadily to his feet. He pointed at a table in a far corner where four teamsters were dealing cards. "I ain't going until I teach those drovers how to play poker."

The dragoons laughed, and one of them grabbed at him. "You ain't in no condition to play cards, Gray. You ain't even in no condition to stand up."

There was more laughter but Gray shook his arm free and lurched over to the table where the teamsters were sitting. They looked up, staring suspiciously at him.

"Something on your mind, soldier?" one asked in a strong Irish brogue.

"Taking your money," Calvin replied. "Won't take much playing, neither."

"You got any money—cash money?"

"Got government scrip," Gray answered. "Good as gold."

"Not with us, it ain't," a teamster sneered. "You soldiers been printing up your own scrip, the way we hear it. We only play for hard specie."

Calvin's face darkened with anger. "You sayin' I'm tryin' to cheat you?"

The teamster stood up, leaning forward until his bearded face was inches away from the dragoon. "And if we is," he grated, "might you be thinking of doing something about it—?"

Calvin stared at him for a moment, then suddenly slammed a fist into the teamster's face. It knocked the man backward onto the floor. The other teamsters jumped to their feet and lunged for Gray. That brought the other men from D Company leaping forward. In seconds, bodies were crashing everywhere.

Billy Hickman and the men at his table scurried to get out of the way. Hickman scooped up the pile of dollars and stuffed them into his pocket just before the table got knocked over. One of the men in the game glared at him. Hickman glared back, eyes glittering threateningly above the black mass of beard.

"Drew two to a royal flush," Hickman hissed at the man. "Pot's mine."

Since the cards already were scattered on the floor, there was no chance for anything but gunplay, and the man didn't want that, not with Billy Hickman. Other teamsters in the saloon joined in the battle, as did all the soldiers. Everybody was so drunk, they could hardly feel the blows they got and gave. The owner stayed behind the heavy bar, watching in frustration as tables and chairs splintered, keeping his hand on the double-barreled shotgun under the counter. It wasn't good for business to kill customers, even if they were breaking up his place, so he didn't want to use the shotgun unless it became absolutely necessary. Besides, every saloonkeeper figured the cost of an occasional fight like this into the prices charged.

Outside, Billy Hickman straightened his coat, put on his hat, and looked for his horse. He'd left it tied to the hitching rail outside the saloon but it wasn't there now.

Hickman looked up and down the street, fury gathering on his face. This wasn't just any horse—it was his favorite horse. A blooded horse. Didn't matter that Hickman had stolen the horse himself months ago in Kansas. Someone had taken his horse. The hell that broke loose on Front Street almost paled the brawling going on inside the saloon.

It was the kind of night that made Frogtown famous all the way back to the Missouri frontier.

The Carson Inn was full, reserved exclusively for the ladies who had come to Cedar Valley for the dedication ceremonies. Carn Tregale spent the night on the post with the other men in quarters provided for officers' guests. All were awakened at five in the morning by the post buglers sounding reveille.

After breakfast, Carn looked up Colonel Cooke, who already was on duty in the administration complex.

"Wonder if I might ask a favor, Philip," Carn said.

"Do whatever I can—"

"I'd like to speak to Calvin Gray. I promised his wife I'd look him up and convey a message for her."

"Gray—he's in D Company, right. Shouldn't be a problem." He called out through the open door. "Sergeant, find Calvin Gray, D Company, Second Dragoons. Bring him here, or at least let me know where he is."

Cooke turned his attention back to Tregale. "You went easy on Edwards yesterday. Don't think I would be so calm about it."

Tregale gave a little shrug of his shoulders. "Not much I can do, not until I talk to Heather."

"You're doing that when you get back, right?"

"Heart to heart."

Cooked nodded approval. "I'll wager that's all it will take."

"Heard a lot of commotion last night," Carn grinned. "Sounded like the men were taking advantage of the general's generosity."

"He's regretting that, I can tell you," Cooke muttered. "He's steaming mad this morning. Wants discipline restored right now. Ordered some examples set—some of the men arrested are going to be real sober by the end of this day."

It wasn't long before the sergeant sent to find Calvin Gray stuck his head through the open doorway.

"Found him, Colonel. He's in the regimental stockade, him and a bunch of others from D Company. Had themselves quite a night in Frogtown, from what I was told. Tore up a saloon and put some teamsters in the hospital. Sergeant in charge ain't about to let any of them out, unless it's a written order."

"Thank you, sergeant. I'll take it from here." The colonel glanced quizzically at Tregale. "You still want to see Gray?"

"Would it be upsetting the general's discipline?"

"Only thing that's going to be upset is your stomach," Cooke grimaced. "You've never visited one of our stockades, as I recall."

"Not since they put in prisoners."

"Not a pretty sight, Carn," Cooke told him quietly. "It's a side of military life not many people get to see—and almost nobody wants to see twice."

Colonel Cooke and Tregale were admitted into the guardhouse of the Second Dragoons regiment a short while later. Beyond the small office area, Tregale could see out an open door into the stock-aded yard beyond. There were at least fifty men crowded into it.

The sergeant in charge saluted Colonel Cooke. "Gray's out in the yard, sir." His glance slid to the civilian, then back to the colonel. "Might be best not to visit him just yet, Colonel—"

"There's a problem—?" Cooke asked.

"Yes, sir," the sergeant replied. "The prisoner was real troublesome when he was brought in, sir. Broke loose and beat up the lieutenant on duty. He's—well, he's under restraint at the present, sir."

"What kind of restraint, Sergeant?"

There was a brief hesitation, then the reply came soft-spoken. "Gray's been bucked and gagged, sir."

"That's harsh, isn't it—"

"Not the way he was acting, Colonel. Short of smashing in his head, there was no other way to control him, sir."

Cooke looked at Tregale. "Sergeant's right. Maybe you should talk to Gray later."

"Unless it's violating rules, I'd like just a few minutes with him," Carn said. "I promised his wife, and I know she's in dire need of knowing what his intentions are."

Cooke nodded, and turned to the sergeant. "I'll take responsibility, Sergeant. Take us to the prisoner."

They found Calvin Gray off to one side of the stockade, near the stone building that housed the cells. Hardened as he was to harsh military discipline in the British army, Tregale was shocked as he stared at Calvin.

Gray was lying on his back, knees in the air. His wrists had been tightly bound together, then while in a crouching position, his knees had been forced up between his arms. A long stick was thrust through the crook of his knees, preventing the arms from raising or the legs from straightening. Any attempt to break loose from the numbing position resulted in what had happened to Gray; the prisoner ended up on his back, unable to move.

Gray saw Tregale standing over him but couldn't say anything. In addition to the bucking, as the soldiers called it, Gray had undergone the gagging. Tregale could see a stick had been placed in Calvin's mouth between the teeth, then drawn back and fastened tightly. Blood was caked on each side of Calvin's mouth where the stick had torn into skin.

Cooked looked at the sergeant. "How long has he been like this?'
"About five hours, sir."

"He should be sobered up by now. Take off the restraints, Sergeant."

The bindings around his arms were taken off, the stick removed from between his knees, and finally the rope holding the stick in his mouth was cut loose. Calvin rolled over onto his side, groaning in pain as he tried to straighten his legs. The other men waited for a few moments, then the sergeant kicked a boot into his ribs.

"On your feet, Gray. Officer present."

Gray tried to get up, but couldn't. Cooke motioned the sergeant back.

"It's all right. Mr. Tregale has a couple of questions for the prisoner, then you can take him to the cells. Think he's had enough bucking and gagging."

"Yes, sir," the sergeant said. You could tell by the tone of his voice that he didn't agree with the colonel.

Calvin looked up at Tregale, shaking his head to clear it. "Ashamed to have you see me like this—"

"Don't matter," Carn said. He squatted down beside him, seeing the cuts and bruises. It must have been a wild time in Frogtown, he thought. "Promised Harriet I'd look you up. She's wondering about you, Calvin."

"She and the baby all right?" Calvin asked.

Tregale nodded. "Staying with us. They're both doing fine. Baby's growing fast."

"Ain't no good," Calvin muttered, wincing in pain as he massaged his legs. "I ain't no good as a husband nor a father. Harriet's well rid of me."

"That the way you want it, Calvin?"

"She deserves more'n me," he said. "Tell her to divorce me and find herself a good Mormon. She needs a Mormon to make her happy. I cain't never be one—not now nor ever."

"You sure about this?" Tregale asked again. "She still loves you, Calvin. You two could make it if that was what you wanted. Harriet wanted me to tell you she'll forgive you for everything—"

"That's just it, Mr. Tregale," Calvin said, using a finger to tenderly explore the bloody corners of his mouth. "It ain't in me to go crawling back—and the truth is, I don't want to. Best thing she can do is forget me. If I ever get out of this army, I'm headed for California. Never should have turned back the last time."

Tregale stared at him, seeing the truth on Calvin's face, swollen and bruised as it was. This wasn't the Calvin Gray that Harriet had married, wasn't the man any of them knew. Calvin had jumped into military life and sunk to the bottom. Carn looked around the stockade, taking in sights that made him even more aware of the world to which Calvin now belonged.

He saw most of the prisoners were wearing leg irons, another length of chain fastened to them, and what looked like a cannon ball secured on the end of that. Tregale guessed the ball weighed about fifteen or twenty pounds. In order to move, a prisoner had to pick up the ball and shuffle along while holding it off the ground. Wasn't anybody going to get very far with that kind of restraint, Tregale figured.

Some of the soldiers were being forced to jog back and forth along the base of the stockade. Not only were these men carrying the iron balls, but they also had timbers strapped across their shoulders. The timbers were heavy, judging from the way the men were leaning to keep their balance. A corporal trotted beside them, shouting curses and lashing legs with a mule whip. One of the prisoners fell to the ground, and despite the threats and yelling, couldn't get back onto his feet. The corporal stood over him, giving him several kicks with his boot. The prisoner lay on the ground, unmoving. Finally the corporal called for help. A couple of guards took the timber off the downed man's back, then carried him into the cells, dragging the heavy metal ball fastened to the chain between his feet. The corporal barked an order and the rest of the prisoners again started jogging.

Tregale looked at the sergeant. "Those men commit some bad crime?"

"Deserters," the sergeant clipped, "waiting a court martial. After that, they'll be flogged, branded, stripped, and drummed off the post."

Cooke saw the frown gather on Tregale's face. "A hard example needs to be set, Carn," he said, "or we'd have more deserters than soldiers."

"Did I hear right," Carn asked the colonel. "Those men will be branded like cattle?"

"Branded like deserters," the sergeant said defensively. "Seeing a big D burned on a man makes others think twice about going over the hill."

Tregale's attention was drawn to two men, bare to the waist, balancing on the edge of beer barrels. They tried to keep stiffly at attention, staring straight ahead. A guard with a whip stood near them, seeming to be waiting for an excuse to use it.

Cooke saw Tregale looking at the men on the barrels. "We call it being on the chimes," the colonel said quietly. "Those men were caught with liquor in their possession, on the post. They'll stand there for eight hours, or until they fall off."

"If that happens," the sergeant added, "they'll get strapped to a caisson wheel and draw fifty lashes."

Tregale shook his head. "Seems excessive for having a bottle of whiskey in your kit."

"It's better than having to bury the bottle, sir," the sergeant said.

"Bury the bottle—?"

"A man has to dig a deep trench, bury the liquor bottle, then fill the hole up again. He keeps doing that, sir, until the officer of the guard feels a lesson has been learned. Sometimes he keeps digging all day and through the night."

"I take it this is what the general means by setting an example—" Carn muttered.

"Can be worse," Cooke said grimly. "Men die under a flogging."

"We got three set this afternoon, Colonel, if you care to witness. A hundred lashes, all of them."

Cooke swiftly shook his head, looking at Tregale. "You have any more questions for this prisoner, Mr. Tregale?"

Calvin motioned for Tregale to lean closer. "Come back to the cell," he said hoarsely. "Got something for my son—"

Tregale looked at Cooke and the colonel nodded. "Sergeant, get this man to his cell. Mr. Tregale will accompany you. He'll only be a moment or two," he added pointedly, looking at Gray.

"Thank you, sir," Calvin told him. "Won't take a minute."

"For reasons you'll soon discover," Cooke told Carn, "I'll wait out here."

Gray was half carried, half dragged into the brick building housing the cells, his legs still almost useless. As soon as he entered the building, Carn felt nauseated by the smell that engulfed them. There obviously were no latrines in the building, and the stench from the cells was revolting. The cells were small, barely large enough for a man to lie down on the dirty straw strewn on the ground. The only ventilation came through the narrow corridor between two rows of cells, the walls on each side solid and windowless. Everything was so dirty and smelled so foul that Tregale had to force himself to follow the guards dragging Calvin to his cell. He couldn't imagine being confined in such hellish quarters for weeks and months.

Calvin was tossed onto the straw. Leaving the ball and chain attached to his leg irons, the guards locked Gray to another chain fastened to the wall. Then they backed out and left Carn alone with the prisoner.

Calvin fumbled under the straw and pulled out a small piece of cloth, handing it to Carn. Unwrapping it, Carn was startled to see four large diamonds.

He looked questioningly at Calvin, who gave a weary shake of his head.

"Don't matter where they came from," he muttered. "Folks what owned them are dead now, thanks to the Shoshones. Give these to Harriet, and tell her I was thinking about her and the boy."

CHAPTER EIGHTEEN

SALT LAKE CITY

I consider this a personal attack on me—and on my office. It was no random theft, sir. I want those responsible tracked down and punished to the fullest extent of the law."

Cummings was red in the face, eyes bulging wide as he shook a finger angrily in the face of U. S. Marshal Peter Dotson. The marshal squirmed uneasily. He knew this was going to be an unpleasant meeting from the moment he received the summons to report in person to the governor's residence.

"We're doing all we can, sir—" he began, only to be cut off by another outburst from the governor.

"If you were doing all you could, Marshal Dotson, those horses would be back in my stable. Do you have any leads whatsoever—?"

"No, sir," Dotson muttered.

"A pair of prize horses is stolen from my own house—a matched pair of white mares that stand out anywhere, mind you—and you can't find them?"

"I've assigned over half my men to this, Governor—"

"Then assign all of them. Have you looked in Camp Floyd?"

Dotson didn't want to be caught in the middle between Cummings and General Johnston. "We have, sir. General Johnston personally ordered a search of all stables, on the post and at all the outposts. Your horses aren't in Cedar Valley, governor, nor any of the outposts."

"Did you check the trail east, back to the frontier?"

"Yes, sir. All military outposts and civilian way stations are alerted. Anyone having a white horse, paired or otherwise, will be stopped. The California trails are closed, so it's unlikely they've gone that way. I'm sure it's only a matter of time, Governor, before we recover them."

"The damnable insolence of whoever did this," Cummings growled. "Do the Territorial judges know about it?"

Dotson nodded. "Chief Justice Eckles, as you know, has taken up residence at Camp Floyd. Judge Cradlebaugh, who arrived only recently, has joined him. I personally briefed Alexander Wilson, the new U.S. Attorney. He arrived in Salt Lake with his bride only a few days ago. I'm assuming, sir, that even though the theft occurred here in the city, you will want the case handled in a federal court."

"Absolutely," Cummings snorted, "absolutely. This is an offense against a federal officer. It's my understanding the Salt Lake police are also giving this their attention—"

"Yes, sir. They've assigned a special marshal full time to the recovery of the horses, governor."

"Good. Do I know the man—?"

"Believe you do, sir. Jim Wilson. He's young, but I hear he's a good officer. As a matter of fact, I asked him to come along in case you had some questions for him. He's waiting outside in the hallway, Governor." He didn't explain he'd mainly brought Wilson along to deflect some of the governor's angry frustration he knew would be directed at him.

"Send him in. I'm interested in hearing what the city police are doing."

"Yes, sir. Mr. Tregale is with him."

"Carn—good. Have them both come in."

"Will that be all for now, sir?" Dotson asked. He felt a great relief when the governor nodded curtly. "We'll find those horses, Governor," he assured him, although he didn't feel anywhere near that confident inside. He had a strong feeling those mares were long gone. "Like you said, a pair like that is hard to keep hid."

Tregale and Jim Wilson entered the governor's living room, noting the sour look on Dotson's face as he waved them in. Tregale ran

175

into Jim as he was riding up East Temple after just returning from Camp Floyd. He agreed to accompany his young friend to see the governor mainly, Carn admitted to himself, because he was headed for the emporium and he wasn't sure who'd be there. He expected Agatha, and maybe General Galloway, because Heather usually didn't go to the store until later in the afternoon. He didn't feel quite ready to confront his wife, and knew Agatha would have some wisdom and insight to offer.

"Sorry to hear you're still missing those mares, Governor."

Cummings shook hands with both of them, saw the dust caking Tregale. "You must have just got back from Camp Floyd. How did the dedication ceremonies go?"

"Well enough," Carn said. "Mighty cold, though. Be grateful you weren't there."

"Oh, I am," Cummings grunted, taking a seat and motioning for the two men to do the same. "Deeply grateful for not having to endure that man's company. I wouldn't have gone even if he'd shown the courtesy of an invitation." The governor fastened his glance on Jim Wilson. "Hear you're working full time on getting my horses back, Mr. Wilson."

"Wish I had some good news for you, Governor," Wilson replied, "but seems those mares disappeared into thin air. We're looking hard, sir—they got to be somewhere."

"I was just telling Marshal Dotson," Cummings said heavily, "I'm convinced those horses were taken as a personal affront. I want whoever's responsible to get the full penalty for horse stealing—that's hanging, I believe."

"We'll find them, Governor," Wilson said, not knowing he was echoing the same assurance just given by Peter Dotson. "I think they might be hid out somewhere close."

Cummings looked at Tregale. "You bring back any communiqués from the general?"

"Getting the camp ready for dedication has taken up most of his time of late, sir. I did inquire if there were any messages to bring back, but there weren't."

"Dotson said the general ordered a search for my mares—"

"He did, sir. The army's been losing mounts, too, and rustlers are taking a heavy toll on the herds of beef grazing in the outer valleys. General Johnston is very upset about those losses, as well as yours, Governor."

"Don't suppose I'll ever hear that from him—"

"Probably not, sir."

"Well, won't keep you from searching, Mr. Wilson," the governor wheezed. He had put on weight since arriving in the valley, resulting in a noticeable shortage of breath. "And I know you must be anxious to get home, Carn. Appreciate all that's being done, gentlemen, though I can't understand how those horses—in your own words, Mr. Wilson—just disappeared."

◆

Carn was relieved to find Heather was not at the store when he arrived. Agatha was helping a customer but she called to Henry, who was working in back, to come out and take over. She took Carn by the arm and led him into the back room. She studied him for a moment, then pushed him down onto a chair beside a small table. She said nothing until after she unwrapped a beef sandwich, putting it on a tin plate and placing it in front of him. She sat down, poured him a cup of water from a pitcher, then leaned back and stared at him again.

"All right, what's going on between you two?"

Carn took a drink, set the cup down on the table. "You mean between Heather and me?"

"No, between you and General Johnston," Agatha snorted. "Of course I mean you and Heather."

"You asked Heather that question?"

"She said to ask you. That's what I'm doing."

Carn lifted the top slice of the sandwich, looked inside, then put the bread back in place. He was stalling and Agatha knew it.

"It's sliced beef, butter, lettuce, and some sweet pickle—and you're obviously not hungry." She reached over and took away the plate. "Now, can we talk about you and Heather—"

A deep sigh lifted Carn's shoulders. "Don't know what to say, Agatha. You probably know more about it than I do. I was hoping you'd tell me what's going on."

"Two people acting very foolish."

"That's how I felt, Agatha—foolish—when I walked into this store a few days ago and found my wife holding hands with an army officer."

"She told me about that," Agatha said. "Not what it looked like."

"That's what Captain Edwards told me."

"Of course, you don't believe either of them."

"The captain also told me he's asked Heather to accompany him back to Boston. Did she tell you that?"

"Yes she did."

"Did she tell you if she's going?"

"Do you think she is?"

A weary, sad look came to Carn's face. "Agatha, I don't know what to think. A few months ago, I thought Heather and me had the perfect marriage. I thought we loved each other deeply—I know I loved her that way. Now she's holding hands with a stranger, and there's serious talk of her leaving me and going back to Boston. It's so sudden, I don't know how to cope with it."

"You want some advice—?"

"I sure do."

"She's lonely, Carn, and she can't understand why you put everyone and everything ahead of her and the baby. She's doubting that you love her, Carn, and that's devastating for a woman so deeply in love herself."

"In love with me—?"

"Who else, you nitwit," Agatha snapped. "It's you who's causing all this, Carn. You're not spending enough time with her, and you're not showing her enough affection."

"She knows I love her—"

"When was the last time you told her that? When was the last time you showed her she was more important to you than Governor Cummings, or General Johnston, or anyone else?"

"Can't help the demands people put on my time—"

"Yes you can. Tell them you got to spend a few days with your wife and baby now and then. Tell them your family has to come first, at least once in awhile."

"Has it been that bad—?"

"If you treated me the same way you've been treating Heather, I'd cold-cock you with a frypan."

Tregale frowned. "Maybe that's what I need."

"We got plenty here in the store," Agatha said. "Be glad to oblige."

The front doorbell jangled and Agatha looked out. "It's Beryl Tate. Looks like she's got something on her mind."

She saw Henry point toward the back room and Beryl hurried back. She looked surprised when she saw Carn at the table.

"Brother Tregale—glad to see you back." She gave Agatha an uncertain look. "Wanted to talk to you, Agatha—"

"Something private—?" Agatha asked.

Tregale stood up. "I was just leaving—"

Beryl waved a hand. "No, you should probably hear what I have to say. I know my parents will be asking you later."

"Sounds like something important," Agatha murmured. "Why don't you sit down and tell us about it?"

Again Beryl waved a hand in dismissal. "I'm going to Camp Floyd," she told them. "Mercy Tuckett has been invited to bring a company there for a few months. She's said she wants me to be one of the group."

"Camp Floyd is a pretty rough place for young ladies," Carn muttered. "You sure you want to do this, Beryl?"

"It's a great opportunity, Brother Tregale. This will give me a chance to really develop my talent as an actress."

"From what I've heard," Agatha said, "those soldiers will be more interested in your legs than your talent."

"We'll be acting, Agatha, not dancing. They have saloon girls for that."

"And prostitutes for everything else," Agatha added. "I worry about this, Beryl."

"Mercy Tuckett is a respected actress, and all of us girls will be shown the same respect."

"Wouldn't count on that," Tregale cautioned. "Soldiers get a couple of whiskeys inside them and they don't show much respect for anyone."

"When does this happen?" Agatha asked.

"Leaving in the morning," Beryl replied. "Mercy just told us. All the girls are so excited, I doubt if any of us will get any sleep tonight."

"Well, it's your decision, Beryl," Agatha told her. "Suppose you want us to tell your parents."

"Would you please, Agatha. There's no way I can get word to them—of course, I wouldn't if I could. I know what father is going to think—his little girl is selling her body to the soldiers. I know he loves me, but I get so furious at him."

"Only natural for a father to worry," Carn said, "especially when his little girl has grown up so beautiful."

Beryl gave him a surprised smile. "Am I, Brother Tregale—am I beautiful?"

"Of course you are," Carn told her. "A lot of dashing young lieutenants will be telling you that, I suspect. Just keep your feet on the ground."

"Good advice no matter how you look at it," Agatha added, her eyebrows lifting into a meaningful curve.

Henry left in the carriage to pick up Heather, and Beryl rode back to the house with him. Agatha didn't say anything but she stood with her arms folded, not taking her eyes off Carn as he got up from the chair, obviously intending to leave.

"I'll talk to her," Carn promised, "but I don't want to do it here. Captain Edwards just might walk in on us, and I don't know how I'd react to that."

"I can appreciate that," Agatha said. "Don't know how I'd react myself."

"Is the General home?"

Agatha shook her head. "He's at a meeting in the Council House. Someone reported a rumor the army was planning an assault on Brigham Young's estate—going to seize him and put him on trial."

"No truth to that," Carn said quickly. "I'd know if anything like that was being planned."

"Well, you might drop in and tell them that." A frown crossed Agatha's face. "Even better, you might kill an hour or so by dropping in on Derek Pitts. Saw him on the street a couple of days ago, and something is troubling that young man."

"Know what it is?"

"Asked him if everything was all right, but he didn't seem to want to talk about it. No doubt he's in need of a friendly smile, though."

"I'll do it." He put an arm around Agatha's shoulders, giving her a warm hug. "I'll try and get all this straightened out—and I'll be taking your advice on some of those things you mentioned. You don't look like my mother, Agatha, but you sure do sound like her sometimes."

Carn found Derek Pitts staring glumly out of the window of the gun shop. There were no customers inside, and like Agatha said, Derek looked troubled. His expression brightened as he greeted Carn.

"Brother Tregale, glad you stopped by. You interested in looking at guns?"

"See too many of them, Derek," Carn smiled. "Just stopped by to check on how you and Gwen are doing."

There was no mistaking the cloud that instantly fell over Derek's face at the mention of his wife. Tregale peered closer at him.

"Something wrong with Gwen?" he asked. "Not sick, is she?"

Derek shook his head. "Not sick like she's got influenza or anything like that."

"So what kind of sickness does she have?" A smile suddenly beamed across Carn's face. "You two finally having a baby?"

The sadness grew even more pronounced. "No baby, Brother Tregale. Wish there was."

"Don't mean to pry into your business, Derek, but you look like you're carrying a weight. Anything I can do to help?"

Derek stared out the window again, thoughts coursing across his face. Then he turned to Tregale. "Might help if I got some of this off my chest. You'd have to promise to keep it just between us, though."

"You have my word, Derek."

Derek began pacing back and forth in front of Carn. "Don't rightly know where to begin—especially with you having such a strong marriage."

That jolted Carn where it hurt. "Never can tell what's going on in a person's heart, Derek. It's easy to put a lie on your face sometimes."

Derek looked hard at him. "You and Sister Tregale aren't having problems, are you? Gwen and me have always looked up to you and Sister Tregale. We've admired the way you've built such a strong marriage—"

"Hope you'll keep on doing that, Derek," Carn murmured. "Isn't any two people who don't have a problem now and then. Is that what's happening between you and Gwen?"

"It ain't nothing Gwen's done," Derek said. "It's me, Brother Tregale. I'm the one who's upset the apple cart."

"Anything you want to talk about? Don't hold myself up much when it comes to dealing with marriage problems, but I'm a good listener."

"I'm in love, Brother Tregale."

"I'd say that's a healthy condition to be in, Derek."

"Gwen don't think so."

"Why's that?"

"I love Gwen, of course—but I've fallen in love with someone else, too."

Carn frowned. "That does sound troublesome. Does Gwen know this?"

"Told her a week ago. She threw me out and I ain't been home since. I bunk down in the back of the store."

"No wonder you're walking around looking like the world fell on you. I'd say it's done just that."

"It's awful, Brother Tregale. Really awful. I really do love Gwen."

"So who's this other young lady?"

"Sarah. Sarah Beezley."

"Charlie Beezley's daughter—?"

"She's beautiful, Brother Tregale. We didn't mean to fall in love— it just happened. I've asked her to marry me."

That put Tregale back on his heels. "How you going to do that, Derek—you being already married to Gwen?"

"Sarah's agreed to be a second wife."

"A polygamous wife—?"

Derek nodded. "Don't matter to her. She's happy to be a second wife."

"But Gwen doesn't feel the same way, right?"

"She went out of her mind, Brother Tregale. Even threw things at me. Never seen her like that."

"Seems like I've seen Sarah—she's about fifteen, isn't she?"

"Sixteen. She's old enough—"

"I agree," Carn said quickly. "Sarah's a mature young woman, as I recall. Has Gwen met her?"

"A few times, here at the store," Derek said. "She didn't seem to have anything against her."

"She's younger, and—forgive me for saying this, Derek—but some might say she's a little prettier than Gwen."

"Suppose that's true. Think it myself, to be truthful."

"So there you have it. No woman wants to bring competition like that into her house."

"Sarah isn't competition," Derek protested. "I love both of them."

"That may sound reasonable to you, Derek," Carn told him, "but there isn't a woman alive who wants her husband telling her how much he loves another woman, or watching him show it. Goes against a woman's grain, so to speak."

"If Sarah isn't jealous of Gwen, why should she be jealous of Sarah?"

"Wouldn't count on Sarah feeling that way after you two get married," Carn said dryly. "Women change the way they look at things—especially a young woman Sarah's age."

Derek looked defensive. "Other men have polygamous wives."

"Usually older men, Derek, providing a home for a widowed woman—"

"That isn't true," Derek said quickly. "There's plenty who take young girls to wife."

Carn scratched thoughtfully at his chin, the back of his mind registering that he would need a shave before meeting with Heather. "True enough. Usually that's in the smaller settlements where there's a lot of marriageable girls and not enough men to go round. That's how it was explained to me. Church leaders frown on a man taking more than one wife unless there's a good reason. Still, if a man's determined to take on some young comfort, that's what he'll do, with or without the proper approvals. Personally I don't agree with the whole concept of polygamy—doesn't seem fair to the women involved. I'm surprised you do, Derek, but can't say I'm surprised Gwen doesn't."

Derek pressed both hands against the sides of his head, trying to ease the aching pressure. "Don't want to give up either one. What do you think I ought to do, Brother Tregale?"

Carn shook his head. "Can't give advice on this, Derek. It's something you and Gwen—and Sarah—have to work out amongst yourselves. All I can say is don't do anything in a hurry. You need to think this all the way through, Derek."

◆

When Carn arrived at the Galloway mansion, only Agatha and Harriet were home. Both women were in the kitchen and the whole house smelled appetizingly delicious from the fresh bread they were baking. Carn saw a platter of fresh-baked sugar cookies cooling on the table.

"Help yourself," Agatha said, seeing him eyeing the cookies. "Dinner won't be ready for another two or three hours. Heather and Henry should be home by then, and hopefully, so will the General."

Carn took a couple of cookies and sat down. Harriet was slicing vegetables into a pot at the stove, but she kept looking back over her shoulder toward Carn. Agatha took the knife from her.

"Sit and talk before you slice a finger into that stew," she told Harriet. "You've been looking out the window for days waiting for Carn to get back, so get on with it."

Harriet gratefully sat down across from Carn, searching his face for answers to the questions both knew were on her mind. Carn thought of trying to sound cheerful and encouraging, but decided it was better that Harriet hear the truth, as painful as it would be.

"Don't hold out much hope, Harriet," he began, "for Calvin ever coming back."

Tears jumped into Harriet's eyes, and she brushed at them quickly. It was a confirmation of fears she had desperately hoped she wouldn't have to face. Carn leaned forward and clasped her hand comfortingly.

"It's a hard thing to hear," he said quietly, "but you and the baby are better off without him. He's changed, Harriet. He's not the man you married, nor the man any of us knew. Not placing any blame for that, but it's happened. I think you knew that after you spent that couple of days with him out at Camp Floyd."

She nodded, again wiping at tears on her cheeks. "I've known it, but haven't wanted to face it. Kept hoping I was wrong."

"The army changed him, Harriet," Carn continued, "and for the worse. Doesn't happen to all soldiers, but it did to your husband. Calvin knows it, too. In his heart, I think he still loves you and the baby, but he knows better than any of us that he can no longer be a husband or a father."

"He told you that?" Harriet asked, her eyes showing the pain inside her. "He came out and said he wasn't coming back to us?"

Tregale squeezed her hand. "It's a mark in his favor. He doesn't want to cause you any more unhappiness than he already has, Harriet."

"So he decides to just abandon us?" Harriet cried, anger flaring into her voice. Carn was glad to hear it; anger would help deal with the pain.

"In his way of thinking, he's doing the right thing. He knows he'd only hurt you more by not facing the truth of it. It's not in him, Harriet, not any more. It's a sad thing to say, but he's turned bad inside, and that won't ever change because he doesn't want it to change."

Harriet suddenly buried her face in her hands and her shoulders began to shake as heavy sobs broke from her. Agatha came over from the stove and put an arm around her.

"It's all right, Harriet. We all love you."

"What am I going to do?" Harriet sobbed. "How am I going to take care of the baby?"

"Take it one day at a time," Agatha said softly. "There's no rush for you to decide what happens in the future. Nothing really has changed, for that matter. You have a home here for you and the baby, you're earning wages—though not much, I admit. We'll talk to the General about that. There's plenty for you to do around the house and at the store. And little Cal and little Carn will find a lot of mischief to get into together."

"Agatha, you're such a wonderful person—"

"Nonsense," Agatha snorted. "You're earning your way, young lady."

"There's something Calvin wanted me to give to you," Carn said, reaching into his pocket. He pulled out the little wrapped bundle and handed it to Harriet. "It's for you and the baby. He said to tell you he was thinking about both of you while he was out on patrol against the Shoshones."

Harriet unwrapped the cloth, then gasped as she saw the four diamonds sparkling up at her.

"These are beautiful," she said, lifting one of the large gems between her fingers. "They must be worth a fortune—" She looked up at Carn, a frown coming to her face. "How did Calvin get these—did he steal them?"

Carn gave a reassuring shake of his head. "Don't know the full story, but he said the people who owned them were killed by the Shoshones. No way of tracing them now, anyway. This is his way of doing something to make up for all the pain he knows he's caused you. I'm not much of a diamond expert, but I think these will provide you and the baby with a good measure of security."

Agatha, leaning over to inspect the gems, nodded agreement. "The General knows people who will pay an honest price. This is a wonderful nest egg, Harriet."

"When the time comes, you can buy a small farm and some livestock, and build a solid life for your son," Carn told her.

"That's if some handsome young man doesn't sweep her off her feet long before she's ready to think of such things," Agatha beamed. "I'm really happy for you, Harriet."

Again Harriet looked at Carn. "Should I try to find the rightful owners, Brother Tregale. Maybe there are relatives back wherever these people came from—"

"Don't know where you'd begin," Carn said. "Just accept them, Harriet, and let Calvin do this for you and his son."

Maybe it was seeing the pain inside Harriet that made Carn decide not to wait to make an effort to hold his own marriage together. After talking to Harriet awhile longer, he excused himself and started for the door.

"You going where I think you're going?" Agatha asked.

"Decided to get it done," he answered. "Beginning to realize how much I'd miss her and the boy. Sooner I do something about that, the better."

"Spoken smartly," Agatha muttered. "Tell Henry to close up. You and Heather take some time together and talk it out. Take the carriage—Henry can ride your horse back."

Carn tied his horse in back of the emporium, beside the carriage. He came in through the back door and walked into the front of the store, his heart thumping and his mind whirling with all that he wanted to say to his wife. He could still hear her accusations about putting everything and everyone in front of her and the baby, and he knew she was right. It was time to straighten out priorities, he told himself sternly, and let his wife know how much she meant to him.

Carn didn't get to put any of those thoughts into words. Heather was in the store, all right, but she was leaning against the counter, a smile on her face as she listened with what appeared to be rapt attention to Captain Edwards. The officer was standing close, not too close perhaps, but closer than appeared proper to Carn. Seeing the officer standing beside his wife, relaxed and obviously enjoying her company, dealt a physical blow to Carn. It hit him like a ramrod in the stomach. Both Heather and Edwards turned as he entered the store, both looking startled and guilty. Carn stood there for a moment, battling with himself about what to do or say. He knew his face was betraying all sorts of emotions. Suddenly he turned and went back into the storeroom. He was on his horse and starting down the alley when he heard his wife run out and call his name. He just kept on going, a terrible, terrible deadness inside him.

CHAPTER NINETEEN

CAMP FLOYD
MID-NOVEMBER

The stagecoach carrying Mercy Tuckett and six young ladies, Beryl Tate among them, arrived at Camp Floyd late in the afternoon. Despite bitterly cold winds blowing the length of Cedar Valley, soldiers were crowded at the bridge entrance to the camp, awaiting the arrival of the company of actresses.

As the stage clattered over the bridge, Mercy leaned out of the window and waved to the soldiers, holding her other hand to a broad-brimmed black hat arched against her head with a tightly drawn black scarf. Mercy's cheeks were brightly rouged, the color almost matching the red velvet of her dress. Starched white lace formed a high collar and fringed the long sleeves.

The coach turned west, making its way toward the now completed theater building on the northern edge of the camp, bordering the creek. Soldiers whistled and cheered as the actresses passed, shouting crude invitations that the women pretended not to hear.

The actresses were greeted at the theater by Sergeant Richard White. Tall and thin, White had a sallow complexion that defied the fierce weather extremes of Cedar Valley, the skin apparently impervious to burning sun or freezing cold.

Wavy black hair was greased close to his head, with long, full sideburns and a slash of mustache above a thin mouth. Richard White looked like a stage villain, a character he had portrayed many times. However, his smile was pleasant and inviting as he greeted the women, taking the hand of each one as they alighted from the stagecoach.

Mercy Tuckett was the last to step down and Sergeant White took an obvious moment to appreciate the striking impression this popular actress made, from her vivacious smile to her hourglass figure. An ample bosom was accentuated by a tight-fitting bodice, a tiny waist, and a full sweep of red velvet skirt. Few people knew it took Mercy, a polygamous wife and mother of four children, almost an hour to encase herself in the corset and uplifts that made that figure possible.

Sergeant White bent over to kiss her outstretched, gloved hand. "A great pleasure to see you again, Miss Tuckett," he murmured.

Their eyes met but no one was close enough to see the electricity that flashed between them.

"The theater is at your complete disposal. The barracks across the street," he said, motioning with a hand, "have been prepared as quarters for you and your company. It lacks many of the conveniences afforded in Salt Lake City or San Francisco, but I hope you will find it comfortable enough."

"I'm sure it will be most satisfactory, Sergeant," Mercy Tuckett smiled, withdrawing her hand. "What of your company—the Military Dramatic Association—will we be intruding upon your rehearsal schedule?"

White flashed a wry grin. "We won't be using this building, Miss Tuckett. There are two smaller regimental halls where our company can perform. As for rehearsals—well frankly, our skits are largely impromptu and need little more than a couple of whiskeys to loosen up the men. Besides, now that the Mercy Tuckett Acting Troupe is on the post," he added gallantly, "there will be no audience left for any show the Fifth might put on."

"You are very gracious, Sergeant," Mercy said. "I wonder if you might find a few volunteers to move our baggage into the barracks—"

White flashed a quick smile. "Probably no more than ten men to a case."

At that moment, a young lieutenant rode up to the theater building. He dismounted and doffed his hat.

"On behalf of General Johnston," he said, addressing Mercy Tuckett, "you and the ladies of your company are invited to join the officers of Camp Floyd tonight at a dinner in your honor. Carriages will be sent, with officer escorts," the lieutenant added.

Mercy Tuckett gave the lieutenant a little curtsy. "Please convey our thanks to General Johnston, and tell him we are most pleased to accept his invitation."

The ring of soldiers looked at each other with glum expressions. The officers were staking their claim. About all an enlisted man could hope for now was a ticket to the performances—unless he got very, very lucky.

Fred and Ted Tate came to the barracks to visit Beryl an hour or so later. To the delight of her brothers, she introduced them to the young ladies in the troupe, although Mercy Tuckett had already left. Then they sat in the small anteroom at the entrance to the barracks and caught up with what was happening in their lives. Since they had not seen each other for several months, there was a lot to talk about.

Beryl told them about how excited she was to be an actress, and how much she was looking forward to performing at Camp Floyd, an engagement that probably would last until spring.

"Next summer, " she told them, "Mercy is going to California to give performances in Los Angeles and San Francisco. She's told me that if I continue to improve like I have, there's a chance she'll take me with her."

"That's what you want to be," Ted asked, "an actress?"

"Yes. I love it. I want to be famous—more famous than Mercy Tuckett—and travel all over. Maybe go back and perform on the stage in London—and Paris."

"We'll go with you," the twins said, almost in unison. "Heard a lot about the girls in France."

Beryl studied them. They hadn't said much about themselves so far, but she knew there were things they weren't telling her. She'd read their faces too long not to know when they were hiding something, or avoiding it.

"So what aren't you telling me?' she asked. "All you've said is you're both still working as civilians here at Camp Floyd. Even if the pay is as good as I hear, that won't get you to Paris. And what exactly have you heard about the girls in Paris, anyway?" she added, a mischievous smile twitching at her lips.

"We've been with a couple," Fred bragged, drawing a frown from his brother. "It's all right," he muttered at Ted, "Beryl's been married. She knows what I'm talking about."

Beryl's eyes widened. "You've been intimate with girls from Paris—is that what you're telling me?" she gasped.

"Whores in Frogtown come from all over," Fred started to explain, but Beryl gasped again.

"Whores—? You and Ted been with whores—?"

"See—you shouldn't have said nothing," Ted muttered sourly. He looked anxiously at his sister. "You won't tell mother—"

Beryl shook her head. "Of course not. She'd probably die on the spot." She studied her brothers more closely, seeing things on their faces she hadn't noticed before. They weren't boys anymore. It was in their eyes—the innocence was gone. More had happened to her brothers than just sleeping with French whores—although that was shock enough.

"So what's the rest of it?" she asked them. "And don't say nothing—I've watched you both telling lies to our parents for years."

"You got to promise not to tell them," Fred said, looking anxiously at her. "You cain't tell no one."

"I promise. You kept secrets for me."

"We got lots of money," Fred confided, his voice lowering as he looked around to make sure no one else had entered the room. "We could go back to England right now, if we wanted. First class cabin, even."

"But I don't ever want to go back," Ted hurriedly added. "Too much to see here in America."

"How did you get that much money?" Beryl asked, her own voice lowered by the looks of secrecy on her brothers' faces. "You didn't steal it, did you?"

"Not exactly," Fred muttered.

"You either stole it, or you didn't."

"We didn't steal the money," Ted told her. "It was paid to us—"

"—for stealin' cattle," Fred added.

Beryl's hand flew to her mouth. "That's rustling—"

"We ride with a gang, most about our own age," Ted said. "Only steal from the army, so nobody figures that's wrong."

"Of course it is," Beryl hissed. "You'll go to prison if you get caught—they can even hang you."

"Ain't going to get caught," Ted said defensively, "and besides, the army don't hang rustlers. Especially not kids like us."

"Besides," Fred added, "we ain't planning on stayin' in the rustling business much longer. We already got enough saved up to do anything we want."

Beryl leaned back in the chair, staring at her brothers. "Well, don't worry about me telling any of this. I'm not proud of my mistakes, but I'm scared to death about yours."

◆

The dinner honoring Mercy Tuckett and the other actresses went well, from the menu featuring venison, pheasant, beef roast, and apple pie, to the short musical program presented by a string quartet of officers, and by Mercy Tuckett singing an impromptu selection of three songs. After that, punch was served and everyone mingled, the largest crowd of admirers always swirling around the vivacious Mercy.

Carn Tregale was among the few civilians invited to attend the dinner, along with John and Elvira Carson, Captain Andy Miller, Sheriff Bill Coates, and the county tax collector, Jim Rodeback. Carn was on the trail between the governor's mansion and Camp Floyd almost constantly these days. Only Tregale and Philip Cooke knew the real reason behind all the traveling—Carn simply didn't want to go home and face Heather before he felt much more in command of his emotions than he did now. Cooke arranged for Carn to stay in guest quarters on the post, rather than risk finding the Carson Inn full, which happened frequently now that Camp Floyd was the destination for a steady stream of vendors and suppliers.

Carn chatted with Captain Miller, encouraged by the merchant's report of steadily increasing prosperity throughout the territory these days. With the threat of an Indian uprising apparently settled, people were eagerly seeking their share of the new wealth pouring into the Territory. Other dinner guests drifted over and joined the discussion.

"I hear Brigham Young is planning a lot of new settlements in the spring," Miller was saying. "Territory needs that kind of growth."

One of the officers standing in the group beside Miller gave an angry shake of his head. "Only thing coming out of that is trouble. We're barely holding those Indians in check, as it is—a whole bunch of them still off the San Pete reservation, even after being ordered back by their chiefs. They see white men taking more and more of their lands for these new settlements, and killing more of their game, and we'll have a war on our hands. You'd think Young could see that."

Colonel Cooke looked doubtful. "He's pretty friendly with the Indians, and they seem to respect him. I'm sure he thinks he can keep them in check."

"He didn't do so good last month when Arrowpeen broke loose—"

"Didn't need to," Cooke smiled, glancing at Carn. "Mr. Tregale took care of that ruckus all by himself."

Tregale lifted his good right hand in protest. "Nothing I did, Colonel. All Arrowpeen wanted was to save face after the death of his son."

"Well, all I want," Sheriff Coates muttered, "is for someone to figure out how to keep the peace in Frogtown."

"Believe Lord Nelson came up with the answer for that when he took on the Frenchies at Trafalgar," one of the officers grinned. "Put the glass up to his blind eye and didn't see defeat coming—so he won the battle."

"Yeah," Coates added sourly, "and died doin' it, as I remember. That ain't exactly what I got in mind. Don't know what it's going to take to bring law and order to that place, but I get the feelin' it's more'n just me."

"You can't change Frogtown," another officer said. "You want it cleaned up, you got to burn it down."

"Make my job a whole lot easier if someone did that," Jim Rodeback said. "Collecting taxes from those people is the same as asking to get your head blown off. I've been told outright that if I put foot into any of their establishments, best thing that will happen is me being tarred and feathered—either that, or getting shot."

"They're just bluffin' you, Rodeback—"

"Maybe they is, maybe they ain't. I don't aim to find out."

Miller grinned at Sheriff Coates. "Sounds like you need to give Rodeback some protection, Sheriff."

"Already told him I can't help—get us both killed. Hard cases, all of 'em. Just as soon shoot you as spit in your eye. Besides, they got a point when it comes down to it. County don't give no services nor benefits to Fairfield, so they don't feel obliged to pay for what they don't get."

"Does this mean I don't have to pay taxes anymore, Rodeback?" Miller asked. "Can't expect a man to pay when his neighbors don't do the same—"

"They will," Rodeback said grimly, "soon as the new tax collector gets here."

The men looked at Rodeback in surprise. "You stepping down, Rodeback?"

"Got me a transfer to Provo," Rodeback told them. "Got no stomach for bracing hard cases. The only way to collect taxes in Frogtown is at the point of a gun."

"This man who's taking your place," Sheriff Coates asked, "anybody I know?"

"Man's name is Richard Keith Johnston."

"No kin to the general, I hope," Coates grunted.

That brought several chuckles but the look that came over Miller's face hushed them.

"You know this Richard Keith Johnston?" Coates asked.

Miller nodded. "Better known on the frontier as Joaquin Johnston. Last I heard, he was in California. Tell you one thing, ain't nobody in Frogtown as hard a case as Joaquin."

"Does he travel outside the law—?"

"He makes his own law," Miller said. "Faster'n greased lighting with a gun, and I seen him kill a rabbit on the run by tossing a blade with either hand. Don't know how you picked him, Rodeback, but he'll collect your taxes. Only problem might be collecting them from Joaquin—"

That brought more chuckles. Carn spotted Beryl standing beside the punchbowl, chatting with two young lieutenants. Excusing himself from the group of men, Tregale crossed to her and nodded at the two officers.

"Hope you'll spare me a few minutes with this lovely young lady," he told them. "Know her family, and they'll be asking about her."

The officers smiled at Beryl. "We'll continue this conversation later, with your permission—"

Beryl smilingly nodded and the officers left. She clasped Carn's hand warmly. "I was hoping we'd get to talk. It's so good to see you, Brother Tregale—"

"Carn," Tregale smiled, glancing around. "Make it Carn. 'Brother' isn't too welcome a sound around here. Have you seen Fred and Ted yet? They're living in the civilian barracks—"

"They came to see me this afternoon." She studied Tregale's face, wondering how much he knew about what her brothers were doing. He saw her scrutiny and knew what was behind it.

"Don't worry too much about them," he told her softly. "They're good kids at heart. Don't think they'll run with that gang much longer."

"Then you know—"

"Important thing is, the army doesn't, not yet. But General Johnston is real upset about losing so much beef—he's going to be coming down hard on rustlers. Your brothers need to get out while they can."

"Will you talk to them—"

"Already have," Carn said quietly. "They listened, and I could tell it got through. I'll be real surprised if they stay around much longer."

She squeezed his arm gratefully. "We just never get through owing our lives to you, Brother Tregale—"

"Carn," he reminded. He stared curiously at her. "You liking this acting life, Beryl?"

"It's wonderful," she gushed. "I want to spend my whole life on the stage."

"Well, I'm looking forward to seeing your performance. Already got tickets for the first two nights—then I expect I'll be heading back to Salt Lake."

On an impulse, she took his hand again. "Would you do a favor for me, Bro—Carn?"

"Pleased to do it, Beryl, if I can."

"I've heard so much about Frogtown—or is it Fairfield?"

"Just call it Hell. That's close enough."

"Would you escort me there?" she asked. "I know Fred and Ted would take me, or one of these officers, but I'd feel much safer with you. Is that brash of me for asking?"

"If you're really set on seeing it," Tregale said, "I'd feel better if I was the one to show it to you. I have to warn you, though—it's not a place for nice young ladies. Frogtown only has a dark side."

"It sounds so exciting," Beryl said, her eyes flashing. "When is a good time to go?"

"How about tomorrow morning? I sure don't want to take you there at night."

"Wonderful. We don't start rehearsing until the afternoon." She paused, then glanced shyly up at him. "There's one more thing. If you see any French whores, would you point them out to me—"

Tregale picked up Beryl at the barracks about midmorning, using a carriage Philip Cooke provided, one used on occasion by General Johnston. At Beryl's pleading, Carn agreed to two of the other young actresses coming along. All were obviously excited at the prospect of visiting the infamous Frogtown.

Carn stopped first at the Carson Inn, where Elvira took time out from the kitchen to escort the three women through the first floor of the inn. The upstairs bedrooms were all occupied. When they climbed back into the carriage, the young ladies were wide-eyed.

"Did you know Billy Hickman is staying in that upstairs room?" Beryl said to Tregale, pointing to the corner room. "He's that killer everyone talks about."

Carn nodded. "Met Mr. Hickman—in fact, he saved my life not too long ago. He's staying in General Johnston's room, as the Carsons call it. Used to stay there myself, until Colonel Cooke provided quarters for me on the post."

"You know Billy Hickman?" one of the other actresses queried. "I hear you can actually see fire in his eyes—"

Tregale chuckled. "Well, they look pretty fierce but I wouldn't say there was any fire. Although I can see how they'd frighten some."

"Is he really a killer—?"

"He's killed some," Tregale shrugged. "Killed three for sure. Those were teamsters who drew down on me and General Galloway. Three clean shots to the heart—that's all Billy needed."

"Why do you think he's here?" Beryl asked.

"Well, there's lots of gambling and loose women here," Tregale answered, "and he recently bought a big ranch in the south end of Cedar Valley. Billy calls Frogtown home now."

Tregale picked up the reins and the carriage continued down Front Street. He couldn't help smiling at the expressions that crossed the faces of the three young women as they passed the parade of saloons and brothels, and saw the dozens of drunks sprawled on sidewalks and street, sleeping off last night's revelry. Some scantily clad women were grouped outside a run-down building, a sign proclaiming it as Polly's Place of Passion. Tregale pointed out the prostitutes to his passengers.

"Don't know if they're from France, Beryl," he told her, "but there's no doubt about how they earn a living."

"It seems so sad," Beryl breathed, staring at the prostitutes. "It must be a horrible life."

"Most choose it for themselves," Tregale told them. "They'd rather do what they're doing than slave over a hot stove for a husband and a brood of kids. Some did that before they came here. It's sad, true enough."

"Do they make a lot of money?" another of the young actresses asked, still fascinated by the prostitutes. The whores saw the women in the carriage staring at them and started to wave, calling out loud and coarse invitations, and beckoning them over to Polly's Place. All three of the young ladies shuddered.

"That's so dreadful!"

Beryl glanced up at Tregale. "Do they—?" she asked, repeating the question from her companion, "Do they make much money?" She glanced at the other young women and shrugged. "I know it's rude, but I'm curious."

This time it was Tregale's turn to shrug. "I'm no expert, happy to say," he told them, "but I don't think they do. They're bought and sold and they're pretty much slaves to whoever owns them. Some get to keep the tips—some don't."

"Bought and sold?" Beryl gasped. "How much—?"

Tregale smothered a grin. The subject obviously was intensely interesting to all three of his passengers. "I'm told the going price is a hundred dollars. Now," he added seriously, "if any of you ladies are interested, I could do some bargaining for you—"

They stared at him in horror, then realized he was joking. All three broke into nervous laughter.

"Makes my skin crawl just thinking about it!" Beryl muttered.

Tregale took them the length of Front Street, then turned around and started back toward the Carson Inn, this time urging the horse into a trot.

"Hope you ladies saw enough drunks and whores to get an idea what Frogtown is all about," he said. "Don't advise going into any of the places we passed. What you can't see, you can imagine—only it's worse than anything you picture in your mind, I guarantee."

Tregale saw Captain Miller walking along the sidewalk, just outside his emporium, and the merchant hailed him. Tregale pulled over and stopped. Miller had met the young ladies the night before at the General's dinner party, and nodded politely.

"Wonder if you might step into the store for a moment, Mr. Tregale," Miller said. "Something I want to show you. Ackley's inside, and he can keep an eye on these lovely young ladies."

Suddenly Billy Hickman swaggered out the open door of the Miller emporium, holding a heavily-rouged, gaudily-dressed young woman on each arm. He smiled in recognition as he saw Tregale.

"Mr. Tregale. You're in Cedar these days almost as much as me."

Tregale nodded. "You're right. Spending more time than I'm comfortable with."

Hickman's deep-set, dark eyes swept the young ladies in the carriage, who were staring at him in wide-eyed wonder.

"Bet these ladies is part of that acting troupe that's performing at the post theater—"

"They are," Tregale said, not bothering with introductions. Hickman did, though. He looked from one to the other of the women accompanying him.

"This here's Mimi," he said, more to the girls in the carriage than to Tregale, "and this is Fifi."

"Bon jour," the one called Mimi said.

"C'est magnifique," Fifi murmured, openly admiring Tregale up and down.

"Sounds like you ladies come from France," Tregale murmured, glancing at an awestruck Beryl.

"Direct from Paris," Hickman said. "These French ladies know things no ordinary—well, let's say ladies get a broader education in Paris than frontier women do."

Tregale decided the young actresses had seen—and heard—enough. He tipped his hat to the French whores. "Pleased to meet you, Mimi—Fifi. And good to see you again, Billy." As an afterthought, he added. "I hear Ferguson is going to trial soon. You think you can get him off? Seems like a lot of people saw him gun down Carpenter in cold blood."

"Not true. Clear case of self defense," Hickman replied. "Don't expect it will ever get to a jury. Poor Ferguson is an innocent victim of Carpenter's friends. They're lying, and I'll prove it. Good day to you all."

Hickman and his two whores started walking toward the Carson Inn. Tregale couldn't help wondering how the religiously strict Elvira Carson was dealing with that situation. He was sure John Carson had already pointed out the reputation of his guest, but allowing prostitutes into the inn would be the hardest concession Elvira had made in her whole life. And somehow, Tregale thought to himself, General Johnston's room would never be the same.

"Somebody's going to brace that man one of these days," Miller said, staring after Hickman. "Sure won't be me, though."

The two men entered Miller's emporium, and moments later, Richard Ackley came out and stood beside the door. He nodded at the ladies in the carriage but didn't say anything.

Beryl and her companions started talking and giggling amongst themselves, sharing opinions about what they had seen in this place of sin. They looked up as a man stopped beside the carriage. He looked admiringly at the young actresses.

"You must be some of those actresses just come to Camp Floyd. I'm Young Nelson—John Young Nelson is my given name, but everybody calls me Young Nelson."

Nelson looked reasonably respectable, at least by Frogtown standards. He was clean-shaven, his shirt and pants rumpled but clean, and he looked pleasant enough. His manner was undoubtedly polite. Watching from the doorway, Ackley made no move. He knew Nelson, and wasn't concerned about the safety of the ladies.

Nelson pointed over his shoulder at one of the saloons on the south side of the street. "That's my place," he said proudly. "Don't own it outright yet, but I will once the pay train gets in from California. Got me eighteen months back pay coming, and it's all going into Nelson's Parlor and Gaming Emporium—that's what I'm going to call it, once I own it."

Beryl and the other young ladies had been staring at him, not saying anything—not being able to say anything, for that matter. Nelson was smiling directly at Beryl Tate.

"Hope you don't mind me saying this, young lady, but I find you amazingly beautiful." His glance quickly took in her three companions. "All of you is beautiful. Never seen so many finely beautiful young ladies in one spot before."

"Don't try nothin', Nelson," Ackley growled from the doorway.

"Just telling these young ladies how beautiful they are," Nelson said. He put both hands on the side of carriage, leaning a little closer toward Beryl. "If you ladies don't mind, I got a proposition to make to you—"

"That's enough, Nelson," Ackley grunted warningly, straightening. "These ain't those kind of ladies—"

"It ain't that kind of proposition," Nelson said quickly. He looked directly at Beryl. "It's plain from looking that you all are ladies of refinement, and no doubt, talented in what you do, or you wouldn't be in Mercy Tuckett's troupe."

"This leadin' somewhere, Nelson?" Ackley asked.

"I'm offering these ladies employment," Nelson said, now staring pointedly at Beryl. "Especially you, ma'am."

Beryl stiffened haughtily. "I'm sure none of us would be interested in any employment you have to offer, Mr. Nelson."

"Just hear me out," Nelson said, glancing up at Ackley. "These ladies is safe with me. You know that, Ackley."

"Better be," Ackley grunted. He relaxed and leaned back against the doorpost.

Nelson addressed the young ladies again. "Like I said, I'll be owning that saloon free and clear soon as the army pays what it owes me. But I don't want it to be just another saloon filled with gamblers and whores. I want my place to be respectable—"

"Hard to make a saloon respectable, isn't it, Mr. Nelson—?" Beryl said, giving Young Nelson a disparaging look.

"No, ma'am," Nelson said quickly. "There's going to be nothing but honest games in my place, and no whores stripping down for entertainment. I plan on having something no other place in Frogtown has got."

"And what would that be?" Beryl asked.

"High class entertainment. Going to put me in a stage, and have real actresses like yourselves putting on real theater plays."

Interested despite herself, Beryl stared curiously at the soon-to-be saloonkeeper—well, parlor keeper, if there was any difference. "That would indeed be different," she said, "from what I've heard about the saloons in Frogtown."

"Won't be no place like it," Nelson said proudly. "Might rub off on the whole town—and this place sure needs liftin' out of the mud."

"That's your proposition," one of the girls asked, "coming to work in your saloon?"

"Won't be just a saloon," Nelson corrected, "and you wouldn't be no working girls, not like all the others in town. You'd be respected, and well protected. And you certainly wouldn't be expected to do nothin' but act on the stage."

At that moment, Tregale came out of the store. He took in Nelson standing beside the carriage, and glanced at Ackley.

"No problems, Mr. Tregale," the burly ex-teamster said. "Young Nelson was just talking to the ladies."

Nelson tipped his hat toward Tregale, then smiled at the ladies in the carriage. "Think about it, ladies. Remember, Young Nelson— that's me. I'll be in touch again, after that pay train gets in."

Carn found an urgent message from Colonel Cooke waiting for him in his quarters when he finished returning Beryl and her friends to the barracks and the carriage to the stables. He went straight to the administration complex and was admitted to Cooke's office.

The colonel rose to shake hands, a worried look on his face. "Got to ask you to head back to Salt Lake this morning, Carn."

"Sounds like trouble."

Cooke gave a despairing shake of his head. "Those people back in Washington seem determined to make life difficult."

"What did they do now?"

"Something that won't sit well with the Mormons."

Carn grinned. "Nothing Washington does, nor what the army does here at Camp Floyd, sits well with the Mormons."

"Courier arrived a couple hours ago carrying word that a new directive is being issued in Washington. Grazing lands in Cedar, Rush, Tintic and Goshen valleys are being confiscated by the government. Local ranchers will have to move their herds somewhere else, because those valleys will be restricted military reservations."

Tregale frowned. "There's no place to move them, Philip."

"Already told that to General Johnston. You know how he is about following orders—and you know as well as I do, he's going to enjoy enforcing this one. We're looking at trouble, Carn."

"Count on it," Carn grunted, pulling out a chair and sitting down. "Those ranchers won't be run off their grazing lands. That's been public domain ever since the Territory was organized."

"We won't be getting official notice to activate that order for at least a couple of months. There's time to work out a compromise," Cooke said. "But Governor Cummings and Brigham Young should be notified without delay."

"Will the general accept a compromise?" Tregale asked, giving his friend a doubtful look. "I agree with what you said earlier—I can see General Johnston relishing giving the Mormons this kind of trouble." He frowned. "I can see him requesting an order like that, for that matter."

"He still hates Mormons," Cooke agreed, "but we have all the problems we can handle. If those young bucks aren't willing to spend the winter on the reservation, you can expect they'll be raising hell come spring. And we'll have to re-open the California trails, which won't be easy. We don't need a fight with the settlers over grazing land on top of that—if a solution can be worked out, Johnston will accept it, like it or not."

Tregale stood up, reached into his pocket and tossed a couple of tickets onto the colonel's desk.

"Seems I won't be needing these," he grimaced. "Look up Beryl Tate for me and tell her it's your fault I didn't get to see her performance."

CHAPTER TWENTY

CAMP FLOYD
MID-DECEMBER

The stagecoach from Salt Lake City pulled up in front of the Carson inn, the wheels splattering mud toward the small group of people standing beside the fence. They backed away as steam rose in clouds from the team of four horses, gushing in labored breaths from flared nostrils, heat and sweat meeting the cold December air.

The door of the coach opened and a dapper looking man stepped down, grimacing as he stepped carefully through the mud pooled in front of the gate. The man was not much over five and a half feet, slender, wearing a long black coat, dusty and wrinkled from his journey. Under the coat was a plain black shirt, buttoned at the collar, with a narrow black cravat. Black corduroy trousers were tucked into the tops of shined black boots. But the most notable thing a person's eyes went to were the silver-handled Colt revolvers slung outside the coat at each hip. They looked like they belonged there, as much a part of the man as arms and legs.

After the guns, you fixed your gaze on the man's face: thin, with high cheek bones and a ribbon of black mustache drooping an inch or two at each side of a slash of thin, colorless lips. The complexion hinted of Spanish blood, but not the features. The man's nationality was difficult to decide, mainly because there was too much coldness in the set of that face to stare too long.

Then there were the eyes. Black and bright, moving constantly, set wide apart under dark, thin eyebrows and a brow without wrinkles.

Those eyes gave the impression of seeing everything, every second, in every direction. If nothing else about the man made a stranger uncomfortable, the eyes did. Somehow, a look became a threat.

Jim Rodeback stepped forward as the man reached the gate. "You Richard Keith Johnston?"

The man in black nodded. "And who might you be?"

"Jim Rodeback. I'm the man you're replacing."

"Don't seem like too big a chore," the man said coldly.

Rodeback ignored the insult. Those eyes were set full on him, piercing into him, and Rodeback was suddenly nervous and uncomfortable. The man could say what he wanted, Rodeback thought. Fifteen more minutes and Frogtown was out of his life forever.

"Got some papers to turn over," he told Johnston, his voice now not even trying to be friendly. "You got any questions, I'll try and answer them. After that, I'm riding out of here."

"Just give me the papers, Rodeback. From what I was told, you don't have answers I'd be interested in."

That was it, Rodeback decided. Johnston obviously wasn't interested in anything he had to say. Let the man find out for himself, and the devil take Johnston and Frogtown.

"Made you reservations here at the inn," Rodeback said curtly. "Papers are on your bed. Good day to you, sir."

With that, Rodeback turned and strode back into the inn to gather his already packed saddlebags. Minutes later, he was heading south down Cedar Valley, vowing never to return to this god-forsaken hole, and enjoying the mental pictures of Richard Keith Johnston walking into the first saloon and asking to collect taxes owed.

Rodeback would have fallen off his horse if he'd known Johnston had walked into that first saloon not three hours after arriving in Frogtown. The saloon owner was pointed out to him, and he walked over to the table where the man was sitting with two companions.

"You Bull Graham?" Johnston asked.

"Who wants to know?"

"Me."

"You got a name?"

"Johnston. Friends call me Joaquin Johnston. You better call me Mister Johnston."

There was something in the cold self assurance of the man confronting him that brought warning prickles to the back of Graham's neck. His glance slid to his two companions, reassured by the belligerence he saw on their faces.

"And you can call me Mister Graham. What business you got with me, Joaquin?" he asked, deliberately emphasizing the use of the man's first name.

"Taxes, Bull. We can call each other by first names, I guess, since this is a friendly enough visit."

"Don't owe no taxes, Joaquin. Just ask that pipsqueak Rodeback."

"Rodeback's gone. And I got papers that say you owe two hundred and twenty three dollars in back taxes. I'm here to collect it, Bull—now."

"You a tax collector, or sumpin'?" Graham growled.

"I'm THE tax collector, Bull. And I ain't no pipsqueak."

"And I ain't paying no taxes—"

Both of Graham's companions went for their guns. A revolver leapt into the right hand of Johnston and bullets ripped into the hearts of both men. At the same time, a knife jumped into Johnston's left hand, and it was pressing hard now under the chin of Bull Graham.

"Those men was resisting taxes," Johnston hissed into Graham's ear. "They're dead legal-like, and you can bet the sheriff's on my side. Only question now is, you giving me that money, or do I kill you and sell this saloon for taxes owed."

It was an easy choice for Bull Graham.

Once the story of Joaquin Johnston's method of collecting taxes spread around, a whole lot of other people decided they owed taxes after all. In fact, it only took Johnston two months to collect every cent owed the county. And once people found out Joaquin was a player as well as an enforcer, a man willing to sit down at a game— and usually win—and pay for the best whores in town, and a man who, despite his size, could drink any teamster under the table, Joaquin became the most popular man in town, tax collector or not.

General Albert Johnston, however, was close to becoming the most unpopular man in the whole territory. Word spread that the army was going to enforce the seizure of all public domain grazing lands in nearby valleys, throwing all private herds off the now official military reservations. It brought people to the boiling point, whether they owned cattle or not. This was invasion of rights—usurpation of rights—and it would not be tolerated.

That was certainly the opinion of Daniel Spencer, owner of a large herd that had grazed in Rush Valley for the past eight years, now sitting in General Johnston's office gripping a notice that his "grazing privileges" had been revoked.

He was staring angrily at both General Johnston and Colonel Smith, sitting stiffly across the table from him. There were three other people in the room, Spencer's nephew, Howard, who ran the herd in Rush Valley, Colonel Philip Cooke, and Carn Tregale, a man Spencer was told was friendly to the Mormons—might even be a Mormon himself. Spencer wasn't sure about that.

Introductions were made all around, formally and with no warmth of friendship. Everyone knew this was not a friendly meeting.

"I asked Mr. Tregale to be here," General Johnston explained, "because he has direct access to Governor Cummings, as well as Brigham Young. I want to assure you a full and impartial account of this meeting will be reported to them as soon as possible by Mr. Tregale."

"You on the army payroll, Mr. Tregale?" young Howard Spencer asked.

Tregale quickly shook his head. "I have no sides in this, Mr. Spencer, if that's your concern. And no, I draw no compensation from the army. Whatever is said here today, you can be sure my report to Governor Cummings will be accurate, complete, and unvarnished."

"Pleased to hear that, Mr. Tregale," the elder Spencer said. "Only natural to be concerned about what goes outside this room."

Colonel Smith bristled. "Are you accusing the General and myself of being untruthful, Mr. Spencer?"

"Don't know you well enough to jump to that conclusion," Spencer snapped back, "but it don't take nobody brilliant to know we're viewing this seizure of our land from a whole different perspective than you gentlemen, Colonel."

"We are not seizing your land, Mr. Spencer," Smith said coldly. "That land was public domain and it is now declared a military reservation."

"We been using it almost since settlers first came to the Great Salt Lake," Howard Spencer retorted. "It ain't nobody's land, and we got a right to graze our herds on it."

"You don't have that right, Mr. Spencer, not any more," the Colonel said. He nodded at the paper in the hand of the elder Spencer. "Those lands are now army property."

"We ain't moving our cattle out of Rush Valley—"

"Your privilege, Mr. Spencer. But if you don't, our soldiers will."

"Gentlemen," Colonel Cooke interrupted, "reason we're here is to talk out the situation and see if we can come up with a solution to the problem—a problem we all share, I might add. This order came from Washington, remember, not from Camp Floyd."

"It's the soldiers from Camp Floyd who've been causing all the trouble in Rush Valley," Daniel Spencer said firmly.

"What kind of trouble, Mr. Spencer?" Johnston asked.

"Those soldiers you got stationed in the north end of Rush Valley—for the life of me, I don't know why—they've been butchering my cattle."

"Didn't know that," Johnston muttered. "I'd be upset about that, if it was me. You tally how many beef they butchered, Mr. Spencer, and I'll see you're fully compensated."

Both Spencers looked at each other, knowing there was no argument against such a fair offer. Daniel Spencer nodded approval.

"Fair enough, General. But butchering cattle ain't all. Those soldiers of yours been tearing down my fences, even tore down one of my barns. I know it's cold, and hard to find wood in all that snow out there, but that ain't no excuse to burn my fences and buildings."

"Sounds like a fair complaint," Colonel Smith told him. "You deserve compensation for that, too. Submit a bill, Mr. Spencer."

Again the Spencers looked at each other. This was going too easy.

"You guarantee to keep your men from repeating those offenses?" Daniel asked.

General Johnston straightened in his chair, clasped both hands together on the table, and fastened Spencer with frowning firmness. "No, Mr. Spencer, I will not give you such a guarantee. You are trespassing on government property and you are breaking several other laws. I want you and your cattle off that reservation. Do I make myself clear, Mr. Spencer?"

Howard Spencer glared at the general. "We ain't breaking no laws—"

"Let me enumerate them, Mr. Spencer," Johnston shot back. Both Cooke and Smith could tell how angry the general was, although the Spencers had no gauge for that. "First, you have constructed permanent buildings on that land against orders specifically forbidding you to do that. Second, you not only are running your own herds on that land, but you are also grazing livestock for commercial freighters—again, strictly against orders. Third, you have turned that log cabin you built—a bunkhouse, as you describe it— into something far more illegal."

Again the younger Spencer protested. "That ain't so, General—"

"Yes it is, Mr. Spencer," Johnston snapped. "That log cabin now serves as a distillery, a tavern, and a resort for rustlers and horse thieves."

Daniel Spencer shot an accusing glare at his nephew. "That ain't true, is it, Howard? You distilling whiskey out there?"

"Course not. Don't know where they come up with that. Our hands bunk there, and nobody else. They see men comin' and goin', that's who it is."

"Nobody else—you sure of that, Howard?"

"Well, maybe a friend or two drop in now and then. Purely social, and they don't stay."

"Don't like to call a man a liar, Mr. Spencer," General Johnston said thinly, "but you're not presenting true facts. That cabin is a tavern, where you keep two young Indian girls to entertain guests. To my frustration, my men have bought those women, and purchased whiskey made on the premises. The man who told them it was home brew, Mr. Spencer, was you. Wouldn't deny it, if I was you." He glanced apologetically at the elder Spencer, who was angrily glowering at his nephew. "Sorry to dip into family matters, Mr. Spencer, but this young man left me no choice. Reports seem clear you were not a party to this."

Daniel Spencer finally looked away from his nephew, who was avoiding eye contact. Howard didn't look contrite, just bitter. Daniel gave the general a questioning frown.

"Take your word that this goes deeper than I knew," Spencer told him, "and those shenanigans is over, as of right now. But we still have the main matter in front of us—will you get this order changed, or at least delay it until we can come up with some other place to run our herds? I'm talking now for all the ranchers in all the valleys you confiscated."

Johnston looked at Colonel Smith, then over to Colonel Cooke. All the men in the room could see how deeply he was churning over question and answer. Finally, he leaned back in his chair, staring directly at Daniel Spencer.

"I'll write to Washington, Mr. Spencer, and see if the order can be changed. Don't hold out much hope for it, but you can keep your herds grazing until I get a final answer. That's the best I can do, sir."

The elder Spencer stood up and leaned over the table, extending his hand.

"More than fair, General. All of us ranchers appreciate it deeply. When might we expect that answer?"

"This is winter, and I suspect there's going to be a lot of questions going back and forth between here and Washington. Probably spring at the earliest, I'd hazard."

Again Spencer shook his hand. "That gives us time to find some place to move the herds, if it comes to that. Surely do hope it doesn't though. People feel mighty aggravated about this, General."

"I'm aware of that, Mr. Spencer. Let's hope an amicable solution can be found."

The Spencers left, Daniel walking stiffly ahead of his nephew. When they got back home would be a better time to get into what young Howard had been doing in Rush Valley.

Sergeant Pike was standing just outside the administration building as the Spencers were leaving. Howard saw him, decided to vent some frustration, and deliberately bumped hard into the sergeant. Pike stumbled and fell to his knees.

Pike got quickly to his feet and reached out to grab Spencer's arm. He whirled him around and shoved his face close to him. "Tell me you was sorry about that," Pike hissed.

"I ain't sorry," Spencer growled back, "and if you don't let go of my arm, you won't be getting up the next time I put you down."

"You got a name, or did they find you under a rock?"

"Name is Spencer. Howard Spencer."

"I'm First Sergeant Ralph Pike, Company I, Tenth Infantry. You got yourself a mean enemy, Howard Spencer."

"I ain't shakin' over it, sergeant."

"And I ain't forgettin' you. Hope we meet again, Howard Spencer, somewhere more private."

"Any time, any place, sergeant."

The two men glared at each other, then Pike dropped his grip on the other man's arm. Spencer wheeled away and went to catch up with his uncle.

Shortly after sundown, the cold mellowed a few degrees in Cedar Valley as the clouds moved in. It started to snow, large flakes swirling in changing patterns as the wind gusted uncertainly in different directions.

In Rush Valley, however, the wind and the snow slashed a clear, cold path from north to south. It was snowing so heavily that the group of eight riders making their way toward the north end of Rush could hardly be made out more than fifty yards away. The riders stayed close, keeping their mounts at a lope, heads huddled down into pulled-up coat collars and pulled-down hat brims.

Fred Tate, riding next to his brother, peered at the rider who came up alongside him. It was Rod Swazey, the youth in charge of this gang of young rustlers.

"We goin' through with this, Rod?" Fred shouted, trying to make himself heard over the wind. "Ain't no weather to be driving cattle."

"Soldiers won't be expectin' no trouble," Swazey yelled, "and they ain't going to be eager to chase us. It's good weather, Fred, for what we're about."

"How far away is the herd?"

"Less than a mile now. Keep your eyes open."

Swazey kicked heels into the flanks of his horse and rode ahead of the rest of the gang. He seemed to know where he was going, so the others just kept their heads down and loped after him. It wasn't long before they saw him pull up, raising a hand in warning to the rest of them.

"The herd is just over the next rise," he told them, speaking as low as he could and still be heard. "Rode out here yesterday to get the lay of the land. Soldiers is a half-mile away, in that stone hut they built. With the wind blowin' the way it is, good chance they won't hear nothin'. We cut out a hundred head and start drivin' south. Then we cross over into Cedar and on down toward the southern end of Utah lake. We'll be met there and the cattle taken off our hands."

"What if we run into Billy Hickman's crowd down in Cedar. There's a bunch of his boys stayin' at that new ranch of his—"

"Drown already told Billy some night riders would be passing through. Hickman won't give us no trouble. Only thing we got to worry about is cutting out our cattle without rousin' none of those soldier boys."

They almost did it. The cattle were right where Swazey said they would be, unguarded. Swazey was probably right again when he said the soldiers would be huddled in that stone hut, trying to keep warm, not really caring if the cattle strayed or got stolen. All they wanted was to get through this miserable week of guard duty and return to the warmth and comfort of their barracks.

The hundred head were cut out and turned into the south, and everyone was feeling good—until a lone outrider appeared out of the storm. No one could see the man's face, but his whole body jerked erect in the saddle, as surprised to see the night riders as they were to see him. If the soldier had just turned and started riding for help, nothing would have changed. By the time the other soldiers got horses saddled and mounted, the rustlers would be long gone. But the guard didn't make the right choice. Instead, he pulled his carbine out from under his slicker and started charging toward the rustlers. He made another mistake in not firing off some rounds to sound an alarm. His last mistake was charging toward the nearest rider, who happened to be Rod Swazey.

Swazey let the soldier get close. When the carbine started to lift into firing position, the youth squeezed the trigger of the revolver in his hand, and kept squeezing it until all six bullets were fired. They all heard the soldier cry out as his arms flew up and he tumbled backwards off his horse.

Swazey rode over to the man sprawled in the snow, swinging out of the saddle to get a closer look. He stood up as others rode up to see for themselves.

"He's cashed out," Swazey told them. "Don't think nobody heard the shots, but maybe they did. Take his horse and get that herd on the run. If it snows heavy enough, they might not find his body before spring. They'll put him down as a deserter."

Ted Tate was staring at the dead soldier. "You gunned him down, Rod," he said, disbelief in his voice and on his face. "We just killed a soldier."

"It was him or us," Swazey snapped. "Don't make nothin' different. Soldiers get paid to take chances on gettin' killed."

"But we ain't just rustlers any more," Ted said, still staring at the dead soldier. "We're killers. We could all get hung for this."

"Nobody's goin' to get hung," Swazey said testily, "not unless we stay around yappin' all night. Start ridin', Tate. We got a long way to go before daylight."

CHAPTER TWENTY ONE

SALT LAKE CITY

T his verdict is an affront to justice, an insult to this court, and a decision that shames the judicial process in this Territory."

Judge Charles C. Sinclair banged his gavel hard on the table, glaring at the nearly two dozen members of the Grand Jury, his face showing anger and frustration.

"You have proved once again that Mormon society does not deserve to be part of the States of America. You have done great harm this day, gentlemen. This far-from-Grand Jury is dismissed."

The Associate Justice of the Utah Territorial Supreme Court once again banged the gavel, making no attempt to conceal his disgust as he looked at the defendants sitting in the second row of chairs in the crowded basement of the Social Hall. In Sinclair's opinion, the case against James Ferguson, Brigham Young, and the Mormon populace as a whole had been adequately, though perhaps not brilliantly, documented—certainly well enough not to allow the sweeping dismissal that had just been handed down. Not one single indictment, after all the evidence presented. Sinclair's mind searched for some way to punish this jury, realizing nothing could legally be done about the travesty. It was bitterly galling.

For a brief moment, he let his anger settle on the portly figure of Governor Cummings, sitting in the front row of benches. It was inexcusable that a federal official supported the Mormons so strongly, as also had the man sitting next to him, U.S. Attorney Alexander Wilson. Both these men had opposed Sinclair at every step in bringing this Grand Jury into session. Sinclair promised himself that he would investigate that matter when the opportunity was presented. He was convinced both men must be involved either in bribery or illegal conspiracy. There must be some reason the two were so friendly with these accursed Mormons.

James Ferguson, the main defendant in the multifaceted case presented to the Grand Jury, rose to his feet. Ferguson was a big man, imposing in demeanor and stature, comfortably wearing the mantle of authority of Adjutant General of the Nauvoo Legion. Ferguson was also a lawyer, the man who two years ago had confronted the former Associate Justice George P. Stiles and sent him fleeing back to Washington in fear of his life. Stiles' exaggerated array of charges had just been used by Sinclair to present his own anti-Mormon agenda.

"Judge Sinclair," Ferguson said, glaring icily at the Justice, "since this court is now dismissed, what I'm about to say cannot be considered contempt—although I assure you, that is exactly what it is."

Sinclair also came to his feet. "Be careful, Ferguson. Your slander case against Judge Stiles may have been dismissed, but I will not hesitate to bring one of my own."

Ferguson glanced down at the man seated next to him. The Grand Jury hearings had continued throughout the week, but the subpoena issued by Sinclair demanded Brigham Young's attendance only on this last scheduled day. Most observers felt Sinclair intended to use testimony from the former governor as a forceful conclusion to his case. Somewhat surprisingly, Brigham Young had not been called to testify. Throughout the day's proceedings, the Mormon leader sat mostly silent, except for a few whispered comments either to Ferguson or Heber C. Kimball, sitting on his other side. Dressed in a dark suit, Brigham Young held his hat in his lap, a dark silk handkerchief tied about his head. The huge basement of the Social Hall was drafty, despite it being crowded from wall to wall with spectators. Word that Governor Young, as he would be forever and affectionately known throughout the Territory, had agreed to attend the Grand Jury session caused widespread excitement. This was the first time the Mormon leader had left the confines of his South Temple estate in nearly seven months, ever since General Albert Johnston marched his troops through the city.

"Say what you got to say, Brother Ferguson," Brigham Young murmured. "Just remember, the more you stir a manure pile, the worse it stinks."

Ferguson looked again at Judge Sinclair. "Sir, you have presented a list of charges against me, Governor Young, the Mormon Church, and just about every God-fearing person residing in this Territory—"

"Every single charge was well founded—"

"Not so, sir," Ferguson retorted. "Every single charge was dismissed."

"By a jury of Mormons—"

"Eleven persons on that jury were not Mormons—"

"And twelve of them were," Sinclair added testily. "Do you have something to say to this Court, Mr. Ferguson—?"

"Not to the Court," Ferguson said pointedly. "That is no longer in session. What I have to say is addressed to you, sir."

"Once again I remind you—" Sinclair began, but Ferguson waved a hand in dismissal of what the Justice was about to say.

"I resent your accusation that injustice was done here today. Justice prevailed, sir. The fact that no indictments resulted from the charges these lawyers of the Court presented," Ferguson said, glancing at the half dozen lawyers seated facing the spectators, "proves the fact that all were groundless. I did not threaten the life of George Stiles, although as was brought out during the hearings, I did point out some illegal actions he'd taken and made a recommendation that he return to Washington. There was no slander, because only the truth was spoken. Neither was there was any attempt to commit fraud against postal regulations. There was no obstruction of justice, no attempt to cover up murders you shamelessly accuse Governor Young of ordering. And not one person in this Territory, especially Governor Young, committed any act of treason. We Mormons love our country, sir, despite the fact we have been persecuted and hounded and driven out of it. We believe this to be a holy land, preserved by God Almighty for His people."

Sinclair's eyes narrowed. Perhaps this arrogant Mormon had just made a mistake that could be used in a court of law. "Are you claiming America belongs to the Mormons, sir?"

"All Americans are His people," Ferguson quickly retorted. "Even you are one of God's children, Judge." The disdain in Ferguson's voice made the intended insult very clear, but Sinclair decided to press the earlier point.

"If there was no treason, why did you people accept the pardon granted by Buchanan—an unconscionable act by the President, I might add."

"To avoid bloodshed, sir. If you read the articles of the Peace Treaty, you will find it clearly states we believe no acts were committed that require pardoning, but Governor Young accepted it in order to bring a peaceable end to the conflict—a conflict we were not responsible for initiating."

"We have heard these arguments," Sinclair said irritably. "I'm tired of hearing you people claim to be persecuted simply because you were granted amnesty. If I have my way, sir, that pardon will be revoked in the halls of Congress. Then we'll see what indictments a proper Grand Jury brings against you Mormons."

There was a swell of angry murmurs from the crowd of several hundred spectators as Sinclair voiced his feelings. Sinclair couldn't help giving a nervous glance about the hall. Most of these people were armed and belligerently protective of their prophet. Any one of them could be provoked into killing, he thought, especially those sitting in the row directly behind Brigham Young and the other top Mormon leaders. Marshal Dotson had warned him before the proceedings began that Billy Hickman and several other men believed to be Danites were in attendance.

The Danites were reputed to be responsible for several murders back in the States, persons believed to have wronged the Mormons but escaped official retribution. While the existence of the avenging order was strongly denied, there was no doubting there was a band of men fiercely loyal and sworn to protect the "Lion of the Lord." Sinclair saw the black-bearded man sitting almost directly behind

Brigham Young, saw his deep-set dark eyes, the set of anger on his swarthy face, and was willing to bet this was Billy Hickman, outlaw and killer—and most recently, attorney-at-law. No doubt Brigham Young was responsible for that. Hickman reportedly had a personal friendship with the Mormon leader that went back to the days of Illinois and Missouri. Sinclair wished that some day he could get Hickman on the stand and question him under oath. The jurist was confident that would bring some dark deeds into the light of day. He turned his attention back to the Mormon lawyer confronting him.

"You people have hidden behind the amnesty you profess was forced upon you," he said harshly. "I find that repugnant, sir, as I do this whole week's proceedings."

"There can be no crime if amnesty has been declared," Ferguson replied, his voice strident with the anger inside him. "You knew that before you insisted on bringing this Grand Jury into existence. Even if evidence of crimes had been presented—and none was—the jury did what it was obligated to do under the law."

A sneer crossed the face of Sinclair. "I hardly consider the men of that jury qualified to interpret the law."

"The law was interpreted by your own lawyers, sir," Ferguson said. "Perhaps they are the ones not qualified."

"Are you questioning the credentials of the state's prosecutors, sir?"

"I am not aware of their credentials. Do they have any?"

Dark fury gathered on Sinclair's face. "That is contempt of this court, Mr. Ferguson."

"It's a question, sir, in response to a doubt you yourself raised."

"Do not misrepresent my words, Ferguson—"

Ferguson could see nothing more could be gained. He had made his point that no wrong had been done by members of the jury. He couldn't expect Sinclair to relent from his hatred of Mormons.

"I have nothing further to say, sir."

Later that afternoon, Cummings and his wife hosted a tea at the former Staines mansion for those who had been the primary targets of Judge Sinclair, along with other civic dignitaries. The Governor planned to move into the old Babbitt estate, near the residence of

Brigham Young on South Temple, in a month or so, after renovations were completed. The Staines mansion would continue to serve as official Territorial headquarters.

Brigham Young attended the tea, looking tired, his string tie slightly askew, his suit badly wrinkled, but giving a warm smile to everyone who shook his hand. This was his first social function outside his own home in those long seven months, a gesture of appreciation for the support the new governor had rendered. Jim Ferguson was there, of course, along with Church leaders Heber Kimball, Daniel Wells, and George Smith. Mayor Smoot came, and several members of the city council. General Galloway and Carn Tregale also were among the guests. Mrs. Cummings supervised a continual flow of hot drinks, sandwiches, and freshly baked pastries, to the gratification of everyone present. There also was a plentiful supply of a good imported port wine, which found many takers.

Governor Young stayed only for half an hour, obviously anxious to get back to his walled estate. He grasped the hand of Mrs. Cummings, pressing it firmly in both of his.

"Your hospitality is very gracious, Mrs. Cummings. The support you and your husband are giving the people of Utah during these trying times is greatly appreciated. I see the Governor is surrounded at the moment, so please pass along our gratitude to him. Good afternoon, Mrs. Cummings."

After Governor Young left, along with his escort of a dozen armed guards, the atmosphere became a little more relaxed. It was amazing how the presence of the man dominated any gathering. People were anxious to please, careful not to offend. The Mormon leader brought an aura into a room, a magnetism that reached out to touch everyone there. Whether friend or foe, or merely among the curious, meeting Brigham Young was an experience no one forgot.

Governor Cummings took a bite from a cream-filled pastry, wiping at his mouth to brush away an excess of cream. He held up a glass half-filled with Port. "Not from Portugal—a French vintner, I believe," he told the people around him, "though equally as sweet to the taste. But I forget, you Mormons aren't supposed to care about such things."

"Abstinence is a point of wisdom," one of the city councilmen smiled. "A glass of good wine now and then might be considered wisdom in itself."

There were chuckles, and several glasses raised in response to the answer.

Cummings took a sip of the Port. "Wisdom to be sure," he told them, "if you compare a good Port like this to that horrible Valley Tan moonshine. That is little more than poison."

"It certainly put more than one teamster under the ground," one of the gathering smiled.

The Governor raised his glass again. "Then it can't be all bad."

General Galloway spoke up. "Speaking of poison, did anyone read the last issue of the Valley Tan?"

Galloway was referring to the newspaper, which had begun publishing three days before the dedication of Camp Floyd. As the name implied, it was a periodical for those who opposed all things Mormon, especially "the Mormon stranglehold on politics and commerce in the Territory." Its editor, a man by the name of Kirk Anderson, could be counted on to publish scathing attacks on anything the Mormons did. It was eagerly read by the Gentile population, particularly those in Frogtown and Camp Floyd.

"I understand there's talk of it going under," someone said. "More papers stolen than sold. The Deseret News won't be sad if it shuts down, I'm sure."

"Still, a lot of people enjoy reading bad things about the Mormons."

Cummings was staring at Galloway. "I understand the editor—what's his name, Anderson, isn't it?—takes me to task for forcing the Territorial legislature to travel down to Fillmore."

"That he does, and as it reads, for the total waste of government money with nothing accomplished. He isn't the only person upset about that, of course," Galloway smiled. "Isn't a member of the Legislature who doesn't share his displeasure at making that trip in the wintertime—as you well know, Governor."

"I merely followed the Territorial charter," Cummings responded defensively. "It says the Legislature must convene at least once a year in the capital—and that's Fillmore, not Salt Lake City."

"I'd advise making the trip in the fall next time," Mayor Smoot grinned. "Legislators will be a lot happier not traveling through snow."

"Or change the charter—" someone said.

"Or change the capital—" another added.

Mayor Smoot spoke up. "At least there's no complaint about prosperity in the Territory, Governor. You've done a fine job, sir, in restoring confidence in the federal government."

"That's very true," Galloway agreed. "Never seen so many folk buying so much merchandise, not in the years I've been in the Territory. This Christmas season has just about depleted our entire inventory, and it's the same for almost every store on East Temple. You might say we're seeing an orgy of spending."

"We have Buchanan to thank for that," Smoot added. "All the money and jobs the army generated has changed the whole Territory from poverty-stricken to prosperous."

"And quite a few from prosperous to downright wealthy," Wilson commented.

"I'm not ashamed to number myself among those," Galloway nodded. "Some of us were fortunate enough to own what the army wanted—lumber, and they got it at fair prices. No doubt that timberland owners fared better than most, I'll admit."

"Can't help being envious," Smoot said wryly. "Brigham Young and the other timber owners like yourself did very well in the construction of Camp Floyd. Though there was opportunity for anyone who wanted to take advantage of it," Smoot added. "Worries me about all the farmers who went to Cedar and just left their crops rotting in the field. We'll pay for that with high prices next year."

"People won't mind, as long as they have the money to pay them."

"Trouble is, there'll be more than a few who don't."

Wilson was frowning. "I worry about all that gold the army is putting into circulation. We have more than enough criminals eager to steal it."

"Better gold than the Church scrip most of us were getting paid with before," someone joked. It did not bring a smile from any of the Church leaders present, although there was no doubting the truth of what the man said. It was the hard value of gold that was vitalizing the economy of the Territory, for gold crossed all barriers.

Mayor Smoot looked at Tregale. "How's General Johnston reacting to seeing all the good he's brought to Utah? He was a man set on bringing mostly harm."

"Don't think the general thinks of things that way," Tregale answered. "The more prosperous the people are, the less complaining they do. He has enough problems dealing with the Indians."

"Understand Arrowpeen still hasn't got his braves back on the reservation. That could bode trouble in the spring."

"I'm helping set up a meeting between the chiefs and General Johnston," Tregale said. "When that happens, probably in the next few weeks, things should settle down."

"Or heat up," Smoot grunted. "Johnston doesn't come across as someone you want as a friend."

"More to the point," Tregale murmured, "he comes across as someone you don't want as an enemy."

The gathering was interrupted by the arrival of Jim Wilson. He went straight to Governor Cummings. "Excuse me for interrupting, Governor, but I have news I'm sure you want to hear quick as possible." A frown crossed his face. "And some not that good."

"Well, let's hear it, young man—Mr. Wilson, isn't it?"

"Found your horses, Governor."

Cummings's eyes widened. "My white mares—?"

"Well, sir, they're not exactly white anymore, but they are your mares."

"Not white—? My mares are white, Mr. Wilson."

"That's how we missed them, sir. We kept looking for two white horses, only the man who stole them dyed them black."

"My mares are black—?"

"Yes, sir. But they're in good shape. Found them in a stable south of the city. Man who took them was a gambler named Black— maybe that's why he chose that color."

"Are they in good condition—?"

"Excellent, sir, far as I could tell. Black was planning on racing them at Camp Floyd when that new race track opened in the spring, so he's kept them in good shape."

Cummings was now so excited he could hardly contain himself as he looked around at the company of men. He grinned as wide as he could grin. "This man's found my mares, gentlemen. Let's give him a round of applause."

There was a noisy burst of clapping, and Wilson went a little red in the face. Cummings put an arm around his shoulder.

"Anything you want, Mr. Wilson, you just come to me. I thank you for not giving up the search."

Tregale pushed forward and slapped Wilson on the shoulder. "Good work, Jim. Have to be honest, I thought those horses were long gone."

"Got suspicious when I heard about this Black fellow secretly training some prize stock. Sure enough, it was the Governor's pair, although I had to look close to see there was white underneath the dye."

"You mentioned some news that wasn't so good, Jim," Galloway said.

The smile slipped off Wilson's face. "Yes, sir. Thought you would like to know what Judge Sinclair just did."

Even through his elation, Cummings summoned a frown. "What was that?"

"He just swore in about two dozen new lawyers, sir."

Everyone was puzzled by that news.

"Where'd they come from?" Alexander Wilson asked.

"Riffraff, mostly," Jim said. "Drunks, gamblers, some Gentile merchants, some teamsters even."

"Was there no one with legal knowledge?" the U.S. attorney gasped. "There had to be some qualification—"

"Other than hating Mormons, don't think so, sir. There were some respectable citizens—a doctor, a couple of army officers. Kirk Anderson, the editor of the Valley Tan, was also sworn in."

The group was looking at each other in angry consternation. Ferguson shoved closer to Jim Wilson.

"He say anything about me?" Ferguson growled.

"Not by name, sir," Wilson replied, "but he said something about teaching those arrogant Mormon lawyers a lesson."

◆

Henry Washington drove the open carriage into the campgrounds on the west side of the Jordan River. Located nearly four miles south of the downtown district, the place was a small town of wagons and people. Close to a hundred wagons, Henry guessed, most lined in rows stretching north and south on the flatlands, with scores of tents of all sizes and shapes clustered closer to the river bank. At least six or seven hundred men, women and children had spent the winter in this open, desolate spot. No doubt all were praying the army would soon announce the trails to California were once again open and safe to travel. Henry could hardly imagine what this place looked like last spring when the thousands of soldiers in General Johnston's army encamped here before moving on to Cedar Valley.

Henry turned the carriage down the fourth avenue between the lines of wagons. He had visited here several times in the last few months and knew exactly where he was going. He started looking anxiously ahead, trying to spot the woman who had been in his thoughts constantly since that first meeting on the sidewalk in front of the Galloway emporium—he knew it was the Galloway & Tregale Emporium, but as much as he liked the Tregales, his years with the General made it difficult to associate anyone with the man who had done so much for him.

Suddenly he spotted Rose Woods ahead, sitting outside one of the wagons reading a book to the small child on her lap. She saw Henry coming, put the child down, and approached the carriage with a warm smile of greeting.

"This is a surprise, Mr. Washington," she greeted him. "A pleasant one, I might add."

Henry climbed down and doffed his hat. "Hope I'm not making a nuisance of myself, Miss Woods—"

She shook her head, smiling again. "Always good to see you, Mr. Washington. The Welches are visiting friends at the other end of camp, so there is no one here but little Dorothy and myself."

Dorothy, a pretty three-year-old, had come over to the carriage and was staring up at Henry Washington. "You're colored, just like Rose, aren't you?"

"I certainly am, little Dorothy," Henry smiled, crouching down so as to be closer to her level. "And you have beautiful red hair, just like your mommy."

"Mommy says it's because we come from Ireland."

"I'm sure she's right." Henry gave her a serious look. "Would you like to sit up in this fine carriage with Rose and me?"

Excitement glistened in green eyes as she looked at Rose. "Can I, Rose?"

Rose lifted her up onto one of the seats. "Just don't fidget too much." She glanced inquiringly at Henry. "I take it we're all supposed to get in. I can't leave the wagon, you know—"

Rose sat next to the child, and Henry sat on the seat beside her. He fumbled with his hat, finally slipped it back on. His hands now free, he took a deep breath then suddenly took one of Rose's hands in his own. She was startled, looked from their hands, up into his face. It was obvious Henry had something on his mind, but was having a difficult time finding proper words.

"Would it be forward of me if I was to call you Rose?" he blurted.

Rose smiled. "I suppose a man who takes my hand can use my first name," she said softly. There was no admonishment in her tone. "I would like that, Mr. Washingt—"

Once again Henry cut her off. "Henry. I'd be very honored if you called me Henry."

"Very well, Henry." She glanced down at their clasped hands, but made no effort to withdraw from his grasp. "Now is there something else that brought you all the way from town?"

"Got me a surprise Christmas present today, Miss Woo—Rose," he said. "Galloway and Mr. Tregale made me the manager of their downtown emporium."

"That's wonderful, Henry!"

"I'm forever indebted to them," Henry said solemnly. "Always been a free man, but I didn't ever see myself as anything more than a servant—although I feel part of the family, thanks to the way all of them treat me."

"I'd like to meet them someday," Rose said. "That is so generous, Henry. Manager of a big downtown store—not many of our color can point to that accomplishment. I'm so pleased you drove out to tell me."

"Well," Henry muttered, "that wasn't exactly the reason."

"It wasn't—?" Rose's heart started fluttering, but she tried to calm it. She'd only spent a total of a few hours with this man. He was older, experienced in life. She must seem like little more than a girl to him. But she felt his grip tighten on her hand.

"I came to ask you to marry me, Rose." She saw his eyes were suddenly brimming wet with tears. "I just never laid eyes on anyone so pretty, and never spoke to anyone who struck me so deep. I know the wagons could head out any day now that the snow's going in the mountains, so when I was told about my new promotion, I decided I couldn't risk waiting. I want you to be my wife, Rose, and be part of this new life I've been handed."

She looked at him, tears now falling down her cheeks. Dorothy saw them, and tugged at her arm in concern.

"You're crying, Rose—"

She put a hand on the child's head, stroking her hair. "Just because I'm happy, Dorothy." She turned to fasten her eyes on the man who had just asked her to marry him. She reached over and gripped both of his hands tightly. "I'd be pleased and honored to be your wife, Henry. And being manager of that store has nothing to do with it. I started going pitter-patter from the first day we met. I just never thought a good man like you would—"

She couldn't finish, because Henry pulled her close and gave her a long kiss. When it broke, Rose could feel Dorothy tugging on her arm again.

"He kissed you, Rose—"

"I know he did, honey," Rose whispered, staring at Henry, tears still falling. "He certainly did—"

CHAPTER TWENTY TWO

SALT LAKE CITY
CHRISTMAS EVE, 1858

I t isn't the same, is it?" Esther Cunningham said, staring out the large window in the living room of the Galloway home. "I mean, we're all so much better off than we were last Christmas, but there's hardly any of us that's happier."

Agatha was sitting in one of the room's comfortable overstuffed chairs. "I'm trying to think of someone who is, but I'm ashamed to say nobody comes to mind except myself. I don't say that with any prideful feeling—I just feel so grateful for all that's happened to me."

Esther turned from the window. "You and the General are an inspiration to all of us, Agatha, now more than ever. Alfred and me should be happier, but I can't honestly say we are."

"But you two are so blessed," Agatha chided softly. "You'll be moving into a fine big house soon, Alfred's business is prospering—"

"—and our marriage is failing," Esther added, her face shadowed with concern."

"That's nonsense—"

"No, it isn't, Agatha. It's my fault, too. I'm not the timid mouse of a wife Alfred had in England. He can't get used to living with someone who speaks her own mind—which I do now, I admit. On top of that, we're losing our only son."

"You're not losing Aaron," Agatha snorted. "He and Lydia are moving to Brigham City—that's little more than fifty miles away, for heaven's sake."

"Might as well be five hundred," Esther complained. "We'll never see them."

"Listen to yourself, Esther. Two winters ago, wasn't one of us expected to live long enough to see Christmas. This year we all have so many blessings we don't know how to cope with them. We must try God's patience something fierce."

Lydia and Harriet entered the room. Both of the sisters were smiling, and Agatha looked at them approvingly.

"A smile looks good on you, Harriet. You two look like you've been up to something—"

"Lydia and Aaron want me to go live with them in Brigham City," Harriet gushed, "and I've said I would."

"Wonderful," Agatha said.

"Oh my goodness," Esther muttered. "Now you and Aaron never will come back to Salt Lake."

"Of course we will," Lydia assured her quickly. "Probably not 'til after the baby's born, but we'll be here for Thanksgiving, if not before."

Esther was wearing a startled expression. "Baby—you and Aaron are having a child?"

Lydia put a hand to her mouth. "I've done it, haven't I. Aaron wanted us to tell you both together. We wanted it to be a surprise."

"It certainly is," Esther muttered. She sank onto one of the chairs, staring down at the floor. "I'll never see my grandchild—"

Agatha got out of the chair and put her arms around Lydia, giving her a big hug. "That's exciting news, Lydia. Esther thinks so too, and she'll tell you if she ever climbs out of that big hole of self pity she's dug for herself—"

Esther looked up guiltily. She stood up and embraced her daughter-in-law. "I'm happy for you, Lydia, I really am. I'm feeling sorry for myself this afternoon, for really no cause. Especially not now—I've been looking forward to becoming a grandmother." She gave a mock frown. "Grandmother—that sounds like I'm getting really old—"

"Don't worry about getting older," Agatha smiled, "because when you stop, you're dead." She looked again at Lydia. "When is the baby due?"

"July—maybe August. It's going to be a long, hot summer."

"Well, Heather and the menfolk will be home soon," Agatha reminded them. "Everything cooking in the kitchen, girls?"

Harriet nodded. "Almost ready. Can't you smell the pies?"

"That I can," Agatha said, "and it smells like you both did your-selves proud."

Esther shook her head. "It's going to be strange, not having everyone here for dinner on Christmas Eve."

"Who isn't coming besides the Tates?" Lydia asked.

"The Tates leave a big hole," Agatha said. "Maude and Willie didn't feel up to coming all the way from Provo, not with a blizzard threatening. I suspect they also aren't eager to deal with questions about Beryl and the boys."

"Something happened to Beryl?" Harriet asked.

"Displaying herself on stage every night to three thousand drunken soldiers and as many evil teamsters," Esther snapped, "and living in a den of iniquity that has only prostitutes and no decent women. As a mother, I'd say that was enough to be happening—"

"It isn't like that," Lydia interrupted. "Beryl acts in a legitimate theater where no drinking is allowed, and she lives on post in a protected barracks with the other actresses. The prostitutes are in Frogtown, and so are the teamsters."

"Well, that woman she works for—Mercy Tuckett—should be ashamed of herself. Not only for parading those girls with hardly any clothes on—"

"That's not true, Esther," Lydia interrupted again. "They wear beautiful dresses and costumes and are fully clothed at all times."

"Not what I hear," Esther said testily. "And did you know Mercy Tuckett is having an illicit affair with some sergeant at Camp Floyd—?"

Agatha was startled, as were the two girls. "You sure that's true? She's happily married, with four children, from what Beryl says."

"Beryl doesn't know what's going on, then. Don't forget the woman is a polygamous wife."

Harriet frowned at her. "What's that got to do with it?"

"Well," Esther said primly, "any woman who willingly shares her husband with other women has to have lower moral standards than the rest of us."

"I'd be careful where you voice such opinions, Esther," Agatha warned. "A lot of those women with 'low moral standards' happen to live down the street with Brigham Young. I wouldn't count on an invitation to any of Eliza Young's parties, feeling the way you do."

Esther gasped in horror. "I didn't mean Sister Eliza—"

"Sounded to me like you were tarring them all with the same brush—"

"That's what it sounded like to me," Lydia added.

"I'll tell you right out, Sister Cunningham," Harriet said coldly, "I'm considering becoming a plural wife and I don't have low moral standards either."

Esther raised both hands in apology. "I didn't make myself clear—"

"Only too clear, Esther," Agatha told her. "Best to let the whole thing drop—and don't ever voice such thoughts again, not here in Utah."

There was an uncomfortable silence for several minutes. But the new Esther couldn't remain silent for long.

"Anyway, I can't help feeling sorry for Maude," she said finally. "She must be out of her mind with worry."

"Why would you say that?" Harriet asked.

"Beryl being in such a terrible situation," she replied. "No matter what you say, Lydia, about everything being so pure and holy, I don't believe it for one minute. Not with the example that Tuckett woman is setting. And those twin boys of hers—who knows what they're doing. Maude hasn't heard from them in weeks."

"Carn sees them all the time," Agatha said. "He says they're doing well enough for a couple of young lads in a bad environment."

"Bad environment—" Esther said caustically. "It's the devil's own playground, from what Alfred tells me."

"Who else isn't coming to dinner?" Harriet asked, trying to change the subject.

"Beth Wilson said Jim will probably have to work this evening," Agatha said. "Beth is worried to death about Jim being one of those special marshals. You should hear the stories she tells about what he has to deal with every day. She wants him to quit, but he's doing so well. People like him, and there's talk of a promotion. Jim is seriously considering making a career in law enforcement, she says."

"Don't expect we'll be seeing Derek or Gwen, either," Esther added. "It's a shame about those two."

"Do you think they'll get through this?" Harriet asked. She had her own opinion, but wanted to hear what Agatha had to say. But it was Esther who answered her question.

"I wouldn't take him back," she said firmly. "Don't know what Derek is thinking about."

"Oh, it's plain what he's thinking about," Agatha murmured. "Brings polygamy close to home, doesn't it? Never thought any of our group would come to grips with such a thing. I confess to wondering about it a few times," she smiled, "but that was before I met the General."

Harriet was studying her closely. "You're not against polygamy, Agatha?"

"It's serves a good purpose," Agatha replied, "when it's used as God intended. I don't think it was revealed so a man could jump into bed with any young girl he fancies, though."

"Exactly what I say," Esther said, anger in her voice. "Derek Pitts has no cause to bring this young tart—"

"Her name is Sarah Beezley," Lydia said quietly, "and from what I've heard, she's a good girl."

"Good enough to throw herself at a married man," Esther snapped back. "I hope Gwen teaches him a lesson. I'd never take him back." She hesitated, looking around as if someone might be eavesdropping. "You know Gwen has taken to drinking, don't you—"

A frown jumped across Agatha's face. "You sure about that, Esther? It would be terrible to spread such a rumor if it wasn't true—"

"It's not a rumor. I've seen it for myself," Esther said. "So has Lydia."

Agatha looked questioningly at Lydia, who gave a reluctant nod. "She's been terribly unhappy since Derek left. He's living in the back of the Beezley gun shop, as you know, and I'm sure that puts ugly pictures into her mind. That's the reason for her drinking, I'm sure."

"I'm really sad to hear that," Agatha said. "Didn't realize she was hurting so much. Is there anything we can do to help?"

"I visit two or three times a week," Lydia said, "but it's got so she doesn't much want to talk to anybody. She can't bring herself to cope with the thoughts of Jim having another wife."

"She shouldn't have to face such a thing," Esther said curtly. "We shouldn't have polygamy. It only makes a man more carnal and lustful, and goodness knows, they're born with enough of that."

"I've been thinking about polygamy quite a bit lately," Harriet said. "I'm not pretty like Lydia—" There was a quick chorus of disagreement, but she shook her head. "Not only that, but I've got a baby. I've accepted the fact that Calvin has gone out of my life, but I don't want to spend the rest of it alone. To be honest, that's one reason I'm happy to be going to Brigham City. My chances of being chosen as a polygamous wife will be better there than here."

"Now don't you start getting into that same hole as Esther," Agatha said, again giving her a hug. "There's plenty of good men who'll be anxious to have a pretty young woman like yourself for a wife—and be a father to your baby."

There was the sound of a carriage in the driveway. Esther looked outside. "It's Heather. She's home from the emporium. No one with her—"

"Good," Agatha said. "She's closed up early, as she should on Christmas Eve."

Agatha whooshed the two girls out of the room. "Looks like we'll be serving before long. Make sure nothing's burning."

Agatha started to follow the girls but Esther reached out to hold her back.

She waited until the girls were out of earshot, then spoke in a low voice, casting a look over her shoulder.

"Is it true that Heather and Carn are having problems?"

Agatha hesitated, not knowing what to say. Esther was a friend, but she had also become a gossip. It was better not to say anything, she decided.

"Don't know of any," she said. "You might ask Heather—"

Esther gasped. "I never would—"

"Not me, either."

Alfred and Aaron showed up a little later, having finished the job they were working on in Sugar House. They had promised a family their two-room addition would be built before Christmas, and they had just barely met the deadline. There would be six very happy young children tonight, they knew. Two to a bedroom was much better than six in one.

General Galloway returned shortly after the Cunninghams. Carn had returned with him, he said, but had volunteered to take the horses out to the barn and put them into their stalls for the night. He and Carn had been in a meeting at Social Hall with several Nauvoo Legion officers, making sure plans were in order if a need arose for an emergency callout during the holiday. No one fully trusted the army, even now.

Minutes later, Jim and Beth Wilson showed up, much to the delight of everyone. Jim was scheduled for duty but at the last minute he was relieved by an officer who was not married and had no family in the city. It made everyone feel a little better, although now Derek and Gwen Pitts were all the more noticeably absent.

In the barn, Carn was stripping saddles off the two horses when he heard footsteps behind him. He turned and was surprised to see Fred and Ted Tate entering.

"Well, what brings you boys here?" he asked, smiling in greeting. "Thought you'd be in Provo with your folks for Christmas."

"Something's happened, Brother Tregale," Fred said, "and we need to talk."

The serious look they both wore made Carn stop what he was doing. He stared at them, trying to read what was on their faces. Worry, that much was plain.

"What happened, boys?"

Quickly, they told him of the raid in Rush Valley and the shooting of the soldier. They had ridden off the next morning, and been camping out since then trying to decide what to do. They were through for good with the gang of rustlers, they told him, but turning themselves in to authorities seemed like it would only make things worse. They had decided to come and ask Carn for advice.

Carn listened until they were through talking, and spent a couple of minutes more weighing their situation in his mind. It wasn't good. A murder had been committed, and they were part of it. But he agreed with the boys that just walking in and surrendering was something that needed to be thought through. The rest of their lives was in balance here.

"I was out at Camp Floyd yesterday," he said finally. "Didn't hear about this raid, nor anything about anyone on patrol getting killed."

They looked at each other.

"Swazey said they might not find the body," Ted said. "It was snowing heavy, and it's kept up ever since."

"If they didn't find it until spring," Fred added, "he said probably wouldn't be much left, after rot and coyotes got to it. They'd just think the soldier, whoever he was, had lit out."

"He's probably right," Carn nodded. "Doesn't change anything that happened, though."

"What should we do, Brother Tregale?" Fred asked. "We been sick with worrying over this. Ain't us so much as what it'll do to our parents. It could kill 'em."

"You had no part in the shooting—?" Tregale asked again.

Both of them shook their head vigorously. "Happened before anyone could stop it," Ted said. "Swazey just kept pulling the trigger. Man was dead before he hit the ground."

"Well, this needs to thought out, and maybe some legal advice brought in," Carn told them. "No direct blame on you two, though the law won't hold no distinction. You're as guilty as Swazey, in the eyes of the law, because you were rustling cattle when it happened."

"That's been eatin' at us real bad," Fred said glumly.

"Tell you what I think," Carn said, reaching a decision. "This being Christmas Eve, I think you should hightail it south and give your parents the best present they could get—you two being home for Christmas."

"Should we tell 'em what happened?" Ted asked.

Carn shook his head quickly. "Don't say anything to anybody about this, not before I have a chance to check out at Camp Floyd, and get some smarter advice than I can give you. Stay at the ranch, and I'll be in touch soon as I have something to tell you."

"We got money to pay a lawyer if—"

Tregale cut him off with a raised hand. "Don't want to hear about money, boys. It's called ill-gotten gains—but if it gets to needing a lawyer, he probably won't mind taking it from you."

The boys left and Carn returned to the house soon after getting the horses groomed and fed. Everyone was glad to see him, although anyone who was watching couldn't help but notice the chill between him and Heather. Carn said nothing about the Tate boys, of course, not even to the General. Time enough to deal with that problem after Christmas.

There was one unexpected guest for dinner that evening. Henry arrived just as they were sitting down. A place was already set for him, because Henry was as much a part of the family as anyone else, but it was a surprise to see he had brought someone with him.

Rose Woods was nervous as Henry introduced her to everyone.

People scooted over and Agatha set a place for her beside Henry. They could tell Henry was bursting to say something, but he waited until they were all seated before making any announcement.

"Rose has agreed to marry me," he told them, grinning proudly. He reached over and put an arm about her shoulders. "She's made me the happiest man in the whole world."

There were exclamations and congratulations from everyone around the table. All of the women got up and came around to give Rose a hug, an act of such sincere friendship that Rose started to cry. Agatha handed her a napkin.

"Save the tears until after you're married, Rose," she smiled. "That's when a woman starts needing them most."

"When is the happy event?" General Galloway asked, the smile of pleasure on his face almost as big as the one Henry kept on his.

"As a matter of fact," Henry said, "we were hoping to be married this very night, General. I couldn't find a finer group of friends to share such a wonderful occasion."

It brought a pang of bittersweet memory to both Heather and Carn. He had said almost those same words two years ago in a snowbound tent high in the Rockies to this same group of people. They had all witnessed his marriage to Heather, and now they would be bound once again in friendship to Henry and Rose.

"We'd be honored, Henry," Galloway said. "This is your home, and we're proud to welcome Rose as your wife." He glanced at Aaron. "Bishop Swann lives just three houses to the east, Aaron. Would you mind letting him know we need a few minutes of his time tonight. He'll be as pleased as we are to hear the news."

Dinner was a happy occasion, Henry and Rose being the center of most of the conversation, of course. Rose told the gathering of her upbringing back East, and it was quickly evident that Henry had found himself not only a beautiful young woman to wed, but an educated and talented one as well. Dinner was cleared and the fresh pies baked by Lydia and Harriet were a delicious dessert. While everyone waited for the arrival of Bishop Swann, they began singing Christmas carols. The spirit of that brought a misty appreciation to everyone in the room of the holy event they were commemorating.

Bishop Swann arrived, and the wedding ceremony was brief and simple. Henry put a ring on Rose's finger that the General had quietly slipped into his hand. Henry had a good idea it was a ring that held sentimental memories of the General's first wedding, but nothing was said. Every woman in the room was crying when Henry finally took Rose in his arms and gave her their first kiss as man and wife.

Later, after most of the guests had retired, Carn went into the living room. It was dark, with no lamps lit, the heavy storm clouds outside allowing only a faint light through the window. He closed the door and sat down, staring into his thoughts. He was painfully melancholy, no doubt from the emotion of seeing Henry and Rose so happy. It brought a knifing realization of the trouble in his own marriage. For the past few weeks, whenever he was home, he slept in a spare bedroom upstairs. That was why he spent most of his time at Camp Floyd lately, for every night here, alone, with his wife and baby son so close, was almost unbearably painful.

The door opened and Heather called his name. He jumped to his feet as she came hesitantly into the room.

"Do you mind if we talk for a moment?" she asked.

"I'd like that. Would you like me to light a lamp?"

"This is fine, thank you." She sat in a chair opposite him, and even in the darkness, he could see her face was troubled. "I'm so happy for Henry and Rose. They looked so—blissful."

"That they did. Henry found himself a good woman."

"I hope their happiness lasts forever. But it usually doesn't, does it."

"I thought ours was going to."

"But it hasn't."

"We've got our problems for sure," Carn muttered. "I'm sorry for my part in that, Heather."

"Seems like I'm more to blame than you for what's between us now."

"One wouldn't have happened without the other. It's hard to place blame," he said, then added quickly, "though I place it mostly on myself."

"I've reached a decision, Carn," Heather said quietly.

For a moment, Carn's heart stopped beating. He couldn't be sure what she was about to say, her voice had been so low. There had been so much hurt, so much pain, he didn't want to feel more.

"What decision is that?"

"The post arrived today from the East," she said, avoiding an answer to his question. "There was a letter from my parents in England."

"Are they well?" he asked, knowing she had a reason for not answering.

"They sent a bank draft," she said, again not giving a direct answer.

"That's interesting. Do they think we need the money?"

"They sent it so I could travel back to Philadelphia and visit my father's brother and his wife. Did I ever mention Uncle Oscar and Aunt Phoebe—?"

"Don't think you did. I would have remembered."

"I thought I did—"

"They live in Philadelphia?"

"I've decided to take little Carn and go visit them. I thought you should know."

"Isn't Philadelphia fairly close to Boston?"

"I believe it is."

"Would you be going to Boston?"

"It's possible. That's not the reason I'm going, Carn. I think we need some time to sort out where our lives are going."

"When do you plan on leaving?"

"As soon as possible. Early spring, I suppose."

"You really want to do this?"

"No, Carn, I don't. What I really want is for us to be happy again, like we were before all this started. I'm not sure that's possible, however. This isn't just for me—while I'm gone, I hope you'll have a chance to decide what's important in your life."

"I already know that."

"I don't think you do, Carn. Don't tell me it's me and the baby—I don't believe that, not anymore."

Carn was silent for long moments, struggling to deal with the turmoil inside him.

"Will you be coming back, Heather?"

"I don't know. I honestly don't know."

CHAPTER TWENTY THREE

CAMP FLOYD
JANUARY 1859

A band of Indian chiefs, led by the stiff, haughty figure of Chief Arrowpeen, loped into Camp Floyd along the trail that cut up through the southern half of Cedar Valley. They were escorted by a company of dragoons from the Second Regiment, Colonel Philip Cooke riding at the head of the column, with Carn Tregale at his side. Arrowpeen had insisted that Tree-With-Crooked-Hand be present at the council with General Johnston, a stipulation the general found galling but acceptable. Carn tactfully omitted telling the general that Arrowpeen had again made it clear he would not trust any promise by Big Soldier but would rely only on the word of Crooked-Hand.

The trail brought the line of riders directly to the administration complex on the west side of the post. General Johnston was waiting in front of the headquarters building, in full dress uniform and looking stiff and stern. He was flanked by several ranking officers, including his second-in-command, Colonel Smith. The welcoming party also included three civilian representatives of various Territorial agencies, and a handful of army interpreters, some of them Indian, some Mexican, some white. Johnston wanted no words misunderstood by either side during this important council.

Jacob Forney's bearded face was smiling as he nodded in greeting toward Arrowpeen and the other chiefs. The beard made it difficult to see how forced the smile was, and that was fortunate. As the newly appointed Superintendent of Indian Affairs in the Territory,

Forney had officially replaced Brigham Young in those duties. So far, however, he found it impossible to convince the chiefs to come to him instead of "The Big Chief." As a result, contact between the new superintendent and his Indian charges was strained and antagonistic.

Forney had another problem, no less aggravating than his run-ins with Brigham Young. Despite the fact that Forney disliked and distrusted the Mormons as much as Johnston, he had not found favor with the general. Johnston was angry at Forney's constant criticism of the way the army was dealing with Indian problems. The superintendent found himself in the difficult position of opposing both the army and the Mormons on their solutions for the crisis, and receiving no support from the Indians for his own proposals. There was little cause for Forney's smile to be genuine.

Standing beside Forney was Garland Hurt, the Indian agent for Central Utah. Hurt, an avowed enemy of the Mormons and especially Brigham Young, was also outwardly smiling as he greeted the Indian visitors. He too was deeply concerned, however. The burning and looting of his Spanish Fork reservation headquarters a few months ago made it plain he no longer held the respect, nor the control, he had commanded a year ago. These days, he seldom went among the Indians without an escort of some of the soldiers bivouacked just outside the reservation.

The other civilian in the reception line was John Hartnett, the new Territorial Secretary. Hartnett viewed the presidential amnesty in much the same light as General Johnston—it should never have been granted. The Secretary had clashed several times with Brigham Young since arriving in Utah. On top of that, it had recently become public knowledge that Hartnett was the principal owner and publisher of the Valley Tan. That alone was enough to earn the respect and admiration of General Johnston. The rumors about secret financial support from Washington, possibly even from President Buchanan himself, didn't matter to anyone who eagerly read the Valley Tan's attacks on everything the Mormons did. Since Johnston refused to invite Governor Cummings to this council with the Indian chiefs, Hartnett was considered an ideal representative of the Territorial government.

As for the Indians, they presented an impressive array of power and authority, representing the Utes, Paiutes, Sanpitches, Pieds, and several smaller tribes. These included the Unintas, from the northeast mountains, the Tumpanowach, from Utah Lake, and the Weeminuches, from the southeast mountains. Even the three new Indian farms, or Indian agencies as Forney and Hurt referred to them, were represented. Indians on the Parvan, Uintah, and Parowan farms would also have to be satisfied if an agreement for peaceful coexistence was to be reached.

Arrowpeen, of course, was the most powerful of all the chiefs in this part of the Territory. Signals from Arrowpeen's San Pete reservation to the rest of the local tribes were rarely ignored.

Riding with Arrowpeen were Chiefs Tintic, Peteetneet, Sanpitch, and Yampants. General Johnston had issued a special invitation to Chief Kanosh, of the southern Pahvants, to attend the council because the word of Kanosh carried almost as much weight as that of Arrowpeen. The southern chief had no intention of riding into the army post, however, for his braves had been the main participants in the massacre of the wagon train at Mountain Meadows last summer. It was no secret that white men in authority were anxious to seize anyone connected to the massacre, red-skinned or white, and Kanosh was not going to risk being taken captive. Little Soldier, chief of the Shoshones living in the northern valleys and canyons close to Ogden and Brigham City, refused to attend for similar reasons. Bands of his braves were largely responsible for the attacks that had closed the northern trails to California and caused so much trouble and frustration for troops under the command of Captain Jim Hawes.

With introductions exchanged, the group proceeded to the large hall nearby that usually served as the officers' dining room. For this special occasion, benches were arranged in a large square, allowing no one to assume greater importance. The chiefs were uncomfortable sitting on the benches in the white man's style, but did not want to sit cross-legged on the ground as they normally would, because then they would be forced to look up to the soldiers.

For the next three hours, the chiefs and the army officers presented their cases, every sentence translated by two interpreters, always one of them an Indian. It became very evident that everyone in the hall was willing to listen and seemed anxious to reach agreement.

Finally, General Johnston looked directly at Arrowpeen and folded his arms across his chest. Two translators moved close beside each man, and the exchange between them was accomplished with little difficulty.

"I would like to summarize the main points that each side has agreed to uphold," Johnston began.

Arrowpeen listened carefully to the translation and nodded. Watching the Indian chief closely, Tregale knew the wily Arrowpeen understood most of what was being said without translation, but the chief had his own reasons for pretending differently. General Johnston began to list the points, using his fingers to illustrate numbers.

"Number One," he said, "the army agrees to protect and safeguard all Indians on lands that have been deeded as reservations."

"Number Two," he said, holding up another finger, "we agree to provide food from army storehouses whenever there is a need. As long as there is peace between us, there will be no hunger. This offer is not made to any band who leaves a reservation without permission."

Frowns crossed the faces of both Forney and Hurt when the offer of free food and provisions was voiced by Johnston. Both agents opposed any such dole to the Indians, claiming it would only undermine efforts to make the Indians self-sufficient. The whites had thoroughly discussed the matter before the chiefs arrived, and the Indian agents knew Johnston's position was unbendable. They were deeply annoyed and disturbed to hear the offer become official policy.

A third finger joined the other two. "Number Three. The army agrees to protect and safeguard all tribal hunting grounds. That means we will stop all white men from hunting on lands given by treaty to the Indians."

Arrowpeen asked a question through an interpreter. His face was expressionless but his eyes deeply intense. "Will soldiers keep Mor-mons from stealing our game?"

Johnston nodded, his manner emphatic. "We certainly will. No white man will be allowed to hunt on your game preserves—Mormon settler, immigrant, teamster, or the devil's own. You have my word on that, sir. Only exclusion is hunting on Indian lands already settled. White folks have rights on those lands."

Arrowpeen's glance slid toward Crooked-Hand even before the general's promise was translated, confirming Tregale's suspicions that the chief understood most, if not all, that was being said in English. Tregale saw the question in his eyes, and nodded. Tregale believed Johnston was being sincere in offering the guarantee of protection against outside hunters.

Johnston caught Arrowpeen's glance and the slight nod of approval that Tregale gave in response. He frowned, not sure what was passing between the two men, but resenting the fact that Arrowpeen was not giving him his full attention.

"Does Arrowpeen have a question about what I just said?" Johnston growled. He gave Tregale a hard look. "Is there something I should know about, Mr. Tregale?"

"Chief Arrowpeen understands your offer, General," Tregale said. "He wants you to know he appreciates it."

Johnston frowned suspiciously. "Didn't hear him say that."

"I've come to know him quite well, sir. That's what he wants to communicate, right enough. He knows I understand that."

Not at all satisfied, Johnston turned his attention back to Arrowpeen. "Chief Arrowpeen and these other chiefs have also made promises." Again a single finger was held up. "Number One, Indians will stay clear of Mormon settlements. No attacks, no threats. Just stay away unless invited. Is that agreeable to Chief Arrowpeen?"

This time Arrowpeen waited until Johnston's comments had been fully translated. Then he nodded, again glancing at Tregale. Tregale had to hand it to him; Arrowpeen was going along with the explanation he'd given the general.

"Arrowpeen understands and agrees, General."

Again Johnston was frowning suspiciously. "Seems he's relying on you quite a bit, Mr. Tregale."

"Like I said, sir, I've spent considerable time with Chief Arrowpeen these last months."

Johnston lifted a second finger. "Number Two," he continued, his stare hardening as he looked at the chief, "all Indians agree to stay clear of Territorial roads, those that run through their reservations, and those that don't."

This time it was General Johnston's stare that fastened on Tregale. "That's a mighty important point, Mr. Tregale. I'd like to be sure Chief Arrowpeen agrees with it—and understands the consequences if the promise of these chiefs is broken."

Anger flashed in Arrowpeen's eyes, but it was quickly hidden. He spoke to the Indian translator beside him, who translated for the general.

"You doubt the word of Chief Arrowpeen, and he is offended by it. If Big Soldier does not trust the word of these chiefs, Arrowpeen says, then there is no trust in the words of Big Soldier. It is time for this council to end."

Johnston realized the thread was in danger of breaking, and that was the last thing he wanted to happen. He nodded deferentially toward Arrowpeen.

"I trust the word of Arrowpeen, and all the chiefs. I only want to be sure Arrowpeen understands that if this promise is broken, much blood will be spilled on both sides."

Arrowpeen leaned over and asked something of the translator, who immediately looked at Johnston.

"Chief Arrowpeen asks if Big Soldier is threatening his people?"

Angry impatience flashed across Johnston's face, but he brought it quickly under control. "My words are not intended as a threat, tell Arrowpeen. I only want to be sure we understand each other." He gave an exasperated look at Tregale. "Mr. Tregale, you seem to communicate clairvoyantly with the chief. Can you make him understand what I'm trying to communicate?"

Tregale looked across at Arrowpeen, who immediately nodded. General Johnston couldn't hold back a scowl of irritation.

"You decide to quit as liaison, Mr. Tregale," he muttered, "and the army will hire you. Seems you got strange powers with Indians."

Again Arrowpeen muttered something to the interpreter. "Chief Arrowpeen agrees with words of Big Soldier," the interpreter said, "but Arrowpeen and the rest of the chiefs cannot speak for Little

242

Soldier. The chief wants to know if you will hold all Indians responsible for what Shoshones might do in the north."

Johnston frowned over that one. His urge was to tell Arrowpeen that consequences for any actions of Little Soldier would indeed fall upon all the tribes, but instinct told him it would not be wise.

"If the other tribes do not join with Little Soldier, they will not be held responsible for what the Shoshones do. And if Little Soldier agrees to what the other chiefs have decided here today," he added, "the Shoshones will be given the same protection."

The looks that passed between the chiefs when they heard his answer told Johnston he had made the right decision.

Arrowpeen had one more point to make with Big Soldier. He reached inside his robe and pulled out a piece of paper. It was clearly a letter, written in English, with a stylish, flowing hand. Arrowpeen made no effort to present the letter, only wanting to hold it up so Big Soldier could see it clearly. This time, the chief made no pretense, and addressed the general in halting, but clear, English.

"This is letter from Big Chief," he began. Johnston knew at once that Arrowpeen was holding up a letter from Brigham Young. "Big Chief tells us we must not attack soldiers. Arrowpeen tells Big Soldier we will do as Big Chief says and not attack soldiers—not unless soldiers break word of Big Soldier, or soldiers attack Indians. That is word of Arrowpeen and all these chiefs."

General Johnston said nothing. He was seething over the realization that Arrowpeen could speak English and his use of translators was nothing but a sham. On the other hand, agreement on the most important points had been reached at this council—or had they? Had Johnston and his officers brought it about—or was Brigham Young the greater force? It was the hardest thing Johnston ever did to restrain himself from crossing and tearing the letter out of Arrowpeen's hand—harder even than keeping on marching through Salt Lake City instead of leveling it to the ground.

The council ended and lunch was served, everyone remaining seated in the square. Cooks brought in several large metal pots of rich stew, generous helpings ladled into bowls. The chiefs had several helpings and obviously enjoyed it. Punch was served, with no liquor in it. The general knew the Indians had a low tolerance for alcohol and wanted to make sure no one felt any ill effects. Most of the chiefs found the punch unpleasant to the taste however, and few drank more than one cup. The stew was followed by servings of a flat cake thickly covered with a maple frosting. It was also a new taste for the Indians but this one they liked, each chief eating two and three pieces and cleaning the last crumbs from their plates.

There was a short break after lunch, then carriages were brought to the administration building and everyone boarded. It was an experience that tested the reserve of the Indians, trying not to show excitement. All had seen these conveyances on the roads but only Arrowpeen had ever ridden in one. That had happened one time while he was visiting the Big Chief in Salt Lake City and Brigham Young had taken him on a tour of the city.

Arrowpeen sat with General Johnston in the lead carriage, along with a single interpreter. The general still was angry over the chief's deception about the language, but this was no time to make a point of it. The line of carriages started out on a tour of the new army post.

General Johnston had one major purpose in showing the chiefs around Camp Floyd. Most had encountered companies of soldiers in the field on occasion, and even seen one or two artillery pieces in action, but none had seen the full force and firepower of this army gathered in one place as it was here.

Johnston wanted these chiefs to be fully aware of what they would be going up against if the agreements of the council were broken.

Two hours later, there was no doubt that General Johnston had accomplished his mission. Seeing the thousands of troops moving about the post, the massive stores of weapons and ammunition, and above all, the long lines of artillery pieces, made a profound impact on every Indian chief who saw them.

Arrowpeen sat staring at the weapons in front of the barracks of the Third and Fourth Artillery, imagining how futile an attack would be against all those cannons. Some were light and swiftly maneuverable, others heavy cannons that looked as if they could reach far and destroy whatever they were aimed at. This awesome array of firepower struck Arrowpeen more than anything else he had seen on the army post. Arrowpeen's face was usually impassive, but Johnston could see the consternation on the chief's face as he seemed unable to break his scrutiny of the cannons.

"Wouldn't want to be on the receiving end," Johnston murmured. "Not much can stand up against that firepower."

Arrowpeen nodded, muttering a rare admission of the inferiority of his own forces. "Indians could not win against all this."

"Hope it never comes to proving it, Chief," Johnston said quietly. "What's been done here today is a good thing, for your people and for everyone else."

That evening, after being served a sumptuous meal in the dining hall, the chiefs were honored guests at a performance of the Military Circus, a group of mostly German performers. Then they watched a skit that portrayed a mock battle, showing how invincible the army was in defeating all its enemies. The message was clear, and it was understood.

A small cluster of Sibley tents was erected just south of the administration complex for the chiefs to spend the night. Both Forney and Hurt assured General Johnston this would be more appreciated than putting them into an unfamiliar barracks environment, and they were right.

The next morning, the chiefs joined the officers for breakfast. It consisted of corn meal mush and fresh cream, squabs from the Second Dragoon's regimental pigeon house, and heaps of fresh donuts smothered in maple syrup. The chiefs seemed to have bottomless pits for stomachs and enjoyed everything the cooks put before them.

Then General Johnston personally led the chiefs, now on their own horses, to one of the larger quartermaster warehouses, one that contained huge supplies of foodstuffs. In a grand gesture, Johnston invited each chief to go into the storehouse and take all the food he could carry. It was difficult for those watching, including Cooke and Tregale, not to break out in laughter as they watched the chiefs scurrying through the warehouse, selecting and discarding as something more appetizing came into sight. Finally, they staggered out of the warehouse carrying huge quantities of foodstuffs in their arms. Slabs of bacon, tins of tobacco, sacks of grain, and small barrels of maple syrup seemed the most popular items, probably because they were more easily handled. When the Indians were once again mounted, the officers helped each one stack the items around them, even providing sacks to carry smaller items. The line of chiefs headed back south, the officers who watched them wondering if any of the agreements of yesterday would hold once the chiefs got home to the reservations.

CHAPTER TWENTY FOUR

RUSH VALLEY
LATE MARCH

A late spring storm raged all week along the Wasatch front, bringing snow, savage winds, and bitter cold. Unfortunately, it was the week that civilian ranchers were supposed to complete the removal of all livestock from outlying valleys, now reserved for grazing only military herds. With the miserable weather conditions, General Johnston might have extended the deadline once again but he was angered by the defiance of the Mormon ranchers. Most had started their spring roundups but showed no signs of preparing to move the herds off federal lands. This made the general determined to enforce this latest deadline.

An infantry company of the Tenth Regiment crossed the low ridges of the Oquirrh Mountains separating Cedar Valley from Rush Valley to the west, marching several miles toward the cluster of crude log and adobe structures that marked the Spencer-Little cattle and sheep operation in the northern part of the valley. Daniel Spencer, after his frustrating meeting with General Johnston last December, had given instructions that the herds in Rush Valley were to stay in place, regardless of any orders from Camp Floyd.

George Reeder, foreman of the Rush Valley ranch, was considering those instructions thoughtfully as he watched the company of soldiers halt several hundred yards from the ranch house. There was a flurry of activity as one of the round Sibley tents was put up. Reeder, a tall, wiry man with a bushy beard, scratched a cheek and weighed the odds. If those soldiers pushed things to a fight, which they probably were prepared to do, wasn't no way to stop them, he decided. No matter what Daniel or his brother Orson wanted, this ranch was closing down. Reeder knew there was no chance going against that many soldiers, and he wasn't ready to get killed for a couple of stubborn old men.

Two men on horseback started trotting toward the ranch house. One was an officer, the other a civilian. Reeder didn't look back at the bunkhouse behind him, but called out to the men inside.

"Don't no one git trigger happy," he growled. "We'll see what these two got on their minds, then we'll decide what's best to do."

The two riders approached to within a dozen yards of Reeder, then reined in. The officer nodded politely toward Reeder.

"You'd be George Reeder, foreman of this outfit." The officer said it like he'd met Reeder before, which he hadn't. He nodded again. "I'm Lieutenant Lou Marshall. This here's Carn Tregale. He's a civilian, sent by Governor Cummings and General Johnston to witness everything is done proper. I'm sure you've noticed the company of Tenth Infantry behind me."

Tregale acknowledged the introduction by a raised hand, but sat silent. As Lieutenant Marshall said, he was here only as an observer.

"I'm Reeder, right enough," the foreman said gruffly. "Can't say I'm pleased to make your acquaintance, Lieutenant. This don't look like no friendly visit."

"It isn't, Mr. Reeder. You and those cattle I see scattered around were supposed to be out of Rush Valley last week. From what I see, you folks barely begun your roundup."

"Maybe it was sunnin' over in Cedar last week, Lieutenant, but it sure wasn't here in Rush. No chance to do anything but hunker down out of those storms."

"It isn't storming now, Mr. Reeder."

"Cattle got pretty scattered over the winter. As you can see, we're startin' to fill up the corrals for brandin'."

"How long do you expect it will take to corral your herd?" the lieutenant asked.

Reeder scratched at his cheek again. He knew what Daniel and Orson Spencer would want him to say, but no sense in hurrying a showdown. "Don't rightly know, Lieutenant. About three, four days, I expect. That's just the cattle. Sheep are all over and they'll take awhile longer."

"You've already had plenty of time to get the job done, Mr. Reeder. I'll give you 'til sunup tomorrow," Marshall told him. "Then you move out with whatever stock you got in the corrals."

"What happens to the rest of the herd—?"

"Confiscated, Mr. Reeder," Marshall said quietly. "Any stock remaining in the valley after tomorrow becomes government property."

Reeder's face grew red, although no one could really tell that through the bushy profusion of beard. "We ain't goin' to do that, Lieutenant. We ain't movin' out without all our stock." He paused, sucked in a breath of courage, then added belligerently, "I ain't sure we're moving out even with our stock."

Both Tregale and Lieutenant Marshall heard the challenge in his voice. The lieutenant stepped his horse closer. "That's a full company of soldiers out there, Mr. Reeder. They all got memories of two winters ago freezing their tails off up in the Rockies. They still got a lot of anger bottled up over that. I wouldn't recommend you give them a reason to spill any of it over you and your men."

"No matter what, Lieutenant," Reeder muttered, his belligerence backed down a notch, "we need more time to round up all that stock."

"Sunup tomorrow, Mr. Reeder. I suggest you get your men in the saddle."

The door of the cabin swung open, drawing the attention of all three men. They watched as young Howard Spencer strode toward them, anger dark on his face.

"Maybe you don't hear so good, Lieutenant," the young man said harshly. "We ain't moving off our land, no matter how many soldiers you got."

Lieutenant Marshall was staring at him, taking in the young man's anger.

"This isn't your land—never was. Always has been government range. And who might you be, sir?"

"Howard Spencer. My father, Orson Spencer, and his brother Daniel own this ranch. We been runnin' cattle in this valley for over seven years—"

"—and now that privilege has been revoked," Marshall said evenly. "I understand how you feel, Mr. Spencer, but that doesn't change any spots. This is now a military grazing reservation, and I have my orders to clear all civilians from it, along with all their livestock."

"The army ain't got no authority to move our cattle off public range. Says that right in the Territorial code. Besides, this ain't public range no more. This is Spencer land now."

"I repeat, sir," Marshall said quietly, "you don't own this land. The government has allowed you to run cattle on it. However, no permission was ever given to build any permanent structures on it."

Spencer started to protest. "Had to build a bunkhouse for the hands—"

"That is more than a bunkhouse, Mr. Spencer," the lieutenant said icily, "as you well know."

"Don't know what you're sayin', Lieutenant."

"You're running a tavern, Mr. Spencer. Ashamed to say some of my own men frequently bought liquor here while they were on seven-day patrol—liquor you claimed to be home brewed. And those Indian girls you keep in that lean-to out back—that makes this a whorehouse as well as a tavern."

"That's a damn lie—"

"Got proof, Mr. Spencer. And my men aren't your only customers. Known rustlers have been seen frequenting your establishment. We're not only closing you down, Mr. Spencer, we're burning you down."

"Over my dead body—"

"That's your call, Mr. Spencer." The lieutenant shifted his attention back to the foreman. "I'll be spending the night up in that tent, with Mr. Tregale and the rest of my officers. Come sunup, my orders will be carried out." His stare hardened. "Don't want trouble, Mr. Reeder, but we're prepared for it."

Early the next morning, before full daylight, a small detachment of soldiers, about a dozen in number, headed toward the silent bunkhouse—or tavern, or whorehouse, or whatever went on inside it. In the lead of the contingent was Lieutenant Alexander Murry, and striding right behind him was Sergeant Ralph Pike. The sergeant had heard about the confrontation yesterday, and was looking forward to meeting Howard Spencer again. He hadn't forgotten being challenged by the truculent young rancher last December. This time, if Pike got the slightest chance, it would be Spencer put on the ground.

Before Lieutenant Murry reached the bunkhouse, the door opened and George Reeder and Howard Spencer stepped outside. Spencer immediately recognized Ralph Pike as the man he'd bumped into back at Camp Floyd. It irritated Spencer to see a slit of a smile on the sergeant's face.

"You come to eat more dust?" Spencer asked.

The lieutenant scowled back. "You threatening me—?"

Sergeant Pike stepped alongside. "That was meant for me, Lieutenant. Me and Spencer here have met before. Told him there'd be another time."

The lieutenant continued to scowl at Howard Spencer. "I was told you're the son of one of the owners of this ranch."

"You was told right."

"That puts you in charge, over Mr. Reeder here," the lieutenant added, nodding at the foreman.

"You could say that."

"Then what I have to say is directed at you, Mr. Spencer. Watched this place all day yesterday, and didn't see anyone out and about. Guess that means you intend to give up your herd."

"You ain't good at guessin', Lieutenant," Spencer growled back. "We ain't goin' nowhere, and neither is our cattle."

"Then you do not intend to comply with the orders issued by General Johnston—?"

"Johnston gives you orders, Lieutenant. He don't give 'em to me."

"That's right, Spencer. And I do intend to comply. You are in violation of official orders of the federal government—not just General Johnston's orders, I might point out. I'm giving you until eight o'clock this morning—that's about an hour from now—to pack up and leave this range. Anything you leave behind will be burned, and any livestock not being driven will become the property of the army. Do you understand what I just said, Mr. Spencer?"

"I ain't an imbecile, Lieutenant. And don't expect us to just ride out of here, neither. You try to put us off this land and someone's gonna get hurt."

Lieutenant Murry turned to Pike. "I'm going back to report to Lieutenant Marshall, Sergeant. You and the men back off and give these settlers room to go about their business. I'll be back in an hour—" he added, turning his head again to stare at Spencer and Reeder, "—with the rest of the company. We'll do whatever has to be done at that time."

Spencer suddenly raised an arm in signal. About a score of men popped out of hiding in various places around the bunkhouse and its clutter of outbuildings.

Another half dozen filed out the open door of the cabin. Lieutenant Murry and the complement of soldiers looked around, surprised by the number of men confronting them. Hands tightened around rifles, but neither Murry nor Pike drew their sidearms.

"You lost your mind, Spencer?" the lieutenant said. "You taking on the army—?"

"Just proving my point, Lieutenant."

"Which is—?"

"Try to move us off our land, and people is going to get hurt."

Murry stared at him a moment longer, then turned again to Pike. "Your orders stand, Sergeant—maybe you'd better back off a little farther, though. I'll bring the rest of the company back on the double."

Less than an hour later, the full complement of infantry arrived at the ranch. Reeder and Spencer had gone inside, and at times, their voices could be heard arguing. Evidently Reeder was not as resolute about defying the army as the younger Spencer. When Lieutenant Marshall rode up to the bunkhouse, flanked by Lieutenant Murry and Carn Tregale, both Spencer and Reeder came outside again. The other ranch hands remained scattered about the yard, rifles at the ready.

"Understand you don't intend to leave voluntarily, Mr. Spencer," Marshall said coldly.

"Don't intend to leave no way."

Marshall looked around the yard, anger on his face. "You or your men fire one shot at my command, Mr. Spencer, and we have the legal right to cut all of you down. We'll do that, sir."

Tregale stepped his horse forward. He studied the two ranchers gravely. "Know how you must feel—"

"Everybody keeps sayin' that," Spencer interrupted. "If they did, all these soldier boys would be high-tailin' it out of here. We ain't bluffin', Tregale."

"If they leave, they'll just come back with three times the number, and probably a couple of cannons."

"Then that's what they got to do."

"No sense anybody getting killed over this, Spencer. I'll see that your claim is put before Governor Cummings—"

"My dad and uncle got plenty of letters from Cummings already," Spencer growled. "He ain't goin' to do nuthin'. He sure ain't goin' to stand up to Johnston. We got to settle this ourselves."

Tregale looked at Reeder. "You can see this isn't going to work, can't you, Reeder? Getting into a shooting match will only get you all killed."

Reeder glanced at Spencer, who glared back at him. "A man has to do what he thinks is right," Reeder replied to Tregale. "Sometimes it don't matter how it comes out."

Lieutenant Marshall cut into the exchange. "That's the long and the short of it, Reeder." He swiveled in the saddle, looking at Pike. "Sergeant, cut that livestock loose from the corrals. If any man gets in your way, arrest him, put him in chains, and haul him to the regimental stockade."

Pike started toward the gate of the nearest corral, but Spencer ran to it and grabbed a pitchfork leaning against the fence. He whirled around and pointed it threateningly at the approaching Pike.

"Ain't goin' to let you do that, Pike."

Pike didn't stop, holding the rifle in his hand loosely.

"Get out of my way, Spencer."

Spencer lunged toward the sergeant with the pitchfork. Pike sidestepped, brought the rifle up in arc, and crashed the butt hard against Spencer's skull. There was a crack that everyone heard. Spencer collapsed on the ground, the pitchfork falling out of his hand.

Pike looked up at Lieutenant Marshall. "Didn't have no choice, Lieutenant—"

Marshall nodded, looking over at Tregale, who also gave a reluctant nod of his head.

"Better than getting shot, I suppose," Tregale muttered.

"Get that man's head looked at," Marshall said. "Something cracked, that's for sure."

Four of the ranch hands came forward and carried the unconscious Spencer into the bunkhouse. There was no doctor in the company, but a medical corpsman came in to look at him. After cleaning away some of the blood and closely inspecting the wound, the corporal turned to the group of anxiously waiting spectators.

"Need to stop the bleeding. Bring me anything you got." He glanced up at Marshall, standing with the others. "This man needs a proper doctor, Lieutenant. Skull's all smashed in."

Marshall quickly gave the order for a rider to return to Camp Floyd and bring a post doctor back to the ranch.

Moments later, Spencer's head was bound in a dirty collection of bedsheets and dusty curtains. They all quickly became soaked, but with some pressure applied by the corpsman, the flow finally slowed. Spencer remained unconscious, his breathing now deep and labored.

"He goin' to die, soldier?" Reeder asked.

"Don't give much for him pulling through," the corpsman muttered. "Don't like the way he's breathing, neither. But I'm no doctor."

Darkness had settled over the ranch before Dr. Charles Brewer arrived from Camp Floyd. He immediately inspected Spencer, who still had not regained consciousness. The young rancher's breathing was slow and irregular, his face startlingly white. For the last couple of hours, Spencer had been having body spasms, jerking and shuddering, but not making any sound. Discarding the bloodied material used to bandage Spencer, the doctor started probing the crushed skull.

"Get me some opiate out of that bag," Brewer told the corpsman. "and those tools wrapped up in the white linen. The wound is filthy, and there's skull fragments poking into his brain. Can't believe this man is still alive."

An hour later, the wound was clean and the doctor had picked out the fragments of bone from the brain. Some gentle pressure in the right places brought the skull mostly back together, although it was fissured with cracks. The main result was the brain being covered and protected again. Brewer administered another dose of opiate, forcing it down Spencer's throat. Relieving the pressure on the brain had brought immediate response, and the young man was now breathing almost normally, his pulse dropping dramatically from the high rate of the past few hours. Brewer looked down at his patient, shaking his head.

"Nothing more I can do here. I'm going to grab some sleep. If he makes it through the next eight hours," he told the corpsman, "he might live. If he does, we got to get him to Camp Floyd—he needs hospital care."

Spencer regained consciousness early in the morning, while daylight was just breaking. He looked around, frowning at the man in military uniform sitting close to the bed. He started pushing himself up, but the corpsman quickly leaned forward and held him down.

"You still got a big hole in your head," the corpsman told him. "Doc says you need to stay flat until we can get you to the hospital."

"What hospital—?" Spencer croaked.

"Camp Floyd—"

Spencer started pushing himself upright again. "Ain't goin' to no army hospital," he muttered.

He swung his legs down, and stood up. The corpsman momentarily was too stunned to stop him. Spencer took a few steps, steadied himself, then continued on toward the open cabin door. He actually made it outside before his knees folded and he crumpled to the ground again.

Reeder saw him come out of the cabin and came running. He stooped over the fallen man. "Damn fool, Spencer," he growled. "You ain't in no condition to walk. You should be dead."

Spencer grabbed his arm. "Don't let them take me to Camp Floyd," he whispered, his eyes rolling as he tried to focus them on Reeder. "No army doctor, neither. Load me up and take me home, George. Promise me you won't let them take me to that army camp—" He didn't hear or see Reeder's reply, because he fell back into unconsciousness.

Brewer re-bandaged Spencer's head and reluctantly agreed to Reeder's insistence on not taking Spencer to Camp Floyd. The doctor watched the carriage leave, and turned to the two men beside him, Lieutenant Marshall and Carn Tregale.

"He's a dead man," Brewer told them. "He won't make it home alive."

Brewer was wrong. Howard Spencer recovered, was even riding in a month. Some thought it was the bitter, consuming hatred he felt toward Ralph Pike that pulled him through as much as anything.

CHAPTER TWENTY FIVE

CAMP FLOYD

The same morning that Howard Spencer got his skull smashed in, Beryl Tate felt like much the same happened to her. She decided to go to the theater building early, to do some extra rehearsing on her part in the new play the group was presenting next week. The building was unlocked and she let herself in through the rear stage door, then went to the dressing room. That was when she got the hammer-blow.

When she walked into the dressing room, she found Mercy Tuckett in a passionate embrace with Sergeant White. The bodice of her dress was unbuttoned, and both the sergeant's hands and arms were up under the skirt of her dress. They were kissing, with Mercy's arms wrapped tightly about White's neck. Beryl stopped like she had hit a wall. For a moment, she couldn't take her eyes off the two of them, as they couldn't take their startled stares from her. Then color flooded into Beryl's cheeks and she turned and ran from the room.

Mercy followed seconds later, catching up with Beryl before she could leave the building. She grabbed Beryl's arm and whirled her around. Beryl looked down at the floor as Mercy hurriedly buttoned up the front of her dress.

"I'm sorry, Mercy," she whispered, cheeks still aflame. "I'm so sorry I burst in on you like that—"

"What on earth are you doing here so early?" Mercy asked, still holding her arm. "There's no rehearsal until this afternoon—"

Beryl nodded. "I came to go over my part. I thought it would help if I did it on the stage—" She looked up at Mercy Tuckett. "I had no idea you were here, Mercy. I feel so terrible—"

Mercy let go of her arm and motioned to a couple of chairs in the room. "Sit down, Beryl. I'd better explain, so you won't go around giving people the wrong impression—"

Beryl quickly interrupted her. "I wouldn't, Mercy. I'd never tell what I saw—"

"What you saw, Beryl," Mercy told her, as both women sat down, "was two people deeply in love."

"I didn't know—"

"—and I was hoping no one would know," Mercy sighed, "not for awhile, at least. I met Richard in San Francisco several years ago. We were attracted to each other right off, but nothing ever came of it. I was, after all, a married woman, and I had a young daughter to consider. Richard was acting then—he joined the army soon after I left to return here to Utah."

Mercy sighed again, staring into her thoughts. "Life takes strange twists sometime, Beryl. Shortly after I returned from that acting engagement in San Francisco, my husband died—the doctor thought it was pneumonia."

Beryl reached out to take Mercy's hand, her eyes saddened. "That's so sad, Mercy. It might have been so different—"

"I was a widow with a young child, and no way to provide for either of us," Mercy continued, her voice now so low Beryl could hardly hear her. "When my present husband offered to take me as his polygamous wife, I was grateful." She finally looked up, giving Beryl a wan smile. "Now I have four children, a husband I have come to despise, and who should I meet on the street in Salt Lake City—Richard, of course. He had never married. He told me he was starting a theater group here in Camp Floyd and begged me to bring my troupe to entertain the soldiers."

"And you still love each other—" Beryl whispered, eyes now shining. "That's so romantic, Mercy."

"Most people will not be so charitable, Beryl. Most will be shocked and offended that a married woman with four children is having an affair with a sergeant in the army. Especially a Mormon woman."

"It's none of their business—"

"It will be, if you tell anyone, Beryl. It will cause serious trouble for Richard, too."

"I'll not mention it to a soul."

"Will you do that for me, Beryl," Mercy asked, staring into Beryl's eyes. "Can you keep this a secret just between us?"

"You have my promise, Mercy," Beryl declared firmly. "No one will hear about this from me."

Mercy reached over and gave her a hug. "Richard's enlistment will be up soon. We'll be going back to San Francisco. He already has an offer to work in a theater there—acting and directing."

Beryl smiled. "I'm happy for you, Mercy."

A shadow crossed Mercy's face. "I'll not be taking the children. You should know that."

Beryl was shocked, but tried to cover it up. "That's your business, Mercy—"

"I know what people will say," Mercy said bitterly. "But the children will be well cared for—they have fifteen brothers and sisters, counting all the other children. They'll be loved, and raised as Mormons. A life in San Francisco, with their mother gone so much, would be worse for them."

"I can see that."

"I love them, Beryl. I really do."

"I'm sure you do, Mercy."

"You still promise not to tell anyone about Richard and me?"

"Of course I do."

Mercy gave her another hug. "Then I have some other news. Richard just told me that the theater will be closed for a week. General Johnston has ordered Richard's whole regiment into the field—something about rounding up cattle on the new grazing reservations. So—we have the week off. And because you have been so wonderful about this, Beryl, I want to do something special for you."

"No need for that," Beryl protested.

"Yes, there is," Mercy insisted. "Not only because of what happened this morning, but because you've worked hard and you've become quite talented. I want you to stay the whole week at the Carson Inn, enjoying some luxury and Elvira's cooking."

"I couldn't do that—"

"I'll make all the arrangements, and it won't cost you a penny." Mercy patted Beryl's hand gratefully. "I'm really grateful, Beryl. It will give me pleasure to do this for you."

Beryl hesitated, then decided to ask what was in her mind. "This probably isn't good timing, Mercy, especially—well, under the circumstances—but you told me once you might take me with you when you went to San Francisco. Since you're moving to San Francisco soon, do you—well, do you think I'm good enough yet?"

Mercy studied her. This was no attempt to take advantage of the situation, she decided. And she had indeed promised to consider taking Beryl to San Francisco with her. She broke into a smile, nodding.

"You're good enough, Beryl. And yes, Richard and I will get you started in San Francisco."

Beryl was beside herself, clapping her hands together in a spontaneous burst of happiness. She was beaming as she looked at her benefactress.

"Thank you, Mercy. I'll make you proud of me."

"I think you will," Mercy smiled back.

With no reason to rehearse, Beryl decided to walk across the bridge and down to the Carson inn. She had meant it when she told Mercy there was no obligation, but she was absolutely delighted at the offer. A few men were standing talking outside the inn, none that Beryl recognized, but that told her breakfast was over. It was Elvira's custom to put food on the table at seven sharp, and it was already two hours past that.

Beryl went into the inn, found the dining room empty and the dishes cleared. A clean tablecloth was already on the table, ready for the noon meal.

Walking into the kitchen, Beryl found Elvira on her knees, scrubbing the floor.

She looked up as Beryl entered, then settled back on her haunches, the scrub brush still in her hand.

"Miss Tate," she said primly, "something I can do for you?"

Beryl shrugged. "Just dropped in to visit, Mrs. Carson. Guess I'm going to be staying here the rest of the week."

"That's more than I'm doing," Elvira snapped. "Soldier was just here. Paid for a week's room and board for you. He made a point to let me know there wasn't anything between him and you."

Color again flushed into Beryl's cheeks. "I hope you believe that, Mrs. Carson—"

"Don't matter if I do or don't," Elvira told her. "Happy to tell you, though, I think you're a good girl, even if you are one of those actresses."

Beryl couldn't quite decide if Elvira had paid her a compliment or not. "Did you say you wouldn't be here these next few days, Mrs. Carson?"

"Leaving in a couple of hours," Elvira replied, looking at the brush in her hand. "Won't be back, so I won't be using this again. Come to think of it, don't know why I'm using it now."

Elvira gave the brush an angry toss and it went flying across the room. Beryl was puzzled.

"Don't think I understand," she said hesitantly.

"Mr. Carson just got himself a new wife," she said stiffly. She stood up, straightening her dress, then brushing at her hair. It was done up as usual in a tight bun so brushing at it didn't do much.

Beryl was shocked. "Mr. Carson has another wife—?"

"Girl by the name of Emma Partridge. Sixteen years old, if you can imagine it. We got a daughter older than that." Elvira was barely holding her composure, and it was plain she was deeply hurt. "Moving me to Orem, with the young'uns. Wouldn't stay here anyway, not with him bouncing that child in our bed."

Beryl didn't know what to do or say. She felt heart-sorry at the pain she could tell was inside the older woman. It was a story repeated often these days.

She thought again of Mercy Tuckett. She obviously didn't like belonging to a polygamous family either, although her situation was entirely different from Elvira's.

"Is there anything I can do?" Beryl asked.

"Nope. All packed and ready to go soon as the wagon comes

around." She glanced around the kitchen, everything in it bearing her stamp of toil and love.

"Don't expect it will ever look this good again," she muttered. She brushed impatiently at the tears that suddenly jumped into her eyes. "Won't miss it more than an hour or two, I suppose. Let me show you to your room, young lady. Last thing I'm doing as hostess of this place."

Carn Tregale rode express back to Camp Floyd, leaving the company of soldiers at the Spencer ranch. Lieutenant Marshall was as anxious as he was to make his report to the proper authorities. If Howard Spencer died, there would be trouble in the making.

Tregale was admitted to Colonel Cooke's office. There was a look of concern on Cooke's face as he greeted Tregale. "Heard they needed a doctor out in Rush. What happened?"

Tregale reported the incident involving Howard Spencer and Sergeant Pike. In his opinion, he told Cooke, the attack on young Spencer was harsh, but justifiable as self-defense. Spencer was trying to put the pitchfork into Pike. Of course, he added, probably wasn't a Mormon alive who would hold Pike blameless.

Cooke told Carn he would report to General Johnston. It was more important, he said, for Carn to get back to Salt Lake City and make sure Cummings and the church leaders knew the true facts of an incident that was sure to be blown up and distorted.

Cooke also had some disturbing news for Tregale.

"Can't confirm this, Carn," he said, "but I believe an attempt is being organized to take Brigham Young prisoner."

Tregale stared at him, finding the news hard to believe. "Johnston's always opposed anything like that—"

"Don't think he knows about it yet," Cooke said, "not officially, at least. There was some plot afoot involving counterfeiting currency plates. All blown over now, but some officers involved are trying to make it look like Brigham Young was behind it."

"Any evidence he was?"

"He definitely wasn't. But a young engraver who worked in the Mormon currency plant was part of it. That's how they're trying to tie in Brigham Young. That crusty one-eyed federal judge, Cradlebaugh, is holding court in Provo and demanding military action. We just sent almost a thousand troops to Utah County, including a company of my dragoons and an artillery battery. Cradlebaugh is out of control. He's arresting people without cause, stirring up a real hornet's nest. He wants Young's hide in the worst way—something to do with that Mountain Meadows massacre. It's a mess, Carn, with a whole lot of people involved."

"How far has this gone, this plan to arrest Brigham Young?"

"Some cannons are gone from the Third Artillery. Just found out some gunnery officers have been scouting out Brigham Young's estate, looking for the best place to blast through the wall."

"It's gone that far—?"

"Doesn't look good. It will finish General Johnston and the rest of us if it happens, especially if Young gets killed. Sentiment's already changed a lot back East—people are starting to believe this whole Utah expedition was just a red herring for treason in the administration."

"What can I do—?"

"Make sure Governor Cummings knows about it, and of course, Brigham Young and his Mormon leaders. I hate doing this, but if some of the junior officers are actually planning on going through with an attack on Brigham Young, this whole command will pay dearly."

CHAPTER TWENTY SIX

SALT LAKE CITY
LATE APRIL

Ideclare, I've never known such kindness." Mrs. Cummings was sitting in the parlor of the Galloway home, with Agatha, Heather, and Esther Cunningham. She took another sip of the herb tea and set the cup down on the small tray on her lap.

"I don't feel good about accepting such a kind offer—"

"Nonsense," Agatha told her. "The sisters will be happy to do it. Might even be considered a little selfish on their part—it will be the only opportunity most of them get to see inside the new governor's mansion."

Mrs. Cummings had dropped in on Agatha to see if she could suggest how to solve a dilemma facing her next week. Heather was still home, although getting ready to spend a couple of days in Sugar House with Gwen Pitts. Esther just happened to be visiting.

Mrs. Cummings and her husband had just moved into the old Babbitt mansion, the new official residence of the Territorial governor. The Staines mansion, in which they had been living for almost a year since arriving in Utah, would now house Territorial administration offices.

The dilemma involved the open house the governor was holding next week. In Georgia, there would be as many slaves as needed to do the cooking and serving and caring for the needs of their guests. In Salt Lake City, it was a different story. There were no slaves, and Mrs. Cummings was at a loss to know how to feed the hundred or so invited guests.

"Don't worry about it," Agatha repeated firmly. "The sisters in the ward put on large socials all the time. The mothers will do the cooking, the young girls will help prepare and serve, and the boys will do the cleaning up. Like I say, they'll be excited at the privilege of being inside your new home."

"But it seems such an imposition—"

"Not in the least," Heather assured her. "They'll be happy to do it—you and the governor are well liked, Mrs. Cummings."

"Well, it does answer what seemed an almost impossible situation," Mrs. Cummings sighed. "Never really realized how much I depended on our Negras. When you grow up—" She hesitated, looking a little awkward. "It must be difficult for you to understand, never having lived in a world where having slaves is an accepted way of life."

Esther Cunningham was frowning as she looked at the governor's wife. "How many slaves did you have in Georgia, Mrs. Cummings?"

Agatha interrupted, not knowing where Esther was going with her question but reasonably sure it would not be a comfortable place for anyone.

"That's not our concern, Esther. Like Mrs. Cummings says, unless you've lived in the South, it's not possible for people like us to understand."

The governor's wife flashed a little smile. "It's like living here with you Mormons, Mrs. Cunningham. Your way of life is very different from people in the East. But I must say," she added quickly, "that you're not at all like the terrible people I was led to believe lived in Utah."

"That seems so strange," Heather murmured. "We just don't think of ourselves as being anything but honest, God-fearing people who love our country. There are so many vicious lies—"

"The aggravating thing is," Agatha added, "that the whole country seems willing, even eager, to believe every one of those lies."

"I'll attest to that," Mrs. Cummings said, nodding her head vigorously. "I must admit, I was one of those who believed the worst about you. I berate myself for that now, of course. Now I can truthfully say I have never met a finer group of people in my whole life."

"We appreciate that," Agatha said. "And of course, the fact that your husband is so well respected is a mark of our esteem for the both of you. There's not too many Gentile officials who have been accepted so warmly in Utah."

Mrs. Cummings smiled again. "That was a pleasant surprise. I thought the Governor was going to his death when he decided to come to Great Salt Lake City without the protection of the army. Now I wish I had accompanied him, as he asked. When I think I could have been here sharing the company of such fine ladies, instead of spending those months nearly freezing to death and constantly fearing for my life in Ecklesville—well, we live and learn, don't we?"

Esther was determined to make the most of this unexpected visit with the wife of the Governor. She gave a quick, almost challenging glance at Agatha and Heather, then asked another question.

"Mrs. Cummings, you've lived among us for almost a year now, and you're considered a close friend by many of us. May I be so bold as to ask what feelings you have toward Mormon women who practice polygamy?"

The governor's wife could see the flashes of annoyance from both Agatha and Heather, but addressed Esther's question with no display of her own feelings.

"Mrs. Cunningham, I really don't know how to answer that question. The practice of plural marriage is strange to me, as it is to hundreds of thousands of other American citizens. It is offensive to many, as you well know. All I can say is that every woman I have come to know personally who lives in a plural relationship, belies every story that is told by those who denounce the practice. I am convinced these women have made a free choice, and seem every bit as happy as any other married woman—in fact, I get the feeling that some of them have a better marriage than some of us."

"But don't you find it repugnant—?" Esther frowned.

"Not at all. I wouldn't want to have that kind of marriage myself—although I'm not so sure about Mr. Cummings," she added with a twinkle. "It's the same thing we were talking about a moment ago. Slavery must seem as strange to you as polygamy does to those outside your faith."

"It's interesting what you said about 'free choice' for women about having their husbands take another wife," Heather said. "I'm leaving this evening to spend a couple of days with a young lady who is having a terrible time with just such a situation. Her husband wants to take a second wife, but she can't stand the thought of that happening."

Esther glanced at her. "You're talking about poor Gwen Pitts, of course. I feel so sorry for her—and someone should take that husband of hers and make it impossible for him to do harm to any woman. I'm sure Gwen would appreciate it—"

"Esther," Heather gasped, "that's a terrible thing to say. Gwen loves Derek—"

"And he loves a young girl of sixteen. It's disgusting."

Mrs. Cummings looked at Heather. "I take it this young woman is having a difficult time—as it would be when the choice is different from her husband."

"She's a wreck," Heather said sadly. "She stopped eating, and started drinking. I'm afraid she's near a complete nervous breakdown. We've known them since they left England and perhaps I can help calm her a little. Not sure if there's anything I can say that will be meaningful, but I know she'll appreciate the friendship."

Esther was shaking her head, the frown deepening. "Gwen Pitts is a good example as to why this polygamy thing bothers me so much. It's so unfair—even if a woman pretends it doesn't bother her. I'm convinced that most of them feel the way Gwen does, even if they don't admit it, and try not to show it. I tell you straight, my Alfred better never get such thoughts—"

Mrs. Cummings suddenly broke into a broad smile.

"I'm sorry to hear about this young lady, but I'm suddenly reminded of the story Mr. Cummings told me just last night. Have you ladies heard what happened to the plural wives of Bishop Aaron Johnson in Springville?"

None of them had. Esther in particular perked up—this would offer a Gentile point of view of polygamy for sure.

"Well," Mrs. Cummings said, "as you know, that horrible Judge Cradlebaugh—I don't know how he ever got appointed to the Territorial Supreme Court—has been down in Utah County investigating murders in Provo and Springville—leastwise, that's what he claims. It's a long story, but a few weeks ago Cradlebaugh arrested the mayor of Provo and two other men on a trumped-up charge of murder, and also issued a warrant for the arrest of Bishop Johnson. A couple of nights later, a force of a hundred and fifty infantry and fifty dragoons crept into Springville and broke into the bishop's home. They also broke into the bedroom of the bishop's nine wives, and from what Mr. Cummings was told, that was a big mistake—"

"What happened?" Esther asked. "Was the bishop there—?"

"He'd been warned and was hiding out in the mountains at a secret camp called Kolob," Mrs. Cummings continued. "The soldiers seized the night pot in the wives bedroom and started doing a war dance around it. That got the women mad and they attacked the soldiers with pillows and blankets—along with some lively language, I understand. Drove those soldiers right out of the house."

Agatha broke into laughter. "That would have been a sight to behold. Nine angry women and all those soldiers—"

"Two hundred soldiers just to seize one man—?" Heather shook her head. "Seems a pity they didn't have something better to do than engage a bed pot in battle."

"That really made Mr. Cummings angry," his wife said. "You know how many times General Johnston has refused to send soldiers when the Governor has requested them—every time for something important, mind you. Judge Cradlebaugh asks for troops to control a few angry settlers in Provo and Johnston sends a force of eight hundred soldiers. Eight hundred! And a battery of artillery! I'm telling you, Mr. Cummings is very upset about that."

"What did Cradlebaugh do after that?" Heather asked.

Mrs. Cummings shrugged. "Let some guilty prisoners go free, just to aggravate the local citizens. Then he went to Lehi to investigate an ax murder."

"An ax murder?" Esther gasped. "In Utah—?"

"Don't know the whole story but it seems a man named Joseph Lance murdered his father, somewhere outside Utah. He escaped and started living in American Fork, where no one knew him. However, he took advantage of a Danish woman and was charged with rape. He never came to trial—"

"Why not?' Esther frowned. "That's a serious crime—"

"The Danish woman got into the jail in Lehi—deliberately let in, some believe—and while Lance was sleeping, she took revenge by axing him to death in his bed."

"My goodness," Esther said, putting a hand to her mouth, "didn't know such things went on in American Fork."

"I can't begin to tell you all the things that are happening in every part of the Territory," Mrs. Cummings said. "It has Mr. Cummings worried sick that there will be a complete breakdown of law and order."

"I hope not," Heather said, "not when the marshals are just beginning to make downtown safe again."

"You people have such a wonderful city," Mrs. Cummings said. "So many amenities that I certainly didn't expect to find in this 'desert wasteland' as it was described to me back in Georgia. In many ways, you put Atlanta to shame with all the culture and refinement you have here."

"Well, you'll have a long time to get to know us and our city," Agatha said.

A frown came to Mrs. Cummings's face. "I'm not so sure, Agatha. There are some troubling signs of late—"

"Like what—?"

"Some communiqués Mr. Cummings is receiving from Washington. There are people back there who don't appreciate the way he is handling the governorship."

"In what way, for heaven's sake?" Heather asked. "Your husband is doing a wonderful job—Brigham Young attests to that."

"Some think Mr. Cummings is being too soft on the Mormons," his wife shrugged. "They want bloodshed it seems, not peace and prosperity."

"That is simply nonsense," Agatha snorted.

"But the most troubling is what is happening politically," Mrs. Cummings said quietly. "That is very disturbing—my husband believes war between the North and the South is almost inevitable."

"Surely it can't be. States would fight each other over slavery—?"

"That's the obvious point of contention," Mrs. Cummings said, "but it goes much deeper. It's not slavery as much as who controls Congress—who controls the direction of our future. The territories will be the key—will they vote for slavery or freemen. And of course, when the Republicans choose their presidential candidate in a few days, it will affect all of us."

Esther was frowning again. "Why would that be, Mrs. Cummings?"

"Because it's almost certain Abe Lincoln will get the Republican nomination—at least, Mr. Cummings seems convinced of that. Lincoln has made his anti-slavery position very clear, and that will cast a shadow over the whole land. If he's elected president, there will be war. And if there's war, Mr. Cummings and I will have to support the way of life we are accustomed to. Our sympathies are well known in Washington so Mr. Cummings will be replaced with a Northerner. It makes me ill to think of all that happening, but it can very easily. If it does, I will miss you ladies of Utah Territory."

"Well," Agatha said, jumping to her feet, "even if it happens, it's a long way off. In the meantime, we need to get your open house organized. Do you have a menu in mind—?"

CHAPTER TWENTY SEVEN

SALT LAKE CITY

Billy Hickman, accompanied by his son-in-law, Jason Luce, came down the stairs from his law office on Second South and saw Charlie Drown passing on the other side of the street. Drown was the flamboyant character who, in addition to several enterprises, ran the youthful rustler gang that Fred and Ted Tate became involved with. Drown was about medium height, a little flabby, with a closely-cut black beard circling his face. He dressed flashily, usually a boldly-striped suit with white shirt and brightly-colored cravat. Perhaps it was the attire, but Drown didn't invite trust. He didn't look like a successful businessman, but then again, he didn't look like a rustler either. Looking at him, words like shifty, seedy, devious all came to mind.

Hickman raced across the street, planting himself directly in front of Drown. Drown looked startled, and then uneasy at the look on Hickman's face. It wasn't the lawyer side of Hickman confronting him, Drown saw, but the rustler-killer side. More disturbing, it was an angry rustler-killer. Drown knew that was not a good combination.

"Billy," Drown said, trying to make himself sound relatively cheerful, "I was thinking you was out in Cedar."

"No, I'm here, Charlie," Hickman replied, staring hard at the man in front of him, "and I was thinking we need to talk."

"Always pleased to do that, Billy. You got something special on your mind?"

"My office is just across the street. It'll be a mite more private talking there than out here on the street."

The three men entered the office and Drown sat down in one of the chairs across from Hickman's desk. Luce took the other. Hickman leaned back in his chair and stared at Drown a moment or two in silence, then got right to it.

"You been rustling my cattle, Charlie."

Fear tingled along Drown's spine. "Ain't true, Billy," he protested. "I'd never take stock what belonged to you. You know me better'n that."

"Two days ago. Off the southwest section of my ranch. About fifty head. One of my night riders recognized Swazey—he works for you, don't he, Charlie?"

Drown started shaking his head vigorously. "Not any more, he don't. I got out of the rustling business almost a month ago, Billy. That Swazey—the crazy kid cut down a trooper. I don't want no trouble like that. Told Swazey I was out of it, and he was on his own. Guess he held the gang together. But he's running it, Billy, not me."

"Who's running with him?"

"The Tate boys are out. Guess it's just Jim Warthers and Ike Hatch, unless Rod's taken in some new blood."

"You say Swazey killed a trooper—?"

Drown nodded. "That's what he said, anyway—on the last raid they did for me. That was in Rush. Still ain't heard nuthin' about it, though."

"My men found a dead trooper in Rush, thawing out in a drift. We didn't know who done it, but we didn't want the army getting riled up about it, maybe even blaming me. The body's hid where it ain't never going to be found."

Drown was visibly relieved. "Glad to hear that. My thanks, Billy."

"This mean you're back in the rustling business?"

Again Drown shook his head vigorously. "I'm out for good. In the spirit business now."

Hickman frowned. "You making moonshine?"

"Not that kind of spirits. You heard about a book telling how to talk to dead people—Josie Arnold wrote it."

"Heard people talking about it."

"Well, me and Josie are in business with Ivy Eddy. You maybe heard about him too. Lectures a lot on spiritualism—some think he's as much a prophet as Brigham Young. People are eating this spiritualism stuff up—willing to pay good money to hear a few words from beyond the grave. Eddy's real good at the seance stuff—and me, I figure I got a natural gift for it."

"That's about as crooked as rustling cattle," Jason Luce grunted.

"But there ain't nothing illegal about it," Drown grinned. "You got anybody dead you want to talk to, Jason?"

"Ain't nobody dead I know who'd say anything I want to hear." He looked curiously at Drown. "Say, didn't you and Arnold just get excommunicated, or sumpin, from the Mormon Church?"

Drown shrugged. "Just a misunderstanding. When Brigham Young heard about it, he undid it. We're both back in the Church now."

"Folks ain't too happy about that, either."

"Arnold—ain't he the guy who says he talks to Jesus Christ?" Hickman asked.

"Well, don't exactly talk to him. Josie says Jesus transmits thoughts direct to him—that's about the same as talking, I guess." Drown was feeling better, reasonably convinced now that Hickman wasn't planning on killing him. "I hear Joaquin Johnston is running a gang out of Frogtown. Well, Lot Huntington's actually running it, I hear."

That brought another frown wrinkling across Hickman's forehead. "Joaquin's competition, right enough. Understand he's running for sheriff of Frogtown—not bad being on both sides of the law."

"Same as you, Billy," Drown said. He was relieved to see Hickman's frown dissolve into a smile.

"'Ceptin' folks don't necessarily consider a lawyer as being on the right side of the law." The smile slipped from his face. "Guess I ain't blaming you for what happened to my cattle, not any more. I'll settle up with Swazey. But I'm recommending you stay out of the rustling business, Drown. Getting pretty crowded."

"I'm out," Drown repeated emphatically, "and I ain't getting back in. This spirit business is looking pretty good."

Drown hurried back onto the street, glad to be leaving with a whole skin. Hickman and his son-in-law were just starting to leave themselves when two men ascended the stairs and entered the office. Hickman recognized them—the two gentile merchants, Gilbert and Gerrish.

"Afternoon, gentlemen," Hickman said, extending his hand. "Is there some legal service I can provide for you?"

The two merchants looked at each other, hesitated for a moment, then Gilbert spoke up.

"Not exactly legal services, Mr. Hickman."

Hickman motioned for them to sit down. Luce brought in another chair and sat close to Hickman. "Can I get you gentlemen a drink?" Both shook their heads, and Hickman waited, but neither of the other two men said anything.

"So what kind of service can I do for you?" Hickman asked finally.

Again looks were exchanged, and again it was Gilbert who answered. "We understand you have successfully recovered stolen property for some of the merchants in town—"

Hickman nodded, beginning to understand what was on the merchants' minds. "Somebody stole something from you gentlemen—?"

"About a thousand head of cattle," Gilbert said. "A few days ago, out in Skull Valley. Rustlers took them."

Hickman knew the exact tally was nine hundred and seventy four head of cattle. That was the count given to him by Joe Rhodes, Billy's ramrod on the raid on the merchants' herd. Couldn't tell that to the men sitting across from him, of course. And neither Gilbert nor Gerrish mentioned to Hickman that they were certain they were talking to the man responsible for the theft of their cattle. Only Hickman had enough men on his payroll to handle rustling a herd that large. In fact, they were willing to bet those cows were grazing on Hickman's ranch in Cedar Valley that very moment.

"We're willing to pay you a sizable finder's fee, Mr. Hickman," Gilbert said, "for the return of that herd. Can you do that for us?"

Hickman looked over at Luce, then scratched at his neck with both hands. "Might be able to locate those cows for you. Fee would be fifty percent of their value."

"That's pretty steep," Gerrish said gruffly. He wasn't talking much because he was afraid he'd say something foolish, like accusing

Hickman of stealing their cattle in the first place. "Twenty-five percent is more reasonable."

"I agree," Hickman replied. "Trouble is, I'd be dealing with people who already got one hundred percent profit. Might talk them into going fifty-fifty, with no hassle of driving those cows to California, or Mexico, or wherever they're planning on taking them. Less than that, and I can't help you, gentlemen."

The two merchants looked at each other, both thinking the same thing.

Half a loaf was better than none.

"It's agreed," Gilbert muttered. "Fifty percent. How soon do you think you can get in touch with these rustlers?"

"Depends if those cows are where I think they might be," Hickman told them, deliberately evasive. "If they are, I'll have that herd back in Skull Valley in a week."

The two merchants stood up. "Appreciate your help, Mr. Hickman. We'll pay in gold soon as the cattle are returned."

"I'll start tracing that herd today."

This time Hickman and Luce made it back to the street. They headed for the jail, where Luce waited outside while Billy went in to visit his first and only client—not counting Gilbert and Gerrish, and others like them. That was a different kind of client. Paying to get stolen property back from the man who stole it wasn't the same as being duped into committing murder.

Tom Ferguson was holding onto the bars of his cell, peering out at Billy Hickman. "You come to get me out, Billy?" he asked.

"Thought you'd be free by now, Tom—I really did. Those new judges just hate everybody in Utah—"

"I ain't from Utah—"

"Told them that, Tom. Told them that several times. And I keep telling them you're an innocent man—you killing Carpenter was a clear case of self defense."

"What did the judge say to that—?"

"He's thinking about it, Tom. Thinking real hard, he told me. I expect to have this whole thing cleared up in a couple more weeks. Just thrown out of court. Won't be no trial, just like I told you."

"It's been six months, Billy—"

"Know that, Tom. Feel real bad about it. Just stopped by to tell you we're making real progress, and it looks good to get you out of here soon."

"How long is soon—?"

"Depends, Tom. Depends on a lot of things. You just rest easy knowing I'm working hard to get you out of here."

"Appreciate that, Billy. Makes me feel better when I talk to you like this."

From the jail, Hickman and Luce went back downtown to Willie's Place, a popular saloon close to his office. It was filled with smoke, and there was a thin man in a striped shirt, suspenders, and a gaudy vest banging away loudly at a piano, making a lot of noise but not playing any recognizable tune. Billy looked around and saw the two men he knew would be there, so he and Luce headed over to their table. Joe Rhodes and Frank McNeil said nothing while the two men sat down with them.

"Frank," Hickman said, "maybe you and Jason should get some air."

McNeil started to protest, saw the look on Billy's face and hurriedly stood up. "Been meaning to do that."

After Luce left with McNeil, Hickman let the full intensity of those dark, deep-set eyes bore into Joe Rhodes. It made Rhodes uncomfortable, but he waited without saying anything.

"Got a visit from Gilbert and Gerrish awhile ago," Hickman said finally. "They was asking about a thousand head of beef that went missing."

"Guess we know what happened," Rhodes grinned.

Hickman nodded. "Know about the thousand head, Joe, but what I don't know is what happened to the three hundred head that's missing from the ranch."

Rhodes heard the threat in Billy's voice and the grin slipped away. "What you talkin' about, Billy?"

"Frank brought me the tally yesterday. Somebody's took three hundred head. You know anything about that, Joe?"

"First I heard about it. Frank should'a told me—"

"Makes me real mad thinking somebody rustled cattle off my own ranch."

Rhodes was thinking fast, knowing what Hickman was getting around to. He decided not to wait until he was asked.

"Come to think of it, Billy," he said, as if just remembering, "one of Joaquin's boys was bragging yesterday about how some cattle sorta wandered onto their place. He was drinking heavy, but he mentioned about three hundred head."

"They still there, you think?"

Rhodes shook his head. "Cowboy mentioned they'd already moved 'em. Could be hid anywhere."

Rhodes tensed as Billy reached inside his coat, but his hand came out holding only some wrinkled currency.

"Fifty dollars, Joe. That's what it's worth for you to find those cattle and run them back to Rush Valley. The whole thousand head. The fifty's over and above your regular cut, of course."

"You givin' that stock back to Gilbert and Gerrish—?"

"Selling it, Joe. Get more profit that way than running the herd to California."

The grin came back to Rhodes's face. He picked up the fifty dollars and stuffed the notes into a shirt pocket. "I'll find 'em, Billy. Wherever Joaquin's got 'em hid, I'll find 'em. Seems like I remember that cowboy talkin' about a canyon up from the Jordan River—"

"I'm counting on you, Joe."

◆

When Carn Tregale rode into the city, after a hard, fast ride back from Camp Floyd, he went first to the Council House, where the Nauvoo Legion was headquartered, hoping to find Bob Burton. He was told Burton was at the Beehive House, meeting with General Wells and Governor Young. Carn got back on his horse and trotted up South Temple to the walled estate.

Admitted through the Eagle Gate, and then into the impressive foyer of the mansion, Tregale waited while one of guards went to inform the officers of his arrival. Just then, Eliza Young bustled across the room. She saw him, and crossed toward him with extended hand and a warm smile.

"Brother Tregale. You look like you've just had a long ride."

Tregale glanced guiltily down at his clothes, realizing he was covered in much of the mud he had splashed through on his way up from Camp Floyd.

"Sorry, Sister Eliza," he muttered. "Didn't realize I was so trail-worn."

"Nonsense," she smiled. "Always glad to see you, Brother Tregale."

Carn had never personally explained to her that he wasn't a member of the Church, but he knew she was aware of it. Being called Brother Tregale just seemed to come natural to folks, and he didn't object. If this latest trouble hadn't come up, he would have been baptized by now, anyway.

"Wonder if you'd do me a favor, Brother Tregale," she smiled.

"Be pleased to do that."

"I'm having a gathering for some of the sisters next Saturday evening—a poetry reading, so I'll not make any of you gentlemen pretend you enjoy such things. I have invitations for your wife and Agatha. Would you mind delivering them for me, since I suspect you'll be going home right after this meeting?"

"Will the reading include any poems you've written?"

Her smile widened. "Why, yes, as a matter of fact, I will be reading a few things of mine. Some of the sisters made a special request—but that's only a small part of the evening."

"I'll be sorry to miss it. Heather has read some of your poems to me, and I really enjoyed them. You have a true talent for it."

"Why Brother Tregale," she said, giving him a steady gaze, "I believe you mean that. Thank you, sir. I accept your compliment with great pleasure."

The guard returned and Eliza Young excused herself. "I'll have the invitations waiting for you after the meeting, Brother Tregale. Thank you kindly."

Tregale was shown into the large office of Governor Young, located in the spacious building that connected the Beehive House and the Lion House. He exchanged greetings with the three men in the room. Governor Young was seated behind a large desk, General Wells and Colonel Burton seated in front of it.

"Your news must be important, Brother Tregale," Brigham Young said, eyeing him with a smile. "Easy to tell you've had a hard ride. Pull up a chair—"

Tregale politely declined. "Need to get home and get rid of some of this mud, sir. Besides," he added with a brief smile, "feels good to stand after being that long in the saddle."

"Then give us your news, Brother Tregale. What's that Johnston fellow been up to now?"

Carn first told them about the incident at the Spencer ranch in Rush Valley, about the large movement of troops into Utah County, and then what Philip Cooke had told him about the possibility of an attack on the governor's estate, and the attempt to take him prisoner. When he finished, there was silence for a few moments as the men in the room absorbed the news.

"How's the Spencer boy?" Brigham Young asked.

"Not sure he'll make it, sir. His head was pretty stoved in."

"Have to be sure that doesn't get twisted in the telling," the governor said gravely. "That grazing situation is bad enough without adding coal oil."

"Bothers me that Judge Cradlebaugh is stirring up so much trouble," Burton grimaced. "The military obviously is planning to step in if that situation gets out of hand—and with the hatred Cradlebaugh's carrying, it certainly could."

"What concerns me is this attack on Governor Young," General Wells said. "Does your colonel friend think the threat is real?" he asked Carn.

"Seems like it is, General."

"Does Governor Cummings know about any of this?" Bob Burton asked.

"Came straight here," Tregale said. "Thought it best to put people on the alert. If an attack is coming, it probably will come soon."

General Wells stood up, addressing Brigham Young. "We'll ask to be excused, sir. Governor Cummings must be informed immediately." His glance moved to Tregale. "Know it's been a long day, but we'll need you at that meeting."

"Of course, sir."

Governor Cummings had recently visited Provo, wanting to see firsthand why so much trouble was being reported during the hearings being conducted by the federal judge. He had left in disgust after watching Cradlebaugh's abuses to the local citizenry, not being able to do much about it other than reprimand the judge about his tactics. Cummings was shocked and angry at learning the new developments.

"That Cradlebaugh," he grunted, "he's a disgrace to his office. Just don't understand why Washington keeps sending such poorly qualified people out here."

He was angry as he turned to General Wells. "This report about attacking Governor Young appalls me, sir. I want you to call out your Nauvoo Legion and be prepared to defend the governor against any such assault on his estate. I'll put it in writing that armed resistance has my full authorization."

"Thank you, Governor," Wells said. "I'll issue the call immediately."

There was an interruption as a tired-looking army corporal was admitted to the governor's office. He too wore the mud covering that spoke of an express ride.

"Looking for Mr. Tregale, sir," he said, addressing the governor. "I was told he could be found with you, Governor."

Carn stepped forward. "I'm Tregale. You have a message for me, corporal?"

"Yes sir," the corporal said, automatically saluting. "From Colonel Cooke, sir. He said it was extremely urgent."

Tregale took the outstretched piece of paper and read it quickly. Then he turned to the other men.

"General Johnston has ordered most of the command at Camp Floyd into the field. Seems he's determined to avoid any further incidents like the one in Rush Valley, and will be deploying large numbers of troops to clear all federal grazing reserves without delay. There's also reports of trouble brewing on Peteetneet's reservation, and a full regiment of dragoons are heading south. Colonel Cooke feels that an attack on Brigham Young has, at the very least, been postponed. He wants us to know there is no longer imminent danger."

"That's good news—I suppose," Cummings wheezed. "Will this territory never be at peace?"

Burton glanced at General Wells. "Even so, General, I'd feel more comfortable with putting our boys around the estate."

"Absolutely agree with that," Cummings replied, before Wells could answer. "General Wells, please call out your Legion. My authorization will be in your hands within the hour."

By two a.m. the next morning, over 5000 members of the Nauvoo Legion were activated and on station over a wide range of territory. They formed a protective cordon around Brigham Young's entire estate; there were observers at the Point of the Mountain at the south end of the valley where signal fires would alert to any force moving out of Cedar; and there were legionnaires stationed on Ensign Peak, the high point above the city to the north, where any alert from the south would be quickly passed on.

After the meeting with Governor Cummings, Tregale left to go home. On an impulse, he stopped at the emporium downtown. He was reasonably certain Heather wasn't there, because she had stopped going in order to prepare for her journey back East. She wasn't needed, actually, now that Rose was working regularly at the store, helping Agatha. It was Agatha that Carn was hoping to see.

Henry Washington greeted him warmly, as did Rose. She seemed radiantly happy, Carn noted. Henry seemed to have a smile permanently attached to his face.

"Sure good to see you, Carn," Henry beamed.

Carn looked at Rose, standing beside her new husband. "You look happy, Rose. Henry must be treating you well."

Rose took her husband's hand and squeezed it. "He surely is. Didn't think I'd ever be this happy."

Tregale looked around the store. "Agatha here today?"

"She was in this morning, but she's gone home," Henry told him. "The General's out visiting properties and won't be back for a couple more days. Is there anything I can do for you?"

"Don't think so, Henry."

Henry hesitated, then said, "Your wife's in Sugar House. Took little Carn with her. She's spending a couple of days with young Gwen Pitts. That girl's been real sick, I hear."

Carn didn't know if he was more relieved or disappointed. He'd been dreading facing Heather, because it was too painful to see how far they'd drawn apart. It was really disappointing, however, that he wouldn't see his son. In a week or so, little Carn would be gone for months, that is if Heather didn't decide to stay permanently back in Philadelphia—or Boston, he forced his thoughts to add.

"Thanks, Henry," he said. "I'll be heading home. A bath and a night's sleep sound mighty good about now."

When he got home, Agatha sat him down at the kitchen table and soon had an improvised hot meal in front of him. She let him eat, even to finishing off a large piece of hot apple pie, before saying anything. Finally, Carn leaned back and gave a contented sigh.

"You're a good cook, Agatha."

"And you're a darn fool," she snapped back.

Carn grinned. "Nothing like getting right to the heart of it."

"You just going to let her go?"

"Not much I can do to stop her."

"Do you still love her?"

"Of course I do. She knows that. Question seems to be, does she still love me?"

"Neither of you won't find out unless you talk to each other."

"Didn't go so good last time we did that," Carn muttered. "Words don't come out right, Agatha, not for me at least. Has she said when she's leaving?"

"Taking the eastbound stage first week in May."

Carn felt the jolt of hearing a firm date. It made the reality of his wife and son leaving him painfully real. "That's only a few weeks off."

"Why do you think she's taking this trip?" Agatha asked.

"Don't think I want to know the answer to that."

"She's going because her heart's breaking. Not over that captain—you're the one who's causing her such pain, Carn Tregale."

"I've done nothing, Agatha," Carn protested. "Heather's the one holding hands with someone else—"

"Just forget that, Carn," Agatha snapped. "That wasn't what it looked like, and you know it as well as I do. You know what I think—"

"I think you're going to tell me—"

"I think you're just green with jealousy, and too proud to admit it."

Carn frowned. "Wouldn't call it jealousy. It hurt a lot—deeper than I thought. I admit that."

"Pride, Carn," Agatha repeated firmly. "Don't destroy your marriage because you let your pride get too big to swallow."

Harriet interrupted them, coming into the kitchen holding an armful of clothing. She saw Carn and stopped.

"Sorry. I was going to iron a few things for tomorrow—"

"What's happening tomorrow?" Carn asked.

A broad smile came to Harriet's face. "I'm leaving for Brigham City with Lydia and Aaron. They'll be picking me up early in the morning."

"Well, I'm glad I'll get to see you all off," Carn said. "Real sorry to see you go, of course, but I think it's the right thing for you to do, Harriet."

"I hope so. I'm looking forward to it, anyway."

"Good for you two sisters to be close," Agatha said. "Although goodness knows, we'll miss having you around. Little Carn will miss you too."

Harriet sighed. "I'm trying not to think about it. You've been such a wonderful family. You'll never know how much you all mean to me."

"Well, no need to get maudlin," Agatha smiled. "You'll only be fifty miles away. We'll see each other a lot." She cast a glance pointedly in Carn's direction. "It's not like you were going back East, is it, where we might never see you again?"

Carn spent a restless night, troubled with thoughts of Heather, and his son, and the prospect of losing both of them. Captain Edwards floated through his consciousness too, now and then, always smiling and looking like he'd just won a prize at the fair. When morning finally came, Carn felt like he hadn't slept at all.

A covered wagon, heavily laden with goods and furniture, brought Aaron and Lydia to the front door just before eight o'clock. Close behind them was a carriage with Esther and Alfred. Esther's face was buried in a large handkerchief, eyes red from crying. They all got down and Harriet's few possessions were packed aboard the wagon. Esther couldn't watch, going inside the house with Agatha supporting her. It was obvious that Esther was convinced her son and the two sisters were going to their deaths.

It was a long, tearful farewell but finally the wagon pulled out and started on the journey north. Aaron and Lydia, and Harriet, were eager and excited; Alfred was misty-eyed; Esther was devastated. She went back into the sitting room and cried for over an hour after the young people left. Agatha started having a difficult time showing sympathy. Carn had to leave, and he poked his head into the room. Agatha was now sitting by the window, preferring to look at budding trees than watch Esther's histrionics.

Carn held out two envelopes. "Almost forgot about these, Agatha. Sister Eliza asked me to give them to you. It's invitations for you and Heather to attend the poetry reading Saturday evening."

Esther looked up, the sobbing suddenly stopped. "Isn't there one for me?"

"She only gave me these two."

"Why wouldn't she invite me?" she asked, looking at Agatha.

"Maybe she did. Probably sent it to your house."

"No. It would have arrived. She hasn't invited me. I don't understand that, Agatha—"

"Well," Agatha murmured, "you expressed some harsh feelings about polygamy the last time. I'm sure you didn't endear yourself to Sister Eliza."

Esther was thoughtful, then defensive. "I'm not two-faced, Agatha. I say what I feel. If Sister Eliza was hurt, I'm sorry. I certainly didn't mean to be personal but I think people should know how you feel about things."

"Well, I think Sister Eliza is letting you know how she feels. She is a polygamous wife, after all, and you let it be known you feel that is a highly unnatural state. If I were you, Esther, I wouldn't count on being invited to the Beehive House anytime in the near future."

CHAPTER TWENTY EIGHT

SALT LAKE CITY
MAY

Carn was waiting in the kitchen when Heather came downstairs, holding the baby, a large canvas bag slung over her shoulder. Carn jumped up from his chair, where he had sat nervously drumming fingers on the table.

"Is there anything I can do?"

Heather gratefully held out their son. "You can take him. He weighs a ton these days." Almost a year old now, little Carn was indeed growing rapidly and putting on weight.

Carn took the baby and held him close, putting the soft little face against his own for a moment, then gently kissing him. Carn had promised himself to keep his emotions in control, but despite that resolve, he felt tears stinging at his eyes.

All he could think of, holding his son, was this was the last day for many long months he would hold him like this. He was going to miss his son's first birthday, little more than a week away. He wouldn't be there when he took his first steps. He wouldn't share the joy of the little things a baby did each day that make parents so proud. He would miss all the pure childish wonderment as little Carn discovered what his fingers and feet and voice could accomplish. It was hard accepting that, a lot harder now that the day of saying goodbye had arrived. Carn brushed impatiently at the tear he felt sliding down his cheek.

It was almost as difficult for Heather, watching from across the room, pretending that she wasn't. How could she take his son away

285

from him, now that the baby was so close to being able to show its love, develop its personality, recognize and enjoy the warmth of being held by his father and mother? Heather's heart was shredding as she watched her husband hold their baby. This whole thing was so terribly sad. How could two people so much in love be pulled so far apart? Yet, even as sadness engulfed her, there was the realization that things were now in motion that could not be stopped.

General Galloway came into the room, taking in the three of them, the sadness he was feeling plain to read on his face.

"All the bags are in the carriage, Heather. Henry wanted to drive you, if that's all right. Agatha and me thought we'd say goodbye here. That will give room for you to ride with them, Carn—and save the two of us from making blubbering fools of ourselves in public." He came over and put an arm around Heather's shoulder, squeezing affectionately. "We're going to miss you, Heather, no one more than Agatha. Never had a daughter, but I consider I have one now. You take care of yourself, child—and you and that baby come back soon."

Heather didn't even try to stop the tears that started to flow. She hugged the General and gave him a kiss on the cheek. "You have been so wonderful, you and Agatha both. I'll miss you so much."

Agatha came into the room, and immediately went to put her arms around Heather. Both women were crying as they held each other.

"Don't you do anything foolish, you hear," Agatha whispered. "This is your home, this is where you belong."

Heather said nothing, just gave her another hug. Then she turned away, and looked at Carn.

"Ready to go?"

Carn didn't answer, not trusting his emotions. He carried the baby out to where Henry stood beside the open door of the carriage. Carn noticed that Rose was up on the front seat, and it looked like she had been crying too. Rose had quickly become as much a part of the family as Henry. After helping Heather into the carriage, Henry climbed up to sit beside his wife. There were more hugs and tears between Heather and Agatha, then the carriage rolled out onto South Temple Street.

There was a touching moment for Heather as they passed the Beehive House. Sister Eliza was waiting beside the Eagle Gate with some of the other "aunts" and a few guards. She came out into the street, waving for Henry to stop. She opened the carriage door and smiled up at Heather.

"Our prayers will be with you, Heather, that you complete your journey safely." She handed Heather a small, bound book. "This is a collection of my favorite poems. Brother Brigham insisted that some of my own words be included, so you'll find them too. I thought it might help pass the time. You'll find an inscription from both my husband and myself. We want you back with us, Heather—you have a lot of friends here."

Heather couldn't say a word. The tears were flowing again and all she could do was press Sister Eliza's hand gratefully as she took the book. The other woman understood, patted her hand, and stepped back. She closed the door and signaled for Henry to continue on.

At the depot, the stage was already waiting. She intended to take the stage to Independence, on the frontier, then take the train the rest of the way to Philadelphia. Henry supervised the loading of Heather's bags, while Carn stood awkwardly beside his wife, still holding his son. He wanted to tell his wife a hundred things, tell her to stay, tell her how sorry he was that things had gone this far, and how foolish it was for them to let such a separation come between them. But he was afraid nothing would come out right, that whatever he said would be misunderstood. So he just held the baby in silence, feeling almost faint from the pain inside.

Heather, too, was feeling the awkwardness of the silence between them. She turned to her husband. "It would be nice if you dropped in to see Derek Pitts," she said. "Gwen is taking their separation very hard. You know, of course, that she's taken to drinking. It's exacting a frightening toll on her, especially now that the Cunninghams have all moved from Sugar House. Lydia used to go see her all the time. Agatha will visit whenever she can, I'm sure—"

Heather stopped, realizing she was rambling just to cover the silence.

Carn frowned. "Do you think Gwen would take Derek back?"

"I'm not sure. Depends on what he has to say."

"General Galloway went to see him a few days ago. He says Derek is still determined to marry this young Beezley girl."

"Maybe you could talk some sense into him—"

Carn grimaced. "Not very qualified in that area. If I was, my wife and child wouldn't be leaving me."

"Don't say that, Carn. I'm not leaving you."

"Sure looks like it."

"I'm going back to visit my parent's relatives."

"Is that the only reason?"

"I told you before, I'm giving both of us a chance to sort out what's gone wrong between us."

He was just about to say more when Captain Geoffrey Edwards approached. He nodded at Tregale, then doffed his hat and met Heather's eyes. She turned to him, her back now toward Carn, so he couldn't tell what her reaction was to seeing the captain.

Captain Edwards looked past her toward Tregale. "I know this is terribly awkward, Tregale, but I couldn't bring myself to let this lady go away without at least wishing her a safe journey. I hope you understand, sir."

Tregale nodded, said nothing. Edwards turned his attention to Heather.

"It will be several months before I'm out of the army and head back East. I've notified my parents that you will be in Philadelphia, and they intend to visit you and pay their respects. I'll not ask if you intend to visit Boston, but I earnestly hope you remain in the East until I return." He bowed and took her hand in his.

"I'll not intrude any longer. A company of dragoons is returning to Fort Leavenworth. I have requested they rendezvous with the stage at Fort Bridger, and escort it the rest of the way to Leavenworth. It should guarantee you a safe journey."

"Thank you, Captain," Heather said quietly. "That's very thoughtful, and I appreciate it. As I have told you, I've made no plans, but I sincerely value your acquaintance. Perhaps we will meet again."

"That is my fervent wish." The Captain bent over and kissed her hand, then quickly released it. "Safe journey, Heather." As he turned away, he looked again at Carn. "I am grateful, sir. You are a real gentleman."

More like a real fool, Tregale thought to himself. Still, it was not the place to make a scene, even if he wanted to. And it certainly wasn't the time.

The call for boarding came, and Heather was helped up the step by the driver. Tregale handed the baby up to her, and for a long moment, they held each other's stare.

"I'm sorry, Carn," she said quietly. "I really think this is best."

"I respect your decision," Carn told her, "though I don't agree with it. I want you to know I'll miss you. This is a poor time to be saying it, but I love you, Heather. You are the most important person in my life, even more than little Carn, as hard as it is to say such a thing. I'm asking you to come back to me, Heather—I need you to bring back my heart."

For the rest of the day, Tregale found it impossible to shake off the terrible depression that his wife's departure left inside him. He excused himself from dinner, not wanting to risk having to discuss Heather, or worse, Captain Edwards.

He barely slept the whole night, tossing and turning to escape troubled dreams—nightmares—of his wife walking down a church aisle, dressed in white, arm-in-arm with Captain Geoffrey Edwards. Little Carn kept crawling down the aisle behind them, which might have been funny in another dream, but not this one.

Dawn was barely seeping over the mountains when Carn got up, went to the barn and saddled his horse, then headed south out of the Salt Lake Valley.

He wasn't sure where he was going, he just needed to get away from all the things that reminded him of Heather and the baby.

It was too early to drop in on Derek Pitts, and frankly, if something was going on between Derek and the Beezley girl, Carn didn't want to know about it.

He decided it would be a good time to drop in on the Tates, down in Utah County. He knew Fred and Ted were staying there with their parents, waiting to hear from him. Carn asked Cooke about any soldiers missing from the Rush Valley patrols, and Cooke said he had heard there might have been a few deserters, but had not seen any official report. Nothing to be gained by the Tate boys coming forward now, Tregale reasoned. There was no blood on their hands, though they had been there when it happened. Carn believed it would be a lesson learned for the rest of their lives. Certainly Willie and Maude would be better off not knowing their sons had ridden outside the law.

From the Provo ranch, it would be a short ride to Camp Floyd. There were serious military upheavals going on in the Territory, and Johnston had already asked him to ride on some of the sorties and report on them to Cummings. Letters passing between the general and the Territorial governor of late were vitriolic, and a showdown between military and civilian authority was brewing. Johnston knew Cummings had appealed to Washington to restrict military participation in matters the governor felt were entirely under his Territorial jurisdiction, and the general did not like the signals that were beginning to come from his superiors. There were broad hints that support for the military was eroding, and drastic changes in the western military commands could be expected soon.

As he rode south, Carn couldn't help but think of his wife and child in the stagecoach, wondering how they were faring. He was relieved that Edwards had arranged for military escort, but felt angry at himself that he had not asked Colonel Cooke about the same protection. He struggled with a nagging fear that he would never see Heather and the baby again. Even more difficult to cope with was the reality that Heather had gone. It just didn't seem possible. Only months ago he had the whole world in his hands, and couldn't conceive how he could be any happier, or more blessed.

A doubt flashed through his mind. He could see nothing divine about losing his family. Perhaps it wasn't a matter of blessings, he thought, only a matter of luck. He'd lived among these Mormons too long. He was losing a proper view of life and its events. The Mormons attributed everything, good or bad, to divine intervention, to a heavenly purpose not easily understood. Well, they were right about that, Tregale told himself bitterly. There was no understanding what had just happened in his life.

CHAPTER TWENTY NINE

CAMP FLOYD
EARLY SUMMER

T his town's got a new sheriff—and don't nobody get in my way." Joaquin Johnston stood in the middle of Front Street, raised both arms above his head, a pistol in each hand, and started firing jubilantly into the air. The crowd around him started whooping and hollering and firing their own guns. A storm of lead filled the sky. At least a score of bullets bit into the sign over the saloon where the ballot count had just been made official. Well, it wasn't exactly a count. Really no need for one. Nobody was going to run against Joaquin, so every vote had to be for him.

Young Nelson stared up at the sign he'd just put up three days ago. The pay train had finally arrived about two months ago from San Francisco and Nelson found more than enough in his account to pay cash and become Fairfield's newest saloon keeper.

Nelson's Parlor & Gaming Emporium. It sounded a lot better than its former name, The Snake Pit. Nelson already was renovating the place, and with the way he and his partner were making money, it would soon become the most elegant gambling hall and whorehouse in all of Fairfield—maybe in the whole Territory. So a few bullet holes in the sign didn't matter much. Gave the place personality, Nelson decided.

Joaquin Johnston slipped his pistols back into the twin holsters and waved the crowd to follow him into Nelson's saloon. There was a stampede and Nelson had to force his way through almost a solid mass of bodies to make his way behind the bar. All that liquor flowing at a dollar a shot for everything but Valley Tan, which went for twenty-five cents less, brought a satisfied grin to Nelson's face. This sure beat army pay.

One man missing the celebration was the former sheriff, Bill Coates. One night last spring, Coates tried to stop a noisy argument here in The Snake Pit. One of four gamblers, a man named Happy Jack Wilson, was standing yelling threats at the other three. When he saw the sheriff approaching, Wilson turned from the table and stalked out of the saloon.

It surprised Coates, because Happy Jack wasn't the sort to back down meekly. The sheriff was grateful, though. It was a busy night and he'd already arrested four drunks and two gamblers who shot men they said were cheating. Coates didn't like to stretch his luck that far, not in Frogtown.

Outside again, Coates found Front Street shadowy but fairly well lit from the lights of the saloons and dance halls lining both sides of the street. Unfortunately, those lights didn't reach into the alleys, and that's where trouble came rushing at Coates.

Happy Jack Wilson lunged out of the darkness, holding the barrel of his pistol and crashing the butt against the sheriff's head. The blow was so hard that the gun bounced out of Happy Jack's hand and dropped into a nearby rain barrel. Coates' luck held one more time; his floppy old hat softened the blow and though he was flung to the ground, he managed to remain conscious. His head cleared in time to see Wilson charging toward him again, this time holding a thin stiletto. Coates pushed to his feet, grabbed at his gun but found it had fallen out of its holster. He jerked out his hunting knife, dodged the deadly arc of the stiletto, and thrust his own blade into the chest of the onrushing gambler.

Happy Jack stopped suddenly, trying to pull out the knife as he glared accusingly at the sheriff. The gambler fell to his knees, still holding onto the handle. He sank back onto his heels and died, remaining balanced upright for a few moments longer, then falling over sideways.

That was it for Bill Coates. He got on his horse the next day and rode out of Frogtown, dropping the sheriff's badge into the dirt.

Keeping the peace wasn't worth dying over, especially since it couldn't be done.

The town went without a sheriff for months after that, until Joaquin thought it might be useful wearing the badge. His own gang of rustlers was locking horns more and more frequently with Billy Hickman's gang, accusations of stealing each other's cattle flying back and forth. Didn't matter that all of the stock had been stolen from someone else beforehand. Joaquin enjoyed imagining the look on Billy's face when he heard about Frogtown's new sheriff.

The noise got louder as the men got drunker. Soon the topic of conversation for almost everyone shifted to the race scheduled to be run tomorrow afternoon at Camp Floyd. Young Nelson started taking bets at a corner table and he had to have help handling the crowd.

This was going to be the first race at the new track put in at Camp Floyd, and it was drawing a lot of money. The big race was going to be between a sorrel owned by Joaquin Johnston, racing against the best horse of the Second Dragoons. The sorrel was sway-backed and ungainly, looked like it wouldn't last down the track. The dragoons had entered a horse named Brownie, belonging to Lieutenant John Sappington Marmaduke. Word around Frogtown and Camp Floyd was that the sorrel had never won a race, was a slow starter, and usually kicked and reared until it was disqualified. That word, of course, was carefully spread by Joaquin. On the other hand, Brownie was being touted as the fastest horse this side of the Mississippi. So the betting was heavily against Joachin's sorrel, a fact that the new sheriff pretended not to notice.

The excitement grew to fever pitch a few hours later when Lieutenant Marmaduke and a large group of officers and enlisted men from the Second Dragoons showed up at Nelson's Emporium with a large sack of money.

Marmaduke searched until he spied Joaquin Johnston, and pushed his way through the crowd toward him. He banged the sack of money down on the table.

"We're calling your bluff, Johnston," the lieutenant bellowed. He was a large man and had a large voice to go with it. The noise inside the saloon quickly died down. Joaquin studied the moneybag.

"Looks like a lot of money," he said.

"Ten thousand dollars," Marmaduke boomed. "You up to taking that bet, Johnston?"

Joachin shrugged. "Can't give no odds. Even up."

"That's good with us," Marmaduke replied. "Every dragoon in the regiment is putting up every dollar they got."

"You boys must be pretty confident of winning."

"My Brownie's fast."

"My sorrel ain't slow."

"We'll take a chance on that." That brought some loud guffaws of laughter from the Dragoons. Marmaduke looked curiously at Johnston. "You taking the whole bet yourself?"

Young Nelson spoke up. "What he don't, I will."

The lieutenant glanced over at Nelson. "Done. Looks like you're holding stakes, Nelson. We'll be over right after the race. Be expecting drinks on the house, too."

"Be here waiting, Lieutenant," Nelson nodded. "Drinks on the house even if it don't go your way."

The dragoons left soon after that, but there was another confrontation moments later when Joaquin spotted Joe Rhodes at a table with Frank McNeil and Jason Luce, all top hands of Billy Hickman. Luce, of course, was married to Hickman's daughter. Johnston walked over and stared icily at the three men. The look on his face caused others around the table to back hurriedly away, leaving a clear space about the table.

"Nice of you boys to join my little celebration," Joaquin said, his words cold and unfriendly. "Guess you know I was just elected sheriff."

"We heard that," Rhodes said, his tone as unfriendly as the other man's. "Won't come as no surprise that none of us voted for you."

"Don't care how you vote, Joe," Johnston answered, "but I sure do care where you ride at night."

"You saying something, Joaquin?"

"I'm saying Billy can steal all the stock he wants from the army, but I'm warning you not to steal any of mine."

"Don't take kindly to warnings." Rhodes stood up, and pushed back his chair. "You accusing us of something—?"

"Missing four hundred head."

"You saying we took 'em?"

"I'm saying your men was seen near my place."

"Our ranch is near your place—can't hardly help riding close. Besides," he added thinly, "somebody stole three hundred head off our place awhile ago."

"Three hundred ain't four hundred—"

"Maybe somebody took a few extra for good measure."

The tension between them was high. McNeil and Luce got to their feet, glancing warily around the room to see who was backing up Johnston. It could easily have come to shooting, but Joaquin wasn't prepared for things to go that far. After all, he admitted to himself, he did steal the stock from Billy in the first place. Besides, he wasn't in the mood for a gunfight. He gave the three one last hard stare.

"You tell Billy I'll be watching. If I catch any of you stealing my stock, we got us a war." He nodded toward a scantily-clad bar girl who still had drinks on her tray that she had been about to deliver to the table. "These men are my guests. I'll be paying for their drinks."

Joe Rhodes tossed some silver dollars onto the table. "You ain't buying us nothing, Joaquin. And we'll be betting against you tomorrow."

A smile slid over Joaquin's face. "Glad to hear that, Joe. Don't want Billy or you men in my camp nohow."

The next day started well for the Second Dragoons. An hour before the race between Johnston's sorrel and Marmaduke's Brownie, the crowd witnessed a marksmanship contest between six riders of D Company and any challengers. One of the Dragoons was Calvin Gray. Three trappers and three teamsters took the challenge, and all twelve riders were now lined up at the starting post.

The men would race one against the other in a straight line, loading and firing two six-shooters, using similar army-issue cartridges, and firing at target bottles lined up on each side of the track. The object was to be first to empty the two six-shooters, hit the most bottles, and reach the finish line in the shortest time. The course was laid out so no onlookers were in danger of becoming accidental targets.

Calvin was the first Dragoon to race. He grinned at the bearded trapper beside him. "I'll have a whiskey waitin' for you when you get to the end of the line."

The horses lined up, empty pistols were holstered, then the starter fired into the air. Calvin brought a roar of cheers from his fellow Dragoons as he galloped recklessly down the track, loaded the pistols and fired, hitting a bottle with every shot. He was first over the finish line, and the trapper, arriving seconds behind him, still hadn't fired all his shots and hit only eight bottles.

It went like that for the whole contest, all six dragoons winning their race.

The excitement lasted awhile, and the barrels of beer kept being brought out from the quartermaster supply building. General Johnston had allowed drinking beer on post for today, but banned all hard liquor. Anyone caught intoxicated, of course, was hauled off to the guardhouse.

The officers were gathered at a wooden grandstand erected at the finish line of a half-mile track. Located just west of the administration complex, the track was already a cause for excitement among soldiers and civilians alike. There was a box seat for General Johnston and his line officers, a grandstand for junior officers and invited civilian guests, and bleachers built for as many soldiers and settlers as could crowd onto them. The remaining spectators, and there were hundreds of them, lined up along the track.

The racetrack was only one of the improvements made at the camp since spring. A large spring of water was dug out and walled up. A mile below the spring, Cedar Creek was dammed and a gristmill constructed to produce better feed for the horses. A small lagoon formed behind the dam, and it was stocked with fish from Utah Lake. A forty-acre garden was planted, each regiment taking turns in weeding and caring for the large quantities of potatoes and vegetables grown in it. An irrigation system was laid out to keep the garden watered. There was now a large circus troupe, a symphony orchestra, a Germanic Singing Club that enthralled even the soldiers with grand opera. The new amenities, and the broadened social activities, improved the quality of life on the post but unfortunately didn't improve the weather. That remained harsh the year-round, whether wind, dust, sun or snow.

The passing of winter and the new stream of money resulting from the soldiers getting paid for the first time in eighteen months had a positive impact on Frogtown, too. The pitiful shelters dug into the ground behind Front Street in those early months had now given way to rows of cabins, some of them good sized and comfortable. There were still a lot of shacks and lean-to dwellings, but for the most part, that part of town was referred to once again as Fairfield. It was sizable, too, with several thousand people living there. The new prosperity also brought more stores, and more conveniences, but Front Street would always be Frogtown.

None of that mattered this afternoon, however. The sun was hot but not unbearable, and for a change, the wind only gusted occasionally. The line officers took their places in the box seats, with Tregale the only civilian present. While they waited for the start of the race, still over half an hour away, the conversation among the officers roamed over many of the crucial issues facing them. The upcoming national election was uppermost, for the outcome of that would affect many things. The Indian unrest was another topic. The California trails had been re-opened a couple of months ago, but there was no guarantee they would stay open. The Indians in Thousand Springs country were reported on the move again, bands already threatening settlers and immigrants.

"Heard Lincoln has made great strides in pulling his party together," Colonel Smith said. "Took three ballots, of course, to get the nomination, but he's got the Democrats worried."

"President Buchanan's probably worried the most," Philip Cooke grimaced. "Word from Leavenworth is that Secretary Floyd doesn't have the influence over him that he did. Heard Floyd's on the way out, regardless of what happens in the elections."

Smith looked at General Johnston. "If there is a change in administrations, General," he asked, "do you see it affecting us out here?"

Johnston gave a gloomy shake of his head. "No doubt about it," he grunted. "Not even sure they'll keep this post activated."

That drew startled glances from the other officers.

"Doesn't look good, gentlemen, in my opinion," Johnston continued. "I won't be surprised at anything. Buchanan's retrenching, trying to win back some of the support he lost since he ordered the army to Utah Territory."

"What might we expect, General?" Cooke asked, a worried expression wrinkling his forehead. "We have a heap of problems facing us."

"Got a feeling that people in Washington don't care about our problems," Johnston replied. It was unusual for the others to hear such openly disgruntled comments from their commanding officer, who usually kept his thoughts to himself. But the general obviously was deeply concerned about the reports he was getting from the East. "Told them about all the Indian problems, and the need to keep the California trails open, but there's still hints of a major troop recall."

"That would cripple us," Smith muttered.

"And put the settlers at major risk," Cooke added.

"Isn't just the Republicans and the Democrats," Colonel Smith said. "This Union Ticket could really upset things."

Smith was referring to the new party just formed by a group of non-Mormons, hoping to wrest political power and control away from what they viewed as complete domination by the Mormon Church.

Johnston smiled. "Was reading their platform a couple of nights ago. According to what it claims, every Mormon in the Territory should be arrested."

"Think they went too far, myself," one of the officers grinned. "They're accusing the Mormons of murder, debauchery, robbery, making eunuchs of their enemies, inciting the Indians to pillage and kill, obstructing justice—the list just goes on and on. Nobody can be that bad."

"Understand the Mormons have ruled that no outsiders have the right to vote in Territorial elections. They mean to keep all of us Gentiles away from the ballot box."

"Won't hold up. Heard that Judge Eckles is declaring anybody can vote, no matter how long they been in the Territory."

"Should be an interesting election."

Johnston glanced over at Tregale. "Governor Cummings have anything to say about the way things are going, Mr. Tregale?"

"Not much," Tregale answered, shaking his head. "He's receiving confusing signals, just like the military. The governor thinks things are out of control in Washington, policies changing with the wind."

"I'd agree with that," Johnston said. He looked quickly at Tregale, a smile flitting across his lips. "Don't tell Cummings I said that. The two of us haven't agreed on anything since we left Leavenworth."

It brought smiles from Tregale and the other officers. "I won't, sir," Carn said. "Not sure the governor could stand the shock."

A carriage rolled into the area at the end of the bleachers. Ebenezer Crouch was sitting on the driver seat, and Young Nelson sat in the carriage beside Beryl Tate. It had taken a lot of talking, but Nelson finally convinced Beryl to accompany him to the races. She made it appear she was reluctant, at least. Inside, she was excited to see the race that everyone in Camp Floyd, Frogtown, and the whole of Cedar Valley was talking about. She made it clear to the saloonkeeper that this did not mean she was even considering going to work for him.

Nelson assured her that had nothing at all to do with his invitation. He was just delighted, he said, that such a lovely young lady was willing to accompany him.

Young Nelson excused himself, telling Beryl he had to see some men about the betting on the race. He'd already bragged about covering the ten thousand-dollar bet with Joaquin Johnston, although he didn't mention Joaquin had only allowed him to put up five hundred of the money. Still, Nelson had covered enough other bets in his saloon to make him a rich man if Joaquin's sorrel won. He didn't even want to think about what might happen if the sorrel lost.

After Nelson left, Ebenezer turned to look at Beryl. "Ain't none of my business, I know, but I was wondering if you was going to work in Young Nelson's saloon?"

Beryl was surprised, and annoyed that anyone even knew about the saloonkeeper's offer to her. "I'm not, Ebenezer. What makes you ask such a question?"

"Well," the youth said hesitantly, "like I said, it ain't none of my business, but I like you, Miss Beryl. Seen you act on the stage about three times already—"

"That's nice of you, Ebenezer—"

"—and I know you come from a good Mormon family. So when I hear Nelson bragging about how he's going to bring a fresh young whore to his place, one who's good at singing and dancing—"

Beryl gasped. "Nelson said that—"

"He sure did, Miss Beryl. Don't mean he was meaning you, of course, but that's why I asked."

Beryl stared up at Ebenezer, anger boiling inside her. "Did he mention my name—?"

Ebenezer shook his head quickly. "No, Miss Beryl, he didn't. But even if he wasn't talking about you, folks see you with him and they might put two and two together."

Beryl put both hands to her face, trying to deal with the shock of what Ebenezer had just told her. "He told me his place wasn't going to have any—any ladies of the night."

"Already got eight of them," Crouch muttered. "They is a notch above most of the others, but they's still whores."

Beryl expelled a deep breath. "Take me out of here, Ebenezer."

The youth looked around nervously. "This is his carriage, Miss Beryl—"

"Just tell him I took faint and ordered you to take me back to the barracks."

Crouch nodded. "That's good enough for me. Hope I didn't do wrong, Miss Beryl—"

"I'm very grateful to you, Ebenezer. You have done me a great service, which I won't forget."

Nelson returned a short while later, looking around for the carriage, thinking perhaps Ebenezer had moved it to a better vantage point. Men in the nearby bleachers told him what happened, that the young lady looked like she suddenly took ill, and left.

There wasn't time to do anything about it now. The race was just minutes away. Nelson climbed up onto one of the high rows of the bleachers, and crowded into a seat beside John Carson. Young

Nelson couldn't help staring at the pretty young girl sitting beside the innkeeper. This must be Carson's new wife. She looked sweet and innocent, reminding Nelson of a young peach that's just been plucked. No wonder Carson looked like a happy man. This new one sure was an improvement over Elvira.

"This is Emma, my new wife." Carson was beaming with pride as he introduced her.

Young Nelson nodded politely in her direction. "Glad to make your acquaintance, ma'am. People admire your husband a lot."

"This is Young Nelson—that's his name," Carson explained to his wife. "He just bought a saloon down on Front Street."

"Hope folks won't think of it as a saloon," Nelson said. "Intend to turn it into a high-class gaming emporium."

There wasn't time for more conversation. Everyone was now fastening their attention on the two horses a half-mile away at the start line.

It didn't take but a moment after the crack of the starter's gun to know Joaquin's sorrel wasn't the sad piece of horseflesh it looked. It leapt away from the chestnut and it became obvious in the first few seconds that it wasn't going to be caught, not in a half-mile, not in a mile. The sorrel was so fast, and so outdistanced Marmaduke's horse, finishing a full two lengths ahead of it, that people knew they had been suckered. Angry shouts rose from the hundreds of soldiers in the Second Dragoons, most of them watching at least six month's pay disappear.

Sitting in the grandstand, taking advantage of his official capacity of sheriff—for General Johnston had earlier banned him from the post as an unsavory character—Joaquin Johnston let a broad grin crease his face. People could think what they wanted, but all he'd ever claimed about the sorrel was that "it ain't slow." The other things, the kicking and bucking and the disqualifications, those weren't true, but he'd never been the one to say them. After a moment of enjoying the victory, and the pounding slaps on the back from those around him, Joaquin got down from the stands, mounted his waiting horse, and left the post. Those dragoons were going to be mighty mad, and no telling what they might do with all that beer inside them.

Beryl Tate got more furious every minute she thought about Young Nelson. There could be no doubt he had lied to her, was attempting to lure her into a horrid life of prostitution. Beryl shuddered at the prospect. It would be better to be dead than live that kind of life.

Arriving back at the barracks, she found it empty. Either the other girls had gone to the races, or they were over practicing. Beryl walked across the road and entered the theater. She found only Mercy Tuckett and Richard White, sitting on the benches in earnest conversation. They looked up as she approached.

"You look troubled, Beryl."

"I'm furious," Beryl snapped. She told them what Ebenezer Crouch had said. "I hate that man Nelson. Every word out of his mouth has been a lie."

Richard White gave a quick shake of his head. "Don't ever trust a saloon keeper, Beryl. They're born snakes."

Beryl looked pleadingly at Mercy Tuckett. "When do you think you'll be going to San Francisco, Mercy? I want to get out of this Territory."

Mercy and White exchanged glances. "We need to talk about that, Beryl," Mercy said. "There's been a few changes."

Beryl was alarmed. "What kind of changes? You're still going to San Francisco, aren't you—"

"No, we're not," Mercy told her. "With the arrival of the pay train and Richard getting all his back pay, and the army willing to let anyone out of the service who wants to—"

"You're not going to San Francisco—?"

"Richard and I are going to Virginia City. We've been offered jobs there, running the theater. It's a small theater and—well, I'm sorry to say we can't take you with us."

Beryl was shocked. She stared at Mercy, then White, in disbelief. "You're just leaving the troupe—?"

"Won't be a troupe, Beryl," White said. "When we go, the troupe folds. Wish it could be different, but that's the way it is."

"What are we going to do?" Beryl gasped. "What am I going to do? I was planning so much on going to San Francisco—"

"We're sorry, Beryl," Mercy said softly. "Truly sorry."

"When are you leaving?"

"In a few days. Richard's papers will be done then, and we'll leave on the next stage for Virginia City. The Mercy Tuckett Theater Troupe has presented its last performance."

"What are we going to do, Mercy?" Beryl repeated

"Something will come up," Mercy said, not able to put any real assurance behind the words. "Maybe you should reconsider going to work for that man Nelson—on your terms, of course. Wouldn't want you to become—well, one of his ladies."

Stunned and not able to think clearly, Beryl left the theater and started across the street. She hardly heard the catcalls and invitations from the scores of soldiers on their way from the races over to Frogtown. It was hard even to see, because now tears were beginning to form through the shock. She turned in alarm as she felt a hand on her elbow. A young soldier was standing beside her. He smiled and tipped his hat politely.

"It's Beryl, isn't it—Beryl Tate?"

She was surprised that he knew her name. Her thoughts stopped whirling and focused on the soldier. She didn't recognize him, and the look on her face said so.

"I'm Peter," he said. "Peter Farnsworth. My family and yours were neighbors in Parowan."

Beryl stared closer. She still didn't recognize him, but the reference to Parowan did jog her memory. "I'm sorry. I don't seem to recall—"

"Pete," he grinned. "I put that frog in your coat pocket at church—"

That brought it all back. He had changed—not the ugly boy she suddenly remembered. He'd grown quite handsome, she thought. Looked a little young, perhaps, although he had to be at least her own age. Still looked innocent, even in uniform. That was it, she decided. Life hadn't started beating on him yet. Not like it had on her.

She smiled at him. "I remember you, Pete. It was the frog that did it—how could I forget anyone that horrible?"

He laughed. "Couldn't believe my eyes, Beryl, when I saw you crossing the road. What you doing at Camp Floyd?'

"Acting in Mercy Tuckett's Theater Troupe—at least, I was until today."

Farnsworth's eyes widened. "You one of those acting ladies? Didn't connect you with anything so grand—"

"I believe you just insulted me, Pete Farnsworth."

There was no sting in her words, but Farnsworth was immediately embarrassed.

"Meant that as a compliment, Beryl. Just didn't make the leap from Parowan to the acting stage. You must be good. I'm impressed—"

"Well, don't be too impressed," Beryl sighed. "I just lost my job—we all did. Mercy Tuckett's Troupe is folded."

"It ain't because of you," Pete said firmly. "Know that for sure, without ever seeing you acting."

"That's sweet of you, Pete. My life is sure in the doldrums, though. Think this is my lowest point so far. What about you—sort of surprising to see you in uniform."

"Won't be after tomorrow," Pete grinned. "They took on a bunch of us right after the army got here. Now there's orders to whittle down and they're letting us go. Got three months pay with a discharge."

"That make you sorry—?"

"Makes me real happy. A year of army life is enough, as far as I'm concerned. It was a way to get out of Parowan, I guess."

"I know that feeling," Beryl smiled. "You going back there?"

Farnsworth shook his head firmly. "Don't know where I'm going, but it won't be back to Parowan. What about you? Heard your family is living in Provo these days—"

"A lot's happened in my life since Parowan," Beryl murmured. "Don't want to turn back into any of it."

Farnsworth hesitated, then drew a deep breath. "Beryl, I know you didn't like me much when we lived in Parowan, but I changed a lot since then. If you ain't got no place to go, and I ain't got no place either—well, maybe you'd consider seeing me. I'd really like talking out our lives." He grinned at her, and Beryl felt a little flutter despite all the tightness inside her. "Promise I won't put no more frogs in your pocket."

A good, warm feeling suddenly flooded through Beryl. She

couldn't explain it, but she felt it. She looked at Peter Farnsworth and admitted he stirred something inside her.

"This is really strange, but I think I'd like that too. There's nobody in our barracks right now. We could sit in the sitting room and start talking." She smiled at him again. "I really would like that."

Later that evening, Carn was sitting in Philip Cooke's quarters, enjoying a quiet visit with his friend. Several times, Philip almost brought up a question about Heather, but he could see how much hurt was in Carn, and always changed the subject. It was good for both of them, talking mostly about nothing serious. There would be enough time to face the problems.

A sergeant knocked on the door and delivered a request for Colonel Cooke to attend an emergency meeting of all staff officers in five minutes in General Johnston's office. Cooke left right after the sergeant, asking Carn to wait. The summons from the general sounded urgent, and under the present circumstances, ominous.

Cooke was gone less than half an hour, returning with a grim set to his face. He sat down and stared silently into his thoughts for several moments, then looked up at Carn.

"Rider just got in from Leavenworth. General Johnston is being relieved of command."

Carn sat upright in his chair. "He's what—"

"Not immediately. Probably not for several months, but it's confirmed that it's going to happen."

"Any reason given—?"

"None. Just that orders will soon be cut for him to return to Washington. Report didn't spell out any details. Johnston told us Colonel Smith will be taking over command here."

"Is this coming from Buchanan?"

Cooke shrugged. "Who knows. He's definitely trying to clean up some of the mess the Democrats are in, before the elections. Personally, I think it's too late. No doubt in my mind that Abe Lincoln will be our next president."

"This have any affect on you?"

A smile came to Cooke's face. "I'm ordered to take immediate leave. Probably want me back before everything becomes official.

Smith gave me a broad hint awhile ago he might be thinking of me for second-in-command."

"That's great, Philip—"

"That's terrible, as far as I'm concerned. This whole Utah Expedition is in trouble, Carn, and it's going to get worse. I'm going to see if I can pull some strings when I'm back East and get my assignment changed."

"Be real sorry to see you go."

"There's something else. Johnston is ordering the entire regiment of the Second Dragoons into the field tomorrow. Most will be headed for Thousand Springs. The Shoshone nation—especially the Bannocks—are on the warpath again, worse than ever. All the settlements in the north are in real danger."

"I should get that news back to Governor Cummings and the Legion."

"Sooner the better. My hunch is, things are going to get bad in a hurry."

CHAPTER THIRTY

BRIGHAM CITY
SUMMER

The Shepard wagon train split off the Oregon Trail and curved westward into Utah Territory. The train was so large, over sixty wagons and almost three hundred people, that it separated itself into three sections. It had traveled through Brigham City a couple days ago and was now headed through Box Elder to pick up the California Trail.

The fifteen wagons of the first section reached Cold Springs, a pleasant camping spot and watering hole in the western part of Box Elder County, late in the afternoon. The wagons pulled off the main trail, wanting to get as close as possible to the springs and make it easier to replenish water kegs. The second and third sections were a mile or so behind, planning on moving onto the Cold Springs campsite when the first section left in the morning.

It was twilight and everyone was getting ready for bed when a small party of Bannocks, of the Shoshone nation, rode into the campsite. There were seven of them, not a large enough force to pose a threat, but their arrival sent mothers scurrying to grab their children. Men reached for rifles, but the Indians showed no hostile intent. One of them spoke enough English to make himself understood.

"Give food, clothes," the Bannock grunted, waving an arm around the camp. "We give safe passage through Shoshone land."

The immigrants looked to Jim Shepard, the wagon master, for response to the request. He saw the Bannocks were painted, had full quivers, and several had rifles slung across their laps. Shepard decided it was best to avoid a confrontation.

"Give 'em food, clothing if you got some to spare," Shepard muttered. "Don't need much. Ain't worth risking a fight."

Bread and stew was brought for the Indians, which they gulped down. A couple pairs of pants, a shirt, and two blankets were piled in front of them. When they finished eating, they picked up the clothing and got back on their horses. People began to relax as the Bannocks rode out of camp and up a small hill beyond, where two of the men from the train were grazing a small herd of cows and some horses. The Indians rode past without stopping, but a brave suddenly whirled his horse around, lifted his rifle and fired at one of the men. The bullet hit him in the heart and he fell to the ground. The second man yelled in fright, turned his horse and raced back into camp. By the time he got there, and the stunned immigrants reacted to the surprise attack, the Bannocks disappeared with nine of the cows and two horses.

Jim Shepard decided against chasing the Bannocks, not wanting to risk more casualties. Instead, he sent word back to the second and third sections that they had been attacked and requested them to catch up without delay. While they waited, burial services were held for the dead man.

At dawn the next morning, the other two sections still had not arrived at Cold Springs. Jim Shepard decided not to wait any longer and started the fifteen wagons westward again. A few hours later, the train entered Goose Creek Canyon, with its narrow trail that followed the twisting course of Goose Creek for some twenty miles. It was a feared part of the California Trail but there was no way around it. The wagon train was forced into single file. Shepard cast several worried looks over his shoulder, but there was no sign of the rest of the train.

The wagons worked their way around a particularly narrow stretch of the trail where the canyon walls closed in until the roadway was barely wide enough to keep a wagon from sliding into the creek. The men bunched up on the lead wagons, doing their best to keep them on the trail.

That was when hell broke loose.

Both sides of the canyon were suddenly filled with yelling Bannocks. Arrows showered down onto the men, along with a storm of rifle fire. There was no place to hide and it became a turkey shoot. Men fell wounded and dead along the length of the train. There had been no warning, although Shepard had put three outriders ahead of the train. There was no way for Shepard to know those men lay dead along the trail, felled by silent arrows before the scouts could sound an alarm. And no way of knowing the second section of the train was still camped several miles back at Cold Springs.

The ambush was deadly, the number of Indians in the assault overwhelming. At least a hundred Bannocks had sprung the trap on the wagon train and it soon became evident to those who still lived that the only way to survive was to run.

When the attack started, most of the women hid themselves and their children in whatever cover they could find. For some it was the wagons, or underneath them. For others it was the rocks along the sides of the trail. Some of those at the rear of the train started to run back along the trail as soon as the attack started. Now the few men still standing let instinct take over. They abandoned the wagons, running or riding back up the canyon. Some stopped to pull women and children up onto their horses, but others rode past, letting fear and panic smother everything but the primal urge to survive. Everyone felt the stark dread of being caught and tortured.

It wasn't long before the firing stopped and the Bannocks streamed down from the canyon walls to pillage the wagons. Wounded men who had not been able to run were chopped down with tomahawks, and scalped. The goods of the wagons were thrown out onto the ground, little of it having any importance to the Indians. A few trinkets were taken, things you might not usually find out in the frontier, and all items that looked as if they might have some value. After taking what they wanted, mostly guns and hardware and livestock, the Indians set the wagons on fire. Nearby bodies were tossed into burning wagon beds to be consumed in the flames.

But the real horror of the massacre came with the discovery of the women and children hidden nearby. The Bannocks were savage in their treatment of these. The lucky ones died instantly under a knife, or a tomahawk, or from a bullet.

One of the women, Mrs. Wright, was among the unlucky victims. She saw her husband fall in that first withering blast of gunfire. She grabbed her two youngest children, an infant daughter and a five-year-old son, and crawled under a wagon. The other five children were sent scurrying to find any hiding place they could.

It wasn't long before she was discovered and dragged out screaming, holding her baby tightly to her chest. Her five-year-old son remained undetected under the wagon. The woman fell to her knees, begging for mercy. Her arms closed even tighter about her baby, trying to protect it from the half dozen Bannock braves who gathered around her. They laughed at her pleadings, taunting her with tomahawks, trying to grab the baby from her. Finally, one of them tired of the game. He stepped forward, tore the baby out of its mother's arms, and holding it so the woman could see, crashed his tomahawk into the infant's skull. Mrs. Wright screamed as he threw the body of her daughter against the stone wall of the canyon.

Then they closed into a circle about her. She looked at them, scrambled to her feet and tried to run, but they grabbed her. Some of them held her as others stripped off her clothing, then threw her naked onto the ground, each taking their turn in raping her. When they were finished, they circled her again. This time, they fired a half dozen arrows into her scratched and bleeding body. Laughing, they left her and continued their search for loot and new victims.

Finally the canyon was quiet except for the crackling of flames from the burning wagons. The Indians, convinced there was no one left to kill and nothing more worth stealing, rode east, hoping to catch up with the immigrants who had escaped. Flushed with their success, the Bannocks were determined to attack the wagons that scouts reported were still camped at Cold Springs. Some of the band trailed behind, herding the oxen and livestock taken in the raid.

Incredibly, the Bannocks were wrong about there being no survivors. Back in the canyon, a few of those left for dead desperately tried to stay alive. Among these was the husband of Mrs. Wright.

Badly wounded with two bullets in the chest and an arrow in his side, Wright probably would have died where he had fallen if it hadn't been for his children, especially his young son. The five-year-old had remained hidden under the wagon while the Indians killed his sister and tortured his mother. Then he scrambled out and ran up into the rocks, where he stayed until after the Indians were gone.

Then the little boy came back to the horror of death and flames and black smoke. He found his mother still alive, moaning in pain, the arrows still sticking out of her. Somehow she held onto life and had crawled up into the rocks looking for her baby. She was holding the pitiful, bloodied little body in her arms when her son found her. He didn't know what to do, of course, but brought her some water from the creek. It seemed to help, so he brought her some more. He took time to search for his brothers and sisters and found them hidden under a partially burned wagon bed. All five of them were unharmed but in mild shock as a result of witnessing the massacre. They all searched for their father, and found him unconscious but not dead. They brought him water, just like their young brother had done for their mother. The children kept caring for their parents all through the night.

Another woman who survived the savage assault was Jim Shepard's wife. She was wounded at the same time as her husband. She managed to take their eight-month-old son and crawl up into the rocks, pulling brush over her and the baby. After awhile, she became so weak from loss of blood that she fainted. The baby fell asleep contentedly on his mother's breast, not making a sound through the whole ordeal. It started to cry in the morning, and that was when the Wright children found mother and baby. Mrs. Shepard was terribly weak, and unable to walk, but she couldn't stop crying as she clutched her baby tightly to her. Sadly, Mrs. Wright died early that morning, but even her children knew it was for the best. Their father died ten days later.

In all, five women and nine children survived the massacre by successfully concealing themselves from the Shoshone attackers.

Now, all anyone in the canyon could do was pray.

The Bannocks were not as lucky at Cold Springs as they were in the Goose Creek ambush. A picket spotted one of the Indians on a bluff overlooking the camp and sounded the alarm. Realizing the advantage of surprise was gone, the Bannocks attacked in full force. The immigrants, fearing they might come under attack, had already dug in and were well protected. Six of the Bannocks were killed in the first assault, and four more in a second charge. Finally the Bannocks broke off their attack and disappeared.

The next day, a small group of Indians wound down out of the hills into the walled settlement of Brigham City. A small herd of about twenty head of oxen, mules and horses trailed behind them. It wasn't an unusual sight, for Brigham City had become a favorite trading post for the Shoshones. Settled eight years earlier, and called Box Elder City until just last year, the settlement had grown rapidly. A lot of farms and orchards sprawled outside the walls, and for the first time since peach trees had been planted four years ago, a bumper crop of the delicious fruit was expected.

Aaron Cunningham was in the central square that morning with Lydia, who was now almost seven months pregnant, and her sister Harriet. All three felt they had made a wise decision moving to Brigham City. They had formed warm friendships, and Aaron already had set up a carpentry shop and was doing well. The three of them watched as the party of Shoshones—a man standing nearby called them Bannocks—came into the square and motioned for people to gather around. The Indians spread out a couple of blankets on the hard-packed ground, and emptied several sacks of items onto it. The settlers crowded closer. They all knew the Shoshones stole the items they brought to barter, but tried not to think about the real possibility that the previous owners might have been butchered on the trail by these same Indians. The Indians often brought trinkets and day-to-day necessities, such as pots and pans, that could not always be found in settlement stores.

While some examined the livestock, others stooped to examine the assortment of goods spread out on the blankets. There was an unusual number of valuable items in the collection. Twelve Colt revolvers, most looking in good condition, several watches, a couple of them with heavy silver chains, some gold coins, and a large selection of women's brooches, necklaces, and chokers. There was no doubt these items had been looted from a wagon train.

An older man picked up a daguerreotype family photograph in a small baroque brass frame. He stared at the picture then looked up at the Indians.

"I seen these folks. They passed through about a week ago—Shepard train. That was it." He glared accusingly at the Shoshones. "That where you got this stuff—from that Shepard train?"

The Indians at first pretended not to understand. A settler standing nearby repeated the question in Shoshone, pointing at the family portrait. Now the Indians shook their heads. The man asked another question. One of the Shoshones answered, obviously reluctantly. The translator frowned at the Indian, then looked around at the crowd.

"He says this stuff came from a small train hit by Flat Heads somewhere near the Goose Creek Mountains. Says the Flat Heads only wanted food, but the Mericats in the train shot 'em dead. Then a whole bunch of Flat Heads attacked the train and looted it."

"What about the people?" a woman asked. "Were they killed—?"

The translator asked another question of the Shoshone, who shook his head.

"Says he don't know nuthin' about that. Flat Heads traded this stuff with them, and now they're trading with us."

"He's lyin'," a man growled.

The translator spat on the ground. "Ain't seen one who don't."

Nevertheless, the trading and bartering went on for another hour. Nothing could be done about the looted train now, and there were family necessities to consider. But a few of the men, Aaron Cunningham among them, drew off to one side.

"I'm thinkin' that Shepard train might be needin' some help," one of the men said.

"They ain't gonna tell us where it was hit."

"Shoshones said it was over by Goose Creek," the translator said. "My guess is the canyon. Not the first to git hit there."

"So what are we gonna do—?"

"I say get a posse together, and see where these Shoshones lead us."

The men in the group nodded, moving off unobtrusively to get their horses.

When the Indians left the settlement, the posse trailed them north toward the Goose Creek Mountains. The Indians knew they were being followed, but paid no attention until they reached the foothills. They were concealed for a moment behind a ridge, and when the posse topped it, there was no sign of the Indians.

The Bannocks had simply disappeared.

"Thought they was being too polite," a member of the posse grunted.

"Don't matter," another said. "The canyon ain't far from here. I say we head there pronto."

The posse, like the wagons, had to ride single file when they got into the canyon. Galloping hard, they rounded a bend and came upon a line of wagons. None of them showed any sign of damage, but about a mile farther on, smoke and haze could be seen still hanging across the canyon. Evidently the posse had come upon a section of the train that had not been attacked. Working their way past these wagons, they finally came upon the scene of the massacre.

Aaron Cunningham felt sickened by the horror around him. It was the first time he had actually seen the results of Indian savagery, and it was something he hoped he would never see again. He would though, not even a month away, with scenes more horrible than anything here in Goose Creek Canyon.

The story of the massacre was told that evening by the women who had survived the attack. If any proof was needed that the Shoshones in Brigham City had lied, it was confirmed in those grim tales the sobbing women told. Some bitterness was expressed as the names of the men who had fled for their lives came out. Still, wasn't a person there who didn't carry a fear deep inside that they might do the same thing if they faced the same choices.

A disturbing accusation was made by two of the women. They claimed to have seen several white renegades in the Shoshone war party, just as vicious and brutal as any of the Indians. It was credible, for whites had been seen for years mingling with Indian war parties. It was generally believed the renegades were largely responsible for much of the more violent acts along the overland routes. The gangs often made themselves look like Indians just to pass the blame along. Many times, no Indians actually took part in the raids. Unfortunately, the army was having little success in tracking down these renegades.

The posse stayed the night, then helped clear the trail of burnt wagon beds so the rest of the train could pass. After helping lift bodies onto a couple of the wagons, the posse left. There would be burial services when the wagons left the canyon about eighteen miles down the trail, but the men from Brigham City had done all they could and needed to get back to their own families. No telling what the Shoshones might do after tasting this much blood. They promised the immigrants they would get word to the military and try to get them protection as they passed through Thousand Springs country.

Back home with his wife and Harriet, Aaron said little about what he had seen in the canyon. The women had a flood of questions but he passed them off by telling them the massacre was so horrible they didn't ever want to carry such pictures in their mind. All the time, he couldn't drive away from his own mind the sight of the Wright baby, its skull split almost in two by an Indian tomahawk. He was soon to see another baby killed in another massacre, this one with its arms and legs hacked off, both ears cut off, and its eyes gouged out. Sights like that never left a person for a lifetime.

Six weeks passed before two companies of dragoons, under the command of a Lieutenant Ebenezer Gay, reached Brigham City. The lieutenant went into immediate conference with local officials, seeking to find out all he could about the Shepard massacre. In response to questions about military presence in Thousand Springs, the officer assured the townsfolk that a large force of dragoons were already protecting that part of the California Trail. Sheriff Sheldon Cutler, who was one of the first settlers in the community, was asked if he would accompany the soldiers to act as guide. Cutler wasn't too pleased about it, but finally agreed.

"Got word a couple days ago that a lot of Bannocks are camped up in Cache Valley," Cutler grunted. "About a hundred of 'em, is what we heard. You able to take on that many Indians, Lieutenant?"

"Twice that many, sheriff," Gay replied, his tone indicating he was offended by the sheriff's question. "These the Indians who attacked that Shepard train?"

"Reasonably certain they is."

"So what's the fastest trail to this Cache Valley? I'd like to attack tonight, if that's possible."

"How many troopers you got?" Cutler asked, not willing to accept such a brash dismissal of his question.

"Forty-two. More than enough, I assure you."

"I take it you ain't fought Indians much, Lieutenant."

"You concerned about that?"

"I'm concerned about a hundred Shoshones," Cutler growled. "They don't think like white men, and they don't fight like white men."

"All men die the same, sheriff. We're ready to leave when you are."

The two companies of dragoons rode out of Brigham City, the lieutenant and Sheriff Cutler in the lead. In the middle of the first column rode Calvin Gray. Calvin had no way of knowing Harriet and his son were now living in the settlement, and it probably was just as good he didn't. A meeting between them would only have brought more hurt.

The column of soldiers rode hard, not slowing even when darkness fell.

They had been in the saddle about four hours when Sheriff Cutler, familiar with the country even at night, leaned over to speak to the lieutenant.

"Getting close, Lieutenant. Might be smart to slow down. Ain't going to be no surprise making this much noise."

But it was a surprise. A real sudden surprise.

The column of soldiers was now in a narrow canyon. They rounded a bend in the trail and rode right into the middle of the sleeping camp of Shoshones, who were bedded down across the trail. There was no telling who was the most startled, the Indians or the soldiers.

The Shoshones scattered, racing up the north slope of the canyon. Calvin Gray saw one of them running past him. With no time to take aim with his rifle, and his pistol still holstered, Calvin flung himself out of the saddle and crashed on top of the fleeing Indian. The man rolled free and Calvin saw the knife in the Indian's hand. He clawed for his revolver but the Indian was too fast. Calvin felt a sharp pain in his chest. He stopped reaching for his gun and fell back. The Indian kept on running up into the rocks.

A dragoon came to Calvin's side, frowning as he saw the hilt of the knife protruding through the uniform. Kneeling beside Calvin, he pulled the knife out and opened the tunic to examine the wound. He couldn't see much in the darkness so he dragged Calvin over to the far edge of the trail, away from the side where the Indians had taken cover. Calvin didn't say anything, just kept looking down at his chest, pushing hard to stop the dark oozing of blood.

The soldiers quickly recovered from their own surprise and started shooting, but the band of Indians were now all up in the rocks. Moments later, the Indians started firing back at the soldiers, who quickly scattered and took positions beside the trail, on the south side. That left the Shoshones on the high ground. Lieutenant Gay silently cursed the bad luck that gave the advantage to the Indians.

The two sides kept firing sporadically at each other all night. The moon was up, but the light from it only served to deepen shadows. There seldom was a clear target for anyone, but an occasional cry of pain proved that some bullets were finding their mark. Just before dawn, the shooting from the south side stopped.

Lieutenant Gay found out why when dawn broke. The Indians were gone.

When he was sure of that, he ordered his men to check for casualties on both sides. Six wounded dragoons were reported, and one dead. That was Calvin. He had bled to death at the side of the trail. There was no sign of the civilian, Sheriff Cutler.

The soldiers found a score of dead Shoshones, and that was some satisfaction. They also found a score of horses, probably belonging to the dead Shoshones. A dragoon, examining the horses, pointed out a

Crooked S brand on the flank of one of them. The Lieutenant was willing to bet that was the Shepard brand. It was the right band of Indians, all right. Now he had to find them all over again.

The soldiers returned to Brigham City, realizing there was no sense in trying to chase down the Shoshones until there was a new lead on their whereabouts.

He was wondering how he was going to tell the folks about Sheriff Cutler being missing, and maybe taken captive, when he saw the sheriff leaning against a fence a short distance away, talking to another man. He halted the troops and rode over to the two men.

"See you're not dead, sheriff."

"Never thought I was."

"What happened back there? You disappeared mighty fast."

"Mighty fast was the best way, Lieutenant. I told you to slow down."

"About a minute before we ran into them—"

The sheriff stared up at the officer. "Something on your mind—?"

"Don't like the way you run out, sheriff."

That angered Cutler. "I'd be careful sayin' things like that. I didn't run out, Lieutenant. Found myself all alone, on the wrong side of the trail. You soldiers was shootin' at anythin' that moved, and I wasn't lookin' forward to some Indian crawlin' up my back. I did the only thing that made sense—I hightailed it out of there. You asked me to take you to 'em, and I did that. You get paid for fightin' Indians, Lieutenant. I don't."

The soldiers continued on into Brigham City. There was no doctor with the dragoons, so Lieutenant Gay had the wounded men attended by a doctor in the settlement. There was curiosity about the one dead soldier, and the dragoons let people know the soldier had a name: Calvin Gray.

Aaron heard about Calvin first, and decided it was the right thing to let Harriet know. She was numbed by the news at first, then picked up little Calvin and hugged him tightly. The shock wore off and she started to sob. Later, Aaron escorted her down to the wagon holding Calvin's flag-draped body. When Aaron explained, the dragoon standing guard let Harriet up on the wagon. He pulled back the part of the flag covering Calvin's face. Harriet thought he looked more at peace than he had in a long time. She knelt beside him, patted his cheek, then leaned over to kiss his forehead. Strangely, amid all the sadness and turmoil inside her, there also came a sense of peace. It was over, and she could finally let go. But that didn't stop a painful sweep of regret as she thought of the goodness and happiness that might have been. She was sobbing as Aaron helped her down from the wagon, and for a few moments, she leaned against him. It was all such a terrible waste.

CHAPTER THIRTY ONE

SALT LAKE CITY
FALL

C arn Tregale was in the courtroom of Federal Judge Charles Sinclair, called as a witness in the trial against Sergeant Ralph Pike. There had been anger and disbelief in Camp Floyd when the charge of attempted murder was brought against Pike for the assault on Howard Spencer last spring. Colonel Smith, acting on behalf of General Johnston, allowed the summons to be served. The officers were so angry, and so convinced there was no case, that it was agreed to send Pike to Salt Lake. Mainly, General Johnston hoped to embarrass both Governor Cummings and Brigham Young by proving in court that civilian authority had no jurisdiction over military authority. Major Fitz John Porter, the post's Adjutant General, was placed in charge of Pike's defense.

The morning hours passed in a calling of witnesses, including Lieutenant Marshall, Lieutenant Murry, and several of the Tenth Infantrymen who had been at the incident in Rush Valley. It got near lunchtime and Judge Sinclair ordered a recess, declaring that testimony from Tregale, George Reeder, and the ranch hands involved, would be heard in the afternoon session.

After lunch at a downtown restaurant, Pike, Major Porter, and four of the infantrymen started walking back. The street was busy with wagon traffic and a lot of pedestrians. Someone called out Pike's name, and the sergeant turned. An angry scowl crossed his face as he saw Howard Spencer a few yards away.

"Got something on your mind, Spencer?"

"Got you on my mind, Pike. Keep remembering the way you snuck up on me and broke my skull."

"Didn't do no sneakin'," Pike growled. "You was tryin' to stick a pitchfork into me, as I remember."

Major Porter was also facing Spencer now. "The sergeant won't be saying anything more, Spencer. We'll do our talking in court."

"You're right," Spencer hissed. "No more talking."

Suddenly Spencer went for the gun at his side. Pike saw the move, grabbed for his own gun but realized the holster was buttoned down. He lunged to get out of Spencer's way, but it was too late. Spencer fired, and the bullet went into Pike's left side, just below the heart. He staggered, then fell.

Spencer gave a howl of satisfaction as he saw the sergeant go down, then turned and ran up the street. One of the infantrymen had his pistol out and took aim, but just before he fired, someone nudged his arm and the shot went wild. Seconds later, Spencer disappeared from sight.

Pike was not dead, but in bad shape. He was carried into the Council House by his companions, and an army doctor who happened to be nearby came to do what he could. Judge Sinclair came out of his chambers and knelt beside Pike, listening to the sergeant's whispered statement. Shortly after that, Pike went into a coma and never regained consciousness.

A furious Major Porter ordered the infantrymen to search the city for Spencer, telling them to shoot anyone who got in their way. The last reported sighting of Spencer was of him jumping onto a horse in a lumber yard and galloping off.

He was never caught or brought to trial.

◆

Other problems were troubling Billy Hickman. Shortly, after the killing of Sergeant Pike, Tom Ferguson, Hickman's first and only client, was found guilty of murdering Alexander Carpenter. Ferguson stared at Hickman after hearing the verdict, not believing it. Hickman had been so sure this would never happen. It must be a mistake. He was still thinking that when the judge sentenced him to death by hanging in two weeks.

Hickman decided it might be best to make himself scarce for awhile, at least until things cooled down. Accompanied by Jason Luce and four other members of his gang, Hickman was walking down East Temple toward the stables a couple of blocks south, when they ran head-on into five members of Joaquin Johnston's gang, just coming from the stables.

Lot Huntington was in the lead, and when he saw Hickman, he drew and fired. A bullet smashed into Hickman's chest, but it hit the big pocket watch he carried. The impact knocked Billy off his feet and left him only half-conscious. The watch splintered into shrapnel and several large pieces flew into his leg. The two gangs opened fire and everyone ran for cover. After several minutes, Lot Huntington and his men broke off and melted away.

Jason Luce and a couple of the others ran into the street and dragged Billy onto the sidewalk. The leg was badly cut, but it didn't seem too serious. They took him to his daughter's home, where his wounds were treated. But the violence wasn't over.

That evening there was a knock on the door. When the door opened, Joe Rhodes was standing there. Hickman, lying across the room, saw him and yelled at his son-in-law.

"It's Rhodes. Keep him off me—"

Jason Luce sprang across the room. He wasn't wearing a gun but he pulled a bowie knife from the sheath at his waist. Rhodes started to draw his pistol but Luce buried the knife in his heart. Rhodes stood erect for a moment, his eyes fastened on Hickman. Changing allegiance and going to work for Joaquin Johnston wasn't supposed to end like this. Then he dropped dead.

It was justifiable homicide, as far as Luce and Hickman were concerned. The next day a city judge agreed, and no charges were brought.

The two gang leaders, Billy Hickman and Joaquin Johnston, would fight each other for months, but neither ever knew the satisfaction of killing the other. It was just a long, drawn-out war that nobody ever won.

CHAPTER THIRTY TWO

SALT LAKE CITY
LATE FALL

Governor Cummings summoned only three people to what some might consider the most important meeting he had held since coming to Utah Territory almost two years ago. These were General Daniel Wells, commander of the Nauvoo Legion and a member of the First Presidency of the Mormon Church, Colonel Robert Burton, commanding the Salt Lake City contingent of the Legion, and Carn Tregale, a man who had provided invaluable service at great personal cost. The three men were sitting in Governor Cummings's office in the former Staines mansion, waiting for the governor to make an appearance.

When the governor entered the room, all three stood up respectfully. Cummings waved them back into their seats.

"Sorry to keep you waiting," he wheezed. "There are urgent matters needing attention." He sat down in a comfortable overstuffed chair, ignoring the chair behind the large desk. He eyed them separately, nodding to himself at some inner satisfaction as he looked at each man. "You have all been loyal friends. I want each of you to know I appreciate the support you have rendered to this office, and the personal respect you have shown to me. It will always be a cherished memory, gentlemen."

"You deserve that respect, sir," Wells said firmly. "You have exercised your responsibilities fairly and with great integrity. We look forward to offering our continued support, Governor."

"That will not be possible, I'm afraid." Cummings drew in a deep breath, expelling it in a long sigh. "My days as governor are numbered. I have just been notified that I am being recalled to Washington."

The three men stared at him, shock on all of their faces.

"That can't be, sir," Wells said. "There is some mistake—"

Cummings shook his head. "All federal officials will soon be leaving the Territory. A firm date has not been set, but it will not be long in coming."

"But why, Governor?" Burton asked. "What possible reason—"

Cummings cut him off. "I've been asking myself the same question, Colonel Burton, but I can't come up with an answer. It makes no sense to virtually abandon the Territory like this."

"Forgive me for asking this, Governor," Wells muttered, "but could this be a personal matter between you and the administration?"

"There's been no disharmony that I'm aware of," Cummings replied. "And if there was personal animosity, it would not explain why all federal appointees are being withdrawn. Washington is saying nothing, of course."

"Something's in the wind," Tregale said. "First General Johnston is ordered back. Then a large part of the military force is recalled, despite urgent needs here in the West. The army is being forced to close the California trails again before the end of the season. Now you, Governor, and all federal authorities. This is a planned exodus."

"I agree. No doubt it's all linked together," Cummings said. "Buchanan is under tremendous pressure and criticism for this whole Utah undertaking, from Congress and the press. My best guess is he's trying to undo as much damage as he can before the elections."

"Has there been mention of who will succeed you, Governor?" Wells asked.

Again Cummings shook his head. "Got the impression there will simply be a void. No plans to replace any of the appointees, as far as I could detect. Not immediately, at least."

"This whole thing is incredible," Wells muttered.

"You people will have to be ready to step in when we leave. As Carn points out, these are troubled times. Looks like you're getting your Territory back, gentlemen."

"Looks to me like the North is getting ready for war," Burton said grimly.

Another sigh came out of Cummings. "That's probably true, Colonel. Hate to even think of such a thing happening, but it does seem headed that way. If Lincoln moves into the White House next March, there'll be trouble. The South won't stand for anti-slavery laws being passed, and Lincoln's sure to push for them."

Wells glanced across at Burton and Tregale. "From what Mr. Tregale has reported about military strength being cut to the bone, and the recent Indian troubles up north, we'll have our hands full. What's there been—two, three massacres of immigrant trains just this past month—?"

"Yes, sir," Burton said. "The Shepard train was attacked first, then the Beal train from Iowa, then the Harrington and Miltmore trains up near the Snake. Bannocks were savage in that one, in particular. That's about when this Bannock witch doctor surfaced—Warahikah, they call him. He'll be causing a lot more trouble, no doubt."

Wells looked grim. "We'll need to get the Legion prepared for that, Colonel." His glance swung to the governor. "Don't hardly know how to prepare for the void you will leave, Governor."

"Well, you managed admirably without government interference for a long time, General," Cummings said, giving a wry smile. "No doubt you people will continue to do that."

"Times are changing," Wells murmured. "We can't hope to remain an island much longer. The railroad is working west, and that new telegraph. We have to change with the times. You've been helpful in preparing us for that, Governor."

"Wanted you to know what Washington is planning, gentlemen. Seems like all of our lives will soon be upset."

"Yours too, Governor?" Carn asked.

"I was born and bred in the South. If it comes to making a choice, I'll be hard put to go against the Union. Still, what's a Georgian to do—follow his head, or his heart?"

After the meeting ended, General Wells went to the Beehive House to report the developments to Brigham Young. Burton and Tregale walked up the street toward the temple block.

"Puts a strange twist on things, doesn't it," Burton mused. "After all the hell everyone went through to keep the federals from taking over, here they are handing it all back."

"Changes the values of things," Tregale said, "at least for me. Don't think I want to stay in the liaison business, Bob. No purpose in it now, not with Governor Cummings and General Johnston both leaving."

"I agree. Not much to be done now. Wish this had happened before—well, before Heather went back East."

"So do I," Carn muttered. "No sense in regrets, though. Did what had to be done."

"It's going to work out," Burton said. "She'll come home soon, and you two will be together just like it was before."

"Not the way I'm hearing it," Carn said, bitterness creeping into his voice. "Her last letter to Agatha said she'd decided to go to Boston. Didn't sound like she was planning on coming back. Agatha let me read the letter. I think I've lost her."

"Not willing to accept that, Carn. Heather just wouldn't up and leave you for good."

"Think she already has."

◆

Derek Pitts' heart was beating louder than the sound of his knocking on the front door of his house, or so it seemed to him. He waited anxiously until Gwen opened the door.

He was shocked. She looked ill and worn, dark circles around her eyes, cheeks bloodless, her hair straggled and uncombed. The housedress she was wearing was badly wrinkled and had stains on it. She obviously was startled to see him. Her hand went automatically to her hair, fingers running through tangles but accomplishing nothing. Aware of how she looked, she tried to back partly behind the door. Not able to think what to say, she stood staring wordlessly out at him.

"I heard you've been ill, Gwen," Derek said. "I came to see if there was anything I could do—and to give you money. I've been sending it with Aaron and Lydia as you know, then with their parents. But since Aaron and Lydia are moved to Brigham City, and

Brother and Sister Cunningham are in Salt Lake now, thought I'd bring it out myself."

"It's appreciated," Gwen said. Her voice croaked and she tried to clear it. "I was sick, but I think I'm better." She hesitated, then added, "Would you like to come in—?"

"Thank you," Derek said. She stood back and he stepped into the room beyond. Once again he was shocked. The room was untidy, things scattered everywhere. The floor looked like it hadn't been swept in a long time. It wasn't so much that the room was dirty; it was so unlike Gwen. She had always been such a spotless housekeeper. She saw him looking around and was embarrassed.

"It's a mess, I know. Haven't felt well enough to do housework."

"All that matters is you feeling better," Derek said quickly. He stared closer at her, and once again her hand went to her hair. He was concerned, and she could see it. "I've worried about you, Gwen. I've—I've wished I could have visited, but you—"

"You hurt me, Derek," she muttered. She pushed aside some things from a worn sofa and sat down. "What you said hurt real bad."

"I just said I loved you—"

"Me and that young girl. I couldn't love anyone but you, Derek— couldn't love two men at the same time, that's for sure. I didn't think you could love anyone but me."

Derek looked sad, moved some clothes from a kitchen chair, and sat down.

"Don't mean I love you any less, Gwen. Couldn't never do that. Don't know how to explain what happened—don't understand it myself. It wasn't because I was unhappy or dissatisfied with you, Gwen. You were a wonderful wife and you made me real content."

"You couldn't be content if you went looking for someone else."

"Didn't do that. I loved you too much—still do."

"You still love me—?"

"Course I do. Never stopped from the first time I saw you. Can't stand the thought of not spending my life with you, Gwen. This past few months have been more hell than I can say."

"Do you mean that—?"

"Never lied to you, Gwen, and I'm not now. You're my wife, and I never want that to change."

"But you still want that girl—"

Derek looked down, not knowing how to explain his feelings. Truth was, he wanted Sarah Beezley more than ever. They'd grown closer since he'd moved into the back room of the gun shop, but they hadn't ever been intimate, or even close to it. Derek couldn't bring himself to do anything like that, because of his wife and because of Church principles. Sarah didn't want it, either.

"Have to be honest," he said finally. "Yes, I still want to marry Sarah. If it comes down to a hard choice, though, I don't want to lose you, Gwen. These past months have made me realize that. I won't see Sarah any more, and I'll get me a new job, if that's what you want."

Tears suddenly came into Gwen's eyes. She started to sob, her whole body shaking with the relief of what her husband had just told her. Derek came across to the sofa, taking her in his arms. Nothing was said for a long time as they held each other, her pent-up emotions pouring out. Derek was crying, too.

They kissed, and for both of them, it was like those first times when they were courting in England. It was thrilling, and tingled through their whole bodies.

Sarah stood up and led her husband upstairs.

Later, as they lay beside each other, Derek reached over and patted his wife's cheek.

"I love you, Gwen.

She rolled over, leaning against his chest. "And I love you, Derek. You sure you never did—well, never did what we just did with that girl?"

He smiled. "Never did, love. That's the truth."

"Well," Gwen said slowly, "I've been thinking a lot about what you said before, about there being a good side to polygamy. Don't quite see it yet, but there must be something or Brigham Young and those others wouldn't be doing it."

"Don't matter, Gwen—"

"What I'm saying is, if you want to marry that girl, I think I could come to accept it."

Derek sat up on the bed, staring at her, not believing what he had just heard. "Do you mean it? You're not just saying it because—well, because we're back together." He let a quick frown cross his face. "We are back together, aren't we, Gwen?"

Gwen laughed, glanced under the sheet at their naked bodies. "I'd say we were back together right enough."

"Do you mean that about Sarah—I mean, really mean it?"

"Well, I'm not really happy about it, not yet anyway. But I'm not happy with us being apart, either. I've been thinking about it, and I can see it working. Won't be easy, and you have to expect me to be jealous at times—specially when you're with her and not me. But if that is what you really want, Derek, we can work it out."

Derek felt like jumping out of bed and rushing down to the gun shop, but he was smart enough to know that wasn't wise, not after what had just happened. But he wanted to yell out, he felt so happy.

The next morning, Derek left for work, leaving a smiling and tearful wife waving to him from the door. It felt so good to be back with her, and he felt so bad about all the pain and suffering he had caused her. But it would be different now.

When he got to the gun shop, he looked for Sarah but she wasn't there. Her father, Tom Beezley, was oiling the guns in the main case and he looked up as Derek came back out into the front of the store.

"She ain't here, Derek."

Derek smiled. "She coming in late—?"

"Ain't coming in."

"Is she sick—?"

"She ain't sick, Derek. She's gone."

Derek frowned, not understanding what Beezley was saying. "Where's she gone? Will she be back this afternoon—?"

"Probably won't never be back."

Alarm flooded through Derek. He could see Beezley was deadly serious.

"What you saying, Tom—?"

"She run off yesterday, Derek, when you was gone. Just up and left. Hardly said goodbye."

Derek was shaking his head, frowning to make sense of what he was hearing. "What do you mean—run off?"

"Some army lieutenant. Said he was out of the army and heading for California. Asked Sarah to go with him."

"She went to California—? We were going to be married—"

"Guess she didn't believe that was going to happen. Don't really know what she was thinking, come down to it. She just gave me a kiss goodbye, and that was it."

Derek sank down onto a stool, his soul shattered. Sarah had run off with a stranger—he couldn't believe it. She wasn't going to be his wife. A terrible bitterness came over him. It would be a long time before Derek came to realize it just might be for the best. Sarah, as young as she was, could have changed her feelings just as easily after they were married.

♦

Carn sat across from General Galloway in the study, looking as down as he felt. The more he thought about the changes that were soon coming to Utah, the more he realized how little it would all mean without Heather and his son. It wasn't hard to read his face, and Galloway knew that Carn was feeling pain.

"Write to Heather and tell her what's happened. She'll be happy to know you'll not be in government service much longer."

"I suppose I could get Captain Edward's address in Boston from the army," Carn muttered bitterly.

"You're looking on the black side, Carn."

"Black on both sides, General. She didn't go to Boston for any other reason than Edwards. We both know that."

"We don't know she went to Boston."

"She said she was going, in her letter to Agatha. She wouldn't have written it if she didn't intend to do it."

"Let's not rush to judgment."

"Been over three months. Don't call that rushing."

"Well, there's a lot for us to be doing. When word gets out about the extent of the federal pull out, things will start happening fast."

"Like what, General?"

"Without the army business, and the federal authorities leaving, Utah won't hold the same attraction for a lot of people. We'll see dozens of Gentile stores closing, with merchants unloading their stock at pennies on the dollar just like Livingston and Kinkaid did."

"Some of that going on already," Carn nodded. "Heard that two hundred dollar wagons were going for as little as ten dollars."

"Already bought some. But wait until the army starts unloading the thousands they got out at Camp Floyd—prices will go even lower."

"So this is the time to buy."

"Wagons, livestock, merchandise—when the panic sets in, those leaving will sell at any price. We'll be able to pick up whole inventories for what it costs now to bring a few wagon loads of goods from the frontier."

Carn frowned. "Does put a different light on things," he muttered. "How so?"

"Well, I was thinking it might be better for everyone if I left. Go to California maybe, or some place."

Galloway dismissed the thought with a wave of his hand. "That's not you talking, Carn. I know you think maybe you failed, that the best way out is to run, but you know as well as I do that you'll feel the same way in California as you do right now. Thing is, you haven't failed in anything. You've done an outstanding job this past year, and everyone knows it. People asked more than they should, but you did everything that was asked. We all owe you a debt of gratitude, Carn."

"My wife doesn't agree, General. No matter what anyone else thinks, she considers me a failure—as a husband, and as a father. She was pretty blunt about making that clear. And no matter how I reason it to myself, I did fail her."

"Sometimes a man can't help the choices he makes," Galloway said. "People put you in a hard place, and there wasn't much else you could do."

"Try explaining that to Heather."

"I will, soon as she gets back."

There was a knock on the door. Agatha looked in.

"The Tates just got here. Willie and the boys wonder if they can have a few minutes with the two of you."

"Have them come in."

Willie entered the room, accompanied by his sons, Fred and Ted. While Willie shook hands, the boys looked at Tregale. They could read nothing in his expression except a friendly welcome.

"What brings you to town, Willie?" Galloway asked.

"Me and the boys got a proposition to make," Willie said. "It's the boys' idea, so I'll let them tell it."

They all sat down and Fred and Ted exchanged looks. Then Fred began, addressing General Galloway.

"You been real good to our family, General Galloway, you and Brother Tregale. We want you to know we all appreciate that."

"Acknowledged. Now what's this about a proposition?"

Ted looked uneasily at Carn, then picked up from his brother. "Me and Fred worked at Camp Floyd for awhile, and we did all right." He looked again at Tregale, then continued. "We saved up some money—"

"A lot of money, when it comes down to it," Fred interjected. "Army paid good."

"So what we'd like to do is maybe buy the ranch from you. Don't know how much you want, but we know it'll be a fair price. Give you all we got as down payment, then work off the rest."

Both boys slid their glance to Tregale. It all depended now on what Tregale might say. He was the only one in the room who knew where that money really came from.

Carn decided to end their worry. "Boys did work hard out there," he said. "I'm real pleased about this, boys. Seems like a good thing to do with that money."

"Might I ask how much you have, boys?" Galloway asked.

Another quick exchange of looks between the boys. Ted answered.

"Four thousand, General Galloway."

The general was startled. "Four thousand dollars—?"

They both nodded.

"Wasn't all just pay," Fred said, casting another quick glance across at Tregale. "We—we did a little gaming." They saw the quick frown from their father. "Wasn't anything much," they added hastily. "We ain't skilled at gaming, but we wuz lucky. Put all our winnin's away."

"Couldn't believe it when they told me how much money they had," Willie said. "Came by it honestly, though, except for that gaming money. Mother wasn't too pleased about that, but seems like no harm was done."

Tregale didn't look at the boys. The looks on their faces told him they were squirming. Nothing to be gained, for anyone, by untwisting their story.

"Glad to see you were smart enough to get out when you did, boys," Carn murmured. "Looks to me you're putting that money to good use."

"Tell you what," Galloway added, "I think this is such a fine thing you're doing to help your family, you can have that ranch free and clear for two thousand."

The Tate's looked at each other, not quite believing what the General had just said.

"Ranch is worth far more'n that, General," Willie said.

"Two thousand is all I want—that suit you, Carn?'

Carn quickly nodded. "That don't include the stock, of course."

"That'll cost another thousand," Galloway said. "What will you boys do with the rest of the money?"

"Put some aside—" Ted answered.

"—and buy some milk cows with the rest," Fred added. "We been talking about how Utah County is a good place for a dairy operation."

"Excellent idea," Galloway nodded. "What about the farm next door, Willie?"

"We'll still run that if you want us to," Willie said. "You sure about such a low price for the ranch, General. Should be two, three times that—"

"You Tates have earned it," Galloway assured him, "and I know Carn feels as good about it as I do."

"Sure do, Willie," Carn added. "The ranch will give you and Maude security, make a fine place to bring up the girls, and provide a good future for the boys."

"Don't know how to thank you both," Willie muttered, his eyes suddenly tearful. "Never expected anything like this, not back in England nor pulling those handcarts."

"No need for thanks," Galloway smiled. "It'll be a lot of hard work, but you and the boys will do good."

Willie stood up and extended his hand again. "Hard work don't scare us none. It'll keep the boys honest."

Out in the kitchen, Maude had already told Agatha what her husband and twin sons were proposing to do. Agatha was delighted, and gave Maude a big hug.

"That's wonderful, Maude. I'm so excited for the whole family."

"The Tate ranch." Maude almost whispered it, then shook her head. Tears jumped into her eyes. "It's such a blessing even to think about it. Do you suppose the General and Carn will agree to it?"

"Course they will," Agatha beamed. "If they don't, I will. The General keeps telling me I own everything he does."

Outside in the driveway, a heavily loaded covered wagon pulled up in front of the entrance. Agatha heard the bells as someone pulled the chain. She hurried to the front door and was surprised to see Jim Wilson and his wife standing there—even more surprised to see the wagon behind them.

"Why, Beth," Maude said, reaching out to give her a hug, "something big must be happening in your lives. What's going on?"

"Just came to say goodbye, Agatha," Beth said. She turned to her husband and took his hand. "Jim and me are leaving Salt Lake."

"Well come on in and tell everybody about it. The Tates are here visiting, too."

Jim reached up and lifted Nancy down from the seat. Their daughter was over three years old now, having been born soon after the couple boarded ship back in Liverpool early in fifty-six. Soon everyone was crowded into the kitchen, the men joining them from the study. Jim couldn't get a word in, his wife was so excited.

"Jim's quit the police force," she told them. "I'm so relieved. He's been shot three times since joining the marshals—"

"Two times it was just scrapes," Jim said, but his wife wouldn't let him lessen the danger.

"Three times," she repeated. "He could have been killed any one of those times. Especially this last time."

Jim glanced at the men and shrugged. "Does appear my luck might be thinning out."

"So tell us," Agatha asked, "where you folks moving?"

"Going up to Brigham City," Jim told them.

"You'll be with Aaron and Lydia, and Harriet," Maude said. "That's wonderful, all you young folks being together."

"You pleased about that, Beth?" Carn asked.

Beth flung her arms about her husband's neck, bringing a wince from Jim as she wrenched his wounded shoulder a little. She backed off quickly, but her face was all smiles.

"I'm so excited I can hardly stand it," she told Carn. "We didn't tell anybody, but Jim rode up to see Aaron a few weeks ago. Aaron's asked him to come work with him in his new carpentry business."

Carn put a hand on Jim's good shoulder. "Good to see the families building a life together. Real happy for you two, Jim."

The doorbell jangled again. Agatha hurried to answer it, and came back moments later followed by Alfred and Esther Cunningham. Esther obviously was upset, her eyes already red from a lot of crying. She saw Jim and Beth and burst into tears again.

Agatha tried to console her. "Everybody's happy here, Esther." She glanced over at Alfred, who was looking almost as upset as his wife. "Something happened, Alfred?"

"Guess we're to blame," Jim muttered. "Brought some news back from Brigham City but didn't tell anyone until just now, when we stopped by their place. Maybe we shouldn't have said nothing."

The Cunninghams had now moved into the Mellencamp mansion, only a few blocks farther east on South Temple Street. Esther broke into a fresh outburst of sobbing.

"What on earth's happened, Alfred?" Agatha asked again. "Something wrong with Lydia?"

"No, nothing like that," Alfred said hurriedly. "From what Jim and Beth tell us, Lydia's doing just fine."

"The baby's due any day now," Beth added. "Lydia's not feeling any better than any woman about to give birth, but not any worse either."

"So what's got you so upset, Esther?" Agatha said, kneeling down beside the sobbing woman. "Maybe if you tell us, it will help—"

"Don't think she can get the words out," Alfred muttered. "It hit her real hard."

"So tell us, Alfred," Maude said, a little impatiently. "We can't help your wife until we know what's wrong."

"Harriet's getting married," Alfred said.

Agatha stared at him, then down at the sobbing Esther. "That's what this is about—Harriet getting married?"

"I'd say that was wonderful news, Alfred," Carn said. "It's what we were all hoping for."

"It's who she's marrying that's got Esther so upset."

"Well, tell us," Agatha said. "Who is she marrying—?"

"Aaron."

It was a shock for everyone in the room. Just hearing her husband say it caused Esther to break out in another loud outburst of wailing. The others stared at Alfred, disbelief on all their faces.

"Harriet's marrying Aaron—?" Maude frowned.

Even Fred and Ted were stunned. "But he's already married to Lydia—ain't he?" Ted frowned.

Willie shook his head at him. "Let the womenfolk handle this, Ted."

Esther took her head out of her hands, looking at Agatha who was still kneeling beside her. "Can you believe Aaron would do such a thing—?" she sobbed. "And Harriet—I knew it was bad for her to go up there with them."

"Well, it's a shock," Agatha said gently, patting Esther's hands, "but it's not the end of the world. Aaron's taking a polygamous wife. A lot of men are doing that, especially in the outlying settlements."

"But she's Lydia's sister—" Anger crossed Esther's face. "She must have set her cap for him behind Lydia's back—"

"Probably wasn't anything like that," Agatha said soothingly. "You know Lydia and Harriet are real close. I'll bet if the truth were known, Lydia is really happy about this."

"She is, Agatha," Jim said. "They was all real excited when they told me about it. You could tell Lydia was really pleased—I got the feeling it was mostly her idea in the first place."

Maude, who hadn't seen Esther much this past year, wasn't as patient as Agatha was trying to be. She frowned at her. "Don't know why you're this upset, Esther. Seems to me you should be feeling happy about this."

Esther glared at her. "Happy—? Happy my son is a polygamist—?"

"It's not a disease, Esther. It's a chosen way of the Lord to take care of His own."

"Well I don't like it," Esther snapped. Her anger was bringing her out of her self-pity. "Just isn't natural for a man to be with more than one woman."

Maude shrugged. "I'd say you don't know much about men, Esther."

Just then, Henry Washington entered the room, with Rose close behind him. Both were smiling but that was quickly wiped away when they saw the faces of the people in the room, and saw how upset Esther was.

"Don't mean to be interrupting—" Henry said.

"You're not, Henry." Agatha stood up again. "Esther here is having trouble making a little adjustment, is all."

"This is more than just a little adjustment," Esther flared.

"Quiet, Esther," Alfred barked. "Maybe you better start seeing that nobody is upset about this but you. Henry looks like he's got something to say."

General Galloway turned to Henry. "What brings you and Rose here, Henry? You both seemed pretty happy a moment ago. Wouldn't be news about Rose, would it—?"

Henry grinned. "No sir, not yet anyway. There is a new arrival, though—"

Agatha screamed and everyone turned to the doorway behind Henry and Rose. Standing there was a tired-looking, but very excited Heather. She was holding little Carn, who looked around at all the people and quickly buried his head on his mother's shoulder. Agatha went flying across the room, arms outstretched. Her arms went around Heather, crushing mother and child. Both women started sobbing at the same instant.

Everyone crowded around and Agatha reluctantly backed away so the others could hug Heather. Agatha took the baby from her, and after a long, suspicious look, little Carn snuggled down on her shoulder. Even Esther looked happy.

Carn stepped forward to take his son from Agatha. The baby was doubtful at first, then decided to go to his father without a struggle. Heather watched them, and a fresh stream of tears started down her cheeks. After kissing his son several times, Carn turned to his wife.

"Can't tell you how good you look," Carn told her, his eyes moist. "Nothing more in this whole world that I'd rather see than you and the boy."

There was an awkward hesitation between them, neither quite knowing what to say. Agatha stepped forward and took the baby from him.

"Think maybe you and Heather ought to step into the parlor and be alone for a few minutes. Words might come a little easier in private."

Carn closed the parlor door and stood in front of his wife. Heather looked so good. He could hardly contain himself from sweeping her into his arms. But maybe he didn't have that right any more.

"Biggest surprise of my life," he told her, a big grin breaking over his face. "So glad you're back, Heather. I missed you so much."

"I missed you, Carn."

"I thought—I heard you went to Boston."

She shook her head. "Didn't go. After I wrote that letter to Agatha, I wished I could have taken it back, but it was too late. Couldn't hardly stand thinking about how you would feel when you read that I was even thinking of such a thing. So I caught the next train to the frontier, and here I am."

"Heather, nothing matters to me except that you're here. I'm so sorry for all that happened between us. You were right in expecting me to be more concerned about you and the baby—"

She put a finger to his lips. "I thought a lot about that, Carn. It was selfish of me. I guess I went back to being a spoiled little girl from London again, who wasn't getting her own way. Maybe Captain Edwards brought that out in me—doesn't matter now. I'm so sorry about all that, Carn. I never did stop loving you."

"Just hearing you say that wipes it all away."

"I realized how much people were relying on you, how much good you were doing for the whole Territory keeping those people talking to each other. I felt real proud of you, Carn. Please forgive me—"

He made no effort to hold back the tears now streaming down his face. "All I want is for us to be together again. If you'll take me back, Heather, I promise things will be different. I know now that nothing is more important than you and little Carn."

"That's all I want, too. That's why I came back as fast as I could."

"It's going to be good for us, Heather. A good life, and I'll make you a good husband."

"Couldn't any woman ask for more than that, Carn Tregale."

CAMP FLOYD

F all of 1859 was the beginning of the end for Camp Floyd. The first sale of surplus goods and materials from the quartermaster's warehouses was held in August, offering enormous savings for buyers and forcing merchants in Fairfield to sell their goods below cost. That specter brought fear to merchants in Great Salt Lake City, and hurried decisions by many to get out of the Territory.

The number of troops at Camp Floyd was ordered reduced from the original twenty-five hundred to only three hundred. It sparked an immediate exodus of thousands of civilians, including merchants, gamblers, prostitutes, and others who relied on the army for their living. Businesses started closing in Great Salt Lake City almost as fast as they had opened eighteen months earlier.

General Albert S. Johnston remained longer at Camp Floyd than expected. It wasn't until March of the next year that he sat on his horse on a cold, snowy parade ground and reviewed his troops for the last time. Twice, Johnston was privately asked to consider running for president, replacing Buchanan as the Democratic Party candidate. Most people in high Democratic circles felt the unpopular incumbent had no chance against Lincoln. The talk about Johnston as a candidate faded, and the general headed west to California, intending to return to Washington by way of the Isthmus of Panama. His orders were changed, however, and he remained in California to assume command of the Western Department of the Army.

General Johnston never visited Salt Lake City after that first time he led his troops through the city. He never visited Brigham Young, or Governor Cummings. And he never got over the resentment that he had not been allowed to fulfill his duty and let the Mormons know who had won and who had lost the war. Of course, there never had really been a war.

Johnston did not realize at the time that he was headed for glory as one of the top commanders of Confederate forces during the Civil War. He would not have believed that when he died of wounds during the battle at Pittsburg Landing, it would be a turning point that would ultimately lead the South toward final defeat.

Colonel Charles F. Smith assumed command of Camp Floyd after the general left. After only a few months, Colonel Smith was transferred to Washington, and Colonel Philip St. George Cooke was placed in command.

It was almost certain the post was headed for deactivation, although it hadn't been made official. The growing tensions between North and South following the election of Abraham Lincoln made it difficult for the small corps of officers remaining at the camp, for their numbers were badly split in loyalties.

In December of the following year, the name of Camp Floyd was officially changed to Fort Crittenden. The former Secretary of War, John B. Floyd, for whom the camp was named, was now openly considered a traitor to the Union and had fled to the South. To make matters worse, the army insisted that all officers remaining at Camp Crittenden sign a pledge of loyalty to the Union. The command disintegrated as officers from the South refused to sign and resigned their commissions. It would not be long before those same officers faced their former friends across bloody battle lines.

It was a very difficult time for Colonel Cooke. A native of Virginia, yet a strong Republican and loyal supporter of the Union, he was torn inside when Virginia joined the other Southern states in seceding from the Union. There no longer was any doubt that civil war was imminent. Cooke, despite being unswervingly loyal to the Union, came under suspicion of disloyalty when his son, John R. Cooke, and his son-in-law, J.E.B. Stuart, both joined the Confederate army. It would cast a cloud over Colonel Cooke's career that would hurt for the rest of his life.

A few months later, Camp Floyd was ordered abandoned. A huge sale of surplus goods was held, during which over two million dollars worth of foodstuffs and materials was sold for less than a hundred thousand dollars. Fortunes were made by a few; hundreds of others went home with bargains of a lifetime. It was estimated that the total cost of the Utah Expedition and Camp Floyd exceeded forty million dollars, depleting the national treasury at the most critical time in the history of the Union. Historians would almost all agree that Buchanan's blunder accomplished absolutely nothing of value to the Union.

It was three years after the army marched into the Salt Lake Valley that a grim Colonel Cooke led the remaining small detachment from Camp Crittenden, now abandoned and already starting to disappear under the hands of scavengers and the relentless onslaught of weather.

Glory and disgrace would touch almost all of the officers and men of Camp Floyd in the conflict that was about to engulf them, and hundreds would die. Colonel Smith, after a series of brilliant victories for the Union forces under his command, would die of a simple accident in Tennessee just nineteen days after death claimed his friend and former commander, General Johnston.

Perhaps the greatest disgrace would come to a former mess cook at Camp Floyd, a man named William Clarke Quantrill. Leading a guerrilla group, Quantrill burned and shot at least 150 civilians in Lawrence Kansas in his wild attempts to punish Northern sympathizers and advance the Southern cause.

Governor Alfred Cummings remained in Utah a full year after he was notified of his impending recall. He and his wife left the Great Salt Lake Valley quietly one afternoon without anyone knowing they had gone, the couple not wanting to go through the hurt of leaving all the close friendships formed these past three years.

Brigham Young was out of the city at the time, visiting settlements in the south.

Fate would decree that both Governor Cummings and his wife would be taken prisoners during the war, kept apart for three long years, then reunited in an exchange of prisoners shortly before the war's end. Both survived in good health, and observers noted that it seemed Cummings might even have put on some weight during his captivity.

Before that great conflict ended, Camp Floyd—or Camp Crittenden—was almost completely erased from existence. Timbers and stone were carried off to become new homes in nearby settlements and finally all buildings and foundations were gone.

Only the post cemetery remained. That held meaning through the passing years, even if most of those buried there had ended their days violently in Frogtown.

ABOUT THE AUTHOR

John McRae was educated in English schools and has traveled extensively throughout the world.

As a writer and producer of trade and educational films and television commercials, Mr. McRae has frequently been honored with top national awards, including such prestigious awards as an Emmy, a New York Art Directors award, top national Telly awards, and several Best In The West awards.

Prior to moving into advertising and filmmaking, he worked as a newspaper feature writer. He retired as president of a Northwest advertising agency, headed his own marketing consulting firm, and now has turned to a full-time career as a novelist.

He has written seven novels, including the best-selling *Trilogy of Fire* series, of which *SOUL FIRE* is the third novel. This series follows Carn Tregale and his friends through historical events occurring in 1856, 1857, and 1858.

John McRae lived for many years in the Pacific Northwest and now lives in Utah.